Night of the Storm

Night of the Storm

Lindsay Townsend

Thorndike Press • Chivers Press
Thorndike, Maine USA   Bath, England

This Large Print edition is published by Thorndike Press, USA and by Chivers Press, England.

Published in 1998 in the U.S. by arrangement with Hodder & Stoughton, Ltd.

Published in 1998 in the U.K. by arrangement with Hodder & Stoughton, Ltd.

U.S. Hardcover   0-7862-1534-8   (Romance Series Edition)
U.K. Hardcover   0-7540-1204-2   (Windsor Large Print)

The text of this Large Print edition is unabridged.
Other aspects of the book may vary from the original edition.

Set in 16 pt. Plantin.

Printed in the United States on permanent paper.

British Library Cataloguing in Publication Data

Library of Congress Cataloging in Publication Data

Townsend, Lindsay.
    Night of the storm / Lindsay Townsend.
        p.   cm.
    ISBN 0-7862-1534-8 (lg. print : hc : alk paper)
    1. Large type books. I. Title.
[PR6070.O8966N5   1998]
823'.914—dc21   98-8440

Acknowledgements

In this book only Rhodes Town and the British locations are real places. Asteri and Antasteri are completely fictional, as are all the characters, companies and organizations mentioned in the text.

The illegal animal trade is, however, real, heartless and still thriving in many parts of the world in spite of the efforts of environmental groups to stamp it out. Wildlife traffickers and their paying customers are a real threat to the survival of many species, and support is essential for those organizations who struggle hard to combat their activities.

Nobody finishes a novel without a good deal of help and support. My thanks go in particular to my family, my editor Carolyn Caughey and her colleagues at Hodder, my agent Teresa Chris, Barbara Lightowler, Pamela Campion, David Glover, Judith and Martin Baker, my friends in the Huddersfield Authors' Circle and the teachers of Mirfield Free Grammar School, especially

Christine Riley, Alec Barker and Basil Christie, who encouraged me in my early writing. Any faults are, of course, mine.

I also owe a debt of gratitude to every library I have ever used.

Prologue

Andrew sat on the cliff below the castle wall and watched the sky. Far below, the Aegean was a deep rust in the setting sun. Wind gusted against his back. At his feet barley and rockroses, a cushion of yellow vetch growing in the ruins, small red and white flowers whose names Melissa would know.

Down on the beach men moved, dark shapes against the sand. A small boat rode at anchor. Stiffly, Andrew shifted position. From the corner of his eye he saw a stocky, dark-haired man standing a bottle of retsina down on a rock, wiping it carefully with a handkerchief. He nodded a greeting.

Then, to his left, another movement —

Two men looked down at him. One pushed at his body with a foot. 'He's out cold, no problem. Do it.' The other spun the cap from the bottle, poured the contents over Andrew, put the bottle between the sleeping fingers. Then they both rolled him over the edge.

A rattle of falling scree, then silence.

Chapter 1

'I should have known I'd find you here.'

The cool voice cut through the beat of straining wings. Gulls, oystercatchers and sanderling were exploding from an English estuary, darkening the ice-blue March sky. Katherine Hopkins had just marched straight across the sands, disturbing hundreds of birds roosting on the beach.

'And a good day to you, too,' Melissa said drily, squinting up at the tall figure. Freezing and cramped after lying motionless behind a breakwater for hours, she had just lost a shot: a vital consideration since nature photography was part of her living.

'You're full of surprises, Katherine,' she observed now through chill-flayed lips. 'I thought you only liked your animals stuffed or sautéed.'

'Always so sure of yourself,' answered Katherine, 'Always so *right*.' She ignored the sights and sounds of alarm around them: birds did not buy anything. Coming to look the site over in private, she had been intensely irritated to realise that Melissa Haye was there first.

'But you've never actually beaten me. I always win in the end. Don't I?'

Melissa shrugged and snapped the cap onto her 600mm lens, fingers tingling with returning life. Unlike her own windswept hair, not a strand of Katherine's dark chignon stirred in the crisp air. Looking over business-dynamo Katherine Hopkins, the trousers tailored to those sleek legs, the scarlet jacket and silken cravat, Melissa wondered why an intelligent woman should find it so hard to accept that anyone was different from her.

What was done was done. Because of local opposition and a campaign spearheaded by Melissa herself, Katherine had failed to build one of her Total Woman Centres on this estuary. To Katherine the horseshoe of cliffs, the closer profile of river and sea, sands and reedbeds, mudflats and marsh, were a barren landscape, evocative as the moon but unproductive.

'Remember the paper which "no longer required" you?' Katherine continued, grinding a razorshell under one green boot. 'Remember the "lost" photo commissions? That was down to me. A couple of phone calls in the right places was all it took.'

'Now you've reminded me . . .' Melissa scooped a beanbag camera-support, hat and veiling into jacket pockets, her back icy where Katherine's shadow fell. It would be great, she thought, if Katherine could let the past alone, but, on and off, Katherine Hopkins had been trying a long time to block her career. Looking back, Melissa acknowledged that Katherine's vindictiveness had actually spurred her on by making her do more, try harder. She laughed softly.

'I never thanked you for that, did I?' She glanced up again at her nemesis. They both knew why Katherine detested her. It had nothing to do with Melissa's work.

Katherine's patrician cheekbones turned a delicate pink. 'What *is* your problem?' she demanded. 'Total Woman Centres provide a service for thousands.'

At fifty pounds an entry ticket, Melissa wondered how many thousands were being favoured. Katherine though was a woman with a mission: already, at thirty-four, one of the wealthiest women in Britain, with her twenty-four-hour shopping and healthcare stores established in every major city in Europe. Her business didn't need more expansion, but Katherine was greedy.

'A pity, then, that the people here voted to leave things as they are.' Cradling her camera, sweeping a rapid look over the area she had been stalking to make sure she would forget none of her photo gear, Melissa rose stiffly to her feet. The waders would not settle now until she and Katherine were gone.

'You can't possibly pretend it ends now,' snapped Katherine. 'This is a prime site . . .'

'I know.' The estuary was a focal point for local families. In summer, these sands rang with children's voices. In winter, mudflats and saltings upstream tingled to the cries of curlew.

Melissa smiled, then frowned, the taste of sea-salt catching for an instant in her throat. 'We should go.' Accustomed to numbness in her legs after a photo-shoot, she started to limp briskly towards the dunes.

'. . . perfect for the sensitive development I had proposed —' Abruptly Katherine broke off, instinctively shying away as a storm of Brent geese flew in overhead. Melissa stopped, throwing back her blonde head to track the birds gossiping and grunting in flight: an everyday miracle. 'Amazing!' she murmured, thirst and cold forgotten.

The dark chattering swarm sharpened her responses to the estuary. *Andrew should have been here to see this,* she thought, hands tightening on the camera.

Memories, too strong to be denied, welled in her. As grief threatened to break out again, it helped Melissa to know that Andrew's favourite place was safe: that she and the local people who had once been Andrew's neighbours had made it safe.

'Wide-eyed enthusiasm doesn't work with me. Is that how you won the locals over, turning on the little-girl charm?' Pausing when she did, Katherine was looking at her sidelong.

Melissa clicked her tongue and chuckled: she was actually grateful for Katherine's presence and sharp comments. 'You'll never know. Meetings are over, and so is the voting. People like their sand and "mud" as it is.'

'So it would seem.' Green eyes showed gold for an instant as Katherine acknowledged that unpalatable fact. Dismissing the estuary development from her immediate calculations with a brisk shake of her head, Katherine moved when Melissa did, keeping pace with her opponent as they left the beach and began to thread through the tall, twisting corridors of dunes.

As they walked, Melissa moving sure as a skier over soft dry sand and clumps of tough marram grass, Katherine's green eyes flashed up her sand-coloured fatigues and gloves, flitted over the younger woman's delicate complexion, gold brows and lashes, shoulder-length silky blonde hair. Her rival would probably have to diet to stop those soft body curves, the round lines of an open face, neat nose, from blurring into flab.

Katherine's lips twitched with satisfaction. Those who thwarted her always paid. Melissa Haye had lost before, but it seemed she had still not learned her lesson. Throughout the last decade, their paths had crossed too often, both professionally and personally.

Andrew Thornhill had been Katherine's personal assistant and occasional lover. Recognising how his attractively uneven, maturing looks and ready enthusiasm could be a foil to her poised, subtle fire, she had given him the chance of a great career. Yet he had been a disappointment, preferring the safe Melissa Haye.

Katherine's lips tensed, umber sculptured eyebrows drawing together as she negotiated a litter of pebbles and feathers on the narrowing dune path. Although it had piqued her to be rejected for some romping teenager, it had cost her nothing. Andrew had been young, and so could be excused his choice. She had wished him well, and it seemed he had been happy — he had lived with Melissa Haye until his sudden death in

14

Rhodes, two years ago.

Old history. Katherine shook herself, consigning Andrew Thornhill to oblivion, and returned to her present enemy now peeling off her gloves, that prying long lens nestled in the crook of an arm.

'I'm watching you, Melissa Haye. One day you're going to make a serious mistake.'

The threat: always a good sign she was doing her job, reflected Melissa wryly. Behind, the distant tide hissed in her ears like an indrawn breath.

'Then we'll see who pays.'

There it was, a gold-plated promise of revenge. Melissa was surprised at how little she felt.

'Nothing to say?' Katherine liked proof of attention.

Melissa sighed. 'Can't we call a truce for once, Katherine?' Fishing into a trouser pocket for her favourite silver seahorse earrings, she hooked them deftly into her ears whilst cresting a dune-top and dipping down the other side. These silver seahorses were special: Andrew had bought them for her on Rhodes . . .

Katherine was coming at her again, leaning forward as she kicked through rabbit-marked sand. Her wide, up-tilting eyes were sharp.

'You disgust me,' she said, scornful of any

15

olive branch. Her rapid gaze, fixing on Melissa's silver seahorse jewellery, became dismissive. 'Everything you are. Everything you stand for. Cross me again and I'll finish you for good.'

Katherine pushed past Melissa, striding on towards the track and her black four-wheel drive, towards civilization and her plans for revenge.

Chapter 2

Clutching her camera, Melissa stared out to sea. She no longer thought of Katherine's threats. The past had returned.

Andrew Thornhill, with his straight brown hair, craggy nose and keen smile. Six-one in his stockinged feet, and broadening. He had blushed when he first saw her at the local wildlife group meeting at Wells-next-the-Sea. Later, walking with Melissa by the sea shore, Andrew had asked her out. He was twenty then, Melissa seventeen.

They had lived together for eight years.

Still the memories flowed. His walk, his voice, his scent. His lethal sloe gin. His listening face. His hilarious imitation of a love-struck diplomat. The way he double-knotted his shoelaces. The way he liked 'messing about' round rock-pools. The way he made love —

'Stop this!' The heavy camera trembled on Melissa's arm. Andrew had died two years ago, and still she was struggling to come to terms with it. She had to get away, find a different direction. But there was something she had to do first: a secret, private mission behind her next assignment.

Her bags were always packed. She loved roving — new places, new people. She was due to go to Greece in April, the peak time for the amazing spring flowering and bird migration in the region, stay on the remote eastern island of Asteri, just off the coast from Turkey, whilst she researched her latest travel series: *Paradise under Threat*. She could bring that trip forward, fly to Rhodes, take the light airplane to Asteri.

It would be expedient to drop out of circulation in England until a certain brunette forgot her. Katherine Hopkins had a spiteful memory and a long business arm.

Melissa laid her camera down and sat on the shadowed side of the dunes, nimble fingers digging into the cold sand. The ebbing, mournful cry of a curlew dragged at her insides as she swallowed, faintly nauseated.

Remembering . . .

Two years ago, due to join Andrew on Rhodes for a holiday, she had been summoned instead to identify his body.

It had been the hardest thing she had ever done: to enter that cold sterile chamber and wait for the fluorescent lights to flicker into hard white brilliance over long grey metal drawers.

Nothing in her twenty-five years of life had prepared her for the moment when the drawer glided open and she must look.

Melissa's father, a merchant sailor, had been lost at sea. At twelve years, when her uncle had met her from school to tell her, Melissa thought she had known the worst. But she was wrong.

Andrew's head was encased in bandages, his face smashed down one side. Staring at the carefully washed, ruined features, Melissa longed to touch, make him whole; run her fingers through his thick brown hair. She had always loved Andrew's hair.

A fall, the police said. A tragic accident.

'No!' murmured Melissa. Andrew had telephoned from Rhodes the day before he died. With a stab of guilt, Melissa remembered how irritated she'd been at the phone call: unlike some people, she was still working, she had told Andrew. She had not been due to join him on Rhodes, a holiday, for another three days.

Full of news, Andrew had persisted. Forgetting her warning about mosquitoes in early May, he had been first wakened by a biting mosquito, then kept awake by several more insects' buzzing passes next to his ear.

Hunting and swatting with a rolled up *Rodos News*, he had finally given up on sleep and gone walkabout in the deserted streets of the Old Town.

Five in the morning and nothing had been moving except for prowling cats, no sounds except the occasional twitter of swallows. Until, walking into a square dominated by a derelict mosque encased in scaffolding, Andrew had seen something strange.

'It was really peculiar, Mel: four men dressed as your salt-of-the-earth Greek fishermen, but not really real — too smooth somehow, and not a smoker amongst them.

'They were struggling with this crate, transferring it from one three wheel truck to another and having to hump it up some steps between the two trucks. There was a dog inside — it started barking like a mad thing — but you have to understand how large this crate was . . . I mean seriously big. And they were treating it with kid gloves; not letting it bump or jostle, though they were obviously in a hurry. I'd the feeling there'd been a serious cock-up in communication, that those two trucks should have met in the square or in the road above the square, but not with the steps between them . . .'

The 'fishermen' had spotted Andrew watching. One had lowered his part of the load onto a step leading out of the square into the narrow alleyway above, and approached.

Thankful he had been using his pencil torch, Andrew had pulled out a map and shone his light on that. After a measuring look at the Englishman, the 'fisherman' had swung round and returned to the others.

'They didn't stir again until I did.' Andrew had said, his voice crackling on the bad line. 'The whole thing was so weird I made sure they weren't following me here.'

Without her being aware of it, Melissa's left foot flexed slightly as she remembered. She had been indignant, but not for Andrew's sake. She had thought he was safe. She had accepted his assurance that he would be careful — anyway, he was driving out that morning from Rhodes Old Town to look over the south of the island — and, yes, he had reported the incident to the police. Melissa's anger had been for the plight of the crate's 'cargo'.

'Smugglers, Andrew. Not of guns or drugs, but of live animals. The dog would be a cover for whatever else was in that box, crammed in some disgusting secret compartment, half-starved and suffocated almost to death. Oh! I hope the police catch those men: it's a revolting trade!'

Melissa winced at the memory of those words. The conspiracy Andrew had stumbled upon in that small Rhodes street was more vicious than either of them realised. By the time Melissa found out more it was too late. Andrew was already dead.

A fall from a sheer pinnacle, an outcrop in the south of the island near to a deserted crusader castle. No one with him. That haunted Melissa most of all — Andrew had died alone.

The police had found no evidence of foul play. No money or cards were removed from Andrew's wallet. Perhaps the thief or thieves had panicked, suggested Melissa.

The police thought mugging unlikely in so remote a region. As for these strange sightings in the Old Town — none of the Rhodes police had received a report from a tourist about smugglers. Perhaps the Englishman had decided he was mistaken and so had done nothing.

Again, the police repeated that they had found no signs of any kind of struggle; no wounds but those consistent with a fall.

The police also revealed that Andrew could have been intoxicated when he was killed — the front of his shirt was stiff with dried-in retsina. Melissa's statement that Andrew disliked retsina was noted, but a significant amount of alcohol had been found in his bloodstream.

'That's impossible,' said Melissa, when told of the autopsy. 'Andrew hates being drunk — he never has more than a single beer, or glass of wine. One of his friends died on his eighteenth birthday pub crawl. Andrew told me about it, how horrible and tragic it all was . . .'

The police had let her talk before observing, tactfully, that Mr Thornhill was no longer eighteen, and that on the day he had died it had been very hot.

He had been seen drinking at the local taverns, two kilometres from the castle.

She could not accept his death as an accident. That Andrew had simply fallen seemed impossible — she knew him. He had the balance and skill of a cat. After a childhood spent scrambling round the West Country cliffs he had a head for heights. For all his zest and interest he was steady, not someone to take foolish risks, least of all round wild, exposed ruins.

And he would never drink to excess.

Throughout the time of their supposed holiday, Melissa kept combing the site where Andrew had fallen, tracking in and around the tiny chapel within the castle walls. She refused to admit he was gone forever. Something of him must remain, some trace.

She had found nothing. When she talked to the owners of the local taverna, they recalled the tall Englishman drinking a glass of wine, possibly retsina, possibly more than one glass: they could not remember exactly.

Andrew's family had wanted him buried and remembered as the living, lovable young man he had been — who had accepted and defended Melissa's wanderlust by referring to his own 'Viking genes'. Andrew's parents had no sense of unfinished business.

Melissa had. Why had Andrew never gone to the authorities with what he had seen in Rhodes Old Town? Why the retsina on his clothes, a wine he detested? It did not make sense.

The questions haunted her. Forced to return to England, to her work at home and abroad, Melissa had slogged through life for the next year. She had packed Andrew's collection of varnished driftwood into the attic, given away his clothes.

Then, five months ago, Melissa heard from a cousin in Piraeus that an Athenian had been caught in Rhodes Old Town trying to sell a juvenile Eleonora's falcon. Under questioning, he had begun to divulge new information — including mention of a wildlife smuggling ring which, he claimed, had murdered a foreign tourist in the south of Rhodes over a year before. The tourist had 'seen something down there' and so had been disposed of, the Athenian said, although he knew of it only through hearsay . . .

Before he had finished telling all he knew, the Athenian had died in prison of a ruptured appendix. No more details had emerged, but Melissa was certain that the murdered tourist was Andrew. What had he seen in the south? What had tipped the smugglers into action there, when in Rhodes Town they had left him alone?

Unfinished business, reflected Melissa, squeezing dune-sand through her fingers, listening to the piping calls of the waders, watching the grey wave-caps Andrew had loved. She wanted to expose the cruel, secret illegal trade which she was sure had cost Andrew his life. To know who had killed him, and why.

The Rhodian police had already admitted, after several lengthy telephone calls by Melissa, that they were reopening Andrew's file and making new enquiries. Melissa meanwhile had started some of her own.

Rhodes island itself was a dead end, she had decided. After the Athenian had been taken trying to sell a rare bird of prey, no doubt the smugglers would lie low in that part of the Dodecanese for a while. She herself was also too well known to the local police, who were beginning their new enquiries and who would naturally resent an amateur. On Rhodes she must let the customs and police do their job.

Melissa reached for her camera and rose to her feet. Time to go, she thought, turning her back on Andrew's estuary. She was to telephone Jonathan Saunders at eight tonight. A wildlife investigator who had been working undercover in the Dodecanese, Jonathan had promised sensational news . . .

Melissa gripped the receiver harder and rammed it tight to her ear. 'You're sure, Jonathan? Asteri?'

'That's where "Spiro" first made contact with me. And where he told me to go to pick up my shipment of orchid bulbs.'

'But the place is practically next door to Turkey! And it's tiny: fourteen miles end to end. The population must be less than two thousand; there's no proper airport, nor a decent-sized harbour . . .'

Melissa stopped, struck by the fact that everything she had mentioned — its smallness, its seclusion, its lack of international airport or harbour security, its closeness to

Turkey — made Asteri an ideal stepping-stone for smugglers wishing to trade from the Far East and Turkey through to Europe and America. And Asteri had no full-time police, only a mayor, Nicholas Stephanides, with whom she had exchanged formal letters of introduction.

'Sorry, I'm babbling,' she said after a deep breath. 'It's just so big a coincidence I can't really get hold of it yet. You know I'm going to Asteri next month?'

'To do those features on bauxite mining, yes. Well, someone needs to draw attention to it before a real mess is made of the place.'

Even whilst trying to concentrate on Jonathan's answer, Melissa's mind went charging ahead. Wildlife smugglers on Asteri. The type of men she was convinced had murdered Andrew. Her fingers tightened further on the receiver.

'Yes, yes, that's right.' *I know what I'm doing, Jonathan: get to the point.* Phone jammed under her chin, Melissa launched herself off the hotel bed to scrabble amongst her worknotes for pen and paper. 'What happened between you and "Spiro"?'

Now she listened intently. After six weeks of posing as an unscrupulous plant collector, shuttling between the Greek islands and the Turkish mainland, Jonathan had been approached on tiny Asteri by a man who introduced himself as 'Spiro'. Spiro had offered to supply Jonathan with over a thousand very rare plants and bulbs, stolen from five Greek island and two Turkish mainland sites, and package them for Jonathan to fly out with them from Asteri to a private airstrip in Northern Greece and then to Germany.

'But I did not confirm the order, and instead called that deal off,' Jonathan said, in his slow deliberate way that made Melissa want to put her hand down the phone line and give his beard a tweak. 'Spiro kept chattering about other "special items" he could obtain. I decided to call his bluff. As you know, Asteri's a breeding site for the Eleonora's falcon . . .'

It was an Eleonora's that the Athenian was trying to sell when the Rhodes police caught him. 'Is that what you asked Spiro for, a falcon?' Melissa asked.

'I raised the stakes.' Jonathan's voice was suddenly harsh. 'Said I was after them and golden eagles: ten of each if Spiro could supply them.'

For an icy shocked instant Melissa was speechless, then — 'Are you mad?' she hurled down the phone line. 'Ten Eleonora's when there are so few thousand breeding in the wild? You know what your "order" means

— for every falcon successfully captured, there'll be another five that don't survive . . . and you go and ask for ten!' Anger gave way to horror and disgust. 'That's sick, Jonathan.'

'It would be, Melissa, if I'd done what you're suggesting. But if you'd allow me to explain . . .'

Breathing in heavily, Melissa listened as Jonathan corrected her first impassioned hasty impression. He had *not* agreed a price with Spiro, and until that first vital part of the deal was concluded, nothing would be set in motion. Spiro it turned out had been 'burnt' before by non-payment and so had determined a simple rule: half-payment first, and only then were the 'goods' obtained, the trappers and middlemen paid for their time and labour.

'We've arranged to meet back on Asteri next week to agree a price,' Jonathan concluded steadily. 'I'm to stay at the Villa Elysion.'

'I see,' said Melissa quietly, feeling somewhat foolish at her earlier flare-up. Asteri was favoured by the super-rich, she now recalled. From her research she knew there were three luxury villas available for hire on the island. One, owned by Asteri's mayor, Nicholas Stephanides, was the Villa Elysion.

'Spiro wouldn't tell me the final date and any pick-up point for my "special items". I'm to wait to be contacted at the villa — naturally with sufficient funds to provide down payment for the transaction.'

There was a moment's silence, then: 'It's a shame, you going there yourself next month. A few weeks earlier and we could have flown out together.'

Melissa's heart began beating faster again. 'Let's do that,' she suggested, with a calmness she did not feel. 'I'll bring my trip forward.' *She had been planning to do that anyway, because of Katherine.* 'If you want, you can tell Spiro when you meet that I adore seahorses. Maybe he'll offer to smuggle those, too.'

Melissa smiled grimly into the receiver as her warm brown eyes fixed on the laughing photograph of Andrew on the otherwise impersonal bedside cabinet. Jonathan didn't know her suspicions about Andrew's death. No one knew.

'I'd be glad to help in any way,' she stressed, sensing hesitation.

Jonathan cleared his throat. 'I know Nicholas Stephanides won't agree but if we posed as a couple I think Spiro might be less wary of me. And more likely to, you know, to answer questions, to show off —'

30

'What's Stephanides to do with this?'

'Nick Stephanides is my local contact, Melissa. I have to consider what he says,' Jonathan answered — reasonably enough, although recalling the terse letter of acknowledgement she had received from the mayor of Asteri, Melissa began to feel annoyed.

Her irritation increased when Jonathan admitted, 'I'm afraid though that Mr Stephanides and I don't exactly get on. Whenever I went to see him he wasn't exactly forthcoming about what Spiro and his group might be doing on Asteri. Seemed to resent what he called foreign interference in Greek affairs.'

Melissa was further irritated at the thought of idealistic, hardworking Jonathan subjected to such a pious little speech. She opened her mouth to respond when Jonathan added anxiously, 'So you think it's a good idea to pose as a couple?'

'I certainly do — and to hell with Stephanides.' Quickly, without giving Jonathan a chance to reconsider, Melissa extracted from him the date of his flight. He was due to go out next Wednesday to meet Spiro the following Friday, only ten days away.

Melissa phoned the airline, then re-dialled Jonathan's number.

31

'See you at Gatwick next Wednesday,' she said.

The evening after, with only a week to go, Jonathan phoned her at home in Norfolk. 'It's off,' he said flatly. 'I've cancelled my flight and told Nick Stephanides and the Villa Elysion we can't make it. Travis is out of the country, so he can't stand in for me . . .'

Travis was Jonathan's fellow wildlife investigator, running their office from his tiny flat in London.

'Of course, even if Travis had been able to get to Asteri, there's no guarantee that Spiro would have dealt with him —'

'Jonathan, you're not making sense,' Melissa broke in. 'What's happened?' Anger made her blunt. 'And what right had you to do anything without asking me? I changed not only my flight but my entire schedule for you.'

Jonathan sighed. 'Without wishing to be over-dramatic about it, Melissa, I can't move; I'm in plaster. Right now, I'm phoning from the hospital, courtesy of a hit-and-run driver this morning. I'll be in and out of doctors' surgeries for weeks.'

'Oh, Jonathan, I'm so sorry.' Melissa was appalled. 'You should have said straightaway. Which hospital are you in? I'll come and see you.'

Jonathan told her, ending gloomily: 'Sorry to have messed it up for you, Melissa.'

'You haven't, because I'm still going,' Melissa said. She thought of something to cheer Jonathan up. 'And just remember *you* have the taped conversations and film of Spiro: probably enough for the Greek customs and police to arrest him.' Jonathan was a careful investigator: he would have met Spiro carrying not only a hidden tape recorder, but a hidden camera as well.

Another sigh gushed down the phone line.

'Sorry again, Melissa. The tapes and films went west in the accident: the car ran over them too.'

Melissa's left foot jerked in an angry frustrated twitch. The thought that perhaps Jonathan's 'accidental' encounter with the car had been nothing of the kind chilled her gut and made her snatch back other reflex questions. She reminded herself she was speaking to a man in hospital, in pain.

'It doesn't matter,' she said. 'The Spiros of the world always make mistakes through greed: you'll have another chance to expose his filthy trade. Perhaps the mayor of Asteri can do something: the island is small, everyone is known . . .'

'Without pictures I've nothing to separate Spiro from a hundred other island Greeks of the same name. The man I met was somewhere between thirty and forty-five, average height, bit stocky, deep tan, black wavy hair, bushy moustache, black sunspecs. Absolutely no distinguishing features — Oh! Except one: he didn't smoke . . .'

Not a smoker amongst them, Andrew had said, when describing the men he had seen in Rhodes Old Town. Melissa said nothing, but her head was buzzing. Coincidence? Possibly. But this new information only made her the more determined to track Spiro down.

'Nick Stephanides was furious when I told him. Said that my identikit picture of Spiro, if produced, would fit half the adult male population of Asteri and that the only good thing to come out of the entire affair was that my "idiot scheme" to involve you in catching the smugglers had fallen through.'

Idiot scheme was it? thought Melissa, feeling the burn of anger sear through her. The chauvinistic old fool . . .

'Forget Mr Stephanides: he's not worth your attention,' she told Jonathan briskly. 'Tell me what you like to read. I'll bring you books when I come.'

★ ★ ★

By the time she arrived at the hospital Jonathan was more comfortable and chatted happily. One of a large family, he was never without visitors. By the end of the week, when Melissa was due to leave, she had no qualms in leaving Jonathan to the loving attention of his sisters, brothers and friends.

'Have you told Stephanides?' Jonathan asked.

Melissa shrugged. 'He should know: my passage to Asteri's not been cancelled.' Her warm brown eyes flashed. 'If the mayor doesn't know, then I'll be a surprise for him.'

'You won't do anything rash?' Jonathan asked anxiously.

Melissa smiled. 'Of course not,' she chuckled, hiding her eyes behind a flick of her blonde fringe. 'You and Mr Stephanides are the wildlife investigators, not me! I'm going to Asteri alone.'

And no mayor of Asteri was going to stop her.

Chapter 3

'*Apó tin Anglía?* No English tourist has such cameras!' Since the last of his regulars had disembarked at Karpathos, Manoli the ferry-man had been bursting with questions. In sight of his final port, his home island, he could no longer stand it.

Melissa grinned. 'But I do this for a living,' she called back in Greek, without taking her eye from the viewfinder. She was enthusiastically soaking in impressions, camera ready.

Already in her long lens, Asteri was more than the smudge that Manoli would see drifting up to them from the sea. It had a dark central mountain and green hills, sharp ridges running down from its single peak, grey and tawny cultivated land.

'What's your name?' Manoli yelled over the engine noise.

'Melissa Haye!' Sitting on a box of fruit and leaning against a crate, Melissa waved a greeting to Manoli in the cabin behind her. Spray and flare would make shots difficult, but she braced her arms to hold her camera steady, keenly aware of the fabric of her Barbour draped over the crate.

Keenly aware of the stranger watching.

A man with a shaggy, charming rag-bag of a dog, sheltering under his legs. Throughout the long boat-trip, Melissa had been tempted to whistle the collie-cross bitch out to fuss her, but wasn't sure how her owner would react.

Considering the man, Melissa reckoned him to be in his thirties and, by the dark shirt and socks — worn in the masculine delusion that these would need less attention than lighter, dye-fast items — probably unattached. In jeans and baggy brown sweater, he sported a blue cap which had plainly seen better days. Like Melissa, he had been on the boat since Rhodes, making himself comfortable amongst the spare bus tyres piled in the bows. Now the man was working with needle and thread on part of a denim jacket but, when he was convinced that Melissa was occupied, he stared at her instead.

Melissa was aware of his eyes the instant she boarded the boat. Like her, the stranger had been obliged to take Manoli's ancient ferry after the scheduled light aircraft flight to Asteri had been cancelled owing to the sudden illness of the only available pilot. The man's interest had increased when she, like him, had remained on board through every port of call visited by *Asteri One.*

Melissa laughed softly. Interest was great, it made her feel good, but she was aware that this man could be Spiro: the wildlife smuggler whom Jonathan had arranged to meet two days from today at the Villa Elysion on Asteri.

Stocky, tanned, blunt-nosed, black-browed and with a Cretan moustache, the stranger glanced up from ripping a clasp-knife through a section of the jacket: at this rate there would be nothing of it left. Adjusting her camera, Melissa felt his eyes quickly fix on her, then withdraw.

'Why are you going to Asteri, Melissa Haye?' Manoli's vigorous call interrupted her thoughts. 'Are you married?'

Straight brown hair and double-knotted shoelaces. Melissa tried for more but Andrew-in-memory vanished. Since setting out from England she had decided to speak of Andrew — not his name, though, nor the time or place of his death — to see if there was any queer reaction from the questioner. It was for Andrew that she took her eye away from the viewfinder and turned her head, wind snagging her fine hair.

'Single. My partner was killed falling from a cliff.' It was easier to admit this in a lan-

38

guage not her own.

Farther along the boat Melissa sensed the stranger trying to listen above the pounding engines. She wished she had the eyes of a hare, to watch everywhere at once. Straining to hear through the strikes of the water and roaring chug of the boat, she sensed no sudden intakes of breath, heard only the tear of cloth ripped by strong hands and a keen knife.

'No children,' she added, anticipating the question.

'Ah!' Steering his ramshackle craft one-handed, Manoli rubbed his unshaven jowls in sympathy. His wind-blown features were guileless yet sharply interested. Making a rapid sign against bad luck he again looked over the pure blonde, nicely rounded young woman with her practical yet delicate shoes, her crisp white top and wool cardigan tucked into orange oilskin overalls similar to those worn by fishermen. Her glowing face and nimble hands were becoming sunburnt: astonishing for March.

With a glance towards the looming island coastline, the sea, the bows, Manoli returned to the woman. 'Are your parents dead too? Do you have brothers? Sisters?'

Most of the Greeks she talked to were like Manoli. Melissa loved the sudden conversational veering off and the absolute directness. 'My father drowned at sea. My mother re-married and lives with my stepfather and my two brothers and three sisters in England. A place called York.'

'Cousins?' shouted Manoli, sucking on a home-made cigarette.

'Lots of cousins, all over the world!' At this rate, Melissa thought, laughing, she was going to be hoarse. 'I've a Greek second cousin in Piraeus: he works in a shipping office.'

They had reached the westernmost tip of the island, one of the five promontories which gave Asteri the rough star shape for which it was named. Panning with her camera, Melissa refocused on the cliffs ahead, searching, stalking —

In the bows the man was shifting. Melissa did not hear but imagined the squeak of a trainer on damp timber as she felt the deck flex underfoot. Her whirling hair cut her sideways vision to the port bows as a limber body prowled sternwards.

To turn away meant a missed shot.

Melissa was looking for more than photo-graphic images. Asteri had an airstrip, a few seaward hamlets and the village port of Khora, the island 'capital', but these were too public for the quarry she had in mind.

Small coves, sheltered beaches were what she was after. Places a team of smugglers might put in to secretly and safely.

Asteri: Star Island, thought Melissa. Already its mountain peak enticed her, already the evergreen blaze of its woods — luxuriant for a small Mediterranean island — excited her. Yet there was sharpness amongst the sweet. It was here Jonathan had tracked down Spiro, the leader of the smugglers who had quite probably murdered her lover.

The silver seahorse earrings were cold against her neck. Melissa's gold eyebrows drew together then flicked apart. Andrew's death made her angry and the anger focused her. Hoping for a glimpse of the smaller islet of Antasteri, the lesser star, she scanned the western rim of the growing island.

In all this she had not forgotten the stranger, but could not hear his approach over the slap of water against the hull.

'Why are you coming to Asteri?' Manoli had recalled an earlier unanswered question.

'I want to photograph the island. To write about it, too. I'm doing a series of newspaper and magazine reports.' As the wind faltered, Melissa heard the footsteps stop.

'How much are they paying you?'

Melissa clicked her tongue and laughed: only the Greeks asked you what everyone else wanted to know. 'Around three thousand pounds. I'm not sure what that'll be in drachmai.'

From the corner of her left eye Melissa watched Manoli let the boat butt its own way on a course parallel to the cliffs as he jerked up both hands to make a 'crazy' gesture. In the eye of the lens, a long steep rocky shoreline replaced the cliffs.

No safe anchorage here in a storm. The thought snapped through Melissa's mind, rapid as a camera shutter. Melissa swept the lens higher, towards the central forest before Asteri's bare mountain peak, and gasped.

Wonderful. No other word encompassed it. Mature, unspoilt Mediterranean forest such as is rarely seen in the islands. Glorious tall pines. Great oaks allowed to reach their full height and spread. Cypress stands, not sad or elegiac but vigorous. And beneath, no doubt, although too far for her long lens, the shrubs and flowers: juniper, honeysuckle, cyclamen —

'Amazing!' Melissa exclaimed, colouring with excitement, ears buzzing with heat.

Suddenly a cap — hewn from a blue denim jacket — was dropped onto her head. The stranger straightened the Robin-Hood style brim over her forehead. 'You're too fair to go without a hat,' he said gruffly, in

American-accented English. 'Down, Chloe!' This last in Greek to his dog, bouncing round Melissa's legs.

Surprised — she'd been on the receiving end of some unusual male approaches before now, but this was the most original — Melissa bent and patted Chloe. 'I'll bear that in mind,' she remarked drily.

'Even old hands can be caught by the spring light,' the man went on, touching his own faded blue cap. 'It's very deceptive.'

He had a gruff, seaman-loud voice. Coupled with fiery light eyes, that luxuriant moustache and the rapid-fire approach of many Greeks, he tended towards benevolent dictatorship. 'People have been sent to hospital with heat exhaustion, and there isn't any hospital on Asteri.' His New England accent broadened. 'Sorry if this seems pushy.'

He was so openly bossy that Melissa couldn't help but be amused. 'Thanks,' she said, laughing, face pink from the sun.

'No problem,' the stranger said — she was sure he was suppressing a grin behind his moustache. Suddenly he thrust out a hand. 'I'm Nick Stephanides, the mayor of Asteri.'

Her free hand disappeared into his, his warm hard grip making his introduction even more incredible. Here was her anticipated

43

adversary, thought Melissa, amazed. Not an old, crusty misogynist, but a smiling man in the prime of life and the peak of fitness. She felt her jawbone go and caught it back.

'Melissa — Pleased to meet you,' she said, amused at her own confusion. The element of surprise had been his, after all.

'Pardon me — you've a leaf caught in your hair.' The man dived forward, and by a nimble sleight of hand unseen by Manoli tucked the dried spear of an olive leaf close to her left ear. As he deftly cupped the leaf to draw it out again, he brought his face close to hers.

'What the hell are you doing here now? Jonathan told me you'd cancelled.'

'I've still my own work!' Melissa hissed back. 'Besides, Spiro's due at your place on —'

The hand in her hair tightened. 'Manoli speaks English,' came the warning whisper. Abruptly she was released.

'Glad to have you with us, Melissa,' said Nicholas loudly. 'I hope you enjoy your stay.'

The moustache made it hard to tell if he was being serious or not, but Melissa was absolutely certain that the mayor of Asteri was furious and that he would one day apologise for pulling her hair.

'Excuse me now, please: we'll be landing in a moment.' Turning abruptly away,

Nicholas started to heave together sacks of potatoes, ready for unloading.

Melissa started as Manoli sounded the horn. Heeling round the southernmost tip of the island, *Asteri One* steamed towards Khora, passing a small private harbour.

The private harbour's natural horseshoe shape reminded Melissa sharply of Andrew's estuary. Throwing off the memory of Katherine Hopkins' threats, she focused on the rambling oaks and run-wild olive and citrus trees at the side of the house, on the drifts of dark purple periwinkles. A sweet scent from narcissi growing near a small stand of trees drifted across the water as Melissa lowered her camera.

Nicholas caught her questioning look. 'My Elysion,' he said laconically, jerking a thumb past the scudding waves to the whitewashed villa at the head of the bay. Manoli revved the engine, ready to strike out for the bigger harbour of Khora.

In another few moments the ship had docked alongside the harbour's central stone jetty and the islanders were swarming aboard to unload the cargo. Slipping the Nikon round her neck, Melissa rapidly retrieved her rucksack and gear. As she squeezed through a crush of dark-garbed women haggling for vegetables on the wide gangplank, Melissa noticed the mayor of Asteri pounding two at a time up a long series of white steps leading from the main jetty into Khora itself, a sack of potatoes slung over one shoulder.

Melissa did not follow him. To gain her bearings, she walked the length of the sweeping harbour front: right, then left.

To the right, a few metres on from the throngling stone jetty, Khora, the 'capital' of Asteri lay quiet under a bright midday sun: pink houses shuttered. At this hour the small loggia where the fish and bric-a-brac market was held was deserted.

Stepping over yellow fishing nets spread across the cobbled harbour road to dry, Melissa approached the closed door of a café, hoping to learn there of somewhere in Khora where she could rent a room. Naturally, Nicholas had not told her anything so useful — opposed as he was to her presence on Asteri a month early, Melissa did not expect any favours from him.

The café was locked.

Melissa wasn't worried. Shrugging off rucksack, tripod and large camera bag, she peeled herself out of her overalls and bundled everything into the shade under the tiny shuttered window of the café. In a Greek

46

village, no one would dream of stealing her things.

Unburdened, she set off for the northernmost limit of Khora. Passing small fields enclosed by drystone walls, she cut across a tiny shale beach littered with old machine parts. Here, fishing boats were drawn out of the water, some yellow caiques balanced on cradles, ready to be repaired. Inhaling the sweet scent of seasoned wood, Melissa strode over a final patch of scrub and, reaching a steep crag whose lower slopes were cloaked in a huge living wall of prickly pear, came to the end of the village. The harbour road stopped here, and above her, the scrub-covered crag threw a black long shadow.

From an ancient Admiralty Pilot borrowed from Wells-next-the-Sea Library, Melissa knew that a three-mile stretch of silver sand lay beyond the crag. Eager to see Lykimi beach, she was tempted to go on, scramble up one of the tiny grey tracks threading through the rampant vegetation, but exploration would be a future pleasure, she promised herself: an adventure for when she was dressed in more substantial clothes than culottes and sandals. Still, she was glad she had dressed lightly: on land there was only the faintest of breezes, wafting the scent of lemon blossom down through the twisting, many-stepped alleys of Khora into the harbour. In this midday sun she was glad, too, of her makeshift hat.

Did Nicholas like her? she wondered, returning to promenade the left-hand side of the harbour, admiring the steps and twists of Khora's intriguing backstreets. Yet why should that matter?

Manoli's ferry was still creaking against the harbour mole, but now the brief flurry of selling and barter was finished, the islanders retiring to their pink-shuttered privacy. A butcher's, a baker's, a chemist's. Melissa slowly read off the Greek shop signs as she wandered alone along the silent waterfront, flitting by identical two-storey, two-windowed, single-doored, flat-roofed houses, Minoan in their simple architecture. No gardens, Melissa noted, except for those chicken-infested olive and vine patches where proud sponge-fishermen's houses, now derelict, had stood.

Suddenly there was a break in this pattern. A new building, metal, not stone, windowless and featureless except for one thing: a steady drone of activity. Only the lapping sea and the complaining wheeze of a donkey interrupted the discreet tapping and hammering filtering from this long grey block.

Life! thought Melissa ironically, measuring the factory as she noted the squat power generator beside it. The building was big enough for wildlife smugglers to use. Whether Mayor Stephanides approved or not she would grab some pictures of its interior.

The rest of Khora swept round the sharper left-hand curve of the bay and was composed of large villas, many here with formal gardens in varying stages of grand decay. The bell tower of a blue-roofed church played hide and seek with her amongst the houses and grey boundary walls, dazzling white steps and leaned-over fig trees. Composing shots in her head, Melissa returned to the café.

It was still closed, but someone had tucked a note amongst her things. 'Room — Mrs Samouri's, just past the plane tree off the main square. N.' Printed in English, the note also comprised a scribbled map and address.

Melissa smiled. Suddenly she felt less alone. Shouldering her things, she set off up the long series of steps into the main village, taking them two at a time as Nicholas had done.

At the top of the steps Khora, in one of its many surprises, levelled off. Melissa walked blinking onto a large sunlit square, fronted by the island's main church.

In the centre of the square was a large circular marble fountain. Melissa paused to drink its cold sweet water before turning towards the spreading embrace of the plane tree at the far end of the square.

At the end of the shadowed street behind the plane tree, as the note had promised, a house with the slogan 'Flat to Let' daubed over the doorway. Sensing a peering of curious eyes through house shutters in the houses opposite, Melissa knocked.

Next morning, having unpacked and settled in to Mrs Samouri's clean and inexpensive two-roomed flat, Melissa was out at sunrise, this time without camera but with her notebook handy. She was going to the office of the mayor, next to the priest's house on the main square, and wanted to be early for what she was certain would not be an easy meeting.

Nicholas Stephanides rose from behind his paper-strewn desk, motioning abruptly to Chloe to stay in her corner basket. 'I didn't expect you for another month,' he said brusquely.

'Yes — you made that plain on the boat.' Melissa remained where she was in the doorway between the inner and outer of the two offices and ignored the mayor's proffered hand. 'In fact, you were generally discourteous, Mr Stephanides.'

'Okay, so I was rude, and I'm sorry, but yesterday wasn't good.' Nicholas remembered how he had tugged on the blonde's hair to shut her up — just like a little kid, he thought, embarrassed. Recalling that silky sun-yellow hair against his rough fingers he felt the blush starting in his ears. How could he explain, he thought, without giving away too much? He didn't want a woman involved.

Trying to gain time he changed the subject. 'How's Jon?'

The blonde in the doorway frowned and the dust between them, lit through the single small back window, swirled, stirred up. 'As comfortable as anyone can be in hospital after being mowed down by a hit-and-run driver,' she answered, her tone dry.

Melissa crossed the tiled floor to the chair the mayor of Asteri had put for her. 'There was no time to send you a letter, Mr Stephanides. Things are moving: Spiro is due to meet Jonathan tomorrow at the Villa Elysion.'

'I know,' interrupted Nicholas harshly. 'What I need to understand here is what

51

business that is of yours.'

'Of course it's my concern!' flashed back Melissa, aroused by Nicholas' consistent bad temper. Her blonde hair blazed in the light through the grimy office window as she flicked her head towards the door. 'I've recorders and a film camera at Mrs Samouri's, and I know how to use them to catch Spiro and his "deals" on tape.' Her eyes looked into his. 'There's no one on this island with my photographic experience, including you, Mr Stephanides.'

Good point, thought Nicholas sourly, waving a warning finger at Chloe as she lolled up from her basket and sidled over to his visitor. All neat and clean and bright. He wondered if she could be put off. 'About our meeting on the boat,' he began, feeling a proper apology was needed.

'If you're going to remind me about wearing a hat, don't bother.' Melissa patted the white floppy cap tucked into her waistband. 'As you can see I've brought my own today.'

Nicholas ploughed on. 'You must have guessed by now how Manoli is: questions, questions. I didn't want him to realise we'd been in touch about certain matters until we could speak privately. As you say, time's of the essence: we don't want to alert anyone too soon.'

He watched the blonde cross her legs. 'We haven't, Mr Stephanides. Corresponded, that is,' she answered crisply. 'When you wrote to me you never mentioned Spiro.'

'You bet I didn't mention him,' Nicholas retaliated, apology forgotten in his irritation. 'Jon and I wrote to each other care of a wildlife group in Rhodes. If we'd used the local post, the whole of Asteri would've known about it. Manoli takes the mail on and off the island.'

'I see.' Unconsciously, Melissa touched the white hat in her waistband a second time. 'Still, do you seriously believe that Manoli could be a wildlife smuggler? Rather old — if indiscreet,' she added, conceding that point.

'In this business I find it wisest to suspect everyone,' replied Nicholas shortly. Including you, he added in thought. Saunders being in hospital and Melissa Haye's sudden appearance alone and a month earlier on Asteri than originally agreed were something he'd not expected.

Melissa leaned forward, jamming her elbows between paperwork on his cluttered desk. 'Oh, I think it's more than that,' she said, a razor edge on her clear voice. 'You've been doubtful about me from the moment Jonathan suggested that he and I team up and pose as a couple — "idiot scheme" was how you described it, I believe. And yesterday on the boat it was obvious you were petrified that this giggly non-Greek blonde might let slip some vital unconsidered remark to the ferryman or anyone else she met between the harbour and Mrs Samouri's about Mayor Stephanides' plans to stop the nasty wildlife traders . . .'

'That is just *not* true.' Nicholas lied, appalled at his own thoughts and the woman's accuracy in revealing them.

'No?' Melissa breathed, 'Prove it, then. Tell me how you're going to help me catch Spiro.'

The man's fierce blue eyes widened. 'I presume you've authorisation from Jon's organization,' he countered.

Melissa fished in a pocket and brought out a sealed envelope. She had no idea of the letter's contents — she was above steaming envelopes open — and waited apprehensively, well prepared to argue, as Nicholas scanned it.

'Says here exactly what you told me: that you're a wildlife photographer and writer doing a series of reports.' Nicholas raised his dark head. 'I'll help you with those,' he promised bluntly, 'although it's not as easy as maybe you think: this island needs some development. Asteri needs a bigger, safer airport. Last year a youngster died because there wasn't a local plane available to take him to the mainland.'

'You mean Rhodes, surely,' commented Melissa steadily. 'Or has Asteri come to an accommodation with her Turkish neighbour?'

'Rhodes or Dalaman, it doesn't matter,' said Nicholas, bayoneting the stale office air with powerful fingers. 'Without a bigger airport Asteri stays off-limits to both.'

Determined not to be put off, Melissa decided to try a direct approach. 'Do *you* think Spiro will put in an appearance tomorrow at the Villa Elysion?'

Nicholas jerked back his head in a sharp negative. 'Not if he sees some girl there instead of a man.' He stared past her at the peeling ferry timetable on the ochre-washed walls of his inner office cell, wondering why the woman threw him off balance.

'Why don't we talk about the bauxite mine first?' Nicholas asked after a long pause. 'If it goes ahead, it'll tear the heart out of our mountain and take most of the old forest with it. I'm trying to persuade the boss of Pindaros Bauxite to invest in eco-tourism instead . . .'

'That's Ari Pindaros, the millionaire,'

Melissa confirmed, running a hand down Chloe's head and along her back. The collie-cross sat down, her tail swishing against the desk leg.

'One and the same,' answered Nicholas. 'His mining company's had a bad press lately and Ari's sensitive about that, so he's interested in the idea of select, expensive holidays that don't damage the environment and pay him a good return. The fact he's Athenian doesn't help him here in the islands either, especially when I pinned up figures in the school comparing what Ari earns to a miner's basic wage. The staff in the Asteri co-operative earn more than the miners.'

He and Melissa exchanged knowing glances in their first moment of under-standing, each trying not to smile. Then Nicholas sighed, drumming the table top with his fingers.

'But Zoe Konstantinou . . . now Zoe's a different matter. That lady is dead set on building her marina development — and who cares if Lykimi's the last nesting beach on Asteri for the loggerhead turtle?' Nicholas jerked a thick black eyebrow. 'You know of course that Ari and Zoe are lovers?'

Melissa nodded. 'And allies,' she added, resigned.

'Then there's Beach International. That's

a big chandlery company — and when I say "big", I mean almost multinational. Well, naturally enough, they want to be involved in the Lykimi marina, and between them, Zoe and Ari, I've my work cut out . . .'

Nicholas talked for over an hour. About his efforts to stop the mine and marina. About ASPW — the Asterian Society for the Protection of Wildlife: an organization he had established. 'Call it Asp if you want; everyone else does.' About there being no proper maps of Asteri and his own mapping of the island, including wildlife sites, times of flowering of all the island plants, and records of every animal spotted. Because of the desperate need for work on Asteri, Nicholas had set up a co-operative in Khora: potters, leatherworkers, lace and carpet makers and other small businesses. All were gathered in that long grey building down by the waterfront in Khora harbour.

Listening, Melissa found herself warming to the mayor of Asteri. He cared, he acted. Such energy was attractive, despite his brusqueness and his rough manners on Manoli's boat.

Stroking Chloe, Melissa remarked idly, 'I passed your factory yesterday afternoon. I must admit I did wonder then if it was being used as a smuggling warehouse.' She smiled, inviting Nicholas to laugh at the idea, glad to cross the factory off her mental list of 'must-get-a-picture-of-that'.

Instead, the mayor's friendly expression changed, growing darker again as his eyes grew fiercer. 'I don't want you prying round Elysion tomorrow,' he said coldly. 'It's too dangerous.'

Melissa's hand paused in Chloe's neck-ruff. 'More dangerous than tracking a hungry puma?' she asked quietly.

Without answering her question, Nicholas continued as though she had not interrupted. 'These men are highly organised and very smart. You're out of your league even more than Jon was — Jon's ten eagles and falcons are just a side order for Spiro's group.' Abruptly he flung back his chair. 'Want a coffee?' he demanded, without smiling. 'They do great Greek coffee at the harbour café down the steps —'

Melissa lifted her hand from Chloe's sleek head and leaned back in her chair. 'When's this very special shipment due on Asteri, Mr Stephanides?' she asked, lifting her blonde head to him. 'And *where* is it coming in?'

Nicholas glowered at her. 'My source didn't know — it's only a tip-off of a tip-off:

third-hand information,' he answered shortly.

'Will you tell me the name of your contact?' asked Melissa politely.

'You know better than that, Miss Haye. My source stays secret.'

'But you can tell me — because you'll know — where the smugglers can't land,' Melissa continued, raising a hand to check that she was still wearing both pairs of silver seahorse earrings. 'And your informant is clearly convinced it's a major item of wildlife merchandise.'

Nicholas inhaled deeply. With his stocky figure blocking the light from the window, his blunt features were in shadow, but Melissa could guess his expression.

'You,' he said, jabbing a finger, 'are definitely too sharp for your own good — and too damn useful to me.'

She was in! Exultant, Melissa bounded to her feet. 'I'll buy the coffee,' she said.

Nicholas snorted. 'We'll argue on the way down about that!'

Melissa laughed and led the way out.

Chapter 4

A week later Melissa was no further forward in her exposure of the smugglers. Last Friday Spiro had not appeared at Elysion. Melissa was frustrated for herself, disappointed for Nicholas.

'Think maybe Spiro was tipped off by whoever ran down Jon?' Nicholas had asked her as the morning star rose on their futile night watch. 'Or is that just the American "everything's a conspiracy" in me?'

'We have to consider both possibilities,' Melissa replied, half-joking as she tried to lighten the mood. But both of them knew the jest was sour. 'What do you think this means for the extra special shipment?' she whispered. 'Is it still coming?'

'According to my informant — yes.' Lying on his stomach in his own garden and propped on his forearms, Nicholas shifted his weight from one elbow to another, sending a scent of bruised narcissi into the lightening air. 'Tonight was no big deal for Spiro: the birds won't even have been trapped. Not till after the money changed hands tonight.'

'Thank God.' Melissa knew this already from Jonathan, but it was a great relief to have it confirmed.

'Yes, thank God. Jon knew that was how these guys operate, so he could bait his trap with an "attractive" order. He'll be glad now, for sure, that all he and Spiro were set to do tonight was settle a price.'

'Poor Jonathan.'

Nicholas shifted again. 'You see now that these smugglers aren't fooling,' he growled testily.

'I've always known that,' Melissa had replied, eyes darkening as she'd thought of Andrew. Yet since that mutual acknowledgement of danger, an uneasy truce had emerged between them, a recognition of each other's awareness of risk.

Nicholas and Chloe were ahead, leading the way in the darkness up through the terraced fields above Khora. Lifting his dog gently over bare rock to the track above, Nicholas clambered from the field onto open heath, placing each foot on the loose shale as carefully as a mountaineer. Scorpions might still be out hunting.

Melissa followed his example. *Step on large stones, and haul yourself up on those roots.* Given the deadly spines and close-packed pin-cushions of scrub on the heath, she was glad to have a guide. Today, she and Nicholas were trekking to the top of Asteri mountain to overlook the proposed site of the bauxite mine, where Melissa hoped to take some landscape shots by morning light.

Nicholas was carrying water, fresh food, and — to provide a base for Melissa's planned four days of solo wildlife photography — camping gear, water and tinned provisions. Melissa was allowed only her camera equipment. A week ago, protesting at this macho arrangement, Melissa received the terse response: 'I'm the mule on these trips. If you aren't fresh, there are no decent pictures.'

Hopelessly old-fashioned, reflected Melissa, as she scanned the black figure prowling the moonlit ribbon of track ahead of her. Several nights ago, waiting undercover at Elysion, Nicholas had been ready to fight if any member of ASPW — scandalously all men — were threatened by Spiro or the wildlife smugglers. Yet she could not fault his commitment, nor his concern for others.

Now she watched him turn, as he often did, ready to stop instantly if she wanted to. Nicholas was surprisingly sensitive to the patient, often painfully slow aspects of her own separate work. Despite the urgency of the threats posed by Spiro, the bauxite mine and the marina, he never hurried her, never asked foolish questions, never made her feel she was holding up the fight against wildlife crime and exploitation.

Melissa turned and gazed down the track, past the terraces of ploughed fields, the orchards bursting with sweet orange blossom, towards Khora and the sea. Cold struck through her boots and camouflage clothing: the pre-sunrise chill. As she looked, the sky changed from black to deepest blue. Over the narrow sea strait, the Turkish mountains were lit by a paling moon. Closer at hand, thrushes were singing from a nearby maple tree, sparrows bustling in a cypress. In the middle distance, Stella the goatherd was leading her flocks up the rising field terraces, a soft jangle of bells heralding their passage.

Heart thumping, hands trembling slightly, Melissa swung her tripod off her back. Dawn, with its gorgeous clear low light, its delicate highlighting of form and textures, its generous spilling of soft pink and gold, was coming.

She worked systematically, bracketing exposures, trying filters, different angles, various lenses. Some time later, having taken several rolls of film, she remembered her guide.

Gathering her things together, Melissa wove her way up the path. 'Thanks,' she said to Nicholas, who was sitting patiently on a boulder, whittling an armadillo from a dry pine cone. The rising sun flared on the sharp knife blade.

'No problem.' Showing his teeth in a brief grin, the mayor of Asteri slipped knife and cone into a jacket pocket, shifted the towering pack on his shoulders and, whistling to Chloe, set out again along the rocky, orchid-lined path.

They worked well together, Nicholas was forced to admit, ducking round a bristling young fir. Behind him, cuddly in her camouflage clothes and hat — dark hat this time — Melissa moved as nimbly as a lizard, breathing steady, brown eyes no doubt winking with anticipation at the thought of a new place. Her enthusiasm was as infectious as it was informed: Nicholas had quickly realised this a week ago when they began to stake out beaches where the smugglers might land. His faint suspicions surrounding Melissa's sudden appearance and Jon Saunders' removal from the picture were now utterly squashed. Watching her operate photographic equipment with a casual ease he envied, Nicholas found himself also questioning his reluctance to involve a woman in this risky investigation. Yet at first he had drawn the line at taking Melissa to the airstrip.

'But that's the most likely place the smugglers will use — if not to bring shipments in, then to get them out quickly!' Melissa had argued — even her flyaway blonde hair seemed to bristle as she stood up to him. Nicholas, on the brink of an apology, reminded himself that Spiro and his group were armed. Last month he'd found a spent sub-machine gun clip on Petra beach in the north of the island, near one of the luxury villas — a detail which left Melissa entirely unimpressed.

'That clip might have been dropped by an over-enthusiastic huntsman for all you know,' she remarked, when told of it.

'The Rhodes police found a chimp's handprint on the clip, and unless baby primates have taken to playing with guns in the jungle I think we can assume Spiro was there,' Nicholas had answered, tugging his cap down low over his eyes, but again he failed to shake his companion.

'Who owns the two villas near Petra?' she asked instantly.

'David Gordon, the same man who owns

Antasteri.' Nicholas permitted himself a wicked grin. 'English.'

'Oh, yes?' Melissa shot him a glance. She'd heard of David Gordon.

'We don't think the smugglers used the villas,' Nicholas found himself admitting. 'Or at least if they did, then only as a stop-over.'

Melissa nodded. 'As with the airport,' she said, returning to their original dispute. 'You need me there, you know,' she went on, ignoring Nicholas' frown. 'I can set up re-mote cameras for you and show your *men* how to use infrared film as well as video.'

'I've been shown the basics,' Nicholas answered gruffly, determined not to give in. 'Zervos and the teacher can use video. And, as you've guessed, there are already *men* on watch, nights.'

Melissa laughed softly and clicked her tongue.

At the airstrip the following night, Melissa had been prepared for barbed wire, but there was only a latched gate to keep the road to Khora and Petra beach from merging into the wider runway. The rest of the site, standing a metre above the fields and fruit trees on a plateau, was not enclosed at all.

Whoever used this airstrip would need an

experienced pilot to fly down between the mountain ridges. Its runway, darker at the edges with what she guessed would be revealed as thyme in daylight, was not long enough to take anything like a jet.

Frowning, Melissa gently snapped the lens cap onto her camera and took the infrared binoculars from her coat pocket to sweep the area. Near the lee of the central peak there was a shape which might be a building.

The airport terminal, Nicholas explained. 'Want a closer look?' he whispered. Melissa nodded.

Watching for scorpions, they ducked round stones and branches, keeping low. If someone were lurking in the 'terminal' and equipped with infrared binoculars, then that person would see them if they ventured beyond the trees.

Nicholas had done this before and so was ready when the olives fanned out more widely, and an old boundary wall gave them a respite from creeping. Scrambling forward in the lead, Nicholas brought them closer to the 'terminal' and the ASPW member on watch tonight, Dr Alexios.

Nodding to the cramped six-foot-four medic, Melissa put her binoculars up to the wall, focusing through a small gap between the stones. There were no signs of spilled water or food for any illegally held animal within the building. She did not think anyone had set foot in there for a while, she whispered to Nicholas. If wildlife traders were using this airstrip, it could only be for small smuggling runs. Light planes could not cope with huge numbers of animals, and this terminal was too modest to use for anything except a rest-stop or transfer point.

'I told you that!' said Nicholas, disappointed yet also relieved that no one was illegally using the airstrip tonight. Wishing he could help, he waited then with nagging, frustrated anxiety as Melissa positioned and hid three remote cameras, then returned to explain how these might be triggered without alerting suspicion. By the end of the night, Nicholas grudgingly acknowledged that she had saved an ASPW member from having to take Alexios' place the following evening.

Melissa grinned, clear eyes twinkling mischievously. 'Good — that means you can keep me company on beach-watch!' she answered, neatly manoeuvring him into missing out on the airstrip, too. Seeing Alexios' lean, handsome features trembling on the brink of laughter, Nicholas had clapped the medic hard on the shoulder, but he could do nothing about Melissa Haye.

Conceding defeat gracefully, next morning he took her to Lykimi beach.

Chapter 5

Seven days after Melissa had met Nicholas in his office, her early arrival on Asteri was being remarked on thousands of miles away in Britain. At the Yorkshire country estate of Sir Oliver Raine, where Katherine Hopkins had been invited for the weekend, Katherine's host suddenly mentioned the wildlife photographer.

They'd been strolling in the oldest part of the Georgian-fronted house, the panelled Tudor long gallery, and until then Katherine had been mildly bored. Sir Oliver was a punctilious host but, like his dun-coloured hair and subdued tweeds, hopelessly drab as a man. Gliding beside him, heads level, an elegant hand tucked through Sir Oliver's brawny forearm, Katherine felt as safe as with a nanny. At forty, her host's passions were fishing — fortunately not indulged in this weekend of pounding rain and wind — and his collection of wildcats.

Katherine had already been shown round his private zoo, housed in the estate's huge stable block. There in special cages were Sir

Oliver's 'kitties', as he liked to call them: a lynx, a bobcat, a Scottish wildcat, a dainty jungle cat and a serval, both from Africa, a Pallas's from Iran and — for sentiment rather than value — a native Egyptian cat picked up by Sir Oliver in a Cairo alley, drugged and then smuggled through Customs inside his coat.

Tactfully, when shown this menagerie, Katherine did not mention that her father, a dour Suffolk farmer, had always drowned any 'kitties' he could lay his thick hands on. Instead, she remarked on the final empty cage, a much larger, stronger construction than the others, and carefully appointed.

Sir Oliver beamed at her, eyes glowing in the dim stable light. 'Yes, everything's ready . . . I can hardly wait for this little beauty . . . the queen of my kitties. Everything's ready — and nobody knows except you and the staff. Materials brought in from all over, you see, and assembled here. I've a little man who can rattle off any documents I need: certificates and stuff like that. The local P.C. tells me if there are any police swoops — not that there have been any for ages. Cages strip down, you see: half an hour and even that big one can come down. Stick 'em in plastic under the manure. And the kitties have a day out at the tenants' farmsteads in their special travelling cages. Police dogs go barmy, I can tell you! But they don't find anything. People are loyal, oh yes. It pays them to be. The staff have worked for my family for years: they're loyal. Oh! I can hardly wait . . .'

The perfect client, thought Katherine, reflecting on this recent memory as they turned at the end of the black-panelled Tudor long gallery for another circuit of the polished boards. Thinking of the half million price tag agreed between her and Sir Oliver for the 'special item' he so desperately longed to acquire, she companionably squeezed her host's arm.

Sir Oliver felt her narrow hand on his arm and suppressed the desire to stroke it. He liked her green eyes and her sleek hair. A pity she was in trade, he thought, ignoring for the moment that he was a director of Beach International, a company busy supplying equipment to marinas all over the world. Yesterday, he and Katherine, in open business, had signed a deal allowing Beach International exclusive rights to supply any of the new Total Women Centre marine resorts due to be opened in Greece and the Greek islands throughout the next decade.

Greece opened another avenue of thought in Sir Oliver.

'You're sure Asteri's the best route?'

Staring out of the draughty long windows at the black, wet March afternoon, counting the minutes to the housekeeper's appearance with the welcome news that tea was now served in the study, Katherine smiled. Client anxiety — a little unexpected from Sir Oliver, who in the past had shown a considerable lack of imagination when it came to worrying about practical arrangements, but perhaps not so surprising, given the value of the item being transported.

She turned her head to face her host. 'Checked and rechecked,' she answered calmly, as she and Sir Oliver slowed to negotiate a large, valuable, hideous onyx urn. 'Would you like me to run through the details with you again?'

It was so simple, thought Katherine, suppressing a yawn as she began to explain. The item was coming in from the East, neatly avoiding Turkish and European Customs by using small private airfields before its final staging post, Asteri. Katherine meanwhile would already have flown to the island to oversee this last change-over — a vital transaction, since Sir Oliver wished to fly with the item out of Greece. The baronet had wanted to accompany the creature for its entire journey: Katherine had persuaded him to adopt her plan to use Beach International's interest in Asteri's Lykimi beach as a screen. He would be sailing in from Rhodes a day or so before the special item had been landed safely, then staying on Asteri on a working holiday before Spiro delivered the goods and Sir Oliver could fly out with his prize.

Katherine's own cover was that of research: she would be staying at one of Asteri's luxury villas to assess the island's potential as a Total Woman Centre marina resort. This gallant, new, well-publicised venture gave Katherine a platinum-plated reason for regularly zipping in and out of the tiny Greek island should any complications arise with her smuggling deal.

Katherine smiled at the thought. She'd already had the pleasure of plunging the opposition into disarray by a few deft telephone calls last night, but still it wasn't often she could combine business and pure fun in so profitable a way. She was looking forward to her month in the sun.

Sir Oliver stopped before one large mullioned window, rubbing at a narrow strip of glass between the leaded lights with his jacket sleeve.

'That should be all right — short, stress-free trips,' he remarked, staring at the rain. 'Your people know about meals and so on? Yes, of course they do, they brought my little

Pallas's out at the same age.' Sir Oliver anxiously wiped the pane of leaded glass again. 'This kitty's so much bigger, and special.'

No seven-week cub was that big, reflected Katherine, grinding the toe of her right ankle boot on the uneven timber floor as Sir Oliver launched into a fevered analysis of the item's feeding patterns. She opened her mouth to reassure the client yet again when Sir Oliver, with a twitch of his brawny shoulders, abruptly changed the subject.

'About that photographer female — you said she wasn't due on the island for another month, but when I talked to Zoe Konstantinou on the blower yesterday morning, she tells me the woman's already there, two days after their Easter.' Sir Oliver's voice become petulant. 'And getting along famously with the mayor.'

Melissa Haye. Everywhere she turned, Melissa Haye. Katherine was suddenly wide awake. 'Really, Sir Oliver, what can one woman do to derail our plans?' she asked lightly without looking at the man, her heart thumping as anger pumped adrenalin through her tall, supple body.

'Quite a lot, I'd say,' came the stiff response. 'She scuppered your estuary development most effectively.'

The top of her perfectly arranged hair

brushed the window frame as Katherine leaned forward to peer into the rainy murk. She wanted to scream with frustration, but instead she responded coolly, 'Spiro mentioned she'd arrived when he faxed me his weekly report from Athens. We know about Miss Haye, and why she's skipped off to Greece so soon.'

It was to run away from me, thought Katherine with a satisfied twitch of her mouth. Yet this time there would be no escape. Since even Thornhill's death had not stopped her investigations, it was time for direct action. Katherine's final solution.

'But a wildlife reporter —'

Katherine shrugged. 'We know every move she makes,' she said, in reassuring tones. 'She'll find nothing.'

She had already told Spiro to kill last Friday night's Villa Elysion bargaining. Bailey, Katherine's personal assistant in London, had discovered just in time that Jonathan Saunders was really working for the Greens. Unknown to Spiro or Sir Oliver, Katherine had instructed Bailey to remove Saunders from the Asteri picture, thereby baiting the trap for her fly, Melissa.

Bailey was anxious about the next stage of her plans, Katherine reflected, but Bailey was a worrier. There was no risk of discovery involved: by the time Melissa Haye managed to stumble anywhere near the truth she would already be enmeshed in Katherine's designs.

Sir Oliver swung round from brooding over his rained-off parkland. 'I'm not happy at her being there,' he mumbled.

Katherine swivelled smoothly on her heels to beam her brightest smile on the fretful client. 'Even as we speak, plans are in motion to deal with Melissa Haye,' she promised. 'There'll be no mistakes. This time she'll be dealt with.'

And Katherine would be there to watch. Even better.

Chapter 6

Beyond the crag marking the northern end of Khora, Lykimi swept in a glistening smooth curve, disappearing round a low point near the turtles' breeding site. Even Melissa's optimism had been dented by the sight of these white sands leading away from Khora crag. A marina would make Lykimi available to every boat operating in the Aegean.

It hasn't happened yet, Melissa reminded herself. Setting her camera-bearing tripod securely into the soft sand, she looked for her companion. In spite of its being only March and early morning, Nicholas had taken off his shoes and socks.

'Good, is it?' Melissa asked, hiding her astonishment.

Nicholas squinted at her over Chloe's head. 'Care to join me?'

Melissa laughed. 'No, thanks!' Settling on the beach, she watched his bare feet digging into cool sand, the strong tendons ridged in white skin as he crouched beside her. There was something innocent about feet, she decided. Naked, they showed a print as fresh and individual as that of any wild creature.

'So — which to you are Asteri's "specials"?' asked Nicholas.

'Everything.' Melissa smiled at her wariness — the mayor of Asteri was hardly a smuggler — then reflected that what she was saying was true. 'To me everything's special.' Raising her head to the sun, she clicked her tongue with anticipation, hearing the lapping sea hiss like an indrawn breath.

Katherine, Melissa thought suddenly, freezing as the sound reminded her of their recent quarrel. And Andrew, now dead, killed near a beach like this.

'Melissa?' A dark, tanned face, looming into hers.

Melissa bounded to her feet. 'The light's wrong here now, and we've a lot of ground to cover,' she said abruptly, reaching for camera and tripod. 'Shall we go?'

Nicholas shrugged his broad shoulders. 'Sure,' he said, rising slowly to his feet. He sensed that a wall had just gone up between himself and Melissa.

The rest of the beaches — Petra, and the pebble cove of Xias in the north, dangerous Hydra in the west opposite the small wooded islet of Antasteri, sheltered Elysion and deserted Kemi in the south — were strictly business. The only thing Nicholas could get Melissa to agree with him about was that there were too many beaches for too few volunteers. Hydra and Kemi had so far been left out. Melissa had already offered to watch Kemi, an offer Nicholas had bluntly turned down.

'But why?' Melissa asked, wanting to scream in the face of such intransigent chauvinism. 'You said yourself that Hydra beach is chancy even in ideal weather, so why shouldn't I look out at Kemi?'

'Kemi was a Turkish settlement deserted in the 1920s — no self-respecting Greek'll set foot in the place,' Nicholas answered, hating how that sounded as soon as he'd said it.

'I'm not Greek,' snapped Melissa. Noting the lusty shadow that anger brought to her merry eyes, Nicholas was resentful of the sudden sharp jab of interest in his trousers.

'It makes no difference,' he said harshly, determined that a woman wouldn't go out alone against men armed with machine guns. 'Nobody can sail into Kemi without engines. We'd hear them coming for miles, and have plenty of time to be waiting with a welcome party.' Planes were also noisy but, with the airfield five miles from Khora, Spiro and his group could set down, pick up and take off again before anyone reached the airstrip. Hence the need for as much round-the-clock surveillance as possible.

As though to emphasise his point, a small plane winked above Nicholas and Melissa as it turned sideways to avoid the island's central point. Chloe looked up at the plane and yapped.

Melissa drew in a deep breath. 'Okay, since the smugglers are clearly off-limits for me,' she said sarcastically, 'I'll tackle the bauxite mine problem. To begin any preliminary studies and research I'd like at least four days: I'll camp in the forest . . . What now?'

Nicholas coughed. 'You'll need a guide in and out of the forest — at least for your first time.'

Melissa stared at him cooly. 'If you're worried I might slip back to watch the airstrip, then perhaps the guide should be you,' she observed. Though why she was even considering spending another day with *this* man —
Tit for tat, Melissa decided. If he was going to treat her as a little woman, then she would make sure he knew how that felt.

Now, a full week after she had first come to the island, and having set out for Asteri mountain with her, Nicholas was altogether more amiable, as though perhaps he was aware of his unfairness and determined to make amends. In fact, reflected Melissa with mingled irritation and amusement, just as she was about to dismiss him as a rampant chauvinist, this human coil of sledgehammer energy would startle her with his patience, his curiosity, his awareness of the island's beauty.

For Asteri was beautiful. Broom, marigold, wallflower: the island was an explosion of yellows and golds. Now it was happening, thought Melissa, lifting eager eyes above their thin grey path to the blooming landscape beyond. Already that morning, as they had walked the steep ridge running up into the mountain, she had photographed courting tortoises, watched a male adder, bright in its new skin, basking beside its mate. Nature was all couples and growth and there weren't enough hours in day or night to enjoy or record every amazing thing.

Nicholas was equally excited, pointing out tree-top nests and sprouting lilies as they crunched their way over dry pine needles, the wind in the firs the only other sound as they climbed higher and the heathland merged into forest.

There, under shade for the first time that morning, they paused. Nicholas produced three bottles of mineral water: one was for

Chloe, he explained, spiriting a cracked china bowl from his rucksack and pouring water for Chloe into it.

'Want some bread and cheese?' he asked Melissa, as Chloe noisily lapped at the bowl wedged between his feet.

Melissa licked her salty lips. 'Just water — it's wonderful.' Raising the bottle thankfully to her mouth again she leaned back against a granite boulder. Away through the trees and far below, the distant sea had a haze on it. As Melissa watched, a dark moving shape between them and the sea became a goatherd whom Nicholas introduced as Stella. Today, Stella wore a flowered headscarf, but her flowing dress and baggy cardigan were still the monotone black of a Greek widow. With a slow smile of acknowledgement, she passed by, smooth-stepping and angular-faced, her goats tumbling around her and bumping against her long staff and the air-rifle slung over her back.

'We'll be able to walk two abreast from now on,' said Nicholas, slicing off a chunk of feta from the block of cheese he'd brought with him. Sensing Melissa's interest, he silently offered her the white cheese on the knife.

Melissa took the cheese from the blade. 'That's good!' she said, as the tang burst in her mouth, making her realise how hungry she was.

'You need the salt,' Nicholas responded, terse as ever as he unpacked the rest of their meal — except that out here in the wilderness his gruffness seemed less spiky, and during these midday pauses he was often quite communicative.

It was in this way that Melissa had first learned that Nicholas was Greek-American, born and brought up in Connecticut, New England.

'Built up my business, married and divorced out there,' he'd admitted briskly, stocky body twitching slightly as he spoke of his marriage breakdown. 'Most of the taxes I pay are in dollars, and my main factory's still in New England, but now I've come back home.'

'What line of business are you in?' Melissa had asked.

'Toys,' rapped out Nicholas, as though expecting Melissa to make a joke at his expense. When she didn't, he added, 'I'm developing a new line of wooden toys on Asteri, based on the puppet-figures that the islanders were famous for in the last century. I'm hoping to update the idea; make a new line of ecotoys that don't need batteries to be fun . . .'

But today, in the forest of Asteri, Nicholas told Melissa the legend of the island's hermit, a monk also called Nicholas, who had lived on the mountain sometime during the Middle Ages. Nicholas the Hermit, it was claimed, still haunted the forest.

'Hear that?' Nicholas paused dramatically as a grouse called somewhere in a nearby laurel thicket. 'Do you think — ?'

Melissa laughed at his wide-eyed feigning. 'I doubt if Pindaros Bauxite are worried by the ghost of a five hundred year old hermit,' she remarked. 'Even another Nicholas,' she added mischievously.

Another hour's walk amongst sage-scented woodland, along twisting goat-paths edged with hyssop, brought them to the north-eastern top of the ridge and the looming shadow of the island's central peak. Stark above them, the mountain top rose from a series of wooded ridges, deep, sudden gullies and everywhere a sea of pines, oaks and cypresses.

Melissa stood beside Nicholas and looked up at the mountain. She was breathing quickly, though not from the climb. A wind fretted the trees and blew against their backs. In the blue sky a falcon swooped earthwards, disappearing in an arch of streamlined wings behind the peak and the western forests. Behind, in the woods they had scrambled through, white and pink cyclamen, orchids and anemones cascaded down the steep hillsides, defying Melissa to capture their sun-and-shade beauty. And everywhere the racket of bees and spiral of birdsong.

'If Pindaros Bauxite come to Asteri, all this will go,' said Nicholas beside her. The forest on the east side of the mountain overlooking Khora would stay to provide an attractive backdrop to the marina, he continued, but the island would lose its trees on the west side. By the time the mine was worked out, half the mountain would be gone, and without its mantle of trees, Asteri would begin to dry out and grow barren.

'Surely your people don't want that?' exclaimed Melissa. 'This island is so fertile; so many fields and orchards . . .'

'All of them hard to work,' Nicholas quietly interrupted. 'Hand hoes and beast-drawn ploughs, backbreaking toil and no certain crops at the end of it.'

To such farmers, working in an open-cast mine would be an easier alternative. Melissa blushed, ashamed at her own good fortune, health and western wealth. She had no right to judge or choose for the islanders.

'The older ones are scared of change. The younger ones, they're not sure. They see on the TV what's going up in smoke in the

Brazilian rainforests, what's being lost to English motorway developments. They're not stupid. But they want a better life: secure work, good health. If we can't give them those things on Asteri, the young are going to leave.'

Nicholas turned towards the sea. 'I've made sure that Ari and Zoe will have to come and face the islanders, answer questions and see for themselves. They're flying in next week: the public meeting's set for the day after. That's when the people will decide.' He took in a deep breath, his face in shadow, uncertain of the result.

Only a week? thought Melissa, totally dismayed. She knew already from Nicholas that ASPW had educational programmes running: talks, rambles, film shows. Her photographs would be the spearhead of a wider campaign, both on and off the island. She was accustomed to working to deadlines, but this news was disastrous. Seven days to conjure the images that had to persuade the islanders and the outside world that Asteri mountain and Lykimi beach were worth saving. The four days she had thought would be just a start to studying and recording Asteri's forest was suddenly all the time she would have — no return trips, no possible chances to shoot seasonal pictures, no patient stalking of animals or birds.

'You should have told me earlier,' she said through gritted teeth, struggling to keep her temper. If the idiot mayor had only written to her six months ago, five months ago — whenever he'd learned — she might have been able to do something. But seven days? 'That hardly gives any professional wildlife photographer — even a man — time to spit,' she said.

Nicholas shrugged his shoulders. 'Ari and Zoe agreed this meeting with me for next October: plenty of time for everyone,' he replied without apology. 'Late last night, I get a phone call from a high-up in government telling me — telling, not asking — that the meeting's been moved forward: as in six months sooner. When I point out that's unfair and undemocratic I suddenly find myself talking to the air. I phone round my contacts in Athens until after midnight — no one can do anything. All the international conservation groups are going to be in Paris next week at the big conference on global warming: they can spare a couple of representatives, but *just* for the meeting. Ari's fixed it to suit himself and now has official approval.'

He shrugged again. 'I didn't say anything earlier because I just felt so sore about it.'

He'd hidden his feelings surprisingly well,

reflected Melissa, but then in her own experience she knew that deep grief, devastating disappointment, could often leave a person numb and curiously detached for a time. Now, seeing his fists clenched in frustration, Melissa's fury against Nicholas faded — there was nothing he had done or not done that would have made any difference. In essence the affair sounded very much like the kind of trick Katherine would pull: shift a vital meeting and throw the opposition into confusion.

'It happens,' she murmured sympathetically.

'It happens — but not to me.' Balanced as a dancer, Nicholas slewed round on his heel and threw a pointing arm over the forest. 'None of the flora or fauna here are rare, I know.' He cleared his throat. 'Not really rare, but, I hope, special.'

And I'm returning for four whole days here, Melissa thought. Determined that four days would be enough, she felt the familiar exultant energy and wonder which she experienced before every assignment. She touched her companion's tensed arm. 'It's beautiful.'

Nicholas glanced at her glowing face, privately relieved that for the next four days at least, Melissa would be busy elsewhere, away from the threat of any possible wildlife smugglers. 'Yes,' he said, his usually gruff voice suddenly quiet, 'it is.'

The wind dropped as they leaned closer.

Chloe, bounding up from scratching at a rabbit hole, cannoned against Melissa for a fuss.

'Down, Chloe!' ordered Melissa and Nicholas together, and the moment passed, both of them telling themselves that time was going by and that Melissa had photographs to take.

By twilight, Melissa had run out of film and Nicholas had run out of fresh food. The western islet of Antasteri, which she had hoped to glimpse from the top of Asteri, was still very much a mystery. She had seen the tiny wooded island once from Hydra beach as it rose out of the water like a low green shield, the sea strait between the two masses dark and narrow as a spear.

'What's it like?' she asked Nicholas as they trudged back the way they had come; the pines seeming to crowd closer and lower now that they were both weary.

Nicholas, his tanned features in shadow, made a gesture of ignorance with a clenched fist. 'No idea,' he said. 'The owner doesn't let anyone near.'

'But surely that must mean security —'

'Correct. Guards, cameras, lights, the full works. No one gets onto Antasteri without Gordon's permission. He's a very private man.' The fading sunlight gleamed darkly in Nicholas' fierce blue eyes.

'Would Antasteri be a large enough base for smugglers?'

Nicholas shifted the rucksack on his back. 'Maybe,' he admitted tersely. 'But then Gordon's already rich.'

'Much can want more,' said Melissa, thinking of Katherine.

'Speaking of more, did you know that Beach International supply almost half the marinas in Europe?'

Nicholas clearly wasn't happy discussing Antasteri with her, but Melissa decided to go along with his clumsy change of subject. 'A formidable opponent, then.'

Nicholas glanced at her sharply, but saw that she was serious. 'Don't forget Zoe Konstantinou,' he added. 'Personally, I think that opposing the marina at Lykimi is going to be even tougher than stopping Pindaros Bauxite: marinas are fashionable right now.' Nicholas paused to climb across a fallen oak. From here, the ground fell away steeply. They would have to climb diagonally, in single file.

Negotiating the oak, he turned to help

Melissa. 'Ever heard of TWC?' he asked, stretching a hand out across the broad trunk of the tree. 'Total Women Centres? Their boss Katherine Hopkins has just signed a deal with Beach International. Katherine wants to build TWC resorts all over Greece, and right now she's looking at Asteri as her possible base for the Dodecanese.'

Chapter 7

With Katherine's face suddenly scornful and laughing in her mind's eye, Melissa launched herself impatiently over the fallen oak. As she did so, the heavy tripod jutting out above her right shoulder caught Nicholas smartly across the chin. In the twilight he hadn't seen it coming. As the bottom half of his face seemed to explode, the pine forest closed round him, growing darker. Suddenly, the place seemed stuffy, airless, too still . . .

Chloe, snuffling and yipping, lunged forward at the slender arm thrusting aside a recalcitrant fir branch.

'Hey, Nick, don't faint on me here.' A delicate face, only a few inches above his, dived closer. 'Shut up, Chloe. He's going to be fine.'

Nicholas blinked as he found himself seated back on the oak, practical fingers undoing his collar, offering him water. He drank and something in his head seemed to pop and his vision swam back and settled.

'Sorry,' he said, surfacing from the rim of the plastic bottle, 'only next time you're going to slug me with something, Bumblebee, I'd appreciate a warning.'

Crouching before him, Melissa murmured something he missed. Heat had slicked down the front of her shirt, making it not transparent but clinging. The bra she had on had two small rose-buds embossed — that wasn't the term but it matched what these roses were doing — one on each side, right above the nipple where the strap met the cup.

Chloe's uncurled tail brushed him like a hundred feathers. Hearing his dog's happy barks and baby growls as she bounded after a particularly pungent woodscent, Nicholas dragged himself back from staring at the rose-buds and tore his gaze upwards into Melissa's blooming complexion.

'Hello again,' she said, with obvious relief at his recovery. 'Are you all right?' For a heart-stopping moment, sturdy, energetic Nicholas had gone quite grey: she'd had visions of dragging him back to Khora, or worse, having to leave him. 'I'm really sorry — Do you want to stay here with Chloe whilst I fetch help?'

'Now you've stopped hitting me, I'm fine. No, serious now, I *am*. Forget it.' Ignoring the temptation to probe the growing bruise with a finger, Nicholas forced a grin onto his throbbing jaw. When Melissa cheekily wrinkled her nose at him, his own smile became more natural.

Suddenly, her expression grew quizzical. 'What did you call me a moment ago?'

'Don't matter,' Nicholas said quickly, embarrassed that his own private nickname for Melissa had slipped out. Nothing would make him admit that he thought bumblebees were busy, bustling, good-tempered little creatures. Cuddly too.

He rose quickly from the fallen tree, thankfully not reeling — for an instant there he'd actually seen green stars. 'You okay to go?' He swept an arm towards the darkening sky.

Melissa nodded, handing Nicholas the rest of the water.

'You know Katherine Hopkins.' Nicholas stumbled against a young cypress and almost overbalanced on the track. Behind him, Melissa grabbed his rucksack and steadied him.

'Thanks,' Nicholas tossed back without looking round. The track was narrow here, where forest merged with heath, full of ruts and loose shale and gorse. They were going carefully again, testing each foothold before stepping forward.

'You do, though, don't you?' he persisted, when they were moving more smoothly.

'Know Katherine?'

'We've met a few times.' Nicholas' use of her rival's first name was instructive. 'Did you meet her in America?'

'Yeah, I saw her in the States last year.' There was a thump as Nicholas lowered himself from one level of track to another — he was as tired as she was, Melissa realised, alarmed again at having hit him with her tripod and ashamed at having thought of him as being hopelessly macho. Smiling and shaking her head against being helped she crouched and skidded down the section of rock-face on her rump, landing with a soft rattle of pebbles beside Nicholas.

'Most impressive.' The Greek-American continued giving his impressions of Katherine Hopkins. 'That lady has some mind: a real head for sharp deals.'

She certainly has, thought Melissa ironically, refusing to admit that Nicholas' admiration for Katherine's business acumen was not what she wanted to hear about. His next remark, however, was even more unwelcome.

'Attractive, too. Great dresser.'

Anyone would be with the amount Katherine spent on clothes, reflected Melissa sourly. Obviously stocky Nicholas had the shorter man's preoccupation with tall women. Jolting along the steep path, sweaty, tired, in dire need of a shower, hair-comb and fresh make-up, Melissa didn't even try to feel guilty about that catty thought.

'We met at a toy fair in New England: Katherine wanted to see my "Stevies" for herself,' Nicholas went on — after that crack on the head, Melissa could only pray that he wasn't rambling. He seemed recovered: his colour was back, and he moved easily enough ahead of her, if stiffly. Glancing anxiously ahead, Melissa noted the spatter of buildings on the rim of the horizon. *Not far now, Nick,* she thought, *just hang on.*

'You're remarkably tolerant of someone who's pitching in with Beach International and Zoe Konstantinou's aims to build on Lykimi beach,' Melissa observed tartly. 'You realise, too, that the bringing forward of the public meeting from next October to next week is just one of Katherine's tricks?'

To her astonishment, Nicholas laughed.

'Maybe you're right there,' he admitted, a note of indulgence, almost admiration, creeping into his voice. 'When I saw her in the States, Katherine admitted to me that she always liked to anticipate the market; that, to her, was the key to success.'

To be a step ahead of the rest, thought Melissa. Was that why Katherine had just become involved with Asteri? Katherine, her most dangerous opponent — *apart from the wildlife smugglers.*

'Do you think Katherine could be connected to Spiro?'

Nicholas gave another good-natured laugh at that idea.

'Don't you think it's rather a coincidence that Katherine Hopkins has decided to invest in Asteri right now?' Melissa continued. 'Just as Spiro's group seem to be using it as their Dodecanese base?'

The mayor of Asteri turned slowly, the black waves of coarse hair thrusting under his cap highlighted by the final rays of the sun. 'That's stupid! It's like saying *you* must be involved in wildlife smuggling because you're here to photograph the island at the same time as a special shipment's due.'

'I've had trouble with this woman before.' As Melissa's mind ran through the clashes between herself and Katherine, the more the possibility of a connection between her rival and the smugglers became not only feasible but altogether in character. 'She really doesn't care who or what she destroys to get her own way.' Her voice quickened as she sensed Nicholas' reluctance to believe that the charming, beautiful young woman he had met in America the previous year could be as vicious as she was suggesting.

Feet apart, arms folded, Melissa stood her ground. 'Listen! I've investigated TWC for years: there's never quite enough to bring a really big charge and make it stick. The nearest I've come to that was last summer, when I saw ocelot fur coats on sale in TWC's Milan store — spotted-cat fur coats, Nick, totally illegal! Unfortunately I couldn't grab a picture before store security threw me out . . .'

'A real *personal* crusade, eh?' Standing before her, hands resting casually on hips, Nicholas slowly ran his eyes over her flushed face. 'I'm beginning to see the picture. Katherine is a stunning woman, isn't she, Melissa?'

'We're not in that kind of competition,' answered Melissa stiffly, instantly regretting the words when Nicholas came back with the soft, killing question: 'Aren't you?'

'And I suppose you assess how sexy you are against Ari Pindaros, and your other business rivals,' snapped back Melissa.

'Sure! That's part of it.' Nicholas gave a smug knowing smile. 'Only difference is, I'm honest enough to admit it.'

'We're not all ruled by testosterone.'

Nicholas' features darkened alarmingly. He kicked a stone off the track with a heavy boot. 'Why don't you crawl back into the pages of one of your Green magazines, Bumblebee, and leave real people — who make real work for others — alone?'

'Do Neanderthals come into that category?' Melissa hit back.

'Buzz-buzz.'

She hated him. That moustache, those keen blue eyes. The bulging muscles on his arms. 'Behold the missing link.'

He laughed.

Obnoxious, thought Melissa.

'Well?' drawled Nicholas, looking her up and down again. 'What does Melissa the bee say now?'

Melissa wasn't going to be put down for wearing the correct clothes for the job. She trailed her eyes over him in return, noting the sinewy figure within the black jeans and brown jacket. 'I say we'll see who's right,' she said. 'If Katherine comes to Asteri, then look out!'

He cocked a bushy black eyebrow, his features hardening. 'Maybe we should leave it there,' he said, and turned his back on her, stalking ahead down the path.

'Glad to,' muttered Melissa.

Stephanides really took the prize, she decided, as they marched back to Khora. Loud, aggressive, brutish — and to complete the picture, hairy. You'd have to vacuum out the bathtub after he'd been in it.

Pricked by the absurdity of that image, Melissa started to laugh. She had been called worse things. 'Melissa' did, after all, mean 'a bee' in Greek.

'What now?' roared her companion, without looking back.

'Nothing!' snarled Melissa, stifling a giggle, caught midway between antagonism and amusement.

If she was exasperated with Nicholas, then he was equally irritated at her. Between heathland, orchards, and fields, they scarcely spoke more than a dozen sentences to each other. Finally, as they were tramping down the steps and twisting alleys of Khora's outskirts, Stella the goatherd thrust her head out of an open upstairs window and called to the mayor.

'Niko! Turkish Gordon's waiting for you in your office.'

Without waiting for Nicholas to respond, Stella nodded to his companion. '*Kaliméra!* May your time here be happy.'

'*Kaliméra!*' Melissa responded gladly, seeing beyond the black clothes and drab greybrown hair to the way the weather-beaten lines of Stella's square face ran into each other. Faced with her first genuine smile of acceptance, Melissa felt her previous anger and disappointment melt away. Stella, she hoped, would be a friend.

Stella meanwhile was staring at her blonde hair. 'You came on Manoli's ferry,' she continued in Greek.

'I did.'

'Me, I do not like the sea so much. It steals people.'

Had Stella lost someone at sea, as she had? wondered Melissa. 'Steals' was perhaps a strange word to use, yet Melissa was sure she had translated Stella's Greek correctly.

'We shall talk again,' said Stella, fiddling with a thick piece of string hanging round her left shoulder. As Melissa's eyes adjusted to the shadows, she realised that Stella still carried her ancient air-rifle, attached to its string. As Stella now leaned farther out of her window, the tip of the barrel scraped against the frame.

Any invitation she might have issued to Melissa was abruptly lost, as Nicholas interrupted their exchange.

'How long has Gordon been waiting?' he demanded.

Switching her dark gaze back to Nicholas, Stella casually folded and scratched her arms through the black widow's cloth. 'Turkish Gordon? Not so long. He's been in there no more an hour.'

The American in him irritated by the Greek island attitude to time, Nicholas swore. 'All I need,' he muttered.

They jogged down the six steps outside Dr Alexios' house.

'Why did Stella call him "Turkish" Gordon?' asked Melissa, piercing the silence between them.

'Just a nickname.' Nicholas tossed her a challenge. 'Want to meet him?'

Surprised to be asked after their less than happy return trip, Melissa nodded. 'Maybe I'll quiz him about Antasteri,' she remarked impishly.

'I'm pretty sure you'll try, but it might be a good idea to be discreet about your work.' Nicholas hefted a conch left stranded on the middle street step, blew in it softly to catch the note, then planted the shell on top of a wall. 'I'd hide those before you get to my office.'

'My cameras?' Even as she spoke Melissa understood. 'The reclusive Mr Gordon.'

'He has his reasons for not welcoming photographers, believe me. Personal reasons . . . but you'll know about that. At the time it was all over the gossip columns.'

'I remember.' In studying what little the outside world knew of Asteri, Melissa had read about the Gordon family, particularly David, former Olympic swimmer and now famous sculptor, the master of Antasteri. It was a pitiful story, she thought, and not one that made her proud of her profession.

'You'll know to be careful, then.'

'Now, Nicholas —'

'I'm serious, Melissa.'

Melissa remembered the crack on the head she'd given him. The mayor had already had a difficult day, she decided. 'Give me a moment to pack my stuff away.'

'I'll give you five.' Nicholas licked his dry lips. Not exactly apprehensive at the thought of meeting David Gordon, Melissa decided, but certainly the Greek-American wasn't complacent. She wondered what the reclusive Englishman was like.

Soon she would know.

Chapter 8

Melissa received a scrupulous handshake, a precise 'Good evening' and the visitor's chair, then David Gordon set his back against the closed inner office door and remonstrated with the mayor.

'For the last two weeks, three caiques have been using Antasteri beach and harbour. I'd appreciate it, Stephanides, if you would remind your people that the entire island is private.'

'Did your guards say how many men were spotted on these occasions?'

'Nine — three to each boat. Dressed in boots and dark overalls and carrying nets.' David Gordon glared at Nicholas. 'They'd blackened their faces.'

The mayor asked further questions, which were answered but which threw no more light onto the possible identities of the trespassers, nor even where they came from. Finally, he leaned back in his chair. 'Naturally, I shall investigate these incidents —'

David Gordon pushed himself off the

door. 'I don't care what nationality these fishermen are,' he said, striding into the room. 'Greek or Turkish, it'll make no difference to how they'll be treated if they trespass again.'

Nicholas, still seated, his chair thrust sideways along the desk behind a flotsam of papers, flashed a what-do-you-think-so-far? glance at Melissa and steepled his fingers. 'We have laws, even in primitive Greece. I suggest you stay within them.'

'If you do your job there'll be no problem.'

'I need no instructions from you.'

Ask him if any of these 'fishermen' smoked, Melissa felt like yelling, forgetting for an instant that she had neglected to tell anyone that detail regarding the smugglers Andrew had spotted on Rhodes. Don't get side-tracked now, she told them in her head: these sightings off Antasteri harbour are possibly the first real clue of what Spiro is up to.

But Nicholas wasn't glancing her way any more: he was eyeball to eyeball with David Gordon, famous sculptor and former Olympic swimmer. Watching the tall David Gordon raise his dark head to glare down from an even greater height at the compact Nicholas Stephanides, Melissa was tempted to walk out — as perhaps she should have done at the start, except that up to a moment ago Gordon had been blocking the door.

Be honest row, Mel, that wouldn't have stopped you. Admit that you like being nosy. Andrew's voice in her head made her blush. It isn't just that, she told herself. I have to stay because Gordon might be . . .

Interesting? . . . teased Andrew in her memory.

. . . involved with Spiro. Melissa determinedly finished her thought. She had always been faintly patronising about Katherine's reluctance to separate 'business' from 'men'. Stuck in this starlit, bare little room with two prime specimens, Melissa discovered to her appalled amusement that she too was not immune to the basics, however crudely strutted.

Yet, as she waited another thirty seconds, Melissa decided that enough really was enough. New information on Antasteri and the caiques spotted within the last two weeks using the island's secret harbour was not going to be forthcoming — these two were too busy sparring off each other. Were she and Katherine this crass? she wondered, bounding to her feet.

'If you gentlemen will excuse me.' Her clear voice stopped them in mid-wrangle as they twisted round to look at her. Both, she was satisfied to note, looked suitably discomforted.

David Gordon spoke first. 'I deeply apologise for my outburst, Miss Haye, and for our behaviour.'

Melissa inclined her blonde head. Standing up beside the strongly built Englishman, she was relieved that she had locked her cameras in the unobtrusive safe in Nicholas' outer office, although, sweeping a long glance over David Gordon's figure, she was briefly tempted to risk a storm and ask the man to model for her. From the tip of his perfectly polished shoes to the crest of his thick black hair he exuded power. Put him in any pack and he would be the dominate male, thought Melissa.

'Apology accepted.' Inclining her blonde head, she sensed Gordon's glossy eyes, black as a swan's, running over her body in return. Even though he was a sculptor, Gordon's scrutiny seemed rather more personal than professional. Not that she minded: as with Nicholas, Gordon's interest made things . . . interesting.

Melissa smiled, and then spoke first to her guide for that day. 'Thanks for coming with me today, Nicholas.'

'No problem.' Nicholas remained seated. 'I don't suppose you need an escort to Mrs

Samouri's at the end of the street?'

'If so, I'm leaving now myself.' David Gordon strode to the door and opened it. 'After you, please?' he asked Melissa, forceful and yet at the same time compliant. By the set of his shoulders, the sculptor was braced for a 'no' and yet he wanted to escort her home — unlike Nicholas, who had obviously had enough of her for one day, decided Melissa, ignoring the spurt of angry hurt that conclusion provoked.

'You can leave your things here for tonight and collect them tomorrow morning,' Nicholas said with a wide smile, jabbing a thumb at the back of photo-phobic David Gordon.

No doubt he was expecting her to protest, but this time Melissa refused to rise to the bait and took him absolutely at face value. 'That's a great idea — see you tomorrow, then.'

With that seemingly guileless exit line, Melissa left on David Gordon's arm.

Outside in the main square, opposite the church, the island band were gathering to begin their evening practice. Arm in arm, she and David Gordon strolled towards the plane tree at the end of the square, past the softly splashing fountain. Melissa, aware that she should be trying to beg, order or sneak an invitation to Antasteri, was overwhelmed by memory. The last time anyone had walked her home had been two years ago.

In the square behind them, the band crashed off into a brash, loud march. Melissa started, jolted into the present again by the raw sound, by the heavy tread of the man beside her. This was not Andrew, but a stranger she had to beguile . . . but how? How? thought Melissa frantically, as the shiny dolphin doorknocker of Mrs Samouri's flat glinted into view. Twenty steps away now, and David Gordon was bending his head towards her as they took an alley step in their stride. He was asking if she was here on holiday.

'Yes, that's right,' Melissa heard herself answering, adding another meaningless, polite phrase about how pretty the place was — how *pretty?* — when every step brought them closer to where Gordon would leave her. Silent again, she found herself no nearer to any key to unlock this mysterious, slightly alarming man, or gain access to his island.

A waft of rigani and lemon drifted from an open upstairs shutter as within the blank-walled house a persistent rumble of voices revealed the family to be at dinner. Now Melissa caught a slight relaxing in the sculptor's jaw. He was hungry.

Disarmed and inspired by this vulnerable touch, Melissa impulsively responded. She'd no food in tonight, but four days from now, when she had completed her assignment in Asteri's central forest . . . 'Would you like to join me for supper next Thursday night? Greek cuisine and keep it simple?'

A lock of black hair fell across David Gordon's forehead, the only sign of his surprise. 'If it's no bother to you, Miss Haye.' His quiet acceptance showed his pleasure.

'Melissa.'

'Melissa.' At the door to Mrs Samouri's the man raised his hand in farewell: she'd been just in time. 'Till Thursday then.'

Chapter 9

Four days later, whilst shopping in Khora for supper, Melissa telephoned the hospital where Jonathan was recovering. Learning that the wildlife investigator was 'progressing nicely', Melissa felt intensely relieved, and celebrated by treating herself to a leisurely coffee at the small quayside café.

She had just been served when the chemist Mr Zervos rushed across the cobbles to say that Melissa was wanted on his telephone and would she come please right away?

Scalding her throat with the rest of her coffee, Melissa bustled after the long-legged Mr Zervos and, at his invitation, stepped through his shop to a small but airy back room full of drying herbs to grope for the black telephone blending into the sage-scented darkness.

'Hello?'

'Melissa, it's Jonathan.'

'Jonathan! What an amazing coincidence — I've only just phoned the hospital. How did you know where to catch me? But never mind that, tell me how you are . . .'

'I'm fine, and I got this number from Nick Stephanides after phoning the mayor's office. Zervos is an ASPW officer, he should be okay.' Jonathan's usually calm voice was suddenly agitated. 'Melissa, listen, I am really glad you telephoned because things are looking bad here.'

'What? Has someone threatened you in hospital?'

'No! It's not me, I'm perfectly safe. It's you. My sister Lucy — you know, the one who's a model — she tells me that Ken Bend's been stirring things round London, tantrums and so on every time your name's mentioned.'

'Is that all?' Melissa was tempted to laugh. Reflecting on Ken with whom she had formed a brief photographic business six months ago, her nose wrinkled at the piquant herbs. She and Ken had finally dissolved their partnership when Melissa had refused to join the talented but stroppy photographer on a trip to Vietnam.

'You're passing up 'Nam for some poxy Greek island?' Ken's bewildered, sullen voice rang in Melissa's memory. 'This is a major chance, why throw it away?'

Still Melissa had refused. Vietnam was a sacrifice; the break-up of her and Ken's

113

fledgeling partnership less so. Ken, she had already discovered, had a nasty habit on location of treating her as his assistant, and of barging into situations without thought or patience. His landscape shots were stunning — it was his work which had caused Melissa to agree to Ken's suggestion of a partnership — but she had made a bad calculation when it came to his character. Artistic temperament was one thing, permanent cussedness and sulks were another.

Could she have repaired their business relationship had she not been so determined to come to Asteri? Melissa wondered now. Quickly, she dismissed the idea.

'As I'm sure Lucy mentioned, Ken having a squall is nothing new,' she hastened to reassure Jonathan. 'And editors know he's always in a foul mood whenever he's back in London from working on location. They never take any notice.'

'I'm afraid that's no longer the case. Lucy has been hearing rumours round the photo circuit that a few glossies are starting to think that maybe Ken has a point.' Jonathan sighed heavily into the phone. 'To be frank, Melissa, you've annoyed several top editors recently, turning down assignments.'

'I didn't turn them down. I just made it clear I wasn't going to be available. It's only for a few months, for goodness' sake!' Melissa felt her cheeks burning. 'They know I'm a safe bet, that I don't just breeze in and out of a place. I've done it lots of times before and no editor has ever complained about the quality of my work.'

'I quite agree that everyone's been really pleased with you — until now. Now, according to Lucy, Ken has got himself a full spread of attention. He's not wasting this opportunity to put down a former partner.'

'How?' demanded Melissa, still incredulous at this turn of events and the speed with which the situation had developed.

'Ken has a new friend. Or rather, he's the new playmate of someone powerful, with connections.'

'Katherine Hopkins.' Melissa leaned against a rack of herbs, her head swirling with the scents. Ken and Katherine. She should have seen this coming. Melissa recalled Katherine's crass threat from a month ago: 'Cross me again and I'll finish you for good.' Was this what Katherine was doing? If so, were her rival interests in Asteri also connected?

'That's right, our old friend Katherine, the fur traders' friend.' Jonathan's next piece of information added to Melissa's disquiet. 'She's really after you this time. Lucy's been having a private word with a few male editors about your work: so far three markets where you've had regular spring commissions have suddenly backed away: your pieces have been "killed". You've got the agreed "kill fee", but the fact is, that's three editors with sudden cold feet.'

Jonathan named the magazines. Each one ran large numbers of advertisements for TWC, and regular features on Katherine Hopkins. 'There's more,' he warned. 'Bruce the Snoop came lurking round the ward yesterday, supposedly to see how I was, but really to ask me in that subtle way of his whether there was any truth in the accusation that Melissa Haye wasn't a genuine conservationist.'

'Hang on? Say that again.'

'Bruce pretended it was only an April Fool joke. But he mentioned a name: Bailey. Nothing else. Mean anything to you?'

'No.' Melissa frowned. Was Bailey connected to Katherine? Or to the smugglers? Did they know she was after them? Was this latest disturbing rumour a ploy to make her return to Britain? If so, it hadn't worked.

Melissa squared her shoulders. 'Thanks for letting me know, Jonathan,' she said, grateful to the wildlife investigator for taking the trouble when he himself was far from fully recovered.

'Don't get in too deep alone, Melissa.' With that final warning, Jonathan put down the phone.

Chapter 10

Melissa raised her head from the baking tray of cheese pies. 'Andrew, do you know where — ?'

She stopped. The room was empty. Shadows thrown by the oil lamp into the corners of the kitchen belonged only to herself and the furniture, cook and cooker. Melissa's left foot twitched. She stirred the lentil soup vigorously.

'I'm an idiot.' Two years after Andrew was gone . . .

Melissa glanced at the picture of Andreas Papandreou hanging to the left of the gas cooker. Her Andrew would have struck a pose next to the photograph to make her laugh. She laughed anyway, the sound thin beside the din of hammering from somewhere towards Khora harbour. In the flat above hers, the throaty voices of Greek women rang out like muffled bells. They were talking to Mrs Samouri's parrot.

Turning, Melissa lifted down the second chair from its nail on the wall, drawing it over the uneven floor to the table. Two glasses, two floral china bowls and plates, two tiny coffee cups and saucers. For David, not Andrew.

Melissa moved saucers of pine kernels and raisins closer to David's place, fingers trembling. For something to do, she checked she had given her guest the freshest tomatoes in his salad.

'It's Greece now, not England. You're here to work.'

'Awrk!' squawked the parrot in the flat above, seemingly in sympathy.

Melissa clicked her tongue and laughed. Twirling in a sunny blaze of yellow silk — her favourite dress — she lifted the new butter from the pink unit hanging precariously above the cooker and dabbed some in a saucepan to melt.

Bounding then from the kitchen into her second room, she caught Mrs Samouri's scraggy tortoiseshell cat lolling on the bed, a paw languidly stretched towards the paraffin heater. Spotting her, the animal leapt in a startled arch up to the window, streaking through the narrow gap in the peeling shutters.

'One day, I'll get your picture, cat!' chuckled Melissa, sitting on the bleached quilt. Reflecting on the photographic side of her present trip, she was so far satisfied. Khora was full of faded splendour and, judging by the postcards on sale at the bric-a-brac and crochet stall at today's market, no professional had set foot on the island. Tired shots of the main church and slightly overexposed views of Khora's gently curving harbour were not what modern picture editors were after.

Melissa frowned. That harbour was too visible for smugglers — every part of the low waterfront and the road running along it could be seen from the rest of the hilly village.

'Forget the smugglers for tonight,' chided Andrew in her head. *'Enjoy this evening.'*

'You're right, handsome.' She used the Norfolk expression which had always amused Andrew.

From the kitchen, cutting through the smog of paraffin, came the smell of scorching butter.

Bouncing up from the floppy bed with its foot supported by bricks, Melissa zoomed back to rescue the pan. For several moments, glazing, stirring and the whole happy melée of cooking took up her attention. She poured David a generous helping of retsina, putting the wine glass in his place, and a saucer ready for the hot cheese pies. The plates were warming, waiting for the fish casserole.

As she worked, Melissa whistled the tune she could hear echoing over the rooftops. In the nearby church square the island band was practicing again.

Opening the rusty oven door, Melissa laid the cheese pies on the shelf above the lemon and garlic scented bream.

A rap at the door. Melissa stirred the soup, then hustled through into her living room.

'Good evening, Melissa.'

'Thank you for coming, David.' Discovering to her amusement that she was holding in her stomach and clicking her high heels, Melissa stepped back to lead the way. Definitely another dark and risky customer like Nicholas, she decided, watching her guest for the evening duck warily under the low ceiling beams. He smelt of turps and a woody aftershave. With his height and his heavy tread he made the room cramped, the bed with its open embroidered covers strangely alarming. It was better in the kitchen. Melissa loved cooking and was good at it: that confidence helped her now to face the former Olympic swimmer.

'If you would cut the bread, please . . . is the retsina acceptable?' Her voice tightened as she mentioned the wine found on Andrew's body, but David Gordon smiled.

121

'Retsina will be fine.' He settled comfortably into his place and picked up the bread-knife. His black, rather blank eyes scanned Melissa's energetic, bouncy way of moving as she stirred soup, opened the oven door, brought out the golden cheese pies, transferred them to a plate.

'You've forgotten one.' He pointed with the knife.

Melissa laughed, flicking the towel she was using as an oven glove off her shoulder to retrieve the final one.

She switched off the gas and poured the soup, aware of David still watching her as he sawed the bread — perfectly. Maybe he worked by touch, she thought, blowing back a strand of golden hair from her flushed forehead.

'You must have worked on this meal all today.' David sampled the wine, took a hot cheese pastry from the plate on the table between them.

'Lentil soup and the baked fish only take an hour and the cheese pies were made up by the baker.' Melissa tasted her soup, nodding that she had got the seasoning right. For an instant, Andrew's habit of always adding salt to any meal she produced — at the time intensely irritating — made David Gordon's reaching for a handful of pine kernels a poignant reminder of her lover, but the sculptor's fingers were longer. Each thing they touched those fingers briefly enfolded. Melissa, reflecting that David owned not only Antasteri — quiet and remote, a possible haven for smugglers — but also the two villas near Petra beach, where Nicholas had found the machine-gun clip, thought of the open traps of the sundew. Those fingers were the same, promising sweetness yet deadly to the naive.

Melissa smiled at her own fancy, well aware of why she had thought of David Gordon caressing anything. Photographs did not do the man justice: they caught only the magnetic looks.

After eating in silence for several moments, David dabbed at the corners of his mouth with his napkin and raised his head. 'This is excellent. Is that what you do when you're not on holiday — you're a chef?'

Here we go, thought Melissa, inwardly bracing herself. 'No, I'm here on assignment. I'm a travel writer and photographer.'

He kept his composure and did not raise his low speaking voice, but his answer showed his feelings. 'A travel writer once photographed me in Rhodes without my permission: I threw his camera into the harbour.' David Gordon balanced his

123

spoon along the rim of the bowl. 'I don't give interviews.'

'Did I say I wanted one?'

He pushed back his chair. 'Goodnight, Miss Haye.'

'Check for hidden recorders if you want.'

Her reply stopped him. A faint self-mocking smile tweaked at the man's mouth. 'You think I'm paranoid.'

Melissa continued with her soup. 'No, I recognise that self-importance is necessary to address a block of stone,' she said evenly. 'With me it's the opposite: animals seem almost to smell egos, so I have to leave bluster behind.' She glanced up at him, his fists clenched round the chair back, his long powerful body supple and focused as a shark's. 'Your supper's going cold.'

David laughed shortly, his eyes sharp. 'You must be married. To put a man down like that takes practice.'

Melissa poured herself another glass of retsina, the wine a tart reminder of why she had to know the sculptor better. Had he lived, Andrew would have been older now than this man.

'Two years ago my partner was killed falling from a cliff.'

The room was suddenly without sound.

David's hands relaxed on the chair.

'You're not saying that to make me feel bad?'

Melissa shook her head: she hated pointless quarrels. 'Please sit down. You said you liked the soup.' She lowered her face. After a moment she heard the chair opposite hers being drawn back. A large shadow darkened her plate as the camera-shy sculptor settled down again.

'I apologise,' began David stiffly, but then he slipped back into bitterness. 'I suppose you people haven't swarmed over Asteri yet.'

'No, I'm the first.' Melissa chewed on a raisin and ignored the barb. David Gordon had reasons — still valid five years after the grotesque events which had resulted in three deaths — for not welcoming any kind of reporter. She looked at him now, feeling the temperature in the room rise as their eyes met.

'Why come now?' *To ruin our peace,* ran the rest of the question. David did not say it, but Melissa read the accusation in his unrelenting face.

'The bauxite mine and marina . . . both will go ahead if people don't know what's worth saving.'

'Isn't that rather an arrogant attitude?' The man suddenly broke off and addressed himself to his meal. When he raised his head again his forehead was knotted. 'I should talk . . .'

Melissa laughed. Without the implied apology she would have told David Gordon to leave without offering coffee, but the show of manners had earned him a reprieve. It was a shame he disliked journalists so much, but now he was clearly biting his tongue. For that effort she liked him.

'From what Nick tells me, some development is overdue.'

Her attempt to be conciliatory worked, and drew a similar tactful answer. 'Yes, I think it is. And we have the Asteri Society for the Protection of Wildlife now, to make sure it's reasonably ecological . . . Yes, Stephanides tries his best but he's up against things here.

'Not that I disagree with what he's trying to do,' David added, interpreting Melissa's shrewd look, 'only Ari Pindaros is one of my clients: he's commissioned a stone carving.'

Melissa took another mouthful of soup, burning her tongue. David and Ari Pindaros: did their relationship go further than a single act of patronage by the Greek businessman?

'How long have you lived on Asteri?' she asked.

'Full-time, about five years.' David's eyes were unreadable. 'But don't expect any tips about stunning views.'

'I'd appreciate it if you didn't. And in return I promise I won't tell you how to take a cast from life.'

Her answer ignited a surprising but pleasant blast of laughter from the man. 'I just meant the natives aren't very friendly.'

He hadn't meant that at all, but Melissa let that pass. 'Oh?' she said, leaning forward on the table, chin on hand.

David finished his soup. 'Excellent,' he said a second time. 'Any chance of more?'

If she wanted to see Antasteri she would have to stalk this subject slowly, thought Melissa, choosing not to pursue the reasons why the Asterians weren't 'friendly'. Refilling David's bowl, she dressed her own salad with oil and picked at the salty feta cheese.

'Were you a naturalist or a photographer first?' David Gordon could be polite, charming even, when he had a mind. At least his smile was charming, thought Melissa, and the genuine article. She'd seen enough model smiles in her work to know.

'Can't say exactly.' Glad to dispose of the pretence, Melissa put down her fork. 'I started really taking notice of birds and plants in Norfolk when I was about seven, when the family used to go on long Sunday walks from Wells along the salt marshes and the pinewoods. Since I wasn't a good enough artist to draw the amazing things I'd seen, I took pictures.' Her light brown eyes glowed as she laughed. 'I suppose the two interests grew together, although to claim I'm a naturalist would be too grand.'

Glancing at the man's smooth chin, reflecting how little stubble he had for a dark complexion, Melissa again recalled what Andrew had said about the three 'fishermen' in Rhodes Town: 'Too smooth somehow . . . not a smoker amongst them.'

Her stomach tingled. One of her eternal regrets was that she had never clarified what Andrew had meant by 'too smooth', assuming that he was simply describing the overall style and appearance of the smugglers, not the degree of facial hair — or lack of it — of the four men he'd seen. Now, fixing on David Gordon's burnished features, Melissa wished again that she had asked Andrew more. The machine-gun clip that had been 'played' with by an illegally smuggled baby chimpanzee had been recovered on Petra beach — near to one of the luxury villas owned by this man. Then there were the caiques using Antasteri harbour. Was David Gordon's anger about them genuine, or were the 'fishermen' in his pay and his protest to the mayor a clever ruse?

Was anyone that obsessively private, or was there something on Antasteri he needed to hide?

These urgent questions remained as Melissa cleared their first course and served the fish casserole. For several moments both ate in silence, David swiftly yet precisely, she more slowly. The retsina and salad went well with the baked bream but she really wasn't hungry.

'Delicious,' David pronounced a moment later, then silently resumed and finished his meal.

Relieved to be moving, Melissa pushed back her chair. 'The yoghurts are keeping cool outside in water. I'll just fetch them.'

'Just coffee for me, please.'

No offers of help from this man, Melissa noted.

Outside, the bandsmen had gone home. The air smelt of hot oil and garlic. Melissa looked up to Hercules, a starry huntsman, pursuing the Dragon across the sea. Tomorrow she would be stalking again herself, Lykimi beach at sunset.

Or possibly, if she could win an invitation tonight, the mysterious — and possibly dangerous — Antasteri?

That would annoy Nicholas, Melissa reflected with grim amusement, as, deciding that she too only wanted coffee, she slipped back inside.

The artificial brightness of the lamp hurt her eyes. Lowering her gaze, she saw with surprise that David had made coffee: hers was ready in her place, with the glass of water custom decreed. She must have been outside longer than she'd realised.

'Thanks,' she murmured, bobbing back down into her seat, disconcerted at having left her guest alone for so long.

'Melissa.' David's black eyes were a deeper darkness in the shadows. Silently, he reached over the table and turned up the flame on the gas lamp still higher. His chiselled features shone out of the brightness.

Wondering what was coming, Melissa held her breath.

'You're beautiful. I want you to model for me. Will you?'

She smiled, shaking her blonde head. David watched the complex tendons stretch beneath the skin as she opened her hands in a soothing gesture.

'I'm . . . flattered.' Her clear voice was soft, appealing. 'But don't you need a professional?' The colour and energy lit her open face. 'Besides, I hate to mention this again but I am on a working holiday. I don't think I'll have the time, and that wouldn't be fair on either of us.'

A pulse showed pale and steady near her ear, close to the long and short earrings. Seahorses in silver, two pairs in each ear. 'Gifts from your lover?' he asked softly.

She glanced at him, surprise showing in her face, and then she nodded.

'They suit you . . . he knew you well.'

Melissa was surprised, then grateful for David's insight. In one evening he had seen what Nicholas had not noticed in a week. 'Yes, he knew me very well,' she answered, thoughts flicking rapidly from Andrew to David as the sculptor rose and stepped round the table towards her, clearly intent on persuasion. To David, Melissa's reply against modelling for him was not a 'No'.

'My request of a moment ago . . . it's for my commission, a "Judgement of Paris",' he said now as, smiling, he watched her face. Melissa's eyes were brown, not grey, but their expression and lively intelligence were perfect. 'You know the story?'

'Yes.' Melissa glanced at the retsina bottle, but David knew he wasn't drunk. The intoxication he felt was not produced by wine. Beauty always aroused him.

'Three women — goddesses,' he continued seriously, stopping several paces short of where Melissa was sitting. 'Each an absolute in herself. I want to celebrate the difference.' He paused, wishing he was handier with words. 'Professional models are often too self-aware: they know exactly how to get an effect. I want something more natural — not less expensive,' he added quickly, catching Melissa's shrewd look. 'It's hard to explain, but you have what I want. Athene, like her home town, Athens, never sleeps. I want a model who suggests that.'

Melissa settled back in her chair, wary but intrigued. 'Someone who never stops?' she joked.

'Yes — no — it's more than that.' His hands carved in air what he was trying to explain, because words were always less. 'An immortal. The goddess Athens was named after, Athene.'

She smiled, her gaze quizzical. 'And how would I pose?'

He was right, thought David, excitement peaking in certainty as he saw her smile. His goddess of wisdom was not solemn but shining. Light.

He guessed her underlying, unspoken question and answered it. 'In a long gown, carrying Athene's sacred olive branch. You wouldn't be naked.' David already knew what she would look like stripped. The thought now of that energetic, bustling little body acted like an electric switch in his body. He wanted, in that apt biblical phrase, to know her.

'That's reassuring,' said Melissa drily, and then, after a pause: 'How much modelling exactly had you in mind?'

'Sessions of two to three hours, no longer.'

'How many?'

'As many as it takes,' replied David, reluctant to put himself on any deadline other than that he had agreed with Ari Pindaros, who had commissioned the work.

Melissa took a drink of her coffee. In the silence that followed, David thought about his recent conversation with Ari Pindaros. The Greek businessman had been very explicit.

'The Goddesses — make them different. Love is different from knowledge, and power is different from wisdom. I want to see that. Use three models — I know you don't have to, but hire three anyway. Let me feel I'm getting my money's worth.'

Pindaros' rasping voice faded in David's mind as Melissa spoke. 'I have a commission, too. And a deadline.'

Staring, David did not immediately absorb that Melissa had just given him a definite refusal. 'What's this?' he growled, hackles rising. No one refused him.

133

'I can't afford to compromise myself. I'm a wildlife photographer, and Ari Pindaros, the man who has commissioned you, controls the bauxite company that wants to —'

'No!' David slapped a hand against the table.

He was gratified to see Melissa start, then shamed when she said quietly, 'You're not my Pygmalion. Did no one ever teach you to control that temper?'

David took a large breath to try to do just that, one part of his mind astonished that Melissa was not frightened of him. Throughout his adult life, whenever he said 'jump', people usually did.

'Of course, I'll pay you.' Blinking fiercely, he named a generous sum of money whilst staring at the oil lamp, not wanting to look at the woman. It was Melissa the photographer he must appeal to. He had to fight to make sure there was no edge in his voice. 'And my home and the island of Antasteri have never been photographed. Both are beautiful, and yours to take pictures of if you want them.' He frowned, his anger at her refusal burning at the corners of his mouth.

'That sort of exclusive isn't usually my business,' Melissa said. At the rim of his vision, David snatched a glimpse of an odd expression ghosting across her features: a

134

look not of curiosity or even triumph but of regret.

He took another deep breath, his temper simmering in his stomach. 'Please,' he said, turning from the light to Melissa.

'I meant what I said about Pindaros. If I model for you he'll find out and he'll use it to his advantage — I certainly would, if the positions were reversed.'

David cracked an uneven smile. 'We'll claim artistic immunity for you,' he said. 'That's the same as diplomatic, only more lasting. Listen, Melissa, I'm not asking you to compromise your principles. In fact, by posing as the goddess of wisdom, you could be said to be sending Ari a strong conservation message.'

'Would you be prepared to state those reasons publicly?' demanded Melissa. 'That Athene is an ecological statement and you support my work?'

'Phew!' David whistled. 'You don't want much, do you?'

'Those are my terms.'

Ari wouldn't be happy but he could handle that, thought David. Insistent on his rights as an artist, David knew that in the end Ari would grumble but comply: he would if he wanted a Gordon sculpture. He could even sell it to the Greek millionaire as a 'courageous choice': dare Ari to have Melissa as a model.

'Very well, I agree. Now, what do you say?'

'My own work won't wait.'

Again he cut across her answer. 'Three days from today. That's when I'll have cleared my studio and have the stone ready. That's when I plan to start and when I'll need to know if my models . . .'

This time Melissa interrupted. 'There'll be three of us?'

'Three ladies — women,' corrected David quickly, nodding. He hadn't found the other two yet, but in three days he would. Usually a great planner in all aspects of his life and work, David was utterly contradictory when it came to choosing living subjects: a believer in serendipity. He liked the spontaneity and risk involved in a rapid search. Not that there would be any problems. The world was full of beautiful women and he had an eye for good models.

'Only three days,' said Melissa, thinking ahead to the vital public meeting where Ari Pindaros, and no doubt Zoe, would be present. Nicholas was caught up in preparations for that meeting, and of course the persistent threat of Spiro's possible appearance on Asteri. She swilled the grounds around her coffee cup. The chance to see Antasteri: why

136

was she even hesitating? She should grab it with both hands. It was exactly what she wanted.

'Yes — why not?' Melissa made herself smile.

'Thanks. You won't regret it.'

Melissa, hiding her face behind her coffee cup, could only hope that he was right.

Chapter 11

Asteri. Katherine ran a finger round the rim of the perfume tester bottle. Her flight to the island was billed as a tax loss but this trip was all gain. A Total Woman Centre resort allied to a marina: this public support for Zoe Konstantinou and Beach International provided perfect cover for more private business.

'Excuse me, please.' A gruff voice addressed her in Greek. Lifting her head, Katherine's cool green gaze was met by a pair of stormy brown eyes set in a lean face. Smoothly withdrawing her legs from the short, narrow gangway, Katherine rapidly assessed the rest that she could see in the dim narrow confines of the plane. Long, jean-clad legs, mean hips, tautly-muscled, lightly-tanned forearm shouldering a rucksack dripping with Greek football team stickers. *Not bad.* Katherine shot a high-powered smile at the youth.

'*Efkharistó,*' A shyly brusque 'Thank you' in Greek.

'*Parakaló.*' It was her pleasure, too,

thought Katherine. 'How long does the flight take?' she asked in English.

Above her the stormy eyes grew large and shy, eclipsing the golden eyelashes and frowning gilt brows. *He doesn't understand*, thought Katherine, rapidly composing a suitable opening line in Greek.

As Katherine opened her mouth to prolong their brief encounter, she noticed the rucksack suddenly slipping from one square shoulder. As the teenager snatched at the battered item to prevent it from slamming into her, Katherine saw the youth's short pigtail come adrift, spilling a fiery bob of red hair around that lean, pink face.

Even before the shadowed outline of a small yet faultless breast appeared amidst the folds of the baggy tee-shirt, the sight of the bobbed hair made Katherine withdraw sharply into her seat, her manicured fingers tightening on the perfume bottle. Resentful towards the androgynous creature who had almost caused her to make an utter fool of herself, Katherine coldly watched the Greek girl striding to a seat at the front of the plane. No longer an appealing native youth, her face was split in an enormous yawn.

Too skinny, too gruff, walks like a man, thought Katherine, raking her pen across the testing chart, striking through the 'too sweet' column. This rose-based confection was the kind of perfume Melissa Haye would wear — not for much longer, though, Katherine reflected, stretching sleekly in the comfortable seat, her flirting mistake now dismissed. Reflecting on her plans for Ms Haye as the plane's engines noisily fired, her green eyes were drawn across the gangway.

Bailey, her companion on this trip, sat primly studying the aircraft's safety instructions, the shadow of Rhodes airport terminal black against his brown suit, the inevitable briefcase snug in the window seat beside him.

Having once glimpsed the contents of that anonymous brown bag, Katherine had no wish to do so again, but now, thinking of Melissa Haye, Bailey and his briefcase were pleasing in their solidity. She, Ken Bend and that odious gutter journalist Bruce Grainge had together produced an elegant trap, yet if her subtle, more satisfying scheme to ruin Melissa Haye should fail, should anything go wrong in the transfer of Sir Oliver's 'special item', her most expensive smuggled piece of wildlife to date, then Bailey would be there.

Nothing would go wrong, Katherine told herself, taking up another perfume bottle from the slim case open on her lap. Now, touching this new scent to her wrist, she consciously relaxed, letting go of the details of where, when and how her major enemy would be destroyed, leaving aside for the moment the where and when and who would meet Spiro on Asteri. Flying always made her feel sexy.

Not everyone responded as she did, Katherine was amused to note. The shudder of the engines had already rocked the skinny Greek girl to sleep, as a white hand, drooping into the gangway a metre ahead of her own seat, clearly showed. Katherine was not in the least surprised when that hand remained limp and unmoved as the ringing of the metal ladder outside the plane announced the arrival of the final two passengers.

Katherine knew who they were. Calmly closing her case of perfumes, she swapped from the inner plane seat to the outer one over the wing. Gazing out of the window, her lips were curved in a perfect smile as she anticipated this meeting, a delightful coincidence on her part, but one she intended to make full use of so as to clarify strategies and demands. Whereas her romantic antennae might not be fully attuned this morning, her business instincts were as honed as ever as she prepared to wait. Dealing with millionaires, it is never a good idea to appear too eager.

So, leaving Bailey to twist half out of his seat and gawp, Katherine studied the weather. Nine in the morning and an hour's flight at least into the sun: her even, subtle tan would be ruined. Sometimes one could have too much of the famous Greek light. Katherine pulled down the window blind.

'Miss Hopkins! May I say how delighted I am to see you in the flesh at last, and looking so much the elegant executive: that tan trouser-suit perfectly sets off the limpid green of your eyes. But allow me to introduce myself . . .'

Katherine smoothly pushed up the blind, the better to see the man who had just complimented her in her own tongue in a manner as extravagant as his thousand dollar clothes were sober. A glance at the tanned features above the navy blazer — the jutting chin, slightly misshapen teeth, wrinkled hook of a nose, dark round eyes and receding grey widow's peak — confirmed what she had suspected: Ari Pindaros paid someone a great deal of money to have those handsome photographs taken of himself.

She accepted his outstretched hand and repeated his name. 'Mr Pindaros.' Katherine let a smile do her flattery.

'Also my associate, Mrs Konstantinou.' His English was perfect, his manners less so as Zoe Konstantinou, a hovering shadow, had to lean round the tall, fleshy chairman of Pindaros Bauxite to bestow an anxious acolyte's handshake. Her companion frowned as a strand of her dull blonde hair attached itself to his navy lapels: the frown made him more menacing, and was sexier than his olive-oil smile, decided Katherine.

'My associate, Mr Bailey.' Introduced, Bailey gave a terse nod of his dark head and murmured a crisp, Australian, 'Good day. One minute to take-off.'

Katherine indicated the two seats opposite hers. There was some hurried shuffling as over the intercom the Captain requested passengers to extinguish their cigarettes, please, and to fasten their seatbelts — no stewards on this flight.

Off at the head of the plane the Greek girl snored softly, her breathing slow between the hectic beats of the plane's propellers.

Still frowning, Ari Pindaros settled in the window seat opposite to Katherine, Zoe Konstantinou tucking in beside him.

'Infrastructure needs serious attention,' he muttered, in a rasping way which reminded Katherine of the sleeping Greek girl. Zoe Konstantinou nodded.

'No doubt they do their best,' she remarked, staring at the flexing aircraft wing as the plane taxied for take-off. Suddenly she turned to address Katherine. 'Mr Pindaros wished to travel on a normal flight to see the conditions for himself.'

Katherine inclined her head, accepting this explanation at face value. There again, millionaires had odd foibles and economies that were usually best indulged. She herself resented the exorbitant prices of private plane hire and so had chosen to travel by scheduled flight. David Gordon, the famous sculptor from whom she had hired her month's luxury accommodation, was meeting her off this plane.

'Are you staying at Petra?' she asked now, guessing her companions were also being met by the same man.

'Yes, we're in Villa Rodin beside Petra beach,' replied Ari Pindaros with a bland smile. 'Are you going to be our neighbour at the Villa Michelangelo?'

These twin villas, separated by the half-mile strip of sand and pebbles of Petra beach, were both owned by David Gordon and rented throughout the year to the rich and famous.

'Of course.' In reality there was no 'of course' about her staying at Petra, thought Katherine, as she felt the aircraft piling on speed, but the only other five-star accommodation on Asteri, the Villa Elysion, was one which Katherine had refused to patronise, owned as it was by the mayor and lately spied on by Melissa Haye.

'Very good!' Ari Pindaros swatted the crease of his immaculately-pressed grey trousers. 'We shall be able to talk there frankly and privately.'

Katherine glanced forward at the sleeping girl — the drooping white hand. 'We are private here, Mr Pindaros,' she observed, heartbeat quickening as she felt the light aircraft rising above the tacky dross of Rhodes.

'Ari, please — Katherine.'

Katherine's large green eyes flashed gold for an instant, then she turned to business, speaking in English, the language of commerce.

'The public meeting — going ahead tomorrow?'

Ari nodded his grey head. 'As you suggested.' He laughed drily. 'And again, as you predicted, the "Greens" are in disarray. No international conservation groups can be present in strength and the local group has no idea: lots of gloomy data but nothing to engage people's feelings or attention. I've been reliably informed that they only have one five-minute video of Lykimi and a few pictures of Asteri mountain.'

Katherine raised an umber eyebrow, the blood surging in her ears as the light airplane levelled out. 'This despite the efforts of the ubiquitous Miss Haye,' she observed, not trying to keep the satisfaction from her voice.

After a glance at Ari for permission, Zoe Konstantinou now spoke up for the first time. She injected a note of caution. 'There may still be opposition at the meeting,' she observed quietly, in perfect English. 'The small businesses of the Asteri co-operative . . .'

'Cut off their primary funds at the bank and they'll fall in fast enough,' interrupted Katherine, staring at the platinum wedding ring on Zoe's sunburned hand. Zoe claimed that Mr Konstantinou was working in Australia, but everyone knew that, married or not, she was Ari Pindaros' lover. She had the full womanly figure that the Greek millionaire admired — his wife was also generously-endowed — and perfect teeth, which she often showed off in a dainty smile.

Katherine now noticed on Zoe's trim, un-crossed ankles the beginnings of several varicose veins running for cover under her baggy harem-style pants and applauded the young woman's good sense in concentrating on her assets. True, her hair was rather coarse and dull, but it was a true egg-yolk blonde, set off nicely by the headband, which complemented Zoe's deep brown eyes. At five four, she was too small to be elegant — short as Melissa Haye — but she radiated a certain homely charm.

'We're not talking about some third-world republic,' Zoe answered sharply, a response which made Katherine blink. Taking in the high forehead below the headband, she sat up in her seat, irritated with herself for having dismissed an ally so lightly.

'I believe we can all agree that we want what's best for Greece,' she dropped nicely into the silence. 'Asteri will benefit tremendously from the building of your marina and Beach International's input. I myself am very interested in a Total Woman Centre resort based at Lykimi. These things cannot be put at risk by a few parochial-minded individuals.'

'Such as ASPW?' challenged Ari, with a ringing laugh.

'The mayor of Asteri may be the greater threat,' said Zoe, ever-serious. 'No one is sure where his true interest lies: one day he opposes the mine because of a few trees, the next he is trying to con the priest into buying children's toys at some ridiculously inflated price. He could support my marina and a TWC resort one week and pay the building workers to go on indefinite strike the next.'

'Nicholas Stephanides,' said Katherine reflectively, crossing her legs; 'I met him last year in the States.' She had been equally taken with both the man's lively personality and his 'Stevie' range of toys. Now, if Sir Oliver and Zoe were correct, and Melissa Haye also had her eye on the Greek-American . . . That would be an added revenge, decided Katherine. To see her rival's face when she renewed her own acquaintance with the mayor of Asteri and she and Nicholas became lovers . . .

'He has much local support,' said Zoe. 'Carpet makers, leather workers, potters and such: they all use his factory and owe him money. His business in Athens is under pressure, however: problems of a legal nature.' Zoe's perfect teeth glinted in the sunshine through the narrow aircraft window. 'These could be increased.'

'Greek bureaucracy can be truly vicious,' said Ari, in case Katherine had missed the point.

'So is non-payment,' remarked Zoe. 'Nicholas Stephanides is owed a great deal of money in America.'

'I can get onto that, maybe,' said Katherine, thinking several stages ahead of the present Total Woman Centre resort on one small

Greek island. Nicholas' 'Stevie' range of toys would after all be a most useful acquisition for her group — as indeed would the man himself. Most promising, decided Katherine, twirling the sandal on the ball of the foot of her crossed right leg.

'As I've already mentioned, my Total Woman group is interested in seeing Asteri sensitively developed for our kind of customer. And if, as you've always said, the mine is to be several kilometres away from Lykimi beach?'

'Any open-cast operations will be totally hidden by the mountain ridge and the remaining trees, Katherine, totally,' promised the head of Pindaros Bauxite. Suddenly, Ari gave a queer little cough. 'That is, of course, if the mine goes ahead. It might be politically more expedient to let Asteri keep its mountain. It's all a question of good public relations and keeping in with the EEC and the World Bank.'

Concerned with image again, thought Katherine, nodding in what she hoped appeared to be an understanding manner.

'The new Pindaros Bauxite mine in Australia is already providing eight million tons of bauxite a year,' added Ari, showing a reassuring sense of self-interest so far as Katherine was concerned. 'The Asteri mine would produce higher grade ore but the seams are not as large, and the ore would need to be processed outside Greece.'

Katherine had already heard and read this lecture many times since the activities of Pindaros Bauxite had entered her calculations concerning the development of Asteri, but she was prepared to listen again in case she had missed something. She leaned back in her blue aircraft seat, noting that, like the Greek girl in front, the super-cautious Bailey was also asleep — or maybe just pretending. One could never be sure with Bailey.

Across the narrow aisle, Ari Pindaros was explaining the wonders and difficulties of bauxite mining.

Bauxite is used to make aluminium. In open-cast mines, the bauxite is first removed by high explosives, then transported to processing plants. There the ore is cleaned and crushed, after which it is ready to be taken to a refining plant. The end product, light, strong and untarnished, is the metal of over a billion drink cans every year.

The island of Asteri had bauxite deposits on its western and north-western mountain slopes — but the cost of extraction had to be balanced against the cost of the product. If the price of the raw ore should go down . . .

Listening, Katherine began to better appreciate Ari Pindaros' hesitancy. A mine on Asteri was a borderline decision: final geological reports, analysed production costs, prospective labour costs, likely political fallout — all these would have a bearing on the millionaire's final choice. And then he would have to persuade the islanders to vote his way.

The issue of Lykimi beach was much simpler. Ari, Zoe, and Katherine were of like mind: Lykimi needed a marina.

'Look!' Zoe leaned across Ari and, with an expansive flourish worthy of her lover, whipped back the window blind. 'Look at it!'

Below them was Asteri and that much-hyped mountain, its western face forested, green and uninteresting, its eastern half pastoral, bucolic. As a Total Woman Centre resort, reflected Katherine, staring hard, it had as much going for it as a score of other rustic Greek islands. She made a mental note to reprimand the TWC team who had covered Asteri: stunning yet contrived pictures and exaggerated claims did not constitute thorough research to her.

In the seat across from hers, Ari suddenly jabbed the airplane window glass with a finger. 'Look at that!' he said, changing Zoe's ridiculously overdone expression by one word.

The aircraft sank lower, banked off the eastern rim of the island and Katherine gasped.

Crisp, blazing white beach sand, the stark contours of Turkish mountains across a jewelled ocean. Already Katherine could envisage a Beach International chandlery on the slow left-hand curve of that gloriously clean sand, money flowing in exchange for designer beach wear, ropes and radios, flares and monogrammed sails and electronic tillers. She could imagine the white yachts gliding into the deep blue of the southern bay to moor in Zoe Konstantinou's marina, bringing discriminating consumers and the old familiar flash of gold cards in the evening sun. She knew where she would lay the foundation stone of her first Dodecanese Total Woman Centre resort. The scent of fresh Greek coffee and bread, the taste of fabulous local honey — this place promised all these things and more.

'Lykimi,' breathed Zoe across from Katherine, saying its name like a charm. 'In summer these sands are covered in white lilies.'

'What a shame,' observed a new voice. Bailey had wakened and, not troubling to look out of his window, was polishing the locks on his briefcase with a silk handkerchief. He now looked up, his gaze untroubled.

'We'll have to deal with those as well as the turtle site,' said Katherine, and now she leaned closer to Ari and Zoe, who also sat forward. 'This is what I propose . . .'

At the front of the plane the tall, wiry, shy, red-haired eighteen-year-old girl whom Katherine had initially taken to be a youth resisted a sudden desire to swallow. Ignoring the agonising pins and needles in her hanging right arm she kept her eyes tightly closed as she listened. It didn't matter that the conspirators were not speaking Greek.

Roxanne Stephanides, American daughter of Nicholas, arriving unannounced from Maine to visit her father, understood English perfectly.

Chapter 12

Ten minutes later, Katherine, Bailey, Zoe and Ari had agreed a course of action and settled back in their seats.

The light aircraft began its final descent to the airstrip under the dark of Asteri mountain.

It was a minute to twelve. Midday sun glistened on white wings as the plane's shadow skimmed over fields and orchards, sliding a smooth course between two ridges of land.

Tense before landing, Zoe sat stiffly, her ringed left hand rigid in Ari's. Bailey studied the in-flight safety manual again. Katherine determined to be the last off the plane: more impact for her first rendezvous with their artistic host.

Roxanne, reserved and wary, still pretended to sleep.

At thirty seconds to twelve David Gordon stepped out of his Rolls-Royce and opened all the doors. The mini bar with its vintage champagne and wine was ready, as was the coffee-making machine he'd specially fixed to run off the car battery. The dainty floral cups poised on the adapted tray on the front passenger seat, the lavishly embroidered napkins, the delectable slivers of bergamot and rose-flavoured Greek delight could be offered or withdrawn in an instant. His Antasteri housekeeper had opened and polished the terminal's washing and plumbing facilities: he'd checked those too. Guests who wanted the latest news were offered a phone and the number of a twenty-four-hour information service. Those who wanted to leave for the villas immediately — so be it. To David, hospitality meant attention, whether to the scented coathangers in the bedrooms or to the networked computer terminal he made available to his busy visitors. As in his own work, the imagining might be large but details were also vital. It was a matter of pride.

Today, high noon, David's one regret was a breakdown in timing, a mistake on his part and one which made him angry at himself. He ought to have known better than to start chipping out that last mould, even if it should have been finished an hour ago. Another security alert on Antasteri beach had meant his breaking off, leaving the studio. Although, why Spiro and the men couldn't have dealt with it . . .

An increasingly loud roaring of engines had David heaving a mental tarpaulin over this morning's fiasco as he checked his suit pockets for the villa keys and spare sun-glasses. With a hard, efficient thumb he drove the pair he was wearing farther up the bridge of his jutting nose and plastered what he hoped was a decent smile on his face. The craft was down, the Greek youths he hired for these occasions already streaming back across the tarmac towards the boot of the Rolls with luggage taken from the rear of the plane. In a moment his guests would be trip-ping down the glinting metal ladder at the front of the plane: tired, excited, rightfully expecting the tedious details of baggage and transport to be taken care of and deserving the best attention he could give.

David strode forward into the blazing light.

Waiting, he noticed a wiry, agile figure slip away through the now-deserted baggage door. Behind his sun-glasses, without any betraying movement of his head, David stud-ied the disappearing redhead. Though he preferred women hour-glass rather than can-dle shaped, that bright head held his atten-tion. Also, although by no means an island regular, the girl was familiar. Yet from where did he know her?

Suddenly, with a fiery flip of that red-gilt bob, the girl turned back. In the swimming noon dazzle David could not clearly see her eyes but sensed her squinting at him for a moment as she tightened the waistband of her rucksack. Then with another flashing movement she swung about, leaving him still puzzled. Who the devil was she?

The aircraft engines had stopped: nothing now but the faint sawing of the wind and grasshoppers. Then a beating of feet on the ladder.

'David, my friend!' Ari Pindaros claimed him, throwing an arm around the sculptor's broad shoulders as they shook hands. 'Do you know my Zoe?' he continued in English.

The last time Ari had stayed at Petra he brought his wife with him. Zoe was a younger version of the same kind of woman: small, stately, generous in hips and bosom. A blonde, Zoe was not so pert in the behind or saucy up front as Melissa.

Thinking of the photographer, David's smile tweaked, then deepened. As introductions and enquiries about her journey passed between him and Zoe, a portion of David's mind was pleasantly remembering the high points of his evening with Melissa. Wonderful food. Conversation. Enthusiasm. Warm yet shrewd brown eyes. Bouncy walk. Flyaway hair. The rounded pads of those clever little fingers.

There was another link between them, David reminded himself, as a memory flash of Melissa leaning over the table, the dip and curve of flanks, waist, backside, threatened to resurrect physical as well as mental recollections. She too had known loss. A lover, not the same as a never-to-be-replaced brother, but Melissa had clearly been devastated.

Two years ago my partner was killed . . . Melissa's clear voice returned to him as though she had just spoken. The strange manner of her lover's death tripped unwelcome bells of resonance in David's mind. With a wrench, he tore all his attention back to the airstrip, momentarily despairing at his polite, bland replies to Zoe's remarks on Asteri's tranquillity. His brother Colin had been a witty conversationalist, *he* was merely conventional.

His work was the original thing and the mould he had begun to chip out was still half-encased in plaster. Reminded of that, David glanced upwards to the shadowed windows of the quiet plane.

'Katherine will be a few moments.' Ari followed his look. 'She told me to let you know that she's changing — no, David, you don't have to make any special arrangements. Zoe and I are quite happy to 'hang about', as you say in English.'

'The view of the sea is so beautiful from here,' put in Zoe.

'There's coffee or soft drinks at the car.' Turning to lead the way, David was intrigued at the woman who could make the boss of Pindaros Bauxite wait; he'd never seen Katherine Hopkins. Reaching the Rolls and ready to take orders, he flipped a rapid over-the-shoulder look.

'Or, if you prefer, there's champagne,' he said.

When she could see Ari and Zoe lounging in the Rolls, contentedly sipping Greek coffee, Katherine emerged from the plane with her handbaggage.

Her travelling companion was already long gone, Bailey's discreet departure unmarked by anyone as he sidled away on a private matter. As Katherine had intended, she was the final passenger to disembark.

David, waiting for her by the aircraft steps, saw a tall, perfectly proportioned figure framed for an instant by the dark rim of the aircraft doorway. For a sculptor, aware of texture, shape, space, the figure was glorious, a strength of curves and absolute straight lines, shown off to maximum advantage by the clothes. A slim straight skirt and collarless straight short jacket in a wonderfully cool, feminine, peppermint green — David checked the colour by a rapid lift of his sunglasses. Sheer silk stockings on long shapely legs, high-heeled ivory court shoes. No jewellery to complicate or cheapen. No bright strand out of place in the simple chignon crowning a face as softly and sweetly imperial as the Venus of Rhodes'. A Venus in sunglasses, carrying handbaggage.

Restrained passion, the complementary opposite to Melissa's exultant enthusiasm, thought David. For another second the sense of difference yet similarity between his Athene, Melissa Haye, and this woman hovered at the edge of his consciousness, an intriguing sameness in the way they projected themselves — both were dynamic, attractive women who knew what they were, what they wanted. But then all thought was knocked out as this magnificent brunette became a form in movement, lissom on fragile ivory heels.

Gliding down to meet David Gordon, Katherine noticed the man's lips moving, talking to himself for an instant before she stepped from shade into light. Then, as the sun flashed up her fresh linen suit, her hair, her skin, his tongue was stilled.

Though not for too long, Katherine noted with approval, as she gracefully put down her business case.

'You're very welcome, Miss Hopkins.' His handshake was firm yet gentle, making some concession for the roughness of his sculptor's hands. He must have looked her over yet again, because he said next, 'I trust you've had a decent flight: no turbulence.'

Katherine smiled. She was struck by the sculptor's robust swimmer's body and dark good looks, chiselled as those of an American Indian. The man's faint Northumberland accent, muted by an expensive education, also attracted her. Liking what she saw and heard, she picked up the business case before David, ensuring he must take it and the vanity case from her. 'The pilot is very skilled, Mr Gordon,' she remarked.

David acknowledged this with a brief nod, causing a shock of blue-black hair to attack the wide expanse of his forehead. Hidden behind tan and glasses, his handsome face showed no expression other than a business-like friendliness, but the way he stacked her vanity and business cases under one arm after taking them from her with scrupulous politeness showed a certain tension.

The tension of two people drawn towards each other by the pull of mutual attraction, Katherine knew. She smiled again.

Abruptly he turned towards the satin-smooth, dust-free, polished royal blue Rolls. 'The name's David,' he said. 'You let me know, please, if there's anything you need.'

They were standing close enough for Katherine to see David's deep-set eyes behind the shades, to catch the man's salty scent mingling with his woody aftershave. Heat rose from the earth and air around them, reflecting back from the hazy sky. She could almost taste his desire.

Katherine removed her sun-glasses, twirled them in her hand. This close, he was even better looking. 'A smile might be nice,' she ventured mischievously. 'Oh, and why not call me Katherine?'

'Katherine.' He smiled now, as aware as she was, showing strong uneven teeth. 'A Greek name, signifying purity.'

'Only in my accounts,' said Katherine, green eyes sparkling.

He laughed then grew serious. 'Listen, Katherine, I'm sorry if I've —'

'You needn't apologise for anything,' Katherine broke in, and now she smoothly gave him an excuse. 'I know how irritating it is when you have to break off from something —'

She paused: right on cue he resumed. 'Chipping out a mould.' Lavishing a look of gratitude on her that made Katherine aware of how sexy she felt right now, David loaded her luggage into the car boot, closed it, moved towards the passenger door.

The front seat, Katherine noted jubilantly, not the back. Empowered by this, she extended her hand for the keys.

'I'd like to drive,' she said. 'If I may? If Ari and Zoe agree? Then you can tell me more about your latest sculpture.'

She had surprised him again, but as he held the keys out, David surprised her. 'You move as well as an African,' he said, brushing her arm with his fingers, tracing the bone beneath the pale skin, a light, sensual touch. 'And you smell fresher than the thyme.'

Chapter 13

Since she was ten years old, Roxanne had been flying from the States to Asteri to see her father for two months of every summer.

At fourteen, she had been allowed to travel part of the journey alone, so long as Nicholas met her at Rhodes airport.

Now Roxanne was eighteen, independent, and making the entire Asteri run by herself. She had worked part-time in cafés to pay for her fares, she had arranged to take some months out of work and school to see a little more of Greece after visiting her father.

Roxanne had kept telling her mother the same little white lie whenever Elizabeth asked if Nicholas knew of her plans, and had Roxanne reminded him that this year she was coming in April instead of July? Since their divorce, Roxanne's parents were civil to each other but did not go out of their way to speak directly. Both also realised that their daughter was now a young woman.

Old enough, Roxanne had decided on the light airplane, to do what she had always wanted to do since age ten and walk alone through the fields and orchards from Asteri airstrip to Nicholas' place in Khora. Although she loved him dearly, having her dad along on this stretch just wasn't the same. He, naturally enough, wanted to talk, ask how she was, tell how he was. Much as she was eager to see him — three months early — Roxanne had also wanted this solo breathing space, this quiet.

So it was ironic to Roxanne that having planned this part of her new independence so carefully she now could not appreciate it and was instead scurrying down the track to Khora as fast as she could — to warn her dad about what she had overheard.

Every scrambled step, Roxanne wished more and more that she had told Nicholas she was coming, that they had arranged to meet as usual at Rhodes. Yet if he had travelled with her to Asteri on the same plane, those people would have said nothing. And it was imperative that Dad knew what was going to happen less than a week from now.

Roxanne ducked under a low orange tree branch, her trainers skidding an instant on the pebbled path in her haste. If only she had contacted him on the flight, had the pilot radio ahead so that Nicholas could meet her at the airstrip! But of course, she couldn't have done that without revealing who she was — and then the conspirators would have guessed that she knew English as well as Greek.

The girl blushed, recalling the innocent question the beautiful, power-dressed Katherine had asked her on the plane whilst smiling at her in a way that was far from innocent. Aware of the older woman's mistake, discomforted for both of them, Roxanne had hesitated to reply and in that moment the rucksack had tumbled off her shoulder, loosening her hair and saving further embarrassment. Thinking back, Roxanne now conceded that the pigtail had been a mistake, too unisex.

Yet, ignominious as it was to be taken for a boy, that was scarcely a matter for anxiety. What did make Roxanne worried, what added a spurt of fire to her heels, was that same woman's probable reaction if she discovered that the 'youth' she had made a pass at had later been listening to her most private and most definitely illegal business deal.

Roxanne had been sleeping. Why she had stirred when she did she had no idea: what mattered was the discussion between Katherine, Ari and Zoe — those three had used each other's first names often and Roxanne knew them all. If she had stayed asleep until the plane had touched down on Asteri, she now thought grimly, she would have been able to stop on this path right here. Settle under a lemon tree, smell the blossoms, watch the azure dazzle of the sea and listen for the cicadas in the tiny hay meadows.

She would have been able to lie down in one of those meadows amongst the tall, sun-ripening grass, oats and wild scabious, and day-dream about the handsome sculptor of Antasteri.

Had David asked Roxanne, she would have been able to tell him exactly when their paths had crossed for the last three years, whenever their visits to Khora had happened to coincide.

Their first encounter — too brief to be called a meeting — had been at a wedding feast held at the schoolhouse in Khora, to which the fifteen-year-old Roxanne and twenty-five-year-old sculptor had been invited. She had worn the local folk costume and, tipsy with retsina and compliments, had lost her reserve and danced. He had worn an immaculate light suit, and had been too shy to set a foot upon the school-hall floor. Three matrons had decided to change that, and dragged the sculptor out from his table.

He had really tried to dance, too, although he moved as though his feet had sprouted ten more toes. Whirling past, partnering her

father, catching the giggles from the matrons, Roxanne had been able to do nothing.

Nothing except speak quietly to the musicians and ask them to change the next
number to an all-women dance.

Nothing except feel for the tall, conspicuous Englishman, who by the end of the evening had progressed to being able to keep up
with the simplest of the dances.

Until then, David's perfectionism had
been off-putting to Roxanne. Now she felt a
certain sympathy for the sculptor and started
looking out for him, cycling on Nicholas'
bike round Asteri, often stopping at Hydra
beach to stare across the narrow strait and
wonder what wooded Antasteri was like, really.

After the wedding, and over the next three
years, she and David had spotted each other
a half-dozen more times, always at a distance, always only for a moment or so.

Really, there wasn't enough between them
to build even a mild infatuation on, Roxanne
now told herself. Striding down to Khora on
a glaring white path between two walled-in
olive groves, the bearer of bad news, she was
relieved that she'd never been tempted to
fantasise about David. It would have been
truly disillusioning to have built the man up

into this marvellous hero-figure on the strength of a few little glimpses, and no conversation at all between them, only to discover that her 'hero' was one of her dad's secret enemies.

Roxanne brought her left index finger up to her mouth and absently tapped her front teeth in time to her pounding feet. Three rapid taps was all it took for her to decide that David couldn't be involved. Otherwise, why had the plotters not waited until they were safely private in David's blue Rolls-Royce?

Smiling, with a tiny nod of relief, Roxanne took her hand away from her face. His hair was as darkly ruffled as a New England pond in autumn, she thought, and the rest of him as pristinely handsome — mysterious — as Maine under fresh snow. Of course David was tanned, but the rest of the image was right. Hidden depths — but whom would he let close enough to study them?

Ahead, the pink roofs of Khora shimmered into view between the silver leaves of olive branches. Across a field of chickpeas, the track used by Stella the goatherd could be seen switchbacking between cypress and mulberry bushes out of the village and up through the cultivated terraces onto the heath. Roxanne was using the other main path into town, which, as it dropped down closer to Khora, turned into a metalled road. This road skirted dangerously close to the island's shooting range, but the route was the quickest from the airstrip to the mayor's office, and Roxanne was in a hurry.

Too much of a hurry. Avoiding a bushy young olive which had seeded itself in the middle of the track, she landed her right foot awkwardly on a large black jutting stone. The rock started a mini-landslide and shunted violently downhill, taking her foot with it.

After that, everything seemed to happen both quickly and yet in slow-motion: her fall seemed to go on forever. Roxanne was hurled forward, desperately trying to keep her balance and not topple head over heels with the sudden top-heavy drag of the ruck-sack. Trying to avoid a steep bank of gorse, she went crashing into an orchard wall. Graz-ing her arm on the dry rough stones and her ear on lemon-tree twigs, she finally came to a stop hung half over the wall, her head in shade, spread-eagled legs in sun, her body jolted, winded and in bone-thumping aggra-vation.

Several moments passed before she had breath to move. Then, unable to prevent a small yip of pain, Roxanne half-rolled, half-pushed herself out of her humiliating, contorted position. Feeling that the rucksack had grazed between her shoulder-blades, she was thankful the damage was no worse: she didn't want her dad worrying about her when soon enough he would have other, more serious matters to consider.

Trying an exercise in damage limitation, Roxanne rubbed several leaves from her hair, smeared a huge cobweb off her jeans and smacked moss off her knees. One good thing about her conspicuous hair was that at least it somehow always kept tidy and fell into place without her having to do a great deal with it. A glance at her forearm, faint specks of blood seeping though the freckles had Roxanne rolling back her tee-shirt cuffs to disguise the widely ripped sleeve. Now she was ready to get going again.

Behind, a sharp metallic click, a slanting shadow.

Roxanne jumped as the reaching fingers came down towards her shoulder. Momentarily amazed at her own speed of recovery she flung herself back from the wall and the overhanging lemon tree and faced the stranger, her features flaming.

The man threw his hands up: he was smiling. 'Sleep under a tree at midday and the bogeyman'll grab you,' he said in English. 'But of course you were asleep all that time on the plane, weren't you? You don't need to rest.'

The one from the plane who wasn't on first-name terms with the others. Katherine had called him Brady — no, Bailey: Roxanne's memory was sprinting. She needed to detach herself from this man as quickly as possible.

'*Lipáme, then katalavéno,*' she apologised as if not understanding. Knowing a smile would be impossible, she tried a shrug. 'English?' she asked, with a heavy Greek accent.

'Australian — Melbourne.' Bailey dipped a brown-suited arm towards the open briefcase at his feet. Standing on a lower part of the path with the briefcase lid towards her, Roxanne could not see what was in it. As someone fired a volley on the nearby shooting range she started.

'We both know what this is,' Bailey said. 'This is a "What do you know that you shouldn't?" situation. This is a language question.' He paused to pick a thread off his suit trousers.

Roxanne daren't take her eyes off him. One of her boyfriends had used weights to work out, and for all that Bailey was only average height and less than average weight, she did not make the mistake of underestimating him. Instead, this compact, sallow-

complexioned man's faintly prissy movements made Roxanne's armpits itch violently
in alarm.

' 'Oliday?' she asked in English, almost
pointing at Bailey but deciding it was probably wisest not to give him any ideas.

'No, you stupid little bitch, work.' The
man's smile split wider to reveal teeth. 'As
in working over.'

Roxanne's mouth went dry as she smiled,
pretending that she didn't know what he'd
just said and had assumed he had answered
differently. 'No problem!' she said in English. 'Very good!' in Greek, as she backed
a few steps farther away from the man and
his open briefcase, edging towards open sunlight. 'I must go.'

'Not till I'm sure.' Bailey's right hand was
reaching inside the briefcase; the light
flashed on the open clasps —

Light flashed from a few metres lower
down the ridge, where the track merged with
the Petra-Khora road, and Bailey froze.

Tumbling from the road and scrambling
up to the two rigid humans, a flock of lop-
eared goats driven by a boy. When the boy
saw Roxanne he shouted in Greek.

'Hi, Roxanne! Great to see you again —
your dad never told me you were coming . . .'

'It's a surprise, Mikhalaki — can't stop, have to hurry —' Giving up on a greeting or an excuse, Roxanne went scrambling down the track, the rucksack heavy on her shoulders and swaying drunkenly as, fighting through the seething flock, she made for the road. Glancing back before she and twelve-year-old Mikhalaki exchanged 'high fives' she saw Bailey rapidly closing the briefcase, holding it aloft out of harm's way as the flock leader paused to nibble a tasty patch of moss by the man's feet.

The twenty-strong herd had given Roxanne a few minutes' lead which she intended to make the most of as, dropping another terrace level out of sight of Bailey, she dumped her pack behind a wall into a prickly pear — a mistake on her part, but one she had no time to amend since she had to get to the road. The Petra-Khora road, where something had been gleaming a moment ago, where an hour ago David had driven his guests to Villas Rodin and Michelangelo, and where, please God, he might now be driving back . . .

Unless he sailed straight back to Antasteri from Petra, not Khora.

There was still no one on the road — whirling round on the concrete trail, Roxanne looked desperately both ways. The range: people were shooting there. Make for the range.

Sprinting, never looking back, she raced round the corner of the Petra-Khora road and straight off it into fields. Left of the road here there was too little vegetation, a few dotted trees. Right side, orchards only fifty metres away — perfect.

Roxanne went crashing through low bushes, gasping as she strove to keep going, keep running, for just a few more moments.

A laurel bush thrust out a branch and caught her — the leathery tendril became an arm, two arms, one braced around her middle, one around her upper body, pinning her own hands fast to her sides.

It wasn't midday yet and she wasn't asleep, but a tree-spirit had trapped her. Even as the thought ran through her mind Roxanne shrieked, convinced Bailey had somehow overtaken her.

'Stop that squealing!' ordered a new voice with deadly quiet in her ear, speaking English with an accent she didn't recognise. She'd only ever heard the voice speaking Greek.

Abruptly she was roughly set down, released. 'Can't a man pee in peace round here without some deranged female trying to kill herself? Can't you see those red flags ahead? Another few paces and you'd have been straight out on the shooting range! No — don't dare look round: this damned fastener's stuck partway. If you're going to prevent my comfort stop, you can still spare my blushes. Now —'

'Ssssh!' hissed Roxanne. 'He might hear!' Visiting only every summer the girl had forgotten this winter's extension to the shooting range. Now, with no chance to reach the orchard without crossing live fire, she crouched in the laurel, desperate to hide.

'Keep still, pet.' The man sat down in front of her, shielding her completely. Several long slow minutes passed. If Bailey decided to come closer off the road, both of them would be discovered. Thinking about the briefcase, Roxanne shuddered.

'Gone,' said David Gordon. 'He's just spotted my car under the tamarisk — you can see the stand from the road. He's decided to cut his losses and turn back.' He glanced round at her, a lock of thick black hair falling heavily across his broad forehead. 'It's over,' he said softly. 'He won't pester you any more.'

For an instant Roxanne experienced a rare spurt of temper and almost snapped back that what she'd just been subjected to was much more serious than pestering. Possibly even deadly.

As the reality of her escape suddenly slammed in on her, Roxanne fought off tears. She still had to get through to Khora, see Nicholas, warn him. Especially now, after Bailey.

Her feelings of alarm were so strong that they overwhelmed any shyness at finally having spoken to the man of her dreams. 'You're sure he's gone for real?' she asked sharply.

'Quite sure.'

Abruptly, both became conscious of how close they were to each other and drew back simultaneously. Roxanne's companion said something under his breath about 'that piece'll keep, anyway,' and loudly cleared his throat.

'You seem to keep catching me when I'm at a disadvantage,' he observed. 'Last time it was dancing . . . The Khora wedding, Manoli's daughter? I owe you profound thanks for getting me out of those fast dances.'

Roxanne nodded an acknowledgement but her hand was hovering close to her mouth as her natural reserve reasserted itself. Three years ago, and he'd remembered. Noticed and remembered.

The man stepped out of the laurel bush and held out his hand. 'Up you come, Daphne. I'll give you a lift to Khora.'

'Roxanne.' She didn't smile: the muscles of her mouth were playing hookey. Please don't make me blush, Roxanne thought desperately.

He grinned. 'David,' he said, drawing her easily to her feet.

Chapter 14

One of the many rooms of the Villa Michelangelo had been decorated and furnished as if for an ancient Greek drinking party. It was there, to the golden splash from a secret courtyard fountain, in deep sunset-purpled shade and the clean aroma of pine and eucalyptus, that Katherine now relaxed.

Tonight was to have been taken up with dinner at the Villa Rodin but, thanks to the lucky chance that Ari and Zoe had chosen at the last moment to travel by the same scheduled flight, her immediate business with them was concluded. There would be time enough tomorrow morning for Ari to set his part of the strategy in motion; then, during the afternoon, she and Zoe could have a last run through their plans for the evening's public meeting.

Smoothly stretching, then sitting up on the opulently inlaid couch, Katherine plucked a kumquat from the black-figured fruit bowl carried by a stone satyr cavorting next to her couch. Taking the ripe fruit into her mouth, she rolled it on her tongue whilst languidly letting down her hair, spilling the bright brown tresses down over the naked brown nipples. Carefully cupping herself, she inspected and approved of the veiling yet revealing effect of her hair, then, sweeping it aside, trailed her fingertips softly down the outer curves of her breasts. No tiny red age blemishes as yet, she thought, relieved, celebrating by sleeking her cool hands lower, across the flat plain of her stomach. Thinking of David, she sucked in her belly to cinch her waist with both hands. Some day soon, she decided, as the sweet rind and tangy juice of the kumquat deliciously hit the back of her throat and she swallowed it and the stone, his long hard hands would be allowed to do this, and more.

'Where are you?' Bailey squawked into the intercom.

It was on Katherine's orders that the villa's butler and maid had taken the evening off — tonight she saw no point in having servants hovering — and by now the cook would be busy in the kitchen. She sighed and quickly slipped back into her sarong.

'I'm in the garden,' she called into the discreet microphone fitted into the carved head of her couch. Leaving Bailey to puzzle his own way through the villa, she stretched now to the bowl held by a second satyr, removing it entirely from the statue's fingers.

'Pass me a yoghurt from the fridge, please,' she said, as Bailey's narrow shadow fell across the spurting fountain. 'Inside the vase,' she explained, pointing to a huge glazed pot set in the middle of the semicircle of couches. 'The ancient Greeks used those to mix together their wine and water.'

'Must have been really disgusting if they had to dilute it.' Plunging a hand into the vase, Bailey flipped open the lid of a tiny fridge inside its wide mouth and brought out a fresh yoghurt in one of the pretty local glasses. 'Mmm, there's a vintage white burgundy in here, nicely chilled . . .'

'Not for me, thanks.' Katherine took the yoghurt and chilled spoon, transferred some to the bottom of the second bowl, began a careful mixing.

'Well, if you change your mind —' Bailey fished two glasses from the bottom of the fridge, set them and the wine bottle on top of the closed lid, and brought out a corkscrew from his briefcase. Watching the cork writhe slowly from the neck of the bottle he said, 'David Gordon gave that redhead off the plane a lift into Khora.'

In the sunset the white burgundy looked rather more of a rose, thought Katherine, as she tossed an amused glance at her compan-

181

ion. 'So our host is kind to teenage hitchhikers.'

'What if the girl heard something on the plane? She or Gordon may have gone to the police.'

Katherine chuckled deep in her throat. 'You've forgotten something, my dear, anxious Bailey. There are no police on Asteri.' She continued smoothly chopping and mixing.

'There's a mayor.' Sulky at being teased in his role as her minder, Bailey was scrupulous in his pouring of the wine.

'And why should Nicholas Stephanides, one of the shrewdest business heads around, take any notice of some girl's half-baked ramblings? Why, for that matter, should David Gordon?' Thinking of both men, aware of their undisguised, trusting admiration for her, Katherine lifted her spoon to jab it at Bailey. 'What's got into you? That girl spoke Greek — we were all speaking English. Besides, she was asleep: I heard her snoring.'

'I think she woke up before we landed,' persisted Bailey. 'If she didn't overhear anything, why did she run away from me?'

'You saw her run?'

'No, but she was walking quickly, and —'

'Did she dump her pack anywhere?'

'Not that I could see: I kept checking over the walls.' Bailey had missed the depression in the farthest edge of the huge prickly pear. 'Gordon did put something into the boot of his car,' he now conceded. 'I couldn't see what because the girl was in the way.'

Bailey had no way of knowing that what David Gordon had lifted into his car was not a rucksack but a section of tamarisk branch: the shape and grain had intrigued the sculptor. As for Roxanne's luggage, that would remain unclaimed within the prickly pear for another day until her father climbed over the wall to retrieve it.

'The only field glasses I'd got on me would have flared and given my position away,' Bailey now added.

'I told you to get rid of those antiques,' Katherine remarked indulgently, not in the least alarmed by anything the man had told her so far. 'Did you meet Spiro at the Pillar, as arranged?' she asked. 'And how was your reunion?'

The Doric pillar, the last remains of a shrine and Asteri's only surviving antiquity, stood two kilometres outside Khora on the Petra-Khora road. Bailey and Spiro had agreed to meet there.

'We saw each other.' Skipping over Katherine's second question, Bailey now raised his glass in a small toast. 'Everything's under control there: the shipment's right on schedule. Spiro likes the new Lykimi angle, too.'

'How very gratifying for Sir Oliver and myself,' remarked Katherine, reminding Bailey whom he and Spiro were working for.

Her companion took a long drink of the white burgundy and did not make any response. 'You going to eat that?' he asked after a moment, jutting a smooth narrow chin towards the bowl on Katherine's lap.

Katherine raised the spoon to dribble the mixture from it. Satisfied with the consistency she raised her head to Bailey. 'My brand new experimental face-and-body mask for part of TWC's summer coolers cosmetic range: crushed cherries and yoghurt, mostly. Should be nicely toning and refreshing.' She kept her voice silky. 'Care to try it?'

Bailey almost recoiled at the offered spoon. 'That's your province,' he said, backing up a step, taking glass and bottle with him.

'Do sit down, Bailey.' Katherine set down the basin and rolled gracefully onto her stomach. 'If you must keep busy, come and spoon some of this onto my back.'

Reluctantly, Bailey put down his briefcase and drained his glass. Katherine sighed as the cool, fragrant mixture was plastered onto her back and rested her head on her arms.

Several moments of blissful peace followed.

'Katherine?' The spoon hovered as Bailey stopped.

'Yes?' Katherine opened an eye into the purple sunset.

'Don't you think it might be a good idea to cancel tomorrow night?'

There was a flash of green into gold as Katherine closed her eye. 'The meeting's fixed: we can't disappoint our public.'

'I meant the other matter.'

'Certainly not!' Katherine snapped both eyes open. It had to be tomorrow night, right after she and Melissa Haye had met. She wanted to see the look on Haye's face when the plan came off. Conscious of a tightening between her shoulders, Katherine turned her head to look directly at Bailey.

'Everything must go ahead as planned,' she ordered.

'Including my visit to Miss Haye?'

'Yes.' Katherine lowered her head, allowing herself to be pampered by the body mask, allowing her mind the luxury of anticipation. She gave a lazy smile.

Tomorrow night . . .

Chapter 15

The following afternoon Melissa, unaware that Katherine was already on the island, was working flat out to a vital deadline. As well as video, she had to capture as many instant Polaroid pictures of Lykimi beach as possible before tonight's 7 pm public meeting. Nicholas would be bringing both islanders and new visitors — business and political — down to the beach to see it for themselves. But that would be just one view of Lykimi, one evening: apart from praying for a fabulous sunset, Melissa thought, what was needed for maximum impact was a really stunning presentation package.

She had already sorted through the photographs and videotape provided by ASPW. Fortunately, most were good, and a few showing the stately white late summer sand lilies were excellent. The very best was a fifteen-minute video, shot by the chemist, Mr Zervos, showing a moonlit night in June when fifteen mature loggerhead turtles had hauled themselves ashore to lay in the soft silver sand of Lykimi's upper beach.

Sadly, the video of the emerging hatchlings two months later was so blurred as to be useless.

The other images would be the main plank of any visual argument. The video and Polaroids Melissa had shot last evening and the final Polaroids she was now producing were more a moonscape of tranquil beauty and peace — a peace Melissa knew would be hard to find tonight, when most of the population of Khora decamped to the spot.

Melissa yawned: lack of sleep was catching up on her. She and Nicholas had worked right through last night to edit the video she had shot during the evening's superb sunset and ASPW's own turtle film. There'd been some wrangling between them over the use of music in the sound-track: Nicholas wanted only natural sounds to go with the commentary, Melissa insisted that music was essential.

'It's a seduction,' she had argued.

'Well, you'll know all about that, now Gordon's come onto the scene,' Nicholas responded, smug behind his bristling moustache, fierce blue eyes brighter than the dawn sky outside his office.

'And maybe you should talk to Katherine,' Melissa quipped back. 'Tell her tomorrow night that her year of voice coaching was a waste.'

'Really? I didn't know that. A full year?'

After that, Nick had taken more notice of her suggestions, a result which had given Melissa satisfaction and irritation in almost equal parts. But then, as she now told herself, working to a deadline was always stressful, and any response was always magnified. What, indeed, had she to be put out about?

'Whatever's between David and me is nothing to do with him,' Melissa muttered.

Whatever's between Nicholas and Katherine is nothing to do with you, either, said Andrew's voice in her head.

Shading her eyes with Nicholas' hand-made cap, Melissa scowled at the wall of prickly pear growing around the cliff between the north side of Khora and Lykimi. Its flowers were still sparse. Another two weeks would have been better, thought Melissa, directing her frustration against the cactus.

If you think Nicholas is so bad, why are you wearing his cap? Andrew asked mildly in her head. In the tender, perky blossoms of the prickly pear Melissa caught a ghost of Andrew's smile.

'The long brim's useful,' she replied absently, accustomed to talking to her lover. The pang of loss she had with each of their

188

'conversations' was as great, her loneliness as intense, as she had always known them. Would catching Spiro make them any less sharp? Melissa hoped not. To feel was to live.

Polite in death as he had been in life, Andrew waited until she had chosen her various angles and taken her readings. She sensed him waiting: a presence in her memory, whether of her own making or not it didn't matter. A friend on this silent, sun-soaked beach, where lengthening shadows stalked like grasping hands.

'What is it then?' she asked. 'Do you want to hear how far I am along in the smuggling stakes? I know no more than what I learned the first day I came. The whole island of Asteri might be involved and I wouldn't know it. Nobody will talk to me. "Ask mayor Niko," Mr Zervos says, whenever I try to introduce any topic other than herbs or the weather. Stella and Mrs Samouri, my contacts with the feminine side of Asteri, are utterly discreet. In time, I think they'd talk about life for island women and allow me to photograph them, but not before tonight's meeting. And even if they allowed me to see into parts of their lives and dreams I don't think they'd ever admit anything they might know about Spiro and the smugglers to a too-smart blonde foreigner.'

Antasteri might be a better place to look, commented Andrew.

'I just wish it wasn't.' Telling herself to keep busy, concentrate, Melissa felt the sun pressing heat against the top of her spine, as Andrew in life had often playfully squeezed the back of her neck.

David's all right.

'You think Nicholas is, too.' Adjusting her Polaroid for a close-up on four beautifully clustered, perfect yellow firecracker prickly pear flowers, Melissa hastily took the shot.

I was a man. I can't help you with the other things. Your choice, Mel.

'I wish you were here,' Melissa said. 'I wish *you* were *now*.' Staring down at the developing Polaroid she discovered that camera shake had spoilt it completely.

Angrily she tore the picture in two, stuffed the remains into a pocket of her sand-coloured camouflage trousers. 'Why did you have to leave me?' she burst out, and then, appalled at her own bitter resentment towards her dead lover, she began to cry.

Melissa wept, oblivious to the perfect golden afternoon, to her deadline, to her tangled feelings towards David and Nicholas and which of these two attractive men was the more compelling — or perhaps, at least in David's case, the more dangerous. Loss overwhelmed her again and brought on a fresh rage of weeping when, trawling her pockets for a handkerchief, Melissa found one of Andrew's old hankies, with the clean, open letter 'A' stamped in blue in one corner.

Melissa sat on the sand of Lykimi and cried, the camera shaking in her hands as her body shuddered. Within the private sweeping bay, the sea, a dark, deeply incandescent blue, shimmering and beautiful as a magpie's wing, rustled in the near distance, hissing softly up the sands.

The sound, relentless as death, penetrated her grief, reminding Melissa first of Andrew's favourite estuary and then of Katherine, their most recent confrontation.

The threat: Cross me again and I'll finish you for good. The action: those subtle, clever moves of Katherine Hopkins in London against her, trying to scare Melissa off, divert her from Asteri. Just because of Katherine's schemes for a TWC resort on the island? Melissa didn't think so. Even for Katherine there had to be more at stake, but what? What didn't she want Melissa to see here?

Reminded of Katherine, Melissa scrubbed harshly at her raw eyes with Andrew's handkerchief. In the ongoing strife between them, a war which Melissa now accepted would never be over until one or other was commercially destroyed, she intended to win.

Grimly smearing the final tears from her cheeks with the back of her hand, Melissa picked herself up and prepared to carry on. She wasn't in an open-war zone, she wasn't in any physical danger, just taking a few easy shots on a gorgeous beach: she should be ashamed at her slow fingers, poor attention. Time for her to get going, get organised, do the business.

A raven, cawing loudly, flew in towards the Khora side of the bay straight over Melissa's head. Turning about to watch its amazing pitching flight, Melissa fixed instead on some stumbling earthbound movements lower on the point.

Not Nick or David. Dismissing disappointment, Melissa moved to meet the figure edging down the cliff path. The name Bailey came into her mind and gave an extra kick to her step, for where the mysterious Bailey was, Katherine was surely close.

With dainty, precise steps, the woman reached the beach and skirted the patch of hottentot figs where Nicholas had once tossed off his shoes. Closing on the stranger, Melissa politely turned the camera strap on her shoulder so that the Polaroid rested astride her hip, pointing away from her visitor. 'Good afternoon,' she said in Greek.

'*Kalispéra*. My name is Popi, I'm a seamstress in Khora,' responded the flushed, slightly dishevelled woman. Looking up from her gloved hands straight into Melissa's clear brown eyes, she said quietly, and all in a rush, 'Manoli, the ferryman who brought you to Asteri, is my godfather. He likes you. He learned something today that he thought you should know, before tonight's meeting. He asked me to tell you.'

Taken aback by this opening, Melissa was at once intrigued, amused and yet instantly on guard. But Popi herself seemed genuine — her fear certainly was. When Melissa glanced behind the seamstress to make sure the woman was not being followed, Popi whirled about, right arm raised protectively in front of herself. In a navy tailored suit and high-heeled court shoes, she was dressed for the later evening promenade along Khora waterfront, yet she had just come scrambling over the cliff path to Lykimi. To speak with Melissa, a foreigner. Because Manoli *liked* her — did whoever had sent Popi really think she would accept that sentimental twaddle? thought Melissa, briskly snapping the fastenings on her camera bag. The Greeks were a people of fierce friendships, strong loyalties, instant passions, but the only thing that rang true right now was the slender messenger's alarm. Disliking the entire situation, but feeling that she had no choice except hear the message — in case it turned out to be her first clear clue to Spiro and the wildlife smugglers — Melissa firmly took Popi's arm.

'Walk with me,' she said. 'Then if anyone comes we'll look like two chattering females exchanging pleasantries. That's right, smile! Now, tell me what your godfather thinks I should know.'

Chapter 16

According to Popi and Manoli, Nicholas Stephanides was a smuggler who dealt in antiquities. Operating in a geographical triangle — Turkey, Rhodes, Greece — the mayor of Asteri shipped classical finds to buyers, dividing the profits of this illegal trade between himself and the farmers and shepherds on whose lands the remains were found.

Or so Manoli the ferryman claimed. Yesterday, when Manoli had sailed *Asteri One* into Khora harbour, he'd a passenger aboard: a shepherd called Andreas who lived in a mountain hamlet eight hundred metres straight up from the dangerous Hydra beach. Returning from a Rhodian wedding, still drunk with retsina, Andreas had been bragging to Manoli of his association with such a smart fellow as Niko Stephanides.

The 'stuff', as fifty-year-old Andreas had dismissively called a collection of antique pottery, had been dumped by a woodland shrine. It had been there for years, doing nobody any good, until he and Niko had shifted it out of the forest and down to Khora. Shipped out to Rhodes, to Athens, to Marmaris on the Turkish mainland, those pots would pay for his daughter's dowry, Andreas concluded, so she'd soon be settling down, too.

Rhodes again, Melissa thought, remembering the Athenian who had been caught trying to sell an Eleonora's falcon in Rhodes Town. Even if the shipping of man-made objects was totally different from trading in living creatures, she wished she hadn't heard about Nicholas' clever trip to Rhodes. Which of course was probably the real reason why Popi had been sent to tell her — to throw doubt into her mind about her relationship with the mayor, and just before tonight's vital meeting.

Wondering aloud why Nicholas should take the risk of smuggling in Greece when he had money and factories in America, Melissa received a curt answer: Popi was telling her all she knew. Yesterday on Manoli's ferry, Andreas had been too far gone on retsina to say anything but the truth.

Perhaps Popi really did believe that, thought Melissa wryly. Certainly the seamstress wasn't expecting her to ask for proof — clearly for Popi, her godfather's word should be enough.

So Melissa asked a different question. What would a wildlife photographer have to fear from an antiquities smuggler? Was Manoli afraid that the mayor might sell her a fusty old vase?

'It's not funny!' Popi hissed, slender figure rigid with irritation. 'My godfather is worried for you. Niko Stephanides can be charming. You're a woman alone, without a man —'

So, the urgent news was that Manoli thought Nicholas wanted to seduce her. Faced with this 'revelation', Melissa found it hard not to smile: the ferryman's sensibilities were so amazingly antique. Almost as old as the relics Nicholas was supposed to be trading. In fact too old-fashioned.

Wary, Melissa repeated the question she had already asked: 'Why have you and Manoli taken the trouble to tell a stranger anything? No one else on Asteri has been so forthcoming.'

'Many people owe him money. My godfather owes mayor Niko nothing. Manoli is free.'

Melissa raised her eyebrows. 'Except for some obscure feeling of obligation to me, it seems.'

Popi's elegant features, serene in repose, took on a blush.

'It's the blonde hair, I think,' she mur-mured.

Recalling the tiny faded pin-up of Melina Mercouri stuck in Manoli's ferry cabin, her answer struck Melissa as being sad enough to be real. It wasn't only people of fashion who hankered after golden women and men.

Sad and probably true, reflected Melissa, but not enough to convince her that the rest of Popi's message was genuine.

She made herself smile. 'Please thank your godfather for his concern,' she said, hoping her voice sounded warm. She thanked Popi for delivering Manoli's 'warning', adding, with seeming casualness, 'May I call on you sometime?'

'But of course.' As Popi was already back-ing away, her reply lacked conviction, but it was a possible beginning, an opened door in this shuttered community. Heartened by that, Melissa watched the seamstress slip away, scrambling up one of the many grey paths until her form and shadow were swal-lowed by the larger mass of prickly pear. Another ten minutes and Popi would be back in Khora, no doubt reporting to her god-father that the blonde foreigner had been shaken by his news.

Startled, not shaken, amended Melissa. She wanted Manoli and whoever else might be involved to think she believed him.

Perhaps speaking of Andrew's death had not been a good idea. Melissa's left foot flexed slightly at that thought, her throat drying. Abruptly she moved forward, bundled up her things. Andreas might not speak to a foreigner, but Nicholas would have to answer when she confronted him with what she had just learned from Popi.

Facing Melissa across an unnaturally tidy desk in his squeaky-clean office, Nicholas heard her out in silence. When she had finished, he reached across the freshly polished pinewood for her Polaroids.

'These are brilliant,' he said gruffly, hands shuffling the shining pictures as deftly as a pack of cards. 'The rest is just a heap of garbage.'

He'd been brusque all of yesterday, too, and Melissa wasn't about to be put off, however disconcerting the newly transformed office and its owner. The mayor of Asteri, in dark blue two-piece suit, white shirt and eye-catching tie was even more astonishing than his pristine workplace. In the corner of the room in a blitz-cleaned dog-basket, the freshly brushed Chloe dozed, fluffed mop head on paws.

Just who was the mayor expecting? Melissa

wondered, glancing at the three chairs ranged alongside hers. Perhaps before the start of the public meeting he was seeing the conservation and wildlife experts, who were flying in tonight — in a few minutes, Melissa amended, checking her watch. Or was this huddle of chairs connected in any way to Spiro and the wildlife smugglers' 'special shipment', due any time now on Asteri? Whatever, Nicholas hadn't told her a thing about this meeting, and clearly didn't want to include her.

Not sure whether she was hurt or just plain angry, Melissa nevertheless tried to put these intriguing — and irritating — issues to one side to concentrate on the matter in hand.

'Garbage?' she questioned, running a fingertip lightly down the slick grain of her visitor's chair.

Nicholas shot forward in his seat, making it see-saw ominously on the tiled floor. 'I believe we've a deadline here, and more important things to discuss than some dumb piece of gossip you've picked up on. Don't let the farmers and shepherds round here fool you: these guys love the rattle of money in their pockets. Someone's paid them to tell you that load of horse-manure.'

'You don't have to explain that part of the affair,' Melissa remarked mildly. 'I'm merely curious about one or two things.'

Her voice faded, as, holding her companion's gaze, she was struck afresh by the vividness, the movement, of Nicholas' blue eyes, so different from David's black, unblinking gaze. Thinking of the sculptor, Melissa realised she had missed him over the last few days. It was a great pity that her agreed trip to Antasteri was to pose for a piece commissioned by Ari Pindaros.

'So, what do you want from me?' Nicholas brusquely shattered her reverie. 'My daily diary for the last six months so you can cross-check dates with those of your source?'

Melissa, about to tease a little, remembered her own furious reaction to the news that Bruce Grainge was 'investigating' her commitment to wildlife. She felt a blush starting to squirm up her neck.

'This is important,' she resumed patiently. 'I mean, if you have any particular enemies, then I think I should know.'

'So you can go buzzing around, stirring things up? No way. I can take care of myself.'

Melissa, reminding herself to be fair, bit down on her first retort. 'I didn't mean it like that,' she said, still patient. 'I just wondered why —'

Nicholas interrupted again. 'Who is this "source", anyhow? And don't give me any mealy-mouthed hogwash about not revealing: you started this thing when you hurled yourself into my office.'

'Hurled yourself.' That sounded rather too close to 'throw yourself', which was one thing she would never do — throw herself at Nick Stephanides. Faced with the pictures of Lykimi, the vital reason why she and the mayor of Asteri had to be allies and had to be able to trust each other, Melissa's good humour abruptly evaporated.

'Speaking as someone who won't tell me the first thing about the man or woman who gave ASPW the tip-off about Spiro's special shipment, I wonder why you expect me to be forthcoming.'

'That's different: I promised discretion and there's real danger for the guy involved if Spiro finds out.' Nicholas, driving home the point, seized and jammed the knot on his tie closer to his throat. Abruptly his fingers turned and thrust at Melissa. 'Petty malice and rumour-mongering are something else, so why don't you come clean and start talking?'

'Why can't you ever give me a straight answer?' Melissa demanded, shoulders cracking as she sat up stiffly in her chair, ignoring Nicholas' question. 'I hate it when you're so terse. All I want to know is why anyone should think you're a smuggler: I mean, it's not something you immediately latch on to. The thought didn't suddenly strike me on the way to the harbour that the mayor of Asteri ran a few antiquities into Turkey and Rhodes. Why antiquities, for goodness' sake? Why not' — Melissa stopped herself within a gasp of saying 'something special from an ASPW site,' and finished, 'Why not contraband cigarettes?'

'Don't use them myself.' With a touch one might use towards porcelain, Nicholas set aside the Polaroids, rested his elbows on the table, chin on hands. His face held the deviously mild expression of a bull before it charged. 'No smoke without fire: that's what you're suggesting.'

'Maybe.' Curiously exhilarated, Melissa would not now back off.

'What can I say then?' Nicholas answered bitterly. 'How do I convince you?'

'Tell me you're not a smuggler.'

'What difference will that make if you don't believe me?'

'Swear to me,' Melissa persisted. Suddenly, though she could not reasonably say why, it was vitally important that he did this for her. 'Say it!'

Nicholas slapped both hands flat onto the table. 'In the name of my saint, I'm not a smuggler!' he roared. 'Happy now?'

They were so close that she could feel his breath on her mouth, almost taste the coffee he'd been drinking. There was a tang of cinnamon on his lips.

Meeting Melissa's widened eyes, taking in her heart-shaped face, the flushed tip of her small neat nose, engagingly sunburnt, Nicholas leaned still closer. 'Your sting's in your tongue, Bumblebee,' he said gruffly, his warm breath lightly stirring the smaller bristles of his moustache.

Spiro had a moustache. Unwelcome as any double exposure, the rest of Jonathan's description of the wildlife smuggler — tanned, stocky, black-haired, a non-smoker, sunglasses to cover those fierce blue eyes — superimposed itself for an instant on Melissa's image of Nicholas.

And the moment was lost.

As though it was a dance long understood between them, both sighed, drew back simultaneously, glanced round the room for something to look at, comment on, break the mood.

In her basket Chloe's paws jumped as she dreamed.

'Wish I could be like her,' said Nicholas. 'No worries. I'm seeing Ari Pindaros in here in less than an hour, hence the glad rags.'

He flicked his jacket with a thumb.

There was a crisp rap at the door. Melissa and Nicholas looked at each other.

'Come in!' called Nicholas in Greek.

It wasn't the head of Pindaros Bauxite but David Gordon and a young flame-headed girl, the girl teasingly insisting on holding the door for the man.

Frowning, Nicholas left his seat. 'You've picked a rare time to call,' he said tersely to the girl in English. 'Alexios and the others ready?'

'Dad, for the billionth time, it's utterly under control.'

'Good evening, Melissa,' David gave her a smile, black eyes fixing on her hips, breasts, the curves of her face. Ignoring a thunderous glare from Nicholas he approached Melissa, his eyes now reminding her of their appointment the following day. 'How are you?' he asked softly, crouching smoothly before Melissa's chair as the red-haired girl and Nicholas — was he really old enough to be her father? — spoke in a series of hurried whispers.

'Very well, thank you.' Melissa was marvelling at the man's balance. Squatting on his heels whilst still keeping intact all the lines and planes of his suit, he looked as elegantly terrifying as a native American warrior. She wanted to put out a foot, try to push him over, though instinct told her it would be impossible. 'And yourself?'

'Not bad.' David cast an eye over her sand-coloured trousers and top. 'Are you going to the meeting now?'

Melissa grinned at him. 'Relax, David. I'm going home to change first,' she said, adding mischievously, 'Tell me, do you work in your pin-stripe or is it just for show?'

'Oh, entirely and completely for show.' Utterly shameless, David smiled again. 'May I walk you home — as before?'

The room rumbled as Nicholas loudly cleared his throat. 'Melissa, I'd like you to meet my daughter Roxanne.'

As tall, slender and darkly sheathed as a bulrush, the girl flashed across the room, the candle-brightness of her hair reflected in her smile. 'Pleased to meet you,' she said.

Her extended hand trembled slightly, reminding Melissa of herself at eighteen, how keen she'd been to like and be liked. She smiled back, rising from her chair as David got out of the way and stepped back. As his eyes ran from one womanly form to another, he gave so acquisitive a smile that Melissa wanted to pour some cold water over his handsome head. David and Nicholas — both had a lot to learn, she thought, in the single leaping instant it took her to clasp Roxanne's hand and speak.

'Hello, Roxanne.' She shook hands with the girl. 'Are you here for the summer?'

'Yes, I am. Dad's told me how much you've done for ASPW,' continued Roxanne shyly, 'and I know how hard you've been working these last two days for the meeting.'

'Thanks, although we've all been busy, no one more than your father,' replied Melissa sweetly. 'All these extra unscheduled meetings . . .' She looked then at the mayor, to make sure her shaft had gone home. His ears were gratifyingly pink.

'Father — I like the sound of that. Shows respect.' Nicholas came to Roxanne and, without a hint of self-consciousness, stretched up to kiss her. Standing beside his daughter, Nicholas was shorter but altogether broader, as sinewy as David, who, resuming what seemed to be his favourite position in Nicholas' office, had leaned himself against the door.

Moving, Nicholas had placed himself between Roxanne and the sculptor, Melissa noted. The girl had also noticed.

'David and I just met outside,' Roxanne said now, unable to resist a glance at the looming figure on the threshold. 'David's coming to the meeting.'

'A rare honour,' said Nicholas. 'If I'd known I'd have polished the schoolroom doorjamb.'

'Dad, please!' murmured Roxanne, but neither man was taking any notice of the softly agonised plea or her scalding blush.

'The only things you need to polish are your arguments,' answered David. 'Pindaros Bauxite are a tough consortium.'

'For which, fortunately, we are absolutely ready,' said Melissa steadily.

From the flagged square outside, the sound of footsteps.

'They're early.' Nicholas glowered at the closed door of the outer office, then snapped his head round. 'I'm sorry, but I'm going to have to ask you to leave. All of you.' He threw an arm round his daughter's narrow shoulders, gave her a quick squeeze. 'Don't be frightened, it'll be fine,' he murmured in Greek. 'If you all go out the back way, he'll not see you.'

Nicholas straightened and pointed to a small side door. 'If you could leave by that door —'

'What's going on?' Melissa demanded, scooping up her things. What hadn't the man told her now?

'Catch you later. Believe me, Melissa —'

Nicholas whirled round in the doorway, his dark blunt features glowing like an excited youth's, 'You'll thank me for this, you surely will.'

In a swish of blue energy the mayor was gone. At the other side of the door Melissa heard Nicholas calling: 'Art! Zoe! Katherine not with you then?' and for the first time that evening was truly alarmed.

Chapter 17

Katherine was already on the island and Nicholas had trotted out in his best suit to meet her. Forget Ari Pindaros, forget the need to impress the millionaire owner of the company which planned to blow up half of Asteri mountain for the sake of a few drink cans: the mayor's sartorial efforts were entirely on behalf of the female side of this delegation. Not for Pindaros had Nicholas waxed his office, teased and combed Chloe's coat into a glossy, tangle-free lustre. Not for Pindaros had he brushed his teeth to a limescale whiteness, groomed his hair neat as panther-fur. No, for Katherine, Melissa reflected furiously. Never for herself, but for *her* —

A hesitant tap on the door of her flat at Mrs Samouri's froze the young woman partway through yanking her grimy, sweated-up tee-shirt over her head. Enveloped in the stale clothing, she paused. 'Yes?'

Roxanne's voice: 'Melissa? David's gone down to the harbour café to borrow a torch in case the street lights go off again tonight.

I'm just slipping across the square to young Mikhalaki's house to make sure he and his family know where to go. I'll see you down on the harbour front, okay? Oh — and Dad told me to remind you to bring your cameras.'

Cameras and what else? Flash units? Tripods? What kind of film? What was she supposed to be photographing — people, close-ups, landscape? How conspicuous or discreet was she supposed to be? Damn him, thought Melissa, aggrieved.

'I will — See you down there in five minutes,' she called back merrily. She liked Nicholas' daughter. Choking down the blast of fury that Roxanne's final request had ignited, Melissa finished pulling off the tee-shirt, face flushed.

Ten minutes later, in yellow silk dress, high heels, and — this a killer to elegance — small black camera bag and shoulder-slung tripod, Melissa was bustling down the endless sequence of steps to Khora harbour, wondering why, on the evening of a vital public meeting, the 'capital' of Asteri was like a ghost town.

As she passed shuttered windows, narrow sidestreets, only swooping swallows and the odd prowling cat were evidence of life. Were people already at the schoolhouse, or wasn't anyone coming? she thought, alarmed by the silence. Swinging round suddenly, hoping to catch someone lurking, she was met by only the sun, lemon trailing to purple tips, the low light shooting at her from the pink and white stone walls like spouting water. Facing ahead again, there was no sign of David or Roxanne yet. But there, on the stone jetty, dangling his feet over the edge towards the limpid sea, sat her 'well-wisher' Manoli, a 'Lucky Luke' comic book rolled in his pocket.

Chance, or had he been waiting? thought Melissa, quickening her step. No matter, she wanted to speak with him and a few moments now, before David and Roxanne appeared, was as good a time as any. If Manoli fancied blondes then she should be able to pump him for information.

Her own cynicism caught Melissa for an instant by surprise. Essentially good-natured, easy-going, it wasn't like her to lose her sense of proportion, or humour, even where Katherine was concerned. But the stakes here were so much greater: Andrew's life, the wildlife smugglers, Andrew's death. Look golden, look young and smile! Melissa told herself, feeling inside as sour as a gold and pink crab apple.

Setting her tripod, camera already attached, on the middle of the jetty, she settled beside Manoli, dangling her legs alongside his over the smooth stone. At the shallow side of the harbour, where the windows of Khora's grander houses flashed out in the weltering sun through tangled gardens and antique iron gates, she could see sea-grass flowering in the limpid water.

'No use asking if you'll roll me a cigarette,' grumbled Manoli as a greeting.

'None,' said Melissa pleasantly. With Andrew's comments on the smugglers' non-smoking habits in Rhodes Town engraved into her memory, she was actually relieved that Manoli smoked. Now she broadened her smile. 'Popi gave me your message.'

'It was better she came. A man and woman walking together on a lonely beach — people would talk,' said Manoli piously. 'But I thought you should know that mayor Niko's a wild one.'

'And just before the meeting, too,' agreed Melissa evenly.

Manoli knuckled his unshaven jowls and then his eyes. 'The damn border patrol put their lights on me last night for a joke. My head's been spinning ever since,' he muttered, avoiding meeting Melissa's eye.

Melissa flicked a hand through her blonde hair. 'How wild?' she asked.

Manoli sighed, swinging his worry beads

in his fingered hand. 'My goddaughter told you all I know.'

'Of course! But I'm sure you can introduce me to Andreas the shepherd tonight.' Melissa gave the weather-beaten sailor a charming smile. 'The ferryman knows everyone on his islands.'

'Sure! No problem.' Attempting to puff out his chest, Manoli finished on a cough, and then let fall what Melissa hoped would be her first real break. 'Andreas and his family are in Khora for the meeting.'

The shepherd's family, thought Melissa, lowering her face so that Manoli would not see the gleam in her eyes. If Manoli had been sent by someone — Spiro, for instance — he would probably also have paid Andreas and told the shepherd what to say and more importantly what *not* to say. Such discussions, however, might not have included Andreas' family. If she could talk to the shepherd's wife alone, decided Melissa, there was a slim chance of finding out if Andreas had been visited recently by any special visitors.

'I noticed that the fishermen seem to have brought in a decent haul.' Melissa had a reason for mentioning this. She also knew now that direct questions — 'For what reason really did you tell me that Nicholas is a smuggler?' 'Who are you working for?' 'Who told you to approach me?' 'What else do you know about smugglers?' — would bring no answers at all.

As she hoped, Manoli took the bait. 'Not bad, although I didn't see their lights in the straits between here and Antasteri. Fishing's good there, if you've the skill to ride the current.'

If Manoli was now telling the truth, the 'fishermen' David had complained of had not been operating near Antasteri last night, thought Melissa. But did that mean the special wildlife shipment would come in to David's island or not?

Aware that time was pressing, Melissa decided she had to risk a more pertinent enquiry. She leaned back, the yellow silk caressing the soft curves of her body as she clasped her knee with her hands. 'Do you ever ferry anything special in for Mayor Niko?' she asked casually. 'Or for any of the islanders? Something like a wardrobe or a bed, say, or a gas fridge?' She deliberately named large packages: objects which may in reality have served as cages.

Manoli coughed, smoker's gargle rumbling in his wiry chest. 'I don't know what you mean.' He coughed again, shoulders shaking, face a picture of grizzled innocence. 'Tax men can read,' he said after a moment.

215

'Off the record.' Melissa smiled: she had always wanted to say that, but never had reason to till now. Turning her head from Manoli, she watched a shoal of flying fish dazzle-dive-dazzle across the mouth of the harbour. Out there in the sea dolphins would be bearing their young, although seahorses, her favourites, were not quite ready yet to spawn.

In real life, in nature, everything was happening, thought Melissa, and *she* had to be in Khora, arguing a case at what was quite possibly by now a rigged public meeting, monitoring these people — Katherine, Pindaros, Zoe, Spiro the smuggler — dabbling their fingers in Asteri's pie.

Manoli's slow reply made her turn to look at him.

'Big stuff? No, not for years. Not since I brought three freezers over from Rhodes for Mike the butcher's shop, back in '89.' Manoli pointed with his worry beads. 'Shall we go?'

Clearly, Manoli wasn't worried about anyone seeing them walking alone together tonight, thought Melissa, amused. Torn between strolling with the ferryman to the schoolhouse — hopefully beguiling more information out of him on the way — and waiting as arranged for David and Roxanne,

216

Melissa hesitated. 'Excuse me a moment: I just need to check that I have something,' she answered easily, opening the camera bag on her shoulder and delving inside whilst she made up her mind.

But in the end the decision was not hers.

'What's he want?' muttered Manoli, rippling a warning hand at Melissa to stay behind him as they both rose.

London clothes, Melissa noted, guessing the city from the cut of the man's brown suit, and beneath the dark brown hair a city face, sharp and sallow. Possibly an official, or a wildlife representative, but instinct warned her otherwise.

'Miss Haye? Will you come with me, please? Someone's waiting for us.' Without introducing himself the man stepped closer.

Manoli barred the way. 'You know this man?' he asked Melissa.

'Beat it, Grandad,' said the stranger softly in English.

'It's all right, Manoli,' Melissa said quickly in Greek, not wanting the old man involved in any trouble. 'He's a friend of someone I know only too well.'

'*Adío*, Melissa, and safe journeys.' Manoli was already leaving — he had accepted her explanation so quickly, the whole confrontation was so small, so slick that for a moment

Melissa wondered if the ferryman knew the man and had been told to delay her until he came. But then common sense reasserted itself. Manoli was going, but already he was looking round, staring with that frank curiosity which to Greeks was not ill-mannered but the interest one showed to strangers.

Melissa was also looking, but she already had a good idea who this brown-suited man was. 'I'm sorry, Mr Bailey, but I've already made my arrangements for this evening,' she said steadily. 'You can tell Katherine I'll see her at the meeting.'

'And a good day to you, too.' The new speaker stood on the steps behind Melissa, bringing the wholesome scent of lemon with her. 'I must say you're looking well, Melissa: in the pink.'

Cool in her pristine peppermint suit, Katherine smiled down at the smaller woman. Her large eyes studied Melissa an instant longer, and then she handed the man a brown briefcase.

'Why not also take the lady's camera for her, Bailey?' she suggested, her voice soft, controlled.

'No, thanks.' Melissa firmly took hold of the tripod before either Bailey or Katherine moved, hiding her face by lowering her head to check that the camera was completely secure. Her heart was hammering fiercely within her breast, thoughts going off in her head like flashguns. She was right: this was the Bailey whom Jonathan had warned her against, but first things first.

'How did you manage it, Katherine?' Melissa asked pleasantly, raising her head. 'Moving the meeting from October to tonight?'

'Ah, you appreciated my little coup,' replied Katherine, leaning for an instant against her associate to steady herself as she shook a tiny pebble from one elegant sandal. Her actions beautifully displayed her long legs, and Melissa was amused to see how Bailey was totally taken in by the show. For an instant she felt a feeling of rapport with Katherine, an emotion totally destroyed by the woman's next statement: 'Nicholas Stephanides and I are having dinner at Elysion tomorrow night: I might tell him, but I won't tell you.' Katherine smiled.

Melissa felt herself blushing. Jealousy was supposed to be green, she reflected, trying to inject humour into her reaction. Nicholas' villa invitations were nothing to do with her.

'How grand,' she remarked, laughing to irritate her adversary. Meeting and holding the woman's large green eyes, she knew that Katherine was thinking of her 'killed' magazine commissions and the clandestine investigations of Bruce the Snoop. She recalled Jonathan's warning not to get too deep in alone. 'Are you planning to stay long this time?'

'As long as is necessary,' came the calm response.

A smell of petrol from the island's only station drifted along the harbour front on the prevailing breeze. Melissa smelt the petrol and below that the sea. She thought of Andrew and her father.

'Of course, you'll have met Nicholas?' Katherine continued sweetly, probing any possible weakness.

'You know I have.' Melissa stared for a moment at Katherine's mouth; at the tiny dark hairs beside those glossy lips. She shook her head slightly, knowing how Katherine hated her seahorse earrings: the jewellery Andrew, Katherine's former lover, had bought for her.

And you think Katherine is malicious? Andrew's voice questioned ironically in Melissa's head. Still the younger woman could not resist another thrust. 'Strange you should mention Elysion. Tomorrow, I'm visiting *your* host's island hideaway.'

'David Gordon's invited you to Antasteri?' The tone said it all: Katherine was mortified.

Beside her Bailey shuffled his briefcase from one hand to the other. 'Almost time, Katherine,' he warned.

'Nothing can start without me,' replied Katherine crisply, 'But you go on ahead — tell them we're coming.' As Bailey moved off, striding smartly along the harbour road, briefcase in hand, Katherine looked Melissa slowly up and down, taking in the floating yellow silk, the flying mimosa-yellow hair. 'I'm surprised; scarcely model material, I would have thought.'

Clearly, Katherine knew nothing of David's latest piece.

Melissa caught a sideways movement just beyond the drying fishing nets. The torch the man was carrying flashed in the sun. 'David's coming,' she said. 'Why not ask him?'

Stepping heavily round the drying nets on his way back from borrowing a torch from the unlocked yet deserted harbour café, David was looking out to sea and had not noticed the figures near the steps. He was thinking not 'meeting' but 'models': by tomorrow he intended to have his three and pose them, starting with Melissa.

Tough, plump almond, thought David, guessing how the blonde would tan. She knew how to take care of herself, even down to that delicate complexion. And Rodin would have adored that body.

David's broad shadow fell across the bright harbour water. He strode on without really seeing the tiny brown fishes, talking softly to himself as was his habit when thinking.

What would Rodin have made of Roxanne? Melissa was his Athene, but Roxanne?

'She's from Maine but she's like the young auburn-haired Elizabeth the First,' he was saying, his mind a montage of red and gilt. And those large, stormy brown eyes . . .

'Hera!' A lock of David's thick black hair fell across his forehead as he slapped the wall of the nearest house with the flat of his hand, astonished not to have seen it before. Hera, the goddess of earthy power, 'ox-eyed Hera' to the ancients, who painted her statues with the appealing brown eyes of a young heifer. 'Star-queen, queen of heaven. Yes!'

Quickly, he reined in, hid the jubilant surge by a lengthening of his stride over the cobbles. Looking ahead now, he saw the perfectly proportioned figure of Katherine Hopkins. 'Pure Katherine,' he murmured, touched by the firm fresh body, the spill of hair over slender bronze arms, the look of welcome in a face the ancient Greek artists would have killed for. As well as Katherine, Melissa — fair, bonny — and behind Katherine, now coming down the steps, the bright Roxanne.

The three. *His* three.

Striding down the steps, unaware that she had just missed meeting Bailey again, Roxanne watched David approach Katherine and Melissa. She sighed: the two were so fine, so shapely, so assured. When they moved it meant something: it caught attention. When they spoke they had something to say.

Admiration a knife-edge away from envy, Roxanne admitted to herself, ashamed of her feelings. David deserved the best, and Katherine and Melissa were surely that.

Yet the sick feeling in the bottom of her stomach was not the worst, Roxanne admitted, as David caught her gaze and smiled at her. She had not forgotten — could never forget — their meeting after her eerie encounter with Bailey. Now, watching David with the elegant Katherine, it seemed that her former companion had almost dismissed that occasion from his mind. Almost but not quite . . .

Tall, dark, handsome in immaculate cream trousers and light jacket, sporting a gold wristwatch, a silk handkerchief in top pocket, David Gordon appeared to be your conventional hero material, right up to the glossy black hair and eyes. As such, he was as remote to Roxanne as a fabulous beast: a creature to be admired but never touched — not by her. It was the faint chicken-pox scar, in the middle of his smooth chin, that brought David down to human, Roxanne level. And he was looking at her, his face strangely shy.

'I believe you all know each other?' he asked, glancing from Roxanne to Katherine then Melissa.

'We've met,' replied Katherine laconically. She was about to add more, but David spoke first.

'I've a favour to ask.' He stared at his hands a moment, then raised his dark head. 'It concerns the three of you.'

'Do tell.' Relaxing, Katherine smiled.

Anticipating the request, Melissa suppressed a sigh. She could only hope that Roxanne also agreed to it: so far as Katherine's participation was concerned, she had no doubts.

David spoke slowly, precisely laying out his request. 'I would like you, Katherine, along with Melissa and Roxanne, to be my guests tomorrow on Antasteri. To see my island and my studio, and to be my models for a stone sculpture. I'm calling it "Before the Judgement of Paris".'

'That's a wonderful idea!' said Katherine.

'We'd have clothes on?' Roxanne asked, blushing hotly as Katherine looked at her with sharply narrowed eyes.

David nodded.

'Well,' Roxanne stopped herself just in time from adding 'I'll have to check with Dad', '. . . all right.'

Melissa silently let go her held-in breath.

Katherine, flicking her eyes from Roxanne and now fixing on David, asked, 'You have us in mind for specific roles?'

The sculptor smiled. 'You shall be my Aphrodite,' he said quietly.

'The goddess of love.' Katherine looked as sleek as she sounded. Stretching her arms above her head, she shot Melissa a glance of total victory, before rounding on the taller Roxanne. 'You understand English!'

'She is my daughter, after all.'

Silently, Nicholas had appeared from one of the back streets and stepped in at a crucial moment. Again Melissa marvelled at his quiet stalking skill, but Nicholas' attention was gripped by the latest visitor to his island.

'Great to see you again, Katherine,' he said, not shaking hands but kissing her lightly on both cheeks.

'The pleasure's definitely mine.' Dismiss-

ing Roxanne, asserting the rights of friend-
ship, Katherine slipped her arm through his.
'I see you're wearing the tie I chose for you.'

Nicholas grinned. 'Where colour's concerned, Katherine, I know your taste is immaculate. Now, if you'd like to step this way
. . . He pointed towards the cliff and Khora
point. 'We're needed on the beach.'

Chapter 18

The beach was full of children, all in their best suits or skirts, embroidered waistcoats, bolero tops. Bright as patches of scarlet and blue pimpernel, boys and girls skipped and cartwheeled on the shining sands. Squeaking like dolphins, they chased and raced up and down Lykimi, weaving round parents, aunts and uncles strolling by the sea's edge, the adults calling after them, 'Try to stay tidy!' but to no effect.

Picking her way down the narrow shaly track, arms pinned to her sides to protect the yellow silk dress from snags on broom and prickly pear, Melissa paused to take in the scene through her viewfinder. A few paces ahead David twisted back, saw what Melissa was doing and frowned. Out in front, Nicholas and Roxanne kept up with Katherine's determined lead. The head of the TWC chain was marching down to Lykimi by the quickest possible route, gyrating like a slalom racer to avoid the thorny shrubs. By the crossbow-taut set of her rival's shoulders, Melissa guessed that Katherine was longing to put a flame-thrower to the entire hillside so that she could get down there the faster.

Melissa had known that Nicholas was bringing everyone to Lykimi tonight, but so far as she'd understood the plan, the meeting was to have started in the schoolhouse, then moved out here. Why had the sequence been changed? Why had the villagers of Khora and the rest of Asteri been told to gather at Lykimi instead? Hundreds were already on the beach and clearly waiting for something.

'The family of Manoli Pavlides the ferry-man, please. Kýrio Pavlides' family to the photo set . . .' The voice of Dr Alexios, blurred and amplified, drifted up to Melissa. Tracking the sound, she easily spotted Alexios, clean-shaven and a head taller than the other islanders, moving through the throng with a megaphone. Sweeping her lens in the direction Alexios was going, Melissa focused on a group of chairs carefully positioned against a backdrop of prickly-pear flowers. Whoever had set it up had used her pictures of the scene to grab the best angle and time of day, Melissa realised at once, feeling flattered and amused. Waiting in front of the chairs, old-fashioned plate camera at the ready, was the chemist and ASPW member Mr Zervos.

Meanwhile the schoolmaster, another

ASPW member, was videoing the entire event.

Reaching the beach, Katherine turned on Nicholas. 'Why the pictures?' she demanded, clearly displeased with this turn of events.

'Asterians love formal family snaps, Katherine,' replied Nicholas, clambering down beside her. 'Promising a free picture each was a great way to make sure lots of bodies would be here.' He glanced up the track, looking past Roxanne and David. 'Mr Zervos is the man the older ones trust,' he said, speaking directly to Melissa. 'I'm sorry to say that they find you and your modern gear pretty scary.'

'Or should that be intrusive?' Katherine asked, with a meaningful glance at David. Despite the sun being low in the sky, the sculptor had put on his dark glasses. Now he said and did nothing to deny or shrug off her suggestion.

Nicholas cleared his throat. 'If you want to join Mr Zervos tonight, the older ones'll accept you,' he said, continuing his explanation and partial apology to Melissa. 'I didn't say anything about this because I wasn't sure how you'd feel about having to work with an amateur. I figured you might prefer to be independent, take more natural — and by that I mean informal — shots.'

So far, his eyes had not left Melissa's face. His right hand, stretching out slightly towards her, suddenly dipped sharply, lightly touching the top of Chloe's groomed head. Melissa found herself wondering what those fingers felt like: an absurd thought in the circumstances.

'Next time, ask. You may be surprised,' she answered drily. When Nicholas lowered his eyes, Melissa knew he'd taken her point.

'Shall we get on?' Katherine was bored, and Nicholas was instantly attentive.

'Sorry, Katherine, I should have explained at once. The press are here: we've reporters and photographers out from Rhodes and Athens.'

Although speaking to Katherine, Melissa sensed that Nicholas was also addressing her, giving another reason why he thought she would prefer to mingle with the crowds rather than keep with the chemist photographing stiff little family groups of solemn-looking women and grim-moustachioed men. Did all the male islanders except for Alexios have those bristling moustaches? she wondered now, quietly astonished by what she had so far seen. Stocky, swarthy, tanned: most of the menfolk of Asteri, including its mayor, could be described in the same terms as Jonathan had used to give a picture of the wildlife smuggler Spiro.

Looking at them gathered together at Lykimi beach, Melissa had a sharp reminder of the difficulties in tracing the individuals she and Nicholas were after. All the more reason, then, why Mr Zervos' formal pictures of family groups would provide a vital record, pictures ASPW could perhaps use to check against any possible sightings of smugglers or suspect 'fishermen'.

Good work, Melissa mentally complimented Nicholas. She would take photographs tonight too, Nicholas' suggested 'informal shots'. Then she and ASPW would have the complete picture: not only who was who but who might be associated with whom, who might be working with whom.

After Nicholas' mention of the reporters, Katherine's expression did not so much soften as become more alert, the very image of a dynamic business personality. 'Why, that's George Tanis over there!' she exclaimed as she recognised the news anchorman of one of the Greek radio stations. Instantly, Katherine sashayed forward to grab TWC's share of media attention.

'Look at them,' David said grimly to no one and everyone, his harsh, handsome profile caught by the setting sun as he jerked his head dismissively towards a particularly dense knot of people. 'The vultures have already fixed on Ari and Zoe.'

'Excuse me.' Melissa snapped her first picture of four middle-aged island men standing together. 'I'm on a roll here with this light, so I'd better take advantage.' She skipped away in soft clouds of beach-dust.

'I saw a condor back in Maine once: it had been blown off course by a storm,' said Roxanne quietly beside David, her voice bland as smoothly flowing water. 'Vultures are really very beautiful birds.' Now she glanced up at him.

It was nicely done, and in a couple more years, when she had learned not to hide her mouth with her thumb, would be most effective, thought David. The sculptor, himself hidden behind dark sunspecs, studied the strong lines of Roxanne's face: the lightning-narrow mouth, the fire-lashed eyes. Melissa, with her easy laughter, that engaging sprinkling of freckles over her ripe upper lip, was, although the elder, the more approachable.

Or was it simply that being older and used to working with images, the photographer had perfected her technique?

Who cares, you prat, she's a beautiful woman who likes you. The voice in David's head was almost Colin's, except that his older brother would never have used the word beautiful. Colin would have said stylish. Colin had always admired style in people. To Colin, Roxanne's appeal would have been less than Melissa's open-hearted energy, because the American hadn't yet refined her individual fashion. And maybe Roxanne was too young, thought David, blowing gently down his nose, whereas Katherine Hopkins —

'Stylish,' murmured David, speaking for his brother.

Whilst David was considering his models, Roxanne was keeping an anxious eye out for Bailey. Tonight she knew that Alexios had locked the schoolroom before coming here, but even so she was uneasy. Much as she didn't want to see Bailey again, she disliked the idea of his being back in Khora, free to do whatever he wanted. But then, she had also promised her dad to fill Melissa in on what was about to take place here in a few moments. Wondering what she should do, which should be her biggest priority, Roxanne started back towards the cliff.

A few steps on, David caught up with her. 'Hold on, your dad's finally got things moving,' he said, smiling down at her in a way that made Roxanne's heart do a fast march in her chest.

She tried to explain. 'But I think Bailey's

back there and if he's got inside the school-house —'

'Too late for anyone if he's done that, my pet.' Lightly cupping her bony shoulder with his hand, David turned Roxanne back to the noisy throng. 'We'll walk back in a moment, shall we?' he asked. 'I want to see what's going to happen here first.'

'Right — and I need to talk to Melissa.' Backing away before her blush and excitement both went nova, and she did something really stupid, like maybe yelling with delight, Roxanne spun herself round hard and blazed off to find Melissa. To keep her word before she *and David* went back to town.

In the middle of the crush, where Katherine was still networking amongst the reporters, Melissa was discreetly tracking Manoli and Popi, hoping one or both might lead her to someone interesting. Andreas, for instance, or one of the shepherd's family. It was best not to think about the chances of meeting Spiro, Melissa found: the feelings provoked by thoughts of such a possible encounter were too explosive. Much better not to think of Spiro, just concentrate on taking pictures, doing her job.

One thing she knew she had to do after tonight was congratulate the mayor. Melissa was already aware that somehow Nicholas had scored a major coup, something the invited delegation of conservation officials, hovering close to George Tanis, were still in the dark about. As she was herself, Melissa thought, with renewed irritation. Glancing at the smiling, sleek Katherine, Melissa wondered how much she had been told. Had Nicholas told Katherine everything?

Nicholas, struggling with the logistics of crowds, settling everyone down so that the meeting could begin with the announcement he had been promised by Ari Pindaros, sensed a pair of warm, expectant brown eyes fixed on him and cursed gruffly. Not so much a bee as a gadfly, he thought: Melissa was always after him for what he should be doing. By contrast, although less easy-going in nature than Melissa, Katherine was less demanding. With her he didn't have to do anything — just be a man. Relations were much simpler and more restful.

He shrugged his powerful shoulders. After tonight and Pindaros' announcement, things between Katherine and himself might be more complicated, more of a challenge. His moustache twitched in wry amusement. It would certainly keep the brunette thinking about him instead of sculptor Gordon. The only reason he'd agreed to Roxanne's modelling for Gordon was because Melissa and Katherine would also be there, keeping an eye on Roxanne — and each other.

Aware of the crackling rivalry between the two women, Nicholas grinned, then frowned. He wasn't really happy about this trip to Antasteri for several reasons. He didn't want Katherine or Melissa entangled with Gordon. He didn't want Melissa buzzing round alone on the sculptor's island.

And if Gordon hurt Roxanne, took advantage of an eighteen-year-old girl's infatuation, then he'd pay. A Cretan father's revenge would be nothing to his, Nicholas vowed, trying to tug his cap low over his fierce blue eyes and cursing when his hand met nothing except hair. In Greece wearing formal clothes made him feel uneasy, overdressed, although in the States he swanked with the best. Maybe he should try to find out who dressed Ari, although Nicholas knew that he'd not be able to afford what the Greek millionaire paid, toy factories in America or not. Perhaps though, after this summer, when all his business deals were concluded . . . Nicholas smoothed his moustache.

'Quiet, everybody!' he bawled for the umpteenth time and was only a little astonished when finally the hubbub switched off. Seizing the megaphone from Alexios, Nicholas thrust it at Ari. 'Mr Pindaros of Pindaros Bauxite has an announcement!'

Slowly the taller man stretched out a fleshy hand, reluctantly took the instrument. Beside him, blonde, plump Zoe Konstantinou, in purple trouser suit with black accessories, looked like an artist's earlier, cruder version of Melissa: a sour, pouting version, Nicholas noted, wondering how Ari dealt with sulks.

Right now, Ari had his hands full facing the crowd. 'My company and I have pledged —'

'To grab all you can and pay no taxes!' roared a heckler from somewhere up the beach, hidden in the shadow of the cliff. Zoe sucked in a long breath, but Ari continued without so much as a blink of an eye.

'Pindaros Bauxite have pledged their full support for the Asteri Society for the Protection of Wildlife and its work in preserving this superb beach for the benefit of the wildlife and people of the island. Lykimi beach is a jewel in the Dodecanese and must remain as it is, undeveloped, undisturbed and utterly unspoilt. To achieve this end, Pindaros Bauxite will supply funds to maintain Lykimi and promise to look into other possible sites at Hydra and Kemi . . .'

Melissa noticed Katherine's shrug when Ari Pindaros mentioned the deserted village of Kemi, and then her more public reaction to Pindaros' closing statement: '. . . for a future marina development.'

'Why was I not informed of this sudden change in your company's plans?' Katherine demanded in Greek, every line of her patrician face hardening as she glared at the head of Pindaros Bauxite, her ally. 'What possible expertise has a mining organization in advising the people of this island about any marina?'

'Who cares, so long as he's paying?' roared the unseen heckler, which provoked a huge shout of 'Yes!' and several loud cheers from the crowds.

'Carried, I believe, by popular assent,' remarked Nicholas over the cheers, smiling down Katherine's furious look. Had they been alone, he had no doubt that the woman would have flown at him: their quarrel would have been cosmic and the making-up pure heaven. Unable to resist, he blew her a kiss.

Bad move there, Nick, reflected Melissa, capturing on film the moment when Ari Pindaros acknowledged the applause, and again when he was congratulated by the wildlife delegates. By this very public declaration, by his tremendous orchestration of local support, Nicholas had ensured that Lykimi beach was safe for now — and yet how had he persuaded Pindaros to go so totally against the wishes of Zoe and Katherine? Katherine who hadn't known anything, who had been as surprised as she'd been.

Nearby, Dr Alexios was being interviewed by George Tanis and several newspaper men. 'Yes, Mr Pindaros' late conversion is a wonderful breakthrough and we of ASPW are going to make full use of his generous help. We're setting up a twenty-four-hour rota to guard this unique wildlife site, and tonight at the more formal public meeting we'll be asking for volunteers . . .'

'That meeting's still going ahead, then?' asked a radio interviewer.

'It most certainly is!' replied Alexios. 'We must try to get Mr Pindaros to change his mind about the mine, too!'

Melissa, knowing that somehow this concession had been won by force from the boss of Pindaros Bauxite, thought that would now be very unlikely and braced herself for a lively meeting at the schoolhouse. Leaving the press photographers still clustering round the stiff figures of Katherine and Zoe, she jostled through the islanders towards the fiery head of Roxanne, who was clearly also heading her way.

They met as a huge battery of flashes exploded amidst another spontaneous cheer, but neither Melissa nor Roxanne joined in the general revelry. Roxanne was already drawing her away from the main body of people; she was explaining softly in rapid English how Pindaros' 'conversion' had really been achieved.

'Two days ago, when I flew in . . . they were on the plane with me. They thought I was asleep, or that I only spoke Greek, and so they talked about how to make the marina happen here at Lykimi. A couple of Pindaros' top mining experts were due to fly in this morning and there was going to be an explosion tonight whilst everyone was at the schoolhouse: enough ripple-blasting to bring down half the cliff. Then the bulldozers would have moved in to clear up the mess . . .'

'Making sure at the same time they ripped through all the sand lilies, and sheared off most of the beach,' added Melissa.

'You've heard of these tricks?' asked David. Arriving with Roxanne, he was now staring at Katherine, shaking his dark head as though he could scarcely credit his model capable of such a conspiracy.

Melissa nodded. 'Heard and seen for myself,' she answered. 'Usually the developers strike first. This time, because of Roxanne, Asteri was lucky.' She gave Roxanne a shrewd glance. 'So that's why Ari Pindaros and Zoe Konstantinou came to the office today: to be informed in no uncertain terms that the mayor of Asteri knew about their little scheme and that if it went ahead the whole of the Greek business world and media would know, and shares in Pindaros Bauxite and Beach International would hit bottom.'

'Dad didn't tell you because whilst you were on the beach this afternoon Pindaros' men couldn't be,' added Roxanne hurriedly, 'but he didn't want you to stay on all through the evening in case they tried to fix explosives.'

'And in case things maybe got out of hand?' remarked Melissa ironically. *Thanks a lot, Nicholas the chauvinist.* The arrogance of the man was mind-blowing. It was as much as Melissa could do to speak evenly.

'I hope your father appreciates what you've done for ASPW.'

'He does,' replied Roxanne loyally.

'But Bailey suspected, and now he and the others will know,' said David. Again his black eyes fixed on Katherine.

'It should make our modelling sessions interesting,' remarked Melissa, with a lightheartedness she did not feel. Katherine was a bad loser, and she had lost hard and publicly tonight. 'Shall we go on to the official meeting?' People were starting to drift away: in a few moments Pindaros, Katherine and Zoe would be moving. Mr Zervos and a small group of radio reporters would be staying behind to take up the first watch.

'Sure — we'll go together,' said Roxanne quietly. Telling herself not to be childish, she smiled to hide her disappointment at not walking back to Khora alone with David. Also — where was Bailey, and what had he been doing?

When she thought of possible answers to those questions, Roxanne felt not only uneasy but scared.

Chapter 19

It was deep twilight as the last of the villagers filed into the single large high-roofed barn which served as Asteri's infants' and primary school. Now the adults shifted nervously on plastic chairs borrowed from the café and from nearby houses, their children revelling in freedom outside in the dirt yard as they played games of hopscotch and football under the holm oaks. The air, intense with jasmine, tumbled with tiny pipistrelle bats hungrily hunting early insects.

Above the roofline the dark blue evening was unsullied by torches as David and other men slipped their lights into their pockets. Only Nicholas was laggard in switching off the beam of his lamp, running it once round the inside of the building as he experimented with hands and fingers to see how shade and light picked out the coloured posters on the uneven grey walls.

'Jupiter,' said David to Roxanne, pointing to the planet glinting brilliantly through a narrow gap in one of the schoolhouse's high shuttered windows. 'Spying on his consort.'

Roxanne hid her face for an instant as she patted Chloe, stationed sideways under the formal rows of chairs. Then, as Melissa sportingly gave no sign of having heard, Roxanne moved the conversation on a little more. 'The Big Dipper's not up yet, I see. Are you interested in astronomy, David?'

Settled between Melissa and David, Roxanne was much more relaxed than she had been on the scramble over Khora point and through the unlit streets. When the three had reached the school yard and seen the doors thrown open, the first of the lanterns inside blooming into life, Roxanne had let a long breath escape through her teeth. 'I'd forgotten the teacher would be staying here until we came,' she said to Melissa, catching the older woman's speculative look. Melissa, studying the other men and women as they arrived, was aware of Roxanne still looking out for someone as she took her seat alongside Melissa and David. Sensing the redhead's slight withdrawal as the neat agile figure of Bailey — clasping that brown briefcase — scuttled down the central aisle towards the long trestle table at the head of the building, Melissa thought she understood. She decided not to reassure Roxanne: sometimes fear was better, especially where the fright concerned one of Katherine Hopkins' agents.

If Roxanne and her father were unaware of how vindictive Katherine could be when crossed, they would soon have to learn, reflected Melissa bleakly. She would have to speak to Nicholas, try to make him understand the dangers, although at present the mayor of Asteri had enough trouble. If Alexios and Mr Zervos and the others of ASPW were to guard Lykimi beach, who would look out for the wildlife smugglers?

Again Melissa scanned the menfolk in the schoolroom and again was overwhelmed by the ranks of warm-skinned, dark-haired, deep-chested males, all different yet all fitting Jonathan's description of Spiro. Were there any here who did not smoke, who, under the moustaches were 'too smooth' in overall appearance? Melissa looked more closely, squinting fiercely by the lantern light.

It was a blow that the electricity was down in the schoolhouse and one which Melissa had not expected. Khora's street lighting was known to be unreliable but power to private and public buildings was another matter. Now, as Nicholas and the rest of the 'top table' people filed through the long barn, she was horrified and alarmed to see the mayor of Asteri jerk his head back in a sharp negative as Manoli 'from the floor' asked if the power had been fixed. Worse than a blow, it was a disaster.

Without electricity, ASPW's careful wall displays were fuzzy blurs, the strongest of pictures weakened by shadows. The wonderful turtle video would not be shown. Worse, Melissa's video and slides of Asteri mountain, the strongest visual argument ASPW had to offer against Pindaros Bauxite, were now useless. For this, she and Nicholas had stayed up all night, choosing and sorting her footage, choosing and sorting slides and pictures from ASPW's own tiny archives, agonising over the final order so as to go for maximum impact. For nothing. Redundant, the projection screen hung behind the gathering figures of the top table: Ari Pindaros, Katherine, Zoe, Bailey, two mining experts from Pindaros Bauxite, the international wildlife delegate, and Dr Alexios.

'Why haven't they been able to fix it?' Roxanne's whisper showed that she was as puzzled as Melissa, and as surprised and suspicious. Power cuts to the main supply were infrequent but not unknown: usually normal service was quickly resumed. And there had been no storm, so why was the supply down in the first place?

'Quiet backhanders, perhaps?' murmured David, speaking Melissa's thought. 'I wonder which of that lot up there knows?' Abruptly his head came round, the seat beneath his heavy frame scraping on the cement floor. 'Hello! And who do we have here?'

Twisting on her shiny red plastic chair, Melissa took in the latecomer standing illuminated in the arched doorway of the schoolhouse. 'Not a conservationist, that's for sure,' she whispered. 'See the ivory cufflinks?'

Raising her camera and firing off a couple of shots was automatic. As she lowered it again she spotted Nicholas' face set in an expression of distaste: whether for the sudden flash or the ivory cufflinks Melissa couldn't tell and at that moment didn't really care. When Katherine protested from the top table: 'Really, Nicholas! Is this paparazzo reception what your visitors should expect?' Melissa's disgust boiled over — this fool was Nick's guest?

'I'm sorry, Katherine. It's nothing to do with me.' Nicholas' words bit deep into Melissa. Shocked, she lowered her camera, saw the stranger extending a hand to the mayor, say a name so softly she did not hear it — not against the background of English and Greek muttering and 'Who the hell do you think you are, blondie?' from the official press on the front row. Stock still, ignoring press complaints and the chatter of island voices, she saw Nicholas shake hands, smile, indicate a free seat on the second row where the man might sit.

David's hand firmly cupped her elbow. 'You want to be the whole show, or will you let the platform start?'

'Take your paw off me, David.'

David flung up his hand. 'Sorry, I thought you were different,' he said. 'I thought there were feelings behind that camera, but you're no better than the rest. It's a shame, Melissa, and I'm disappointed.'

The meeting opened and Nicholas, to Melissa's alarm, allowed Ari and the mining experts from Pindaros Bauxite to speak first. True, she had agreed with him yesterday that ASPW should speak last, but that was before the power cut had ruined their presentation. Watching Nicholas throw an arm over the defunct television and video recorder stored behind his seat and cross his fingers on top of the TV set when he thought no one was looking, Melissa knew they were both praying that the electricity would be restored before their turn came.

Ari had also brought video and slides, but the head of Pindaros Bauxite appeared remarkably sanguine about not being able to show them, Melissa noted.

'Cool, isn't he?' Roxanne muttered bitterly, as Pindaros patted his widow's peak of grey hair and rose smoothly to his feet, conference smile wide across his prominent jaw.

'He's a clever man,' remarked David. Sitting beside Roxanne, the sculptor studiously avoided Melissa.

A clever man who was David's latest patron, Melissa reminded herself. David might be sitting near to a 'Green' but he had already shown the people on the top table that he did not approve of certain of her tactics. Leaning back in his chair, the sculptor seemed to be physically distancing himself from her too.

David and Nicholas, Nicholas and David — whose side were they really on? Melissa reflected bitterly, as Nicholas exchanged a smile with Katherine. By all means be civilised, lull your opponent into a sense of false security, but as Melissa knew from stalking wildlife: however patient, cunning and careful, in the end what mattered was the shot, the clean finish.

How much of a killer instinct had Nicholas for Katherine? Melissa had no doubt that were the positions reversed, Katherine would have no hesitation in dispatching Nicholas as her latest victim. But then, as Melissa recognised in herself as well as in nature, females were often tougher and more ruthless than males.

Pindaros meanwhile was talking seamlessly, flawlessly, without a single hitch as he paused with modest politeness to acknowledge each ripple of applause, each call of 'Yes!' from the floor.

First, he addressed the economics of any mine on Asteri mountain. A borderline case, he admitted, wrinkling his nose: there would only be modest profits. As he continued to explain, the two mining experts chipping in with technical details to which he would then add a human gloss, the Greek millionaire was gradually making it appear that if any development were voted for tonight, this would be a courageous decision on the part of Pindaros Bauxite and a favour to the islanders.

Nothing was so seductive as allowing people to persuade you to sell them something, Melissa acknowledged, suppressed anger simmering in the dryness of her throat, the ache in her eyes. These lanterns were not only blurring her photographic work, they were blinding the islanders to Pindaros' true purpose. In the soft glow of hanging oil-lamps, their light dropping in a tender arc from walls and roofbeams, the scent of honest hot oil spiralling slowly to the ceiling and down, Ari Pindaros became a true man of labour. A miner, whose thousand dollar suit was made plain and ordinary in the dim light, whose rugged features were given depth and dignity by the many shadows. To many he would be little more than a voice; and here Pindaros' cleverness came to the fore as he sharpened the Piraeus accents in his speech: a stranger from the mainland, yes, but from the workplace of Athens' port, not the smooth rich suburbs of Kolonaki.

An honest man, promising honest work — real jobs — for other men. There would be a new road, right from Khora into the mountain. A special bus. A small hospital for workers and their families, of which no doubt Dr Alexios would approve and to which he might offer his excellent services . . .

Very clever, thought Melissa, left foot twitching slightly as her rigid fingers tightened on the camera in her lap.

Khora port would be deepened to take cargo ships of the necessary tonnage. Khora school would be enlarged and the single present teacher would become a teaching head, able to appoint more staff: Pindaros Bauxite were committed to a highly educated, highly

251

motivated workforce.

The teacher, Mr Stoulis, another key ASPW member, presently filming the entire public meeting on a hand-held, battery-driven video camera. Pindaros certainly knew where to direct his sweeteners, thought Melissa, stabbing a glance at Katherine seated next to the Greek millionaire. No doubt Pindaros would have already held out these juicy offers to Alexios and Mr Stoulis, but now they were publicly revealed, another chance to tempt, another opportunity to create envy in those less publicly favoured.

The mine site would be landscaped and later replanted with native species. For which read: no more mountain and a monoculture of a few scraggy pines, the cheapest to plant and grow. Melissa clicked her tongue but did not feel like laughing.

This would be a Greek mine, owned by the Greek people. For too long, Pindaros stated, his voice rising to a sudden shout, for too long Greece had been at the bottom of Europe, lower even than Turkey —

Mutters of angry disquiet at that statement.

Greece had been ignored and for why? Because Greece had no natural resources. No oil, little coal, no gold. But bauxite meant aluminium, and aluminium was a valuable commodity. 'Look how many Pepsis and Cokes the *Amerikáni* drink,' he continued. 'Our children even parade in sweatshirts showing the cans!'

There was laughter and vigorous nodding. Pindaros stretched out his hands, rippled his fingers for silence and the whispers subsided. The man waited another moment, letting the audience hold their breaths.

And the bauxite was theirs, he then roared out suddenly. 'Yours!' Pindaros shouted at the meeting, striking the table with both fists. 'Do you need to go look at the mountain? No — because it's yours!'

Thereby neatly scuppering any chance that the mayor might have of persuading the islanders to delay making a decision until they had at least visited the site, seen what they would lose, Ari Pindaros sat down amidst overwhelming applause.

Nicholas tried to burst the bubble. He cross-questioned the mining experts, extracting from one the grudging admission that the mine could well be worked out after twenty years. He passed round Melissa's pictures of the forest. He and Dr Alexios spoke passionately of the wild creatures and plants which lived there. These were Asteri's heritage: this was what truly belonged to the islanders. And they did not have to lose it.

Swiftly Nicholas explained the benefits of eco-tourism. The pine-resin collectors did not have to choose between back-breaking work in a stifling pine forest or back-breaking toil in a dark stifling mine. They could market their skills to tourists, rich north Europeans and Americans who would pay handsomely for a holiday where they would be close to nature and working with their hands. Look at the Agricultural-Tourist Co-operative at Arakhova, where two hundred tourists could stay at one time, helping the local people with the farming and weaving. There were other similar ventures on Khios and Lesvos — if those islands could make it work, why not Asteri?

The forest would bring birdwatchers, photographers, walkers, Nicholas went on, all of whom would need beds and food and would be eager to spend their money on the local retsina wine — made with Asteri wildwood pine resin — and on traditional wooden bowls, furniture, toys.

The mayor spoke eloquently, but he had two major disadvantages: no film or video to remind the Khorians of their mountain wilderness, and no chance to postpone the vote. An attempt to bring a motion to delay any decisions until the wildlife delegate and the islanders trekked into the mountain area was soundly defeated.

'We know what's out there — tons of trees!' bawled one man, summing up the feelings of the rest.

'At least wait until the power's been restored,' pleaded Nicholas, blue eyes dark in the light of the lanterns. 'See what you're about to throw away!'

'We've made up our minds, Stephanides. Get on with the vote!'

Nicholas put his palms on the trestle. 'You can't do anything without a mayor: it won't be recognized. And there's no way I'm going to let you take that vote tonight: this whole meeting's been fixed!'

Then he was out of his seat, off the dais and on his way to the door. Men were on their feet, chairs toppling. Nicholas stopped in front of a huge fisherman, as broad as he was tall.

'You don't like it — get another mayor!' he hissed into the man's face, standing up on his toes. No one attempted to stop him as he stalked forward, shoulders hunched.

Leaving the schoolroom in tumult, Nicholas walked out.

Chapter 20

Zoe rose to her feet, breathed softly into her lover's ear: 'Ari? Surely the vote can go ahead?'

'Not when half the electorate are chasing after the mayor,' said Katherine.

Folding her arms, Katherine took in the scene of chaos in the hall below their table. The door was hanging wide, moths blundering in as people streamed out, men and women calling after Nicholas and arguing with each other.

It had been quickly and shrewdly done, the kind of lightning strike which Katherine herself excelled in. Acknowledging this and responding to it, Katherine smiled: at least now Ari would not be able to patronise her over the Lykimi beach fiasco. If only for that she was grateful to Nicholas. And in standing up to the meeting he had been so very rugged. Most attractive.

Anticipating their dinner for two tomorrow night at Elysion — she'd plans involving Bailey that would keep Sir Oliver out of the way — Katherine stretched her arms above her head. 'Constitutional or not, I'd say that Niko has won hands down for tonight. Not a bad evening's work.'

'We've been too complacent,' murmured Zoe. 'I knew we shouldn't have talked on the plane. I should have insisted we waited.'

Ari clasped her shoulder. 'There, now —'

'Ari, I'm so sorry.' Zoe's voice sank to a whisper as she leaned against her lover — pretending to need support whilst in reality shielding the man from his own stupidity, thought Katherine, irritated beyond measure by the Greek woman's servile assumption of blame. One plan had failed so try another attack: breast-beating was a waste of energy.

'What exactly happened between you and Stephanides, Ari?' she asked, interrupting his and Zoe's little reconciliation. 'What did he say to you this afternoon — it was this afternoon you met him, I presume — that made you change your mind about Lykimi?'

Pindaros' eyes flicked across to George Tanis and the press, for the moment crowded in a chattering body round the international wildlife delegate who was speechifying about 'sustainable development' and 'quiet consultation with the local people'.

Katherine, understanding the millionaire's single glance, was quietly incensed. The old bad publicity threat, but so what in this case? It would have been the girl's word against theirs.

'There's been some confusion about a tape,' an Australian-accented voice spoke close to her ear. Katherine jumped, turned on Bailey.

'I hate creepers,' she started to say, but Bailey caught her wrist, drew her sharply back from the table and against the unused slide screen at the back of the hall.

'Here come the press,' Bailey warned. 'You want Mr Pindaros to deal with his own?'

Katherine snorted. So far as she was concerned, if Pindaros was crucified by reporters in the next few moments that would be too good for him. 'You said nothing about any recordings!' she hissed at Bailey, speaking under cover of the press hubbub.

'Relax, Katherine, there isn't anything. That girl wasn't wearing any kind of wire. But then Mr Pindaros didn't talk to me: he just assumed the mayor was telling the truth and panicked — Mr Pindaros has been caught before by people with hidden microphones.'

'But the engine noise on that plane —' protested Katherine.

'Mr Pindaros obviously felt he couldn't

take any chances.'

'What a fool!' Katherine said bitterly. 'Stupid cowardly fool!' Her eyes gleamed. 'Unless —'

'Maybe Stephanides called in some favour,' remarked Bailey mildly.

'Exactly!' said Katherine. 'That makes more sense: we did after all get Kemi in what must have been some serious horse-trading between Nicholas and Ari this afternoon.' Her bright brown head snapped up. 'Get onto that,' she ordered decisively. 'I want to know.'

Bailey nodded his narrow head. 'The girl left with the first stampede, chasing after Daddy,' he said, changing the subject as he changed grips on his briefcase. 'Do you want me to get after that, too?'

Katherine vigorously shook her head. 'As we've already agreed, Bailey, nothing more.' She shrugged her elegant shoulders. 'Don't worry: Roxanne's burned out. She's said her piece and it's over.'

Suddenly, as a battery of flashguns fired, Katherine touched Bailey's shoulder. 'By the way, Sir Oliver didn't like having his picture taken.' Staring into the schoolroom, Katherine fixed on Melissa Haye. 'I want the film.'

Bailey started to edge away.

'Don't squash the fly yet,' Katherine

warned after him. Thinking of tomorrow's modelling sessions with the handsome David Gordon she laughed, softly. 'Just brush it aside, Bailey. Tweak its wings a little.'

Why had she done it? Melissa wondered, packing away her camera now she had shot the last frame on the film. Why had she drawn attention to herself earlier in the evening in that way, simply to snap a latecomer? Anger directed at the wrong target in a foolish, self-indulgent move.

'I'm disappointed in you.' David's reaction made Melissa burn again as she remembered. No one more naive than an artist, she concluded wryly, trying to dismiss the remark. She wished he hadn't used the word disappointed; that he'd been straightforwardly furious. It would have been easier to pretend then, to justify herself. But David's censure only shadowed her own. Impatience in the field and disturbing the subject were the two worst sins in her line of work. She'd been unprofessional tonight.

The schoolhouse was still half full of people curious as to what the top table would do now that the mayor had left: some uncertain whether the meeting was over or not, others frankly trying to catch a reporter's eye, give an interview, have their moment of glory. Of her two companions of the evening, Roxanne had taken Chloe and followed after her father, but David had not budged. Checking quickly the whereabouts of Katherine's shadow Bailey, Melissa was relieved to spot the man outside in the schoolyard: he, thank goodness, had not followed Nicholas or Roxanne.

David meanwhile was waiting until George Tanis had finished questioning Ari Pindaros. As Tanis spoke a few closing remarks into a microphone, the sculptor closed on the Greek millionaire.

'David!' Pindaros was clearly glad of the diversion. He shook hands with the taller, more sinewy man, his conference smile flashing into one of genuine pleasure. 'What a night!' he exclaimed in English, showing off his language skills. 'What do you think of our Greek democracy, eh? No doubt more extravagant than the model you're used to.'

'Just a little,' replied David drily. 'I can't think of many MPs who could move as fast as that without doing themselves a mischief.'

Listening, Melissa smiled at David's turn of phrase, although Pindaros looked momentarily nonplussed and disguised it with a hasty, 'Of course, Niko's a character, as you say in England, but even he knows that tonight's cheap trick only postpones the inevitable.'

'It was a cheap trick,' David agreed, taking his sun-glasses and Liberty handkerchief from the top pocket of his blazer and scrupulously polishing the lenses. He lowered his quiet speaking voice still further so that only Pindaros would hear. 'Almost as cheap as sabotaging the power supply so that the opposition can't put on their film show.'

Pindaros' tanned face darkened a little, or perhaps it was simply the lanterns dimming. 'Have you met Sir Oliver Raine?' he rasped, backing up a step. 'Sir Oliver's just sailed into Khora this evening from Rhodes; he's looking forward to the Villa Michelangelo. Come, I'll introduce you: two Englishmen should get on . . .'

Sir Oliver Raine. Melissa had missed whatever else David had said after agreeing that Nicholas had ended the meeting by a crude stunt, but she certainly heard all of Pindaros' throaty bonhomie and clearly caught the name. As recognition swiftly followed, a shock wave passed straight through her. Sir Oliver Raine, head of Beach International, supplier to all Katherine's Total Women Centre marine resorts. Sir Oliver Raine was now on Asteri and staying at the same villa as Katherine. What were David, Pindaros and Sir Oliver talking about? thought Melissa, frustrated as she saw the three men greet each other and begin to talk in soft swift voices, their backs half to her, their features in shadow. Perhaps tomorrow on Antasteri she would be able to find out.

David's private island, where strange 'fishermen' came calling. Where tomorrow she would be a model for a goddess. Melissa frowned. Glad as she was to be going to Antasteri, to see and map David's secret domain — a gift withheld from Nicholas and ASPW — she certainly did not feel wise enough for Athene, goddess of knowledge.

Abruptly, sensing a presence near her, Melissa turned.

'Look at Turkish Gordon and the Athenian!' Speaking Greek, Popi emerged from the shadows. Slender and winsome as a girl of twenty, she deftly side-stepped the chairs and walked up to greet Melissa. 'Many are unhappy about tonight. They think Niko the mayor and others such as you wish them to keep their poverty.'

Melissa shook her head. 'In England I live in a house with running water, central heating and electricity. I'm not going to preach to Asterians about how they should live with less. Ecotourism means having your cake and eating it.'

For an instant Popi paused in the shadow-patterned hall, dark slanting eyes nimbly hunting after the expression on Melissa's face like a shrew stalking worms in the grass.

Finally Popi touched Melissa's hand with a cool cotton glove and pointed the direction they should walk.

'I support the Athenian. Ari Pindaros is building a mine — so what if a few trees are lost?'

Melissa was shaken by the sudden venom in Popi and dismayed: had Popi and other villagers understood nothing of Nicholas' arguments tonight? 'It's not that simple,' she began.

'Just like Turkish Gordon,' Popi said coldly. 'But Ari has fixed Gordon this time: the workman cannot complain about his master. Now Pindaros owns Gordon — and he will make him pay!'

Melissa wetted her dry lips. Since meeting David she had been wondering where he really stood on Green issues, but Popi's graphic description had put the matter vividly. David was working for the very man who was planning to wreck Asteri mountain — he had taken the commission on, knowing that.

'I hate him.' The seamstress' elegant features were frozen in an expression of distaste.

'His family come here before my grand-father's time and steal our land, buy from those dogs of Turks when we are oppressed and cannot stop it, and then tell us how we must live.'

Victorians buying Greek estates from Turkish pashas: Melissa had heard of other families being embroiled in modern Greece as a result of such historical transactions. With both sides feeling that right was on their side, resentments were often deep and violent. It was no wonder that David 'Turkish' Gordon did not feel accepted or welcomed by many in Asteri.

'I hate him,' repeated Popi. 'Though not as much as I loathe Nicholas Stephanides.'

Obscurely, Melissa felt compelled to defend Nicholas. 'Why should you dislike him? He seems an excellent mayor.'

Popi's thin mouth pouted slightly. 'Niko's a hypocrite. I told you what my godfather learned.'

'Yes, from Andreas,' said Melissa easily. 'Is the shepherd here tonight?'

Popi waved an arm across towards one of the high windows. 'That's Andreas and his wife over there.'

Not repeating her earlier mistake, Melissa committed the heavy features and shining long plaited hair of Andreas' wife to her memory, not a photograph. Debating whether or not to ask Popi to introduce her, Melissa sensed a new stir in the schoolhouse. Stella the goatherd glided past, nodding slowly and wishing the younger woman a good evening in her cracked, weather-beaten voice, but only good manners made Melissa respond to Stella's *'Kalispéra'*. Katherine was coming down the aisle, flanked by Zoe and the fair-haired, golden tanned George Tanis. Behind in their wake strolled David, Pindaros and the russet-cheeked Sir Oliver, still talking animatedly: *only* about tonight's drama? thought Melissa, frustrated she could not hear. Sensing trouble now Katherine was on the march, she squeezed Popi's slim wrist, murmured a quick *'Adío'*, then stepped forward so that the seamstress was not caught up in the oncoming storm.

'George, this is the woman I was telling you about, Melissa Haye.' Katherine blinked her long-lashed eyelids at the anchorman. Smiling back, his slim, clean-shaven, classic face arresting in this island of dark, broad-featured, moustachioed men, George Tanis did not notice Katherine's deliberate rudeness but Melissa knew.

'Ah, the lady who does not want a marina on Lykimi.' George had been briefed, and rose to Katherine's unspoken cues like a well-trained small dog, reflected Melissa un-kindly, bracing herself.

'Kemi is as beautiful, and much easier to reach.' Melissa swung her camera bag over one shoulder, brown eyes twinkling. 'There's already a road.'

'I wouldn't call a cart track a road,' said Zoe, glaring at the Englishwoman who had blighted her original plans.

'Melissa's being naughty.' Katherine's voice chimed like a bell, drawing many heads. 'She knows that deserted Turkish vil-lage —' Katherine paused delicately as she reminded onlookers of the island's share of recent strained Greek-Turkish relations — 'is sited on a pebble beach.'

'And once the concrete paths and sun-loungers are in place, Kemi's pebbles will be as hidden as Lykimi's sand would have been tonight.' Melissa swapped from Greek to English. 'You know what I'm talking about, Katherine.'

Katherine tilted her head slightly to one side. 'I always wonder why you insist on wearing seahorse earrings,' she remarked, totally changing the subject. 'Of course, they make a nice little earner for you, sea-horses. Used dried in Asian medicine, I be-lieve?'

Before Melissa had time to respond, Zoe

piled in: 'Did you buy the earrings with your Chinese sales?'

'Don't be ridiculous,' Melissa answered sharply. Tugging at a silver earring, she glared at Katherine. 'Is this part of your campaign against me? Some trick you've picked up from Bruce Grainge? It won't work, Katherine. These earrings were a gift.'

As Melissa spoke, memory twisted deep in her gut, a bitter poignancy unrelenting as steel. Andrew's last gift, bought for her on Rhodes.

Katherine smiled. 'If you say so, Melissa,' she answered.

Chapter 21

Melissa stalked out of the schoolroom, bounded angrily up and down the narrow steps and dark alleyways of Khora's backstreets. No David to walk her home to Mrs Samouri's flat this time: the sculptor had still been talking with Pindaros when Melissa left.

She was not sure if David had heard what Katherine and Zoe said to her, if he had registered what they were implying. Tomorrow, on Antasteri, Katherine would no doubt try to ensure that David heard her version of their final exchange of the evening.

Melissa ducked under a low balcony support, passed a half-ruined house full of crown daisies, their petals now closed down, umbrella-fashion, for the night. A breeze sneaked through the alley from a tiny square. Chickens complained somewhere behind a church no larger than a goatherd's hut. In other, broader streets, people were walking home together to the click of worry-beads, the scrape of boots on cobbles and stone, the flash of cigarettes and smiles. Talk was constant: a rumble as persistent as the rock and drag of the tide along Khora waterfront.

Katherine, Zoe, Bailey and Sir Oliver had already been transported out of these homely streets by car: two new blue Nissan Micras driven by two of David's security team, who took bumping up the occasional step or the rapid avoidance of a sleepy donkey as all part of the service.

Melissa, offered a lift, had declined it. In another few hours — too soon — she and Katherine would meet again in the harbour. The arrangement had been confirmed in a few words of casual farewell between David and herself just before Melissa had left the schoolhouse. Dawn on Khora waterfront, morning on Antasteri.

'Do join us for a night-cap at Petra,' Katherine had said, green eyes all innocence and appeal.

'Maybe Melissa needs her sleep,' Zoe had remarked acidly. Since David had obviously not considered asking her to be a model, Zoe could not resist a comment perhaps as envious as it was malicious.

Walking down towards the oil-dark jetty now shining blackly below her in the sweeping harbour, Melissa contemplated the puzzle of Zoe's exclusion from Antasteri. Perhaps the reason why Pindaros had not insisted that his lover be the template for

270

David's three goddesses was respect for the sculptor's judgement. Perhaps Pindaros feared his wife's reaction if Zoe posed for the piece.

Or perhaps the fact that one of the models was a wildlife photographer was too juicy a piece of information for the boss of Pindaros Bauxite to miss using in his campaign to win the right to mine Asteri mountain, reflected Melissa, shoulders tensed in nagging alarm.

Yet her promise to David had given her access to Antasteri. With the wildlife smugglers' special shipment due at any moment, Melissa felt she had no choice but to keep her word, whatever the consequences.

Besides, Mel, a promise is a promise. 'I know, Andrew. I know,' Melissa muttered under her breath. David too had made a promise: to explain in public why he had chosen a 'Green' as Athene, goddess of foresight and wisdom.

Was that what David and Pindaros had been speaking of so energetically as she left the hall tonight? The sculptor had drawn Pindaros away from Sir Oliver Raine: Melissa's last image of them that evening had been of the two tall men leaning against a child's dolphin wall-poster, heads close as they talked in soft rapid whispers.

Tonight, though, to Melissa's unease,

David had not made any formal announcement. A special midnight plane to Rhodes had been laid on; George Tanis and the other reporters had already left Khora for the airstrip before the sculptor took his patron to one side. Now the sound of a light aircraft climbing slowly into the star-filled night was final and decisive.

At least their leaving meant that Katherine couldn't steal a march and leak any slanted news to the media about Lykimi, the mine or David's latest commission. Attempting to extract some humour from that, Melissa found little to smile about. Zoe, Katherine and Pindaros had not given up yet. As for Katherine and Nicholas, they had their intimate dinner tomorrow night to look forward to.

'Don't even think of it,' Melissa told herself, scowling at the Lion constellation lunging towards the stark Turkish mountains.

She hated feeling nettled. She detested the clarity of vision it brought, as though life were suddenly simple, black and white. She distrusted the false sense of security, even superiority, that came with being angry. But she hated failure even more.

Tonight she had not been able to speak to Andreas or the shepherd's family about Nicholas' supposed smuggling. She had taken numerous photographs of island men chatting together but could do nothing more until the pictures were developed. Manoli's possible links with Spiro remained unexplored. She had not had the chance to take up Popi's earlier offer of hospitality and go calling on the Greek seamstress. And where, if anywhere, did Katherine or tonight's new player, Sir Oliver Raine, fit in? Sir Oliver's cuff-links, which had so incensed Melissa, had, upon discreet closer inspection, turned out to be heirlooms. No proof there of any present-day illegal purchase of ivory.

The butcher, the baker, the chemist. Trudging along the waterfront, her feet beginning to rub slightly in her high heels — unusual for her — Melissa read the names off again as she had on her first day in Khora. For days and weeks she had been here since then, and still no further progress in her secret quest to expose the men who had caused Andrew's death.

Tonight she was to watch at Kemi beach: against Nicholas' wishes but no doubt with the same lack of result as all her other previous midnight beach watches. Mr Zervos was standing watch at the airstrip, checking and, if necessary, changing the films in the various remote cameras which Melissa had set up and which until the last few days she

273

had always insisted on looking after herself. Today, with light breezes making any *sail-boat* landing at Kemi a possibility — albeit a slim one — Melissa was happy to leave the remotes to the chemist so that she could concentrate on possible action. Dr Alexios was at Hydra, the schoolteacher at Lykimi.

Nicholas was meant to be watching Petra beach tonight. All the closer to the Villa Michelangelo and Katherine, concluded Melissa savagely, despising her thought. Reaching the long flight of steps from the harbour up to the main square, Melissa attacked them three at a time, running despite her party shoes and sore feet.

The street where she lived seemed gloomy after the sparkling fountain of the main square, and Melissa was glad that she was only dropping in to change. Tramping around in camouflage clothes was both conspicuous and uncomfortable in daylight but tonight she would need them. If by his statement earlier this evening — 'You'll thank me for this, Melissa' — Nicholas had meant she should be grateful to him for saving her from meeting the power-dressed Katherine, Pindaros and Zoe in her working gear then the man was misguided. It was important to establish her credentials: people already knew who she was, and why she was here.

At least part of the reason why she was here.

Melissa shivered. She dropped off her small camera bag to shoulder-butt the stiff door —

— And was wrenched back into darkness.

She was thrown to the cobbles, the breath knocked from her. A shoe was aimed at her face — Melissa jerked aside, and shielded her head with an arm before she even registered that she was being kicked.

The main force of the blow missed her completely but the shoe still glanced along her forearm, searing a bruise. The foot stamped at her ribs, missed and caught her thigh instead. A vicious, spiteful kick at her mouth grazed her ear as Melissa jerked and rolled, trying to keep out of the way.

Grunting with frustration, the man switched his attack, diving towards her camera bag. Melissa snatched at the flailing foot, hung on desperately. Trying to protect her work, the means of her livelihood and the only evidence she had, Melissa kept hold as the man tried violently to shake her off.

A hand smacked her face towards the cobbles. The sudden sickness and pain almost made her black out. Through a choking mist,

Melissa scrabbled upwards with a hand and tugged.

Her fingers struck inner thigh, not hanging flesh, but the twist and shock were enough. Sucking in a harsh breath, the man loosened his grip on the back of her neck.

Voices called from a nearby house.

Stumbling over the pavement, the man fled.

Coughing, Melissa clawed for the door-step, dragged herself to her knees and seized her partially ransacked camera bag. First law — always have a loaded camera ready. Not this time: she had assumed she was finished for the night.

Too late now. Don't compound your mistake, Melissa told herself, staggering to her feet, forcing herself to run down the alley. Get a proper look at him. Listen where he goes.

A starlit shadow thrown on a wall blinked out as her attacker vanished round the corner. Footsteps running hard under the plane tree towards the fountain echoed then faded as the man sprinted across the square and disappeared into the darkness of the Khora-Petra road. Then nothing.

Swallowing, Melissa forced a rising sickness back down her burning throat. Above her reeling head, oblivious to the drama in the street outside, Mrs Samouri's parrot was squawking raucously.

Legs trembling, Melissa crashed the door open and dragged herself inside the flat.

Chapter 22

She had intended standing watch for part of the night at Kemi, but after the attack it took Melissa over an hour simply to sort through her camera bag. Dazed and in shock, she laboriously turned out the films, lenses and camera bodies onto the bed. Sitting on the quilt, Melissa remembered to bring the lantern from the kitchen, find matches, light it, look.

Everything seemed to be taking a very long time, she thought at one point, slowly lifting a lens to her eye. Several films, including the final one she had shot that evening, were gone, probably smashed into the cobbles outside. The cap on her wide-angle lens was fractured. A flash unit was ruined. Beyond scrapes, no other equipment was damaged. She'd been lucky.

Melissa's mouth twisted at the thought. She glanced down at her yellow silk dress, sunny no longer. Dirt and bloodstains were sprayed from hemline to waist. The right sleeve had been partly torn out, the front panel ripped, shredded and hitched, the left back waist-tie missing altogether, the breast buttons torn off. It was fortunate she'd not been wearing tights or leggings, Melissa concluded: either would have been annihilated. Along her left thigh spread a darkly glowing purple bruise, streaking to a lurid mottled yellow. Both calves were crisscrossed with welts, grazes, cobble marks, heel and toe prints. Her right foot was branded across the instep with a spongy blood blister, grotesque to touch and painful to walk on. But then everything seemed to hurt, her grazed ear worst of all. Strangely her face was numb, or stiff, Melissa wasn't sure which and wasn't about to find out why. Right now, a mirror was certainly not her friend — but then who was?

Maudlin! Melissa snapped at herself. Rolling awkwardly off the bed, battered arm hanging limply against her bruised thigh, she stood up to consider her options. Bed or bath? Police or priest? Mrs Samouri would help her: she need only rap on the ceiling beams. Mrs Samouri and her friends would fetch the authorities: it would be a midnight adventure for them, because they wouldn't have to go out alone.

Melissa shuddered. The room swung her round, jerked her knees from under her and slumped her back on the bed. She couldn't recall where Nicholas was supposed to be watching tonight, which was stupid, because she'd known. And she needed to talk to Nicholas because she'd just remembered that there were no regular police on Asteri. Authority here was the mayor, the school-teacher, the doctor and the priest.

She didn't want any of them to see her like this, certainly not the priest or teacher, guardians of spirit and mind, of higher things unconnected to this dirty business. Worse than the beating, Melissa felt soiled. She had allowed herself to be invaded. Whatever evidence was printed onto her flesh and clothes, Melissa felt as filthy as a rock sprayed by an old tom cat. A bath would only scrape the surface. What she really wanted to do was to return the compliment, grind her attacker into the dust.

Grimly she limped to the door.

Nicholas, back in his old jeans and work-ing shirt, had just spent the night out of doors. It had been sleepless, boring, cold and cramping, but none of that mattered. Noth-ing had happened, the people who worked for him were still safe and Spiro had not put in an appearance.

Signing off radio contact with Zervos on Hydra beach after hearing the chemist's,

'Everything's quiet here,' Nicholas punched a fist into the air in celebration. Jerking his hunched shoulders, rolling his head to ease the tension in his stocky frame as relief poured through his tired muscles, he padded quickly into Khora along the inky black smoothness of the Petra-Khora road. Thinking back over the start of his long night, he broke into a fast energetic sprint. 'Come on, Chloe!' he encouraged his companion of the evening, snatching playfully at a whirling tail as she drifted past on snowflake paws.

His desperate move to avoid having the islanders take a vote on future development had, to his delighted relief, been a total success. As he had hoped, many Asterians were bitterly resentful of their mayor's highhanded action and had not hesitated in chasing after him to tell him. Next time, however, it would not be so easy, and Pindaros would be forewarned. But when it came to the electricity and other vital aids and services, he too would be wary.

Grinning at Chloe as she raced off ahead, Nicholas caught his loosening cap and slowed to a rangy walk reminiscent of his daughter. By the restored but enfeebled street lights of the village outskirts, the thick waves spilling down over his forehead formed a purple-black fringe to his stark blue eyes.

'Down, Chloe! It can't hurt you!' he reassured gruffly, as his dog skidded to a bristling halt and woofed and whined anxiously at a blown scrap of paper tumbling round the first alley corner they'd come to. Padding forward, Nicholas gently rumpled Chloe's neck ruff. 'See? It's just garbage, you silly girl. Ah —' His fingers tightened warningly. 'Leave that alone, now: old tom's on the prowl as we are.'

Eyes yellow slits in the darkness, the cat slithered bonelessly across the alley, vanishing under a yard gate. Its feral slimness reminded Nicholas of Roxanne. Hours ago, Roxanne had done a Melissa on him and argued to go on smuggler patrol. He'd had a hard time persuading her to remain at home beside the phone.

'Bet if I were your son you'd take me!' Roxanne had flashed at him, stalking into the house.

'No way,' Nicholas had rasped back. 'Eighteen-year-old boys are trigger-happy sulkers — I've been there, so I know. I need someone responsible to stay here to take messages now the answering machine's on the blink.'

'Really? How long's that been down?'

'Day or so,' Nicholas had lied, relieved that the power had still been off, so the message light wouldn't show. One thing he hadn't lied about was his reluctance to take a youngster with him: one hard lesson he'd learned as a seventeen-year-old father was that old heads never fit on youthful shoulders.

He most definitely wanted Roxanne to grow up, to survive, and each night on smuggler-watch Nicholas was never quite sure what would happen. Old rifles matched against modern automatics was a dangerous equation. He'd asked for more official help, more professional assistance, but so far had received only promises. More proof was needed, it seemed.

Would one of his team riddled dead with machine-gun fire be proof enough? Nicholas now thought angrily, vastly relieved that the night watch had again passed without incident, that Roxanne was tucked up safe at home on the large blue sofa, head nodding against the cushions as she fought sleep and lost. If it weren't for the fact that Gordon was under suspicion himself, he'd have spilled the beans to him, asked the man to help provide cover from some of his Antasteri guards. There again, why hadn't the Englishman offered ASPW any assistance in *any* way? Lack of interest? Maybe it was more than that. Maybe Gordon knew exactly what was going on.

Tomorrow it would be interesting to know what Melissa found out about Mr David Gordon's secret island hideaway. Today, corrected Nicholas, seeing the black rim of the horizon tinged with blue. He swore and, without breaking stride pattern, kicked a loose stone down the cobbles into the black wheely-bins at the end of the street.

No, thought Nicholas, he most definitely was not happy about Roxanne and Melissa going to Antasteri, modelling — posing, for goodness' sake — for the sculptor. He hadn't been able to think of any good reason to say 'No' to Roxanne going, but he didn't like it any more than he felt comfortable with the idea of Melissa scouring those unknown woods, photographing the camera-phobic Gordon's personal kingdom.

Duke Bluebeard without the beard, reflected Nicholas, thinking of Gordon as he sprang lightly down four steps into the main square. Scooping silver water from the fountain and vigorously washing his face, he found himself wishing that he didn't know the rest of the Bluebeard legend: the forbidden room, the murdered women. Melissa for her life couldn't resist a secret, he wagered, and as for Roxanne, all he could hope was that she changed her mind about Gordon. 'If he hurts her I'll kill him!' Nicholas swore to himself extravagantly as a small inner voice added, *If Gordon touches the bee, I hope she stings him.*

Katherine's presence was a different matter. She would keep them all out of trouble. Today he'd find out if their dinner was still on — Nicholas hoped so. It would give him a cast-iron excuse to offer Pindaros not to reconvene the meeting for that evening: Ari Pindaros would be expecting Katherine to work her considerable wiles on him and would readily agree to a night's postponement.

Another day would give him vital extra time to lobby opinion. And a night with Katherine.

Licking his lips, Nicholas filled his canteen and set off from the fountain for the office. He wanted an early-morning foray on paperwork before he met Roxanne for breakfast at the fisherman's café and saw her and the others off at the harbour.

Flipping open the door to the outer room, holding it on fingertips for Chloe, Nicholas assumed at first that he'd left the light on in his private office. As he prepared to curse his

285

own stupidity a shifting shadow, racing across the roof at him through the crack in the closed inner door, had Nicholas melting back against the darkest wall.

Someone was in there. Going by the rapid pattern of shadows, and now the sudden absolute stillness, Nicholas guessed a figure had ducked down behind his desk. Who'd been going through his papers?

Whistling softly for Chloe to stay back, Nicholas waited, listening. Until he'd been deep frozen like this, Nicholas reflected with grim irony, he'd never realised how noisily his dog snorted through her nose.

Outside, as if tripped by some invisible switch, the dawn chorus warbled out of the plane tree. An early workman, bumping his moped down the long steps to Khora harbour, suddenly gunned the engine.

Inside his office, silence. With a decent high-velocity rifle he could have been shot through the wall by now.

Unless he was careful he still might be.

Stealthily, Nicholas stretched for the polished doorknob.

'Thank God it's you.' The figure seemed to be addressing Chloe, now lying on the spotless floorboards, ears and body totally relaxed.

Chloe slowly wagged her tail.

'Of course you know me.' Melissa sounded strangely muffled. 'Where's Nick, eh? Still slinking at the back of the door?'

Nicholas pivoted briskly off the wall into the room. 'Thought it was more of a skulk, myself,' he was saying, when Melissa rose from behind the desk.

The sight of her as she stumbled forward broke him like a blow to the balls, low deep pain, and his mind reeled. Sickness filled the pit of his stomach, chilling his anger for a moment.

'Who? Tell me and I'll —'

'Kill him?' Her tone was tired. 'He came from behind, from the shadows. Made sure I never really saw his face. Smacked me around, smashed some film.' A grimace flowed across Melissa's face as she lifted a shoulder. She gave up on the shrug and made herself smile instead, a straight, wry smile. 'A neat job, I suppose. Maybe I took Spiro's photograph tonight and he didn't like it.'

The rage arrived. Nicholas snatched up the nearest object he could find and hurled it, wishing the thing were a spear aimed at Spiro's guts. The staple gun exploded against the ceiling, causing a huge clump of plaster to fall off and splinter onto the floor.

'Bastard! Sneaking bastard! Let me get him, give me ten minutes with him. No, fifteen minutes, give me fifteen!'

'You going to blame me next? In my experience that's the usual male pattern.'

Melissa's heavy irony dropped on him like chains, stopping him dead in mid fingerjab. Jerking his head up, Nicholas registered her anger against him, read in her stiffened body her distaste for his dumb male response, way way too late, just a stupid waste of time. His impotent show of force.

'Come on, then? Why don't you say it? That I shouldn't have been out at night alone.' Her voice hitched higher, then suddenly lower, harder. 'That this is my own fault!'

Boiling anger in a flash changed to a brutish sullen resentment, primitive in its nastiness. 'Yeah — I warned you what you were getting into but you wouldn't listen. Miss Barbie Doll had to get involved.'

Scarlet streamed into Melissa's face and she swung at him.

Nicholas did not budge, although she socked quite a wallop, smacked the stuffing and everything else out of him. 'Sorry,' he said, when his ears stopped ringing.

'Even for you that was low.'

'I know.' He prodded his aching face. 'Thanks, I think.'

'What? For knocking sense into you? Or

for sharing the pain?'

Nicholas acknowledged both with a sigh. 'Times, Melissa, when you're too sharp for everyone's good.'

'So I've been told.'

As her bruised face patterned its careful smile into the backs of his eyes, something more in Nicholas shattered when he felt he had nothing left to give. He moaned and put his arms around her.

Their heads leaned together.

'Wait!' Nicholas suddenly froze. 'What about a doctor? What about the police? Alexios can take swabs.'

'I was kicked on my arms and legs and slapped round my head, nowhere else. Shut up and hold me.'

'Am I too tight?' Nicholas asked once.

'A bit. But it's nice.'

'We need to get you to a doctor.'

'In a minute.'

'Want me to carry you?'

Melissa shook her blonde head, flinching as her grazed ear caught against his cheek.

'Sorry!' Nicholas could not stand the thought of her being hurt more. He kissed her softly on the forehead. 'I'm sorry.'

'The man who hit me was about your height.' Melissa coughed, rested more of her weight against him. 'It wasn't at Kemi: I never made it to Kemi.'

'I know — the dress gave it away.' He'd never told Melissa how good she looked in it, and now it was ruined. 'How long you been waiting for me?'

Melissa's gold brows drew together. 'I've been asleep in your chair.' A glance at the office clock. 'Got in here around one, I think.' She wrinkled her nose. 'I was a bit mazed.'

'You've a wonderful capacity for understatement.'

She coughed again, a hand clutching her middle. Hugging Nicholas she'd actually forgotten the kick in the ribs. 'Anyone watching at Elysion last night?' she asked, sharp with herself.

Sensing she'd keep on for a reply, Nicholas shook his head. 'Only your remotes,' he said. 'With Lykimi having to be watched now, we just haven't the people. At least nothing happened at Petra, Hydra or the airstrip.'

'Where are they? When are they going to come in?' Melissa frowned. 'Maybe your informant was wrong about the smugglers.'

Nicholas had heard enough. He pointed to the door. 'Doctor's for you,' he said, 'and then bed.'

'Can't. I'm going to Antasteri.'

'You're not serious!' Nicholas ducked

slightly to glower into her eyes. 'Are you?'

'A lot of this is surface, Nicholas.'

'That's what Gordon's going to be looking at.'

Melissa breathed heavily. 'Have you thought that perhaps whoever did this doesn't want me on Antasteri? I need to find out if that's the case, and if so, why.'

Nicholas released her, drew back slightly. His look was speculative. 'It's not just the smugglers, is it?' he said. 'There's something more.'

For an instant, Melissa almost told him about Andrew. Then, as she recalled Manoli's clumsy 'warnings' about the mayor and more especially Nicholas' continued admiration for Katherine, she decided to adopt a more flirty approach. She grinned a crooked smile at him. 'David's quite a dish.'

Nicholas grunted. 'You most definitely need a doctor.'

At Melissa's insistence they walked to Dr Alexios' surgery, where alone with the tall medic in his consulting room, she ran through a full account of her attack for the first time.

Alexios immediately made a good impression on Melissa. After listening to her, photographing and examining her injuries, he searched her clothes for clues to her attacker's identity, putting each item of clothing into a sterile plastic bag. The bags were regularly supplied by his wife Eleni, who worked for a pharmaceutical company on Rhodes. As evidence of Melissa's beating, they could be shipped directly to Rhodes police.

'Do you often have to do this?' Melissa asked.

'You're my very first.' Cleaning under her fingernails for any traces of her assailant's hairs, blood or flesh from which the Rhodes police might extract DNA, Alexios gave Melissa a glowing smile. 'That's it. Eleni's been checking the hot water: there's enough for a shower here, if you want. I'm sure our mayor wouldn't mind jogging to Mrs Samouri's for fresh clothes.'

There came a soft knock on the inner surgery door. Opening it, Alexios was handed a garment which he presented to Melissa. After she had covered the loose medical gown with Eleni's bathrobe, Alexios allowed a fretful Nicholas back into the room.

It was obvious that the mayor was less impressed with Alexios than Melissa had been. 'You mean that's it?' he demanded. 'That's all you're going to do for her?'

'The bruising on her body is fortunately

not severe. The grazes and bruising on her limbs will heal quickest exposed to the air,' said Alexios. 'And Miss Haye's jabs are all up to date. Unlike some I could mention,' he added.

'But what about internal injuries, broken bones, shock?'

'Niko, she's fine.'

Still seated on the couch, Melissa felt it time she put in a word. 'Nicholas, I have to leave in an hour. What about my clothes?'

Nicholas began pacing.

'Antasteri! A day trip to Antasteri!' Nicholas smacked his forehead with a hand. 'Say something, Alexios!'

'I think it's an excellent idea,' replied the doctor evenly. 'A day of relaxation and change. I imagine it might be quite interesting.'

Stunned silence from Nicholas.

Alexios lifted the largest bag from the floor tiles, twirled it in his steady fingers. 'Pity about your dress having to go to Rhodes, especially as I doubt the police will find anything,' he said now to Melissa. 'Whoever roughed you up wore gloves, I believe.'

'He did — I'm certain of that even though it happened quickly and he kept to the shadows. Black leather gloves.' Melissa clicked her tongue. 'I certainly never felt any nails.'

Alexios nodded solemnly. 'You've not been scratched by fingernails.'

Nicholas spoke up. 'What about the shoeprints? He stamped on her, remember.'

'A common Greek shoe and size,' said Alexios.

'Yet he never spoke,' Melissa observed. She was interested in expressing certain suspicions to a neutral audience, to see if the doctor picked up on a trail she herself had been wondering at but dismissed as tilting at shadows.

As she hoped, Alexios was on it instantly. 'Perhaps not an islander?' he suggested. 'Or Greek?'

Nicholas shrugged. 'That's been an obvious possibility from the start. Last night's events and meeting pulled a lot of strangers in.'

'But the reporters and miners had already left: I heard the plane fly over the harbour front long before I reached Mrs Samouri's,' said Melissa.

'Then who?' demanded Nicholas, striding forward.

Melissa swallowed, conscious of the mayor's keen blue eyes on her grazed ear and faintly purpled jaw.

'Two spring to my mind,' remarked Alexios, leaning against Melissa's couch. 'You said your assailant was about Niko's height? Probably in a dark suit?'

'That's right.'

'If you're thinking of accusing Sir Oliver Raine or Mr Bailey, then I'd be very careful.' Nicholas now broke in. 'Sir Oliver in particular has a lot of — let's call it — "influence" in the Greek tourist industry.'

'I saw Bailey leaving with Katherine Hopkins in a car,' said Alexios. 'Of course,' he added, 'cars can be stopped.'

Nicholas shook his dark head at both of his companions. 'Without proof, it's slander,' he warned. 'And both appear to be supplied with witnesses.'

'But what do you think?' breathed Melissa.

The mayor of Asteri stared down at his watch. 'If you're going to Gordon's you need to start moving soon,' he said. 'Of course, if you don't feel like it —'

Melissa interrupted. 'I'm curious to know, Nicholas.'

Nicholas raised his head. 'What's their motive?'

'Whoever it was spoilt several of my films.'

'Sir Oliver has thousands of photographs taken of him every year. Including ones wearing those gross cuff-links.'

'Bailey, then.'

'Why? Because he's Katherine's associate?'

In the silence that followed Alexios also glanced at his watch. 'Our hot water should be boiling by now,' he said. 'If Melissa wants a shower before Nicholas brings some more clothes from Mrs Samouri's?'

Melissa nodded wearily, resigned that the subject was closed for the moment. 'If I may,' she said.

Chapter 23

Katherine sat cross-legged on the stone jetty of Khora harbour, slowly combing her unbound hair. She was first: Roxanne was staring blankly into a cup of coffee at the fisherman's taverna, Melissa was totally out of contention.

It had been Roxanne who, flashing past Katherine on the way down the long steps to Khora harbour, had suddenly stopped, spun back. Her pale lean face and large stormy brown eyes had Katherine guessing the news before it burst from the American's colourless lips.

'You not heard? Melissa was attacked in the street last night, straight after the meeting broke up! I've just seen Dad by Mrs Samouri's, fetching more clothes for her — he says she was lucky to escape only with bruises. They're both at the doctor's right now: it may be she won't be able to come today.' Roxanne paused. Bringing her thumb up to her mouth, she bit on it in her distraction. 'I really can't believe it,' she murmured. 'Attacked on Asteri, the very last place anything ever happens.' She glanced over Katherine's head at the open sea. 'I really hope Melissa makes it.'

'Oh, so do I,' Katherine agreed fervently, hiding her face as she resumed her graceful progress down the steps, leaving Roxanne to do whatever naive shocked teenagers did whenever their world had been dented. The effect she was after this morning would be lost if she weren't there to meet David.

Katherine never wasted time in recriminations or regrets. Last night hadn't brought what she wanted but today might, especially after the good omen of Roxanne's news. As she always did with any important meeting, she had planned this encounter, right down to her final throwaway line on the jetty to Nicholas: 'Until tonight, then.' That should make the current, most interesting men in her life nicely aware of each other's competition — and of her.

Not like Roxanne: a passive prize or dutiful daughter. Nor as a ludicrous equal: Melissa's 'best-friend' syndrome. Katherine knew her superior worth.

Roxanne had been awake and deciding what to wear, how to look, for at least an hour before this early-morning rendezvous. Katherine recognised the signs: a faint shadowing and look of strain round the eyes, done and redone with mascara. Scrubbed, painted toe-nails, peeping through determinedly polished heelless sandals. Newly washed and fiercely combed hair. Four carefully hung gold chains. A new padded bra thrusting stiffly under the freshly ironed tube dress.

Katherine inventoried Roxanne's final choice of clothing. A black cotton round-necked, sleeveless number with small shiny black buttons — not the original cream buttons, thought Katherine, who retailed the simple dress in her more basic TWC stores. Roxanne had replaced all twenty-two of those fasteners this morning. And — despite being a redhead — no hat or sun-glasses. Fortunately, she had a spare pair she could lend Roxanne.

Katherine smiled. It would be interesting if Melissa came today. Like Roxanne, Melissa had been awake for a large part of the night. However picturesque and pitiful her bruises, the overall effect would be stale, insipid.

Katherine's skin glowed. Her eyes, after a good night's sleep, were limpid. Her loose hair was, she felt, suitably alluring yet mysterious, flowing through the wide teeth of her comb with the sensual smoothness of musquash fur. She had swum before breakfast, after which it had taken her exactly thirteen minutes to decide what she would wear and put it on.

No jewellery, naturally, no make-up or perfume. The clothes loose, comfortable, deceptively practical: they were, after all, travelling to Antasteri by boat, on the open sea.

Fighting down the faint swell of panic which the final thought had inspired, Katherine checked the fastenings of her shoes. Today her footwear was Roman-style: leather sandal-boots with elegant crisscross thongs. Paisley patterned softly tailored silk trousers were topped by a cream silk camisole, worn with the discreet side slits showing. When she was ready, Katherine would pin back her hair with the two antique combs she was carrying, one of which she was using as a grooming device.

Beside her a wicker basket with hat, sunglasses, tissues, book. Men loved to carry baskets, swinging them along.

A horn sounded in the harbour and Katherine resumed her combing. An early-morning breeze frothed the wavelets in the bay into egg-white stiffness as into Khora harbour a white sailboat came riding.

David was here. As she was, first, to welcome him.

★ ★ ★

Afterwards, Katherine remembered David's white boat with its new sails, the still, glassy sea, her own strong lifeline and the stifling lifejacket glued to her skin. Just being on the sea was for her a victory of courage over fear. She remembered striving not to tremble whenever the boat rolled. She remembered Roxanne's laughter, her skimming around the ship, her crazy liking for speed. She remembered Melissa Haye settled calmly by the starboard gunwale for most of the trip, a hat shading the bruises near her left ear and chin.

David and Roxanne had noticed the bruises at once but neither of them had said much. Roxanne, boarding behind Melissa, had squeezed the blonde's shoulder and quickly murmured her good wishes before stepping aside. David, after a hard unreadable stare at Nicholas standing watching them off the jetty, had shown Melissa to a seat then slipped below for more cushions and a Thermos.

'Rum and hot water's all I can offer, I'm afraid,' Katherine heard him say to her rival, now surrounded by a bower of pillows. 'Don't worry about standing today, and let me know as soon as you've had enough.'

'I will, thanks.' Melissa had said, clipping

her camera bag onto a safety line.

Katherine watched David crouch down on the deck, saw his lips moving. He might have been checking that Melissa really was okay, or he might have been talking to himself again. Or maybe both: Katherine wasn't sure, and wasn't all that interested. As David left Melissa, and Roxanne scrambled eagerly after him to offer help in tacking out of the harbour, it had been left to Katherine to offer sympathy.

But Katherine's mind was already occupied. 'See you here at eight tonight, Nick!' she called down from her place on David's boat, as the Englishman made ready to sail.

'I'll be waiting!' Nicholas roared back, blue eyes flashing as he smiled at her.

'Until tonight, then.' Satisfied, Katherine lounged back against her cushion with a slight nervous intake of breath, bracing herself mentally for the voyage and not thinking of Melissa at all.

Chapter 24

Roxanne quietly surveyed the studio, disappointed by its sterile work surfaces; the glinting chisels, saws, pliers, palette knives, coils of aluminium wire and other tools ranged in strict order of size. Various pieces, covered in plastic bags or cloth drapes, stood against one of the two longest walls alongside benches, boards and easels.

The tools were hanging on or clipped against the opposite wall, along with brushes, plumb lines, complicated callipers and other scaling-up aids. Paint cans, drums of water, plastic bowls and bins crowded near two sinks. No windows in this back section of the studio, yet no cobwebs against the whitewashed walls, no soft lurking piles of terracotta dust on the concrete floor. Even the blades of the overhead electric fans and the naked light bulbs were polished.

Sure, the place was ordered, Roxanne thought to herself, checking that her fingernails were clean. But where could inspiration strike in this chilly, tidy building?

'And the kilns are outside in the yard,'

Melissa was saying. Without looking round at their host she stood on tiptoe to swing open a shutter to see. Light leaping through the revealed window jumped over her hair and flowed along the edge of her matt black camera strap. Compact herself, the photographer seemed fascinated by large things: the kilns, the storage bins, the packing cases in the windowless section of the studio, the shadowy forms under the drapes.

Roxanne recalled Melissa on their way up from the tiny harbour, her exultant 'Amazing!' when climbing up the gravelled path from the bay through a stand of tall cypress trees — rare, she explained, because they were so pure. Although Antasteri was only two kilometres in length and barely one in width, it was obvious to Roxanne that Melissa was excited by the island's photographic and wildlife possibilities. For now though, with the pitiless sun creating midday shadows in the bay, baking the woods and wilting the formal rose gardens that surrounded David's house and studio, Melissa's interest was engaged inside.

Earlier in the day, when they had first docked, Roxanne had not been surprised when Katherine said 'no' to a tour and Melissa 'yes'. Saddled with the deciding vote, Roxanne had opted for a *brief* look round the island — she'd been alarmed by Katherine's faint pallor, and by Melissa's slow, careful walk.

'Naturally after coffee,' David had said, showing he too was aware of the discomfort of two of his models if somewhat insensitive to the third. He had turned to Roxanne and asked if she wanted an ice-cream rather than coffee.

'Just coffee, please,' Roxanne had said, the ice in her voice not matched by the heat in her face. Ice-cream in these circumstances, she felt, was strictly for kids: she noticed that David hadn't offered Katherine or Melissa ice-cream.

Coffee arrived as they lay on sun loungers under a vine trellis, served by the two security guards who had run from the harbour building to catch the lines from David's boat.

'Why Australian security, David?' Katherine had asked a few moments later, green eyes smiling pleasantly at the uniformed man who had brought her a second glass of mineral water.

'I wanted the best,' David answered — rather drily, Roxanne thought — and he smiled at Katherine. 'Joe agrees with me, don't you, Joe?' The guard nodded.

'Unusual, certainly,' remarked Melissa, stretching for her coffee cup. Again her fascination with all things tall seemed to reassert itself as she measured both guards with her eyes, giving a sharp nod which Roxanne took to mean approval.

'I'm glad you approve,' said David, this time without glancing up from his sketchpad. Since settling under the vine trellis he had been filling a page of the pad with drawings of all three of his models — a movement frozen and captured from front, profile and back. No fine details of ears, eyes or hands, but a rapid record of how each carried themselves, the first part of their bodies to move whenever they made a characteristic gesture. Catching a glimpse of her own mouth, drawn partly open and lower lip jutting slightly forward to cushion her thumb, Roxanne had sworn softly and looked away. After that, she had been relieved when the coffee break was over and David, his drink still untouched, had smilingly taken up Katherine's offer and slipped sketchpad and pencils into her wicker carrying basket.

To Roxanne's surprise, Melissa had taken no pictures on their subsequent tour of Antasteri: an hour's stroll on well-marked paths through cypress and pine woods. Once through the thick shade Roxanne had spotted Antasteri's mini-mountain, a bare rockface mirroring Asteri's central peak but thinner, steeper and without even scrub vegetation. Several birds of prey had been darting above this rock and Roxanne had asked Melissa if these were Eleonora's falcons.

'They are indeed,' Melissa had replied, her ready smile replaced by a curiously wistful expression as she watched the roving falcons. In another month no doubt the birds would put on some fine pairing displays, Melissa added.

'They nest on the western cliffs here,' David put in, turning back on the path with Katherine to see what was keeping the others.

'Really?' said Katherine, her arm hooked comfortably through David's as the sculptor swung the wicker basket in his other hand. 'Another picture for you, Melissa. How nice.'

Melissa cracked a grin which Roxanne knew must be hurting her grazed ear and jawbone, but she made no move to capture the Eleonora's' pre-season return to their nesting site.

In fact, as Roxanne recollected, Melissa had taken no shots at all: not the island's shrine, nor its slip of a western beach just under the cliffs, nor the tiny sea cave at the southern tip of the beach.

'I prefer to work alone,' Melissa said, when Katherine had remarked on it. 'Besides,' she added, with a significant glance at David, 'people in pictures are for me never an exposure of an individual but the capture of a mood.'

'Spirit of place?' David asked ironically.

'That's for the viewer to decide,' Melissa responded, warm eyes twinkling.

She and David looked at each other for another moment and then the man's heavy tread again ground the pine needles into the gravel as he and Katherine moved on.

Outside, Roxanne had been in an agony of anticipation, half-wonder, half-dread, in case David should speak to her in so gently taunting a fashion and she have no ready answer. At eighteen, Roxanne was aware of ambiguity, of the quicksilver changes in relations between men and women, but she was also painfully alert to her own laconic, quiet style. Was it a trick of the British to make New Englanders feel provincial? she wondered. And yet David was not a natural flirt as her father was. *He doesn't need to be for you, not even a little.* 'Just back off,' Roxanne told herself, not sure if she meant her words as a warning against negative thinking, or prompt self-advice.

'Talking to yourself's the first sign of madness,' Melissa teased.

'In that case we're all mad, aren't we?' Roxanne laughingly answered, stormy brown eyes looking anywhere but at the man who walked ahead — and never alone, Roxanne acknowledged with a pang.

Entering David's house through the studio, Roxanne felt diminished a second time, slowly crushed inside by her own dashed expectations. Staring round the white walls of the spotless studio, Roxanne was forced to conclude that this man had no rough edges, no unfinished corners, no heroic wilderness in his psyche. Instead all was cool control, an always-wash-one's-hands neatness bordering on Bailey's prissiness. Roxanne shuddered slightly.

'Bet it doesn't look this way when you're working.' Melissa's wicked voice came as a welcome blast of human warmth to Roxanne. Now, as the smaller woman turned from casting a keen eye over the kilns, packing cases and swept cobbles of the side yard, the sun winked on her lens cap and David actually flinched: a small movement, but noticeable to Roxanne.

Why was he so edgy around cameras? she wondered, aware of the warm blood pumping through her as a rush of curious pity made her feel alive once more in this private, mysterious man's presence.

'Where can I store these in safety?' Melissa was already tactfully removing the offending camera and bag from her shoulders, biting her lip as the strap dragged briefly against her left shoulder. Roxanne's eyes twitched as she traced the outline of a huge bruise through Melissa's long sleeved white shirt, but Katherine was not so sporting.

'One spot instantly springs to mind,' she remarked, 'Although I doubt if you'll take my advice.'

'I'd appreciate it if you two would save up your feuding till I've posed you both with Roxanne. Then the three of you can bicker all you want,' said David in mild rebuke, an answer Roxanne found puzzling. She watched as, ignoring Katherine's 'Of course, David,' the sculptor strode over the concrete to Melissa and lightly took her gear from her, laying it down gently on a bench out of the light. 'Will here do?' he asked. 'This table's out of range of thrown pencils, chisels, mallets, chains or clay.'

'Chains?' Katherine's interjection fizzed with erotic connotations.

For an answer, David turned and pointed past Katherine to the farthest roofbeam, from which, sure enough, there hung several long chains, hooks, and block-and-tackle.

'Lifting gear. Stone isn't something I relish humping round my studio even when I'm having a good day.' He grinned. 'Any more questions, ladies?'

'Women,' corrected Katherine, and, after a darting look at Roxanne, 'and girls.'

Giving Roxanne a wink, Melissa tossed a change of subject neatly at David. 'I keep wondering why Ari Pindaros didn't contract a Greek for this work,' she observed guilelessly. 'It is a Greek legend, after all: the three goddesses quarrelling over this golden apple dedicated "To the Fairest".'

Now Roxanne understood David's reference to Katherine and Melissa keeping their bickering going until they were posed together. If the three of them were supposed to desire the same object, then a certain tension between the models would be a very good thing.

Only in their case the sparks weren't about to fly over some golden apple. Roxanne smiled, her lips a taut line in her lean face. She wasn't vying for a piece of fruit. The prize was smack in her eye-line: best Northumberland beefcake. She sniggered at the foolish image, then flushed.

Roxanne had been thinking fast, in the space when David had cleared his throat before answering Melissa drily, 'Well, actually

I'm the second artist to take the work on. Ari had asked the Cretan sculptor Ariadne Kyriakos to undertake the piece, but he didn't like her maquettes and then his wife and Ariadne fell out.'

'I wonder why?' asked Katherine, keeping herself constantly to the fore in any exchange. 'Is Ariadne young, by any chance?'

David laughed. 'Ariadne's an extremely attractive fifty-year-old, and a good friend. It was she who suggested to Ari that since Pindaros Bauxite had been highly satisfied with my aluminium sculpture for head office, I might be a good alternative for this personal commission.'

Melissa stared at the chains and lifting gear behind Katherine. 'You should have told me you'd already worked for Pindaros' company.'

David shrugged. 'Doesn't matter, Melissa. Ari's already sent a statement to the press about your involvement in this piece — I told him last night that having a committed environmentalist pose as wisdom would be seen as a courageous choice.

'I've done everything you asked for, Melissa,' he continued, 'including informing the Greek media that my Athene is an ecological statement and I totally agree with your work here.'

'Great!' Melissa glowed. Bounding forward, she raised her face and kissed David on the cheek, close to his chicken-pox scar, a swift impulsive kiss Roxanne did not deny her for an instant. To her, too, the sculptor's announcement was good.

Instead, Roxanne's fiery head swivelled towards Katherine.

Katherine kept her composure well, Roxanne was forced to admit, feeling a little sorry for her. The older woman stretched out a steady hand and touched a work-bench. 'I understand that a maquette is to a sculptor what sketches and cartoons are to an artist,' she said quietly, her fingers slowly tracing the grain of the wood.

'Quite right,' David explained. 'The sculptor needs a three-dimensional sketch in clay or Plasticine, a first trial or mock-up for the final piece.' A maquette was a way of showing possibilities — both to the sculptor and to the client.

'I have the maquette for the three goddesses set up in the working third of the studio,' David concluded. 'Come and see.'

David's working third was shielded from the rest of the studio by a long corrugated metal screen which he now pushed back. It was in this section, he explained, where he did all his concentrated work, and where Katherine, Melissa and Roxanne would pose.

Here in the final third of the building the walls curved into the shape of an apse and were studded with windows.

David opened all the shutters and light cascaded onto the central table.

'Well!' said Melissa, 'The viewer as the object.'

'Quite, quite superb.' Katherine's low heels scuffed softly on the cement floor as she approached the thirty centimetre high clay maquette set upon a tall mounting block in the middle of the table. 'Ari approved of this, you say? I'm not surprised.'

Roxanne said nothing. Staring at the three figures, their right hands extended down towards her as if reaching for something, she understood David's conception. Seen from this angle, the onlooker became part of the scene, the desired object. Viewer as apple.

'The finished piece will be half life-size, standing in an alcove on a semicircular marble table,' David was saying. 'I decided to show the moment when the apple is thrown onto the table at Thetis' wedding feast. That's why the bodies are shown mainly in torso, rising as if from the table itself.'

'Good idea,' murmured Roxanne to herself. She was horribly aware that her legs were by no means her best feature.

'Yet I see one is more revealed than the others.' Katherine homed in on the left-hand figure, frankly admiring the long sweeping lines in that section of the maquette, the beautifully modelled flank and thigh. 'Aphrodite, no doubt?'

David frowned slightly. 'No, the ancient Greeks believed their goddess of love came from the East: that's Aphrodite, on the right.'

Katherine stiffened. 'That's a very greedy expression,' she remarked, studying the right-hand figure more closely.

Melissa coughed and kept her head bowed for an instant, but David answered Katherine seriously, 'But erotic love is greedy, always grasping after luxury. And it comes from outside. Knowledge, self-awareness is our centre.'

Then the one showing the gorgeous leg is Hera, and it's me, thought Roxanne. But I can't do it.

David turned from viewing the maquette to his three models. 'Now that I have you together, I see straightaway that several major changes will have to be made.'

He looked straight at Roxanne. 'The characteristic tilt of your head will look wrong if I keep Hera on the outside,' he said. 'You need to be in the middle. Then Melissa as Athene will be on your left and Katherine as Aphrodite on your right. It may be Aphrodite will need to be shown in full right-hand profile too, to balance the overall design.'

'An excellent solution.' Katherine glided round the maquette, observing from every angle. 'So what next, David?'

'Lunch.' David's black eyes rested on Melissa. 'Then a swim or siesta by the pool,' he added gently. He raised his head to address Roxanne. 'Swimsuits provided.'

He sounded as though he was laughing inside at her more lurid imaginings, thought Roxanne, irritated afresh.

After consultation with David's daytime housekeeper, Litsa, it was decided that lunch would be taken by the pool. David then directed Melissa, Katherine and Roxanne to separate rooms where they could change in private into their swimsuits and towelling robes.

Later, behind sun-glasses, David studied Melissa, who had finished eating, thanked Litsa, and was now sipping her cold retsina in the sensual, warm comfort of the pool. She didn't want fusses and didn't create them herself. A pleasant 'thanks', for the anti-inflammatory spray and painkillers he'd left in her room was enough for Melissa to show her awareness and appreciation of his concern.

Watching Melissa sip her drink and slowly kick her legs, David felt a great liking for the tough little blonde floating in his pool. Dispassionately, he realised from his experience of sports injuries and his sculptor's knowledge of anatomy and the human form that Melissa was not badly hurt. Flesh, unlike plaster of Paris or clay, was resilient. Drapery would cover the worst of the bruises to her left flank and thigh. The slight swelling to her face would go down in a couple of days. There was nothing that would affect her posing as a model. Yet beyond the superficial wounds there was a longer hurt, a diminishing of trust, which made Melissa's shrewd clear gaze even more poignantly aware. Knowledge he would have spared her, had he been able to.

Some people — Spiro for instance — were always excessive in their use of force.

Katherine spoke from the lounger under the palm tree across the corner of the pool. 'Who do you think will try it first, David — the old "Could you rub a little sun-oil over my back" line?'

David smiled. 'I was hoping it would be you,' he answered, glancing down at the

317

sketchpad balanced on his lap to check that he had the perfect sweep of Katherine's shoulders right.

Katherine shook her bright brown head. 'Too obvious.' She picked an olive lightly from the china plate on her low table and sucked the plump flesh slowly from the stone.

David knew she was allowing him to watch and made the most of the opportunity. Studying Katherine was a rousing experience in all senses: visual, intellectual, physical. He admired her determination in business, even if he could not approve of all of her methods. Still, the way Katherine disdained using personal abuse or lines of attack showed great style and a restraint he envied. And how she ignored setbacks — as she'd had to this morning in the studio, when he'd admitted his public allegiance to Melissa's cause — was absolutely to be applauded.

Right now, though, David's admiration was altogether earthier. Inevitably, given his line of work, he had a highly developed sense of form, size and shape, yet Katherine's emerald costume, laced at the sides with golden cord, not only set her off but set him going as well.

A skinny shadow flitted across his sketchpad as Roxanne stalked past, slim hands tight round a bottle of sun-oil. She dived into the pool, swimming underwater in an untidy breaststroke, and, right hand still clutching the bottle, trod water in the centre, in full sun, away from the comfortable leafy shade of the tree-encircled water.

Aware he was one of the flashpoints of these three young women's rivalry, David would not have been human had he not been flattered by their different ploys to attract his attention. Even so, he was surprised: in the past, when Colin had been alive, his older brother had been the focus of such admiration. Laconic and lanky throughout his teens, David, a swimmer in training, a sculptor by bent, had been a background figure in the Gordon household. Later, after Colin had been killed, after Mum and Dad had died, and he'd moved here to Antasteri, the women he'd seen were mostly older, people like Ariadne. So these sleek figures in and round his pool were a novelty. Smiling, David closed his eyes.

Melissa, sexy in scarlet halter-top, cutaway suit, a rose with faintly bruised petals. Katherine, a glorious bronze, with green patina. Roxanne . . .

'Let him sleep.' Melissa's clear warm voice.

'All right, but the sun's come round now:

319

he certainly won't thank you for leaving him to burn.' Katherine's hands grasped the back of his lounger. 'Help me move this. Goodness, he's heavy — where are the guards when you need one? No, Roxanne, I don't think we need your assistance.'

'Right. Well, since you guys are obviously doing all right, I'll go join Litsa in the kitchen and ask if I can have a drink of water.'

Catching the end of Roxanne's speech, David blinked and shook himself fully awake. He was startled and annoyed to discover that he had been asleep: enough time had already been taken by lunch. Usually he never slept at midday, and never when models were present. He'd been day-dreaming too much.

'I'd like a mug of tea, but I'll tell Litsa myself.' Heaving himself up from the lounger, David asked Melissa and Katherine, 'Would you like anything to drink . . . to eat?'

Both thanked him but declined anything more. Leaving the pool area, David called back over his shoulder, 'The studio, in ten minutes, in what you're wearing now, please.'

Overtaking the hesitant Roxanne, David led the way back through the studio.

'Quicker this way,' he explained, stamping

on a piece of clay he'd missed in his cleaning up. 'Besides' — a sudden burn of anger tugged at the corners of his mouth — 'no doubt Melissa would complain if you dripped water over the house rugs: not very photogenic for her Antasteri exclusive.'

Prowling behind him, her towelling robe snagging against a bench, Roxanne said quietly, 'Just take me to the kitchen, please,' an answer which effectively reduced his attempt at sarcasm to waste.

'My housekeeper will get you some water,' he said meekly at the door to the kitchen.

'Thank you.'

Something in Roxanne's reserve made David want to do more for her. 'Are you a bit peckish? I am. How about a sandwich?'

'A sandwich would be fine.'

'Tell Litsa what you want.'

Opening the kitchen door for Roxanne, David nodded to the plump, dark, middle-aged housekeeper standing by the sink, washing a Greek wild salad. 'A sandwich for Roxanne and tea and a cheese roll for me, please, Litsa.'

Five minutes later, entering the tiled, mirrored kitchen from his 'office' after changing into his working clothes, David was again struck by one of Roxanne's thunderbolts. But this time it was nothing she said.

He stopped short by the fridge, appalled.

Roxanne flashed a look at the silent, watchful housekeeper, then at David. 'Litsa offered, but I made it myself,' she explained politely in Greek, so as to include the housekeeper. 'Want some?'

'You're going to eat that?'

'You're as bad as my dad: he always goes a little hairy when I tuck in to one of my specials.' Roxanne lifted the pitta bread sandwich to her mouth and took a neat bite. 'Yum! Feta cheese, green peppers and apricot jam. Delicious.' Taunting, she smacked her lips.

'Revolting,' David said, plucking his own cheese roll from its china plate.

Roxanne grinned happily at him. The three sets of designer swimwear he'd had flown in from Athens yesterday fitted all his models, but Roxanne's black wrapover had seemed rather too drab. Not any more, thought David, the raised hair on his spine prickling through his shirt.

Quickly, David turned to the more comfortable, motherly figure of Litsa. 'Looking forward to tomorrow?' he asked, putting down the bread roll.

Litsa's half-smile widened in anticipation of a chaotic family shindig in the pinewoods of Asteri. 'Your food is already prepared,' she added, reminding Roxanne that she, Melissa and Katherine would be looked after tomorrow by David.

On their morning sail across, David had mentioned Litsa's absence from the island on the following day quite casually. Now, as Litsa placed the last of the washed salad onto a plate and picked up a long soft brush to sweep the villa's tiled floors, Roxanne felt a mingled excitement and shyness at the housekeeper's sly announcement. Fighting through the last emotion as Litsa left the kitchen, Roxanne decided to prolong her own personal moment alone with David.

'Quite the male model,' she said in English, deadpan.

David looked down at his clay-spattered overalls. 'I can hardly work in a suit,' he began testily, then, hearing the teasing in Roxanne's voice, he smiled at her.

Roxanne's large brown eyes stretched even wider, her lips suddenly full of laughter. She leaned back against the pine work-top, the afternoon sun through the huge east window setting an arrow of gold in her hair, and took another neat bite from her pitta. 'You going to be dressed that way when Melissa takes your picture?'

David stiffened. 'No!'

'You don't want to be shown in working

clothes?' Roxanne sounded genuinely puzzled, as though she didn't know why he detested being photographed — any kind of picture.

David began to explain.

Five years ago, after graduating with honours from Durham University, David had been training as an international swimmer, still torn between the demands of the sport and his dream of succeeding as an artist. In both he had been supported by his parents and his elder brother, Colin.

At twenty-five, Colin was an established professional cricketer, a fluent middle-order batsman tipped for a great career. Tall, with burnished brown hair, frank blue eyes, and his mother's classic good looks, Colin also had his father's ease of manner and a charmingly rumpled way of dressing which women seemed to find irresistible.

When Colin began an affair with the disaffected wife of a politician, his family were uneasy but tried to understand. When the politician set the tabloids scurrying for salacious titbits, David and his parents closed ranks to protect Colin and his lover. The press, however, had other ideas.

Colin and his beautiful new 'friend' were intensely photogenic, and were pursued everywhere. For a time, David and his parents were also under scrutiny. Photographers in every bush, car, toilet, café, cinema, night-club, church — nowhere was safe. After two weeks, the long lenses focused exclusively on Colin and the woman.

With court cases pending against three newspapers, Colin's lover went back to her husband. That same night, his every facial gesture and body posture photographed by the paparazzi camped outside his flat, Colin set off in his Porsche to try to persuade her to return.

Blinded by flashguns close to his wind-screen, Colin failed to spot a van with grubby headlights turning into the street. Still accel-erating, still wrestling with his seatbelt, he hit it full on, broke his neck and died.

A free-lance photojournalist sold pictures of the devastated parents to a European magazine. Before they were published, Colin's father followed his son, victim to a heart attack.

Six months later his mother, never robust, slipped away quietly. His family was gone.

A day after his mother's funeral David competed in the Olympics, coming last in all his heats.

'Photographers bagged that too,' con-cluded David. 'On the anniversary of Colin's death a journalist rang me up for a few quotes describing my feelings, one year on. I put the phone down on her and packed for Asteri. Now you know it all.'

Roxanne threw the rest of her sandwich away.

Chapter 25

Lunch had been at noon and they had lounged round the pool for another hour and a half. Now it was six-thirty and David had been working continuously for three hours. Melissa calculated that in another hour he would have to return Katherine, Roxanne and herself to Khora. Which left her less than an hour today to look round Antasteri.

Not much time, when Spiro's special shipment could be coming into the island that night.

Melissa broke pose and stepped round from behind the 'table' — in reality a large packing case. 'Mind if I take a breather outside?' she asked the startled David. 'It's very muggy in here, particularly now you've opened the shutters.'

David, wrapped up in viewing and sketching, suddenly remembered Melissa's injuries, which would make long standing uncomfortable, and his earlier promise to allow her to explore and photograph freely.

'You're right — sorry.' He lifted his head to Roxanne and Katherine. 'Thank you:

that's it for today. If you'd like to come with me, I'll show you where you can shower and change. Then Litsa will fix us a snack before she and her husband leave for tonight.'

And tomorrow, Melissa reminded herself, aware that the housekeeper and her gardener husband would be absent for all the following day. Right now, though, Melissa was intent on scrambling for the door. 'Nothing for me, thanks, I just need the walk. See you later, by the harbour.'

A cheery smile and she had snatched up her camera gear and gone off to change.

Ten minutes later, Melissa was hurrying down a gravel path towards the lowering sun. David had called Antasteri beautiful and so it was: an ordered loveliness, perfect down to the polished glass in the tiny wooden shrine and the sculptured pine branches arching over the walkways. Given time, she'd want to explore the island's less managed corners, wander off the paths into the woods, scale that craggy ruin of a peak, find and photograph the dreys and babies of the red squirrels she could see racing up the firs at her approach. April was the peak of the bird migration, when the blue and amber bee-eater returned to Greece, the month of the orchids and broom.

A Painted Lady butterfly flitted from a tiny

grassy clearing across the path and Melissa yearned to follow it into the tangle of darkening laurels where a Scops owl was just beginning to call. But now she was stalking more lethal prey. A sudden flash of light in the grass from where the butterfly had emerged made her start, and when the beam flipped on again and stayed on in a dazzling glare she acknowledged with a grim smile what it was: one of the security lights Nicholas had mentioned as part of fortress Antasteri.

A good reminder of the dangers involved in her present enterprise — what was it Nick had said? Lights, security men, cameras. No dogs, though — Melissa was already reassured about that. Men and cameras she had seen round the house, but no trace of dogs: no telltale clumps of fur, droppings, prints round the building; no broken flowers, snapped twigs, torn cobwebs in the woods now in this low clear evening light, where all such details were teased out in a soft glow of gold. Antasteri's largest mammal seemed to be the squirrel.

No dogs would make it easier for her to wander freely.

And easier for smugglers.

Why not dogs? Melissa thought, scrambling down some steps, almost running as she spotted the harbour immediately underneath. Time compelled a direct approach: the harbour which David complained 'fishermen' had been using without his permission was the obvious place to begin her reconnaissance. There had been no guard dogs in evidence here, either.

Perhaps David Gordon considered men, lights and cameras to be sufficient to protect his privacy from photojournalists, Melissa decided, both amused and faintly irritated by the implied low opinion of her peers' intelligence. Or was it that David thought dogs were less reliable than men? Did he dislike the inevitable barking? Had perhaps David had a bad experience with a guard dog on Asteri which had put him off employing them on his island?

Given the ferocity of some Greek dogs, Melissa concluded that this last was entirely feasible, yet a more disturbing and obvious possibility remained. From the point of view of a smuggler dealing in wild creatures, dogs could disturb and distress many of the 'goods'.

Even if such an idea had not occurred to David — and why should it, since he's a sculptor, not a naturalist? rose the rapid thought in Melissa's head — it might very well have figured in Spiro's calculations.

Could Spiro and his men be using Antasteri without David knowing? If the only harbour was here, was that likely?

Melissa swerved off the final bend in the path before she became visible to the guards in the harbour building. 'If only I'd more time!' she muttered, ducking under the low branches of cypress. Considering the possibility of other usable coves on the island, she decided that the entire north-western end — where David had taken them this morning — was not an option. The north-western sand beach was reached only by a goat-track which was highly visible from the sea and could at any time be seen by patrol boats. The sea cave was, according to David, tiny, low-roofed and liable to flood in a storm. The rest of the western half of Antasteri was sheer cliff, used only by the Eleonora's falcons.

Yet, it was an Eleonora's which the Athenian had been caught trying to sell in Rhodes, so how far could she trust anything David said?

One thing at a time, Mel, chided Andrew's voice in her memory. *Concentrate on the harbour.*

She'd already prepared a remote with low-light film, loaded more low-light film into her own camera, and put a short zoom lens on it. Flash was no use in these circumstances and would only give her away to the harbour guards: something Melissa didn't want — yet. David had given her permission to wander and she wanted to be able to do so freely, without a security team breathing down her neck. She wanted to poke and pry around, perhaps in places David and his guards wouldn't want her to see or photograph.

Close by, a single cicada chirruped in the undergrowth. Crouching, Melissa paused, her hands curved round her ears to catch any stray sounds from the bay. Behind her, the Scops owl hooted again. The evening breeze softly lashed the prickly scrub round her calves. She was wearing ankle boots below her knee-length khaki shorts, protection against snakes. Gorse had snagged a thread in her cream top.

Khaki and cream, neutral, natural colours, thought Melissa, glancing down at herself as she listened patiently for the warning calls of blackbirds or other creatures. Whatever his reservations about her stirring things up, Nicholas had been keen for her to go looking round Antasteri and had chosen her clothes this morning accordingly. David in a different way had been similarly considerate: Melissa had liked the way he had not made a drama over her injuries, just given her sprays and painkillers. No fuss, just practical help.

She wished David had swum in the pool that afternoon. It would have been interesting to see how he looked in swimming trunks. Smashing, she was willing to guess, remembering the strongly muscled legs beneath the towelling pool-robe. Enjoying a not unpleasant tingle between her thighs, Melissa told herself to stop fantasising.

The difficulty was of course that in her experience trust had very little to do with sexual attraction. David had things she admired: generosity, skill, a sense of threat with that explosive temper of his, a broad back, a willingness to laugh at her jokes, an amazingly strapping yet lean set of hips and a pair of feet with the second toes engagingly just a little longer than the big toes.

Yes, she liked David a lot, but could she trust him? In some ways the question made him more appealing, not less, but only an idiot would be drawn into the flame of his attraction. Katherine, as Melissa readily admitted, was sexy, but Melissa did not trust her.

Reminded of her rival, Melissa felt her surroundings flood back in a tide of sharp sea tang. The weltering light, glancing off an ancient windsail turning in the evening breeze across the strait along Hydra beach, made her aware of how little prying time she had left. The channel between the two islands churned with white foam close to Asteri, showing again the risks of trying to land on Hydra. No, smugglers would cross that water only if there were nowhere else to go, Melissa decided.

The water outside David's harbour was as flat and sun-golden as the beach sand, where a sparrow bobbed amongst the deserted sun umbrellas and loungers, looking for crumbs.

Andrew had died near a Greek island beach: not this one, but similar in size and remoteness.

Satisfied that neither beast nor man had noticed her, Melissa started down between the cedars for the harbour.

Alert to the slightest crackle of gravel or dry vegetation, she picked her way very carefully, conscious of the security lights hidden near the path. The harbour itself, with stone jetty and long wooden harbour building, seemed determinedly ordinary. Until you spotted the moving shapes through the small square windows, the shifting shadows streaming out through the building's open door.

Two Australian guards, Melissa reminded herself, one of whom was called Joe. Measuring them both in her mind's eye that morning, she had been glad to discover that these two were too tall to have been her attacker of last night. A spry man of middle height, and a non-smoker — strange, thought Melissa flattening herself against a boulder and focusing on the windows and threshold shadows, how she had just made that connection, yet certainly last night she had not smelt the characteristic lingering odour of tobacco.

Clouds filtered from the door: both guards were enjoying a cigar: good quality, too, Melissa realised, the irrelevant thought triggered by relief that down in this harbour, right now, was no one who had done Andrew or herself any harm.

Sheltered from even the worst storm by a natural outcrop of limestone rock which closed off the mouth of the bay to fishing-boat width, the harbour was perfect.

She hid a small remote camera; then, not expecting to spot any spoor, spilled food, bedding or paw prints, but checking in case someone had forgotten to sweep all the jetty, she methodically scoured the stone mole and cobbles in front of the harbour building with her binoculars. As she'd expected,

335

nothing was happening.

Melissa's fingers tightened on the hard black plastic. A stranger was striding out of the building: the Australians hadn't been alone.

'Hey, Spiro!' Joe called after the man, in English, 'Thanks again for not telling the boss.'

Twisting back, irritably flapping away the cigar smoke, the stocky, dark-haired stranger rapped back tersely, 'It's the last time I cover for you, Joe. Any more mistakes and your nuts are for the grinder — you'll be the one to tell Gordon.'

Greek-Australian. The nationality registered in Melissa's shocked mind ahead of the direction in which Spiro was leaving the jetty. She stopped the remote and ran off several shots on her own camera, fingers moving instinctively under pressure. Now she heard the gravel spit and hiss as a stocky figure, jogging swiftly, jumped from the jetty onto the path.

He was coming her way. In another instant he'd round the path and see her crouched in the scrub, frozen like a rabbit in headlights. It didn't need the sudden eerie scream of a nightjar to make the hairs on her arms stand up.

Spiro was armed with an automatic rifle.

The smugglers used automatics. It was an ammunition clip from a similar weapon which Nicholas had recovered from Petra beach. Spiro the *Greek*-Australian guard: dark, stocky and from his reaction to the cigars a probable non-smoker — was this man also the Spiro she was after? Could she risk meeting him now with her cameras? Even given David's permission for her to look round his island, was she so good a liar that nothing of her suspicion would show in her face when she confronted Spiro? What if the guard traced her trail back to a remote? How would she answer his questions — and David's — about that? At the very least, David could accuse her of breaking the spirit of their agreement.

Maybe the man with the automatic wouldn't wait to ask questions. And if Spiro really was a smuggler and he suspected her of shooting more than travel-article pictures, what might his reaction be?

Move! Melissa told herself. Whirling to her feet, grazing her right side on the boulder, she leaped across a sage bush and almost straight into the beam of a newly glowing security light. Just in time, she stopped by snatching hold of a cedar branch. As the branch shuddered slightly Melissa released it and set off into the deeper forest, not caring how much noise she made or alarm calls she started.

She was lucky. Her headlong flight flushed out a red-legged partridge and Spiro, assuming that had caused the disturbance in the woods, could not resist a burst of fire at the bird. By the time the man had retrieved his game, Melissa was long gone.

It was in this, accidental, way that Melissa had discovered the hidden track. Rushing deep into the woods, swatting off droning mosquitoes, she had leaped over a clump of blue pimpernel growing down a dry water course and jumped directly onto a new path, this one as narrow and shaly as a sheep track.

Although running away from both harbour and house, Melissa had followed it. The path's very lack of upkeep in this gravelled, ordered kingdom made her want to find out where it was heading . . . to a place where a stand of spreading umbrella pine shaded out most of the sunlight and vegetation, and hid what lay beneath the dense canopy to planes and birds alike. Cold to her boots, Melissa set up, hid and left her second remote and then with her own main camera photographed the cages.

Five wood and wire and metal constructions, each with a small wooden hutch inside, central high platform and water trough. Rough birchwood poles slotted diagonally across the cage, and resting on the second run of horizontal bars at approximately two metros off the cement floor, might be perching posts for either large birds or small mammals.

Melissa sniffed each of the wooden hutches and the hyssop-scented tufts of scrub outside the cages, but everything was spotless. Whatever animals these had been used for, someone had taken pains to ensure no trace of scent, pelt, print or scat remained. The hutch doors were bolted open, their bare boards mocking in their pristine emptiness.

Above the entrance to the second and third cages, a neat wooden board with the name 'Niko Stephanides' inscribed in Greek letters.

Hidden cages. Why hidden, unless it was for illegal, secret business? Cages built in Nicholas' factory on Khora waterfront — Melissa knew that after reading the address set out below 'Niko Stephanides'. Empty now, but certainly very well maintained and ready for some creature. Some 'special shipment', perhaps?

Melissa knew the iron taste of disillusion in her mouth. No absolute evidence here, but proof enough to deny her peace of mind. At first, Nicholas' help this morning in choosing her clothes did not make sense, but then, in growing anger, Melissa admitted that, once again, Nicholas had underestimated her. No doubt he had assumed that Spiro and Joe and the other security guards would keep her to the well-tended, 'public', paths, so that she would never find this hidden place.

As she slowly wound back the last film she had taken, Melissa's mind was also running back to an early meeting with Nicholas, his reluctance to discuss Antasteri with her, his clumsy change of subject onto less controversial matters. His statement that so far as he was concerned, a Turkish airport was the same as a Greek: 'Rhodes or Dalaman, it doesn't matter.' She had dismissed Manoli's smuggling stories about Nicholas as nonsense, had thought of him and David as natural rivals, yet the proof was here, in wood and steel, that the two men had come to some kind of mutual accommodation.

Unless David did not know the cages were hidden here?

'Then he's a fool!' Melissa burst out, striking the wire of the nearest cage with her small tripod, making it and the wire ring. She had been the fool — for not realising as soon as

David mentioned his earlier commission from Pindaros that the sculptor's first loyalty was to his paymasters. Now that she could see clearly past the dazzle of his good looks she recalled with a lurching coldness that at the public meeting she had never actually seen David talking to the media, only to Ari Pindaros, and the newcomer to Asteri, Sir Oliver Raine.

Sir Oliver just happened to be staying at one of David's villas.

Suddenly her earlier resolution to discover what David had been talking to the two men about became irrelevant against this larger picture of a possible alliance between David and Nicholas. Squinting up at the name plate above the second and third cages, Melissa dropped the final film into her camera bag. So much for Nicholas' claims that he had never set foot on Antasteri, she thought, as disillusion churned into more anger, into action.

She had a picture of a man called Spiro: a man in David's employ who would have to be known by Nicholas. Tonight, as soon as she was off this island, she would send the film to Jonathan in England with the question, 'Is this your man?'

Right now she was going back to the house, but not to rejoin David and his models. To break into his studio.

For Melissa, used to tracking animals, stalking and avoiding the strolling security guards was easy. In the five years since David had settled on Antasteri he had not updated his technology, so the lights and cameras were no real problem. Melissa crawled through the rose beds towards the yard with its kilns and packing cases, glad that the earth was iron-hard and would leave no prints. After hearing and watching Litsa and her husband leave the villa for the harbour through a side gate, Melissa waited until the guards had gone round the front again. Then she hopped onto the top of a kiln and with a penknife prised at the shutter.

The lock gave and the shutter sighed open. Feeling only slightly ashamed at her tabloid slyness, Melissa dropped down into the studio. By then she was so angry with what she had already discovered in Antasteri's woods that she forgot the dull ache in her left side and the throbbing graze on her right.

Breathing through her nose, starting for a second at the faint peal of laughter tinkling through the newly swept corridors as Katherine entertained David and charmed Roxanne, Melissa set about snooping. The studio was, she thought, the most likely place to start searching for documents relating to smuggled wild animals. David was an ordered kind of man. Melissa reasoned that he would keep all his business files, legal or otherwise, in his workspace.

Five minutes later, tracing power points, she found a computer under one of the drapes — not in the studio office, this, but, by some strange, possibly artistic, probably sinister whimsy, close to the ordered clutter round the sink. Flicking back the cloth, Melissa groped and switched the machine on, flinching as the muffled roar of its spinning disk drive split the silence of the black studio.

No choice — she'd come this far: for her own safety she couldn't stop now. For the sake of Andrew she didn't want to. Even if the computer were to burst into life with a fanfare of trumpets, she had to risk someone hearing what she was doing because of the prize involved. David's personal and business records.

'Does that make me another Bruce Grainge?' Melissa asked aloud, pressing the computer's return key. In a perverse way she was enjoying herself, this eerie kind of hunting in the shadows.

Back came the prim message 'Password not known'.

David, Gordon, Accounts, Clients, Artwork, Spiro, Nicholas, Niko, Ari, Pindaros, Zoe — all were met by the flashing, 'Password not known'.

Melissa tried Judgement, Paris, Stone, Wood, Bauxite, Marble, Colin, Swimming, Swimmer, Olympic — same result.

This was proving tiresome and, with ten more minutes already elapsed, increasingly risky. Melissa suddenly remembered to wipe the computer keys — she was not wearing gloves. Burrowing in a pocket for a hanky, she laid the ghostly white cloth over the keyboard and tried again.

No joy.

'Crikey, David, what do you store files under, the name of your latest conquest?' Melissa addressed the stubbornly blank computer screen, black and unreadable as David's luminous eyes. Feeling by now faintly desperate, she typed in Ariadne as a joke, then Roxanne, then her own name, then Katherine's.

'Katherine' set the machine whirring again and up they came: records of dates, of animals, of payment — modest fees as yet, but still significant. Animal shipments, glowing at her, making the hidden cages and the security and the guard called Spiro perfectly understandable.

Whatever areas of his private island David had been willing for her to see, Melissa wagered that the file on this computer and the secret woodland cages were not part of his 'deal' with her. These he would certainly *not* want her to know about.

Scribbling furiously with marker pen onto her freshly bared forearm — the only suitable writing surface she could find quickly in this black hole of a studio — Melissa heard voices.

She yanked the plug at the mains, and as the computer burped off, she flung down its drape, remembered her hanky just in time, and tweaked it away as footsteps began clumping down the corridor. Banging her head on a table, Melissa launched herself past several figures wrapped in rustling black plastic and dropped down behind them, pulling a spare cloth over her own huddled body.

Had she taken her handkerchief off the computer keys? Had she replaced its flowing cloth cover?

Too late to check: they were inside.

Chapter 26

'Next time I call for my daughter and my dinner date,' Nicholas was saying, 'I'd appreciate it if you'd call off your people pronto. I lose my temper when some junior stormtrooper in combat gear threatens to fire a machine gun across my bows.'

Was Chloe here? Melissa's first panicked thought. Unable to breathe, she braced herself for a friendly snout or wagging tail thrust in at her through the coarse heavy cloth. When none came she found herself wondering why David and Nicholas were still continuing the charade of Nicholas not being allowed on Antasteri. And yet tonight, clearly, whatever might or might not happen on other nights, Nicholas' exclusion from Antasteri had been not a feint but a reality. So what exactly was going on?

'My men are professionals. They'd never fire without a direct order from me.' David's stiff answer yielded no apology. 'When the call from the harbour-watch came through here at the villa, I told them to give you every assistance in landing.'

'He did, Dad. I heard him.'

'That's not the point, Roxanne.'

'As I recall, the arrangement was that Roxanne and Katherine were sailing back with me to Khora. My men simply didn't expect you.' There was a thump as David's heavy body leaned against the studio doorjamb. 'Did they continue to threaten you?' he demanded.

Nicholas plainly would not give him the satisfaction of an answer to that one. 'Assault rifles are excessive even for you, Gordon.'

'So invoke some of your laws, or whatever.'

'Gentlemen!' Katherine stepped in, a model of reason. 'We're here to see work in progress, not indulge in unseemly bickering. I'm certain David will take your legitimate concerns into consideration, Nicholas.'

No doubt said with a generous smile to both men, thought Melissa sourly, angered afresh as she thought of the contents of the 'Katherine' file. Yet unless David and Katherine were superlative actors, Melissa would have sworn they hadn't known each other before Katherine had come to Asteri. Of course in this age of faxes and electronic mail they needn't have met each other. There again, the 'Katherine' of the file might not be *this* Katherine, Melissa acknowledged, it was just that she hoped it was: proof that would finally reveal Katherine Hopkins' less savoury trading practices to the world. And, if by some lucky and sadly unrealistic chance he was genuinely *not* involved in any of this murky business, to Nicholas.

Nicholas' indignation over David's use of firearms didn't extend to concern about others' safety, Melissa now noted, nor did David himself seem worried that his men were quite happy to shoot at people whilst she, another stranger to Antasteri, was wandering alone through the island.

But she was wrong.

Nicholas' rasp increased as he cleared his throat. 'Where's Melissa?'

'She's not at the harbour?' David suddenly steamed past within inches of Melissa to jab a rapid series of digits into the wall phone. A terse conversation established that Melissa wasn't where she'd promised she would be at the agreed time.

'Maybe she's gone looking for your bird-of-prey sanctuary,' Nicholas observed wickedly, as David smacked down the receiver. 'The one you had me make cages for but which so far I've had no invitation to visit.'

It was almost as though Nicholas knew she was hiding and was excusing himself, thought Melissa. She glanced anxiously down at her fingers and feet, wondering if either were peeping out of the cloth. For a horrible moment she considered the possibility that not only Nicholas but David, Katherine and even Roxanne knew exactly where she was and were now taunting her.

It took all of Melissa's expertise not to flinch as David's right foot brushed her left boot as he rejoined the others.

'There's nothing to see there right now, man,' he snapped, responding to Nicholas' jibe. 'We've no juveniles in care yet this early in the season and Melissa won't go bothering with empty cages.'

A private sanctuary for young injured birds of prey? Maybe, Melissa admitted reluctantly, tensed under her own hot, enveloping hood, wary of an inner eagerness to seize upon the explanation. Yet it did not account for the presence on Antasteri of automatic weapons, or Spiro, or the animal file on David's computer code-named 'Katherine'. Any 'sanctuary' might even be for cover, in case the police or Customs came calling.

'Surely you've learned by now that Melissa's not always reliable,' said Katherine mildly. 'Or necessarily does what she claims to do.'

'What the hell's that supposed to mean?'

'Temper, David!' Katherine was smiling:

Melissa could tell from her voice. 'You of all people should know that knowledge isn't innocent. Melissa's a great deal more aware, let us say, of business affairs than you give her credit for. In Hong Kong, for instance —'

'None of this matters,' Roxanne broke in sharply. 'Melissa's missing. We should be out looking for her, doing something, not tale-telling like kids.'

Good for you! Melissa wanted to shout. Crouched in her out-of-the-way corner, praying the dark weighty drape she had flung hastily over herself was sufficient a hide, she could only hope that the two men ignored her enemy and heeded Roxanne. Plaster dust, invisible to the naked eye, had begun to congest slowly in her lungs. She was afraid that at any instant she might cough.

'My men are already searching,' responded David decisively.

A scream of chain as Nicholas yanked on a block and tackle. 'So let's join them,' he said.

'That won't be necessary. As I've already mentioned, my people are professional.'

'Then we'll wait,' said Nicholas, ice-cold.

'No — I'll bring Melissa home to Khora later.'

A draught surged round Melissa's feet as

350

David opened the studio door. Any proposed viewing of the day's work was no longer an option, it seemed.

'I believe you and Katherine have a dinner engagement at Elysion?' he now enquired. 'If so, please don't let me keep you. See you tomorrow, pet.'

With this last to Roxanne, the sculptor ushered them from his studio.

The second the lights were out and the door locked, Melissa broke pose, rubbing herself furiously to drive the circulation back into her tingling legs. With Nicholas now leaving with Roxanne and Katherine, she too needed to be on her way.

Why not slip outside and meet David or the guards openly? thought Melissa, shaking one foot after the other. That way she could return to Asteri comfortably in David's yacht.

Yet suppose David suspected her of finding the hidden cages? Seeing that the guards had not found her on any of the marked paths, he might easily conclude that she'd wandered off and seen things she shouldn't. If he were connected to Spiro the smuggler, how far would David go to ensure that their illegal trade remained secret? And in the dangerous strait between Antasteri and Asteri, what better place for an 'accident'? Could she afford the risk of returning to Khora in David's boat, alone with a man who might be capable of murder?

Too smooth, Andrew had said of the men who'd spotted him in Rhodes. Even with his temper, David was smooth, all right.

The sudden contrast between Andrew and David, the dead and the living, decided Melissa. There was no way she would go back in David's boat tonight.

That being the case, the harbour was the only place to find a craft to take her across the strait to Asteri.

Outside the studio the gravel path was empty. Why not use it? Melissa thought. If 'discovered' walking down to the harbour she would be less suspicious than if a guard or — worse — David found her stealing amongst the vegetation like some malign spirit.

Checking that no one would see her emerging from the roses, Melissa launched herself at the broad path, swivelling her hips as she made the small pebbles spit and dance under her feet.

Ahead, Nicholas' small motor boat was rounding the lip of the bay and striking out in open water. The boat's engine drummed above the steady pulse of the sea and the breath of wind in the pines. Down in the harbour the Greek and British flags on David's yacht flapped stiffly in the slow swirling breeze. The lines on the white boat twanged lightly.

With the guards beating the woods for her, staying hidden had become too complicated, too risky. These men were armed and on their 'guard' against her. Tonight, even if wildlife smugglers were planning to land at Antasteri, she could not stay to find out. After what she'd learned in David's studio, Melissa didn't feel it was safe.

Approaching a corkscrew corner where the path dropped steeply after the turn, Melissa stopped and listened. Then she sat down on the pebbles to fiddle with her boot laces in case any of those power torches moving in a steady straight line towards the cages should suddenly twist back and beam into her face.

Of course, if any of David's security people had infrared, then camouflage would be of little use. She hoped that line of bobbing torches meant that no one on David's team had infrared, although the guards might be using open lights as a way of showing her they were looking for her.

Assume they have it, Melissa told herself, double-knotting her bootlaces in the same way that Andrew had tied his footwear.

Watching the waving lights, she wondered if Andrew had been hunted before he was killed.

Had the last thing that Andrew heard before he fell been David's heavy tread behind him?

Hard, fast footsteps on the path below — he was coming back from the harbour. For an instant Melissa listened, mesmerised, then the instincts of survival snapped into play as her body acted on what her mind was too distracted to remember. In a soft flurry of gravel she rolled off the track, scrabbled over the ditch and landed coiled with her hands jammed underneath her, boots in a broom bush. She pushed her head down into a rosemary thicket. As the aromatic scent choked her nostrils, Melissa prayed her desperate gamble would work.

Nearer came the heavy beat of steps. Oh, to be as drab as a nightingale, thought Melissa, as far off towards the now blazingly lit villa she caught a golden scrap of the bird's mellifluous song.

David was close enough for her to hear his breathing, deep and athlete-slow. She could hear him talking to himself, a faint tinge of Northumberland accent rolling from his lips at this moment of stress. 'Daft bugger, she's not going to be there —'

Melissa's scalp, shoulders and spine seemed to want to detach from the rest of her body. Raised over in goose-bumps, she felt sweat engulf her and gritted her teeth.

He was almost past now. Even without seeing, Melissa sensed that David's dark head was turned to the landward side of the path. She was on the sea side. In the midst of blessing her good fortune, Melissa became aware of just how close she was to a final drop into the bay. Now her night vision showed that beyond the rosemary there was nothing.

The sound of the waves broke into her ears, making her reel for an instant. Oblivious to the risk of David hearing, she snatched at the rosemary scrub, fingers closing round the woody stems as a sudden primitive fear of falling threatened to drown her. As a 'rock' beneath her left calf suddenly shaped in her sharpening night-vision to become a tortoise, Melissa knew an overwhelming urge to turn, to look. Not at the impersonal sea but at another human being.

Dreading every tiny rustle, lifting first her upper body, Melissa half twisted, then slowly lowered her torso onto the spiny, shaly ground. A dried twig rocked beneath her flank but did not snap.

Melissa's open, staring eyes fixed on the

nearest stable point — David's back as he strode away from her. In that moment she didn't care what he was: it was enough that he was there.

She wished she had never found that computer in his studio.

A low branch of one pine arch lightly snagged his thick yet fine black hair. Images of David sketching by the pool ran through Melissa's mind's eye, blending into that single moment when the towelling robe had slipped open to reveal fully the hard, active body beneath.

It's a seduction. Her words to Nicholas regarding the importance of presenting their case at the public meeting now returned to mock Melissa as her breasts and loins ached. Tonight David's strong body seduced her. Quickened by fear, she was now aroused by life.

'Wait!' she murmured.

David vanished onto the next sweep of the path.

Get up! Melissa told herself. *Get, up, fool. You need to be out of reach at sea before David realises you're not on the island any more.*

Melissa crept crab-wise out of the scrub, onto the lighted path. With the drop running nearer on one side and an explosion of tough impenetrable scrub on the other there was no choice but to stay on the track as it turned blind round the final corner.

No one noticed her. Two guards were still in the bay, pacing up and down the jetty looking busy, but their heads were cocked for the radio in the harbour building and their eyes patrolled only as far as the two floodlights fixed between the jetty and the start of the path. Since their boss had just gone off up the path they did not expect to see anyone coming down it and did not spot the small figure springing into the path-lights, then out of them a few metres farther down.

Panting, Melissa dropped into a patch of star clover and skidded on her rump the last section down to the harbour area. Keeping out of the floodlights, she walked a little more easily here as she picked a way round boulders, driftwood, a forgotten fuel can. Head bowed so as not to impair her own night vision in the bright lights, Melissa first checked she had all her gear with her and that it was packed so as not to rattle, and then she began her steady stalk towards the bobbing dinghy tied to David's boat.

Again, luck was with her. Creeping in from the rear of the building, Melissa discovered a wooden ladder leading down under the level of the harbour building to the beach.

Slithering down the damp wood to the smooth sand, she found a second small boat — hidden before by the overhanging building — drawn up bow first out of the water.

Shivering, Melissa frantically scoured its insides with her eyes and hands. It seemed seaworthy, though with the port bow gunwale slightly spongy and rotten, but, best of all, the owner had fitted an outboard engine.

Whether it would work was another matter, but an engine it was: another bonus.

Melissa gripped the bow in both hands, lifting and heaving the craft onto the water. Its bottom made a small skidding sound on the sand and then was free, its rowlocks winking at her as it pitched in the sea.

Melissa climbed in, found an oar, pushed on it hard and drifted off beneath David's white yacht. Jerking the outboard down into the sea, she hauled on the cord: once, then again as she came out from the yacht's shadow and the harbour light hit her, then again as the two guards on the jetty came running, shouting at her and into their radios.

The engine fired, the tiller shook under her clenched fist and then she was away, leaving harbour side and running figures behind, leaving the light and fleeing into the dark.

Chapter 27

The sea and the breeze together funnelled Melissa's boat down the strait between the two islands. Their combined force was too strong for the tiny engine, Melissa quickly realised, glad that it was a relatively calm night. Now, just a few moments after clearing Antasteri harbour, she vividly understood Manoli's comments about the knowledge needed to sail these deceptive waters. She also recognised that David and Nicholas must both be capable seamen — useful skills for any smugglers, if items had to be shipped instead of flown in.

But she was not a sailor, and if she made any mistakes tonight she'd have no second chance.

Fearing that she might be followed, Melissa chose to make the crossing between the two islands at the narrowest point. She steered towards the swift-running midstream currents, mentally preparing herself to tackle the rocky entrance to Hydra beach.

The first swell from the churning water almost swamped her boat. By pushing hard on the tiller and screaming the engine at full throttle, Melissa just managed to drag the craft out of the current. Time to stop fighting one threat and work with nature instead of against it, she decided wryly, when her heart and breathing were both a touch steadier. David had brought them round the northern end of Asteri from Khora: she would return the other way.

Melissa turned her craft back towards Antasteri. Allowing the engine to idle, she let the dinghy be pushed by the tail of the mid-stream current past the tip of the wooded islet towards Asteri's westernmost cliffs. Then, surging on what power she had, Melissa hauled the tiller again and set a bow-on course for the open sea.

Easy, she thought, in irreverent relief, as she cleared the black promontory and received another blessing of icy water from the Aegean over the gunwale. With no means to bail, her boots were paddling and she kept her camera gear hung round her bandit-fashion, but these were minor discomforts.

The first sandy beach that looked safe — that was what she wanted. She doubted if the engine had sufficient fuel to take her all the way to Khora and didn't fancy the trip anyway. The dinghy was already taking water and quickly developing a pronounced and dangerous list. Beneath the tiller, the engine gargled and coughed, threatening to cut out at any moment. If the wind rose even a little more she could easily be driven onto some rocky lee shore or out into open waters — both dangerous. On the sea she was at the mercy of the tides, of winds, of the slowness of her boat. A sea chase, against a modern yacht or fishing boat, would see her caught long before Khora. There were bitter memories, too, of her father's death at sea.

Land was another matter. David and Nicholas and the smugglers might be master mariners, but Melissa knew she was their equal and more on land. Asteri was huge compared to Antasteri, certainly large enough for her to lose any hunters if she was followed tonight.

Melissa bobbed past the nunnery on Asteri's south-western point. The Turkish coast was hidden from her by the island's south-eastern point. A plane blinked high overhead — a jet, not a light aircraft. She checked her watch: it was after nine. Nicholas would be at dinner now with Katherine, the two of them luxuriating in the delights of the Villa Elysion, full of good food, comfortable in each other's company. Maybe Nicholas would tell of his trips to Asteri mountain and Lykimi beach, bringing out the amusing parts: Melissa's mistakes. The time she had struck him with her tripod, for instance. After liqueurs maybe he would tell Katherine what Melissa had said about her. He and Katherine would then agree that it was a pity Melissa was so obsessed with this absurd rivalry and imagined enmity, especially when she had so much else going for her.

Melissa's stomach clenched, though not because of the rolling motion of the boat. She was hungry, she told herself, and a touch cold. Without coat or sweater, long sleeves were not enough to stop the knife-slice of night air.

The open sea at night has its own star-adorned beauty and Melissa was pricklingly aware of it, the more so because its vast yet quiet, strangely intimate, mystery was tempting. Shivering, crouched tight by the tiller, Melissa did not allow her eyes to be drawn into the huge dark sea and skyscape, the lowering clear deep blue and silver, the intriguing sparkles of life under the waves but kept her gaze rigidly to land. The breeze from the sea whipped her left sleeve against her bruised and aching flank. Only the flapping of her clothes against her body reminded Melissa that she was not naked. She had to land soon, before she froze. Death by exposure was increasingly becoming not a vivid yet mercifully unlikely nightmare but a real and terrifying possibility.

There! thought Melissa, jamming the steering gear fiercely to port. Straight ahead now, the silver sands sheered softly by the overhead stars: no moon tonight, and calm waters — perfect for fishermen, sailors and smugglers.

And now for me, thought Melissa, as the boat came sweetly to shore. She jumped stiffly out, hauled the craft half out of the water, then left it — no place to hide it on this ribbon of sand. Her time would be better spent climbing the long series of winding steps to the hamlet above the beach, and then away to Khora.

Once in the hamlet, Melissa noticed moving lights in the white church but did not stay to investigate. Finding a pitted track leading off from the back of the bell tower in the direction she wanted she took it, walking as fast as she could to warm herself.

The 'road' kept to the coastline, avoiding the ridged and mountainous interior, the forest and the fields. Melissa was first grateful, then bored, by its monotony. She tried to count bats, then the bleating of lambs calling in the upland meadows for their mothers.

Step followed step but Khora seemed to

come no nearer. One ridge swung back and away to be replaced in the star-lit distance by another. Donkey dung, her own stale sweat and the glorious occasional crush of lemon thyme were the scents of her journey. Her boots rattled the stones. Stars rose, then fell.

What's wrong with you, wimp? Melissa berated herself at one point. Get on, it's only about nine miles, ten at the most. Midnight should see you home, get on.

She had things to do in Khora. Find out when the public meeting had been rescheduled. Find out more about Sir Oliver Raine. There was a convincing lie she had to compose to cover tonight's 'escape' from Antasteri — it would have to be credible, too, since she was due back on the island tomorrow. There was the picture of Spiro to send to Jonathan. She needed to telephone Jonathan, too, tonight, to tell him what was going on, how the public meeting had produced no result. She needed to find out what was going on in London with her various editors and Katherine's stooges, Ken and Bruce.

Tonight was all she had. Tomorrow she would have to go back to David's island, try to obtain a record of the 'Katherine' file. That wasn't enough evidence, she knew.

She should have stayed on Antasteri,

waited to see if Spiro the guard, whose boss was David Gordon, and Spiro the wildlife smuggler, who worked for rich international clients, were one and the same.

Melissa shook her tousled blonde hair. If she were ever to discover if David had somehow been involved in Andrew's death, then she had to work patiently, track the connections carefully.

But she didn't want to see David again, Melissa thought fiercely. Or Nicholas.

She waited for Andrew's voice to speak but tonight memory was silent, she had only the present. Passionate, powerful, perilous: was that Andrew or David? Engaging, energetic, evasive: Nicholas fitted these descriptions and yet there was more to the mayor of Asteri, depths and shallows. Two very different men, both drawn to her and she to them. She didn't want to be drawn. She didn't want to choose, not when the choice could lose her so much: her self-respect, if she later discovered she was sleeping with a murderer, maybe even her own life.

'I won't be the one to choose, if Katherine has anything to do with it,' Melissa said aloud, but that attempt to distract her thoughts failed.

A murderer. David might have killed Andrew. Why was it that, faced with that terrifying possibility, she could only remember the sculptor's beguiling strength? To have those arms around her, that tall powerful body seeking hers . . . was that the ultimate betrayal of Andrew's memory or a final catharsis of her grief?

Or had Nicholas been the one who forced Andrew to drink the retsina before he murdered him? Black hair, blue eyes: storm banners for a stormy man. If David was the stone-still eye of the hurricane, Nicholas was more a tornado, lashing here and there with devastating speed. Tornadoes could destroy everything they touched, yet they could also clear, make free for new life.

Nicholas had certainly blown some cobwebs from her feelings, Melissa acknowledged, irritated yet amused when she recalled the Greek-American's unabashed, non-politically-correct opinions. The man made her laugh and she liked to laugh.

How could she laugh at someone who could be trading in animals? Who could have — ?

You're not safe. Not Andrew's voice, nor Nicholas' nor David's but an eerie blend of all three, a warning which jolted Melissa out of introspection into action. Lips and fingerends tingling, she stopped stock-still, sideways on, to look rapidly down, then up, the mule-and-moped-marked track. The path disappeared a few metres farther on towards Khora, falling off into a long gulley. She had not yet crested the hilltop, which meant she was invisible to anyone on that section of road.

Melissa crouched behind a budding judas tree between the track and the field. Listening and peering in the shadows, she smelt them first; their lighted cigarettes. Whoever they were, these people were walking quietly, but now she began to hear the slow press of feet and guessed that they were carrying something heavy between them.

Suddenly the footfalls changed direction, began shuffling off towards the sea. Stealing out from behind the judas tree, Melissa risked dropping onto her front and elbowing forward over the hilltop, careful to stay always on the shadowed side of the track. Now she could see them through her infrared binoculars: five men, hefting two long unlit braziers between them. They had turned down off the track onto a smaller path towards the deserted Turkish village of Kemi.

'This is the place,' a voice said in Greek, carrying clearly in the still night air. 'Let's make it our own.'

'Andreas knows he's to bring three sheep?' asked another, waving his glowing cigarette towards Asteri mountain.

'If he forgets the right number, as he did last year, then no doubt Popi will remind him.'

There was laughter, a joke Melissa did not understand, although its ribald intention was plain from the shadowed movements of the man's hands and hips, which set the bottles in his rucksack ringing.

'Watch that Amstel,' grumbled a third.

'The women will bring more beer when they get out of church,' was the casual reply. The man drew hard on his cigarette and by the hotly gleaming tip Melissa caught a glimpse of a moustache and a pair of weather-beaten cheeks.

'Where's Manoli?' the man asked.

'Leathering that bastard dog of his, last time I saw him. I just hope he doesn't bring it today.'

'Maybe Andreas will throw it a lamb chop.'

More laughter, then: 'What time's the feast starting?'

'When everything is ready and not before,' said the clean-shaven man. 'But remember it's Andreas' beach party.'

Carrying their braziers, the figures melded

into the shadows and the track was finally silent.

Melissa rose to her feet. The men were going to Kemi, clearly to 'reoccupy' the former Turkish village by preparing and eating a Christian feast down on its beach. Because tonight was the eve of St George's Day, and after the church services the whole of Asteri would be bursting out onto meadows and beaches to eat spit-roasted lamb, drink beer and wine and dance. Easter had been early this year and she had missed its joyous celebrations, but she was here now for St George's Day.

Did these men and their families come to Kemi every year to celebrate the saint's day in this way? It seemed from their conversation that they did: last year the shepherd Andreas had not provided the number of sheep he'd been asked for. More interesting to Melissa was that from what she had heard it was obvious that Andreas, Popi and Manoli were not only acquaintances but friends — and, in Andreas' and Popi's case, more intimate still.

One thing Melissa knew for certain now was that no smugglers would bother trying to land anything at Kemi. Not with a beach party in full swing. Even if only the adults were involved and the children told to 'watch

the wall', the risk of someone talking, someone letting something slip, would be enormous.

Besides, it was an international smuggling
ring she was after, with major clients and
bosses. It was an organised business. Melissa
couldn't see an entrepreneur like Katherine
Hopkins agreeing to any 'special shipment'
being dumped in the middle of an unruly
party of Greek shepherds, ferrymen and
farmers' wives.

Katherine. As she continued walking, always with ears listening and eyes sharpened
for Manoli's or Andreas' possible appearance, Melissa considered her rival.

Why, if Katherine and David, or Katherine
and Nicholas — or maybe all three — were
involved in the wildlife smuggling racket, was
Katherine bothering to try to blacken *her*
reputation with the two men? Jealousy was
the simple explanation, but Katherine wasn't
simple.

Besides, Melissa sensed that her enemy's
remarks were part of a sustained campaign:
part of Katherine's larger tactics in using
Bruce and Ken against her. But to what end?
To destroy her reputation, certainly. 'Cross
me again and I'll finish you.' Was Katherine
making good her threat? And was it out of
revenge or fear?

What did Katherine not want her to discover on Asteri?

If it was David's computer records, then she was too late, concluded Melissa, yet the thought gave no satisfaction. Instead, uneasy, she picked up her stride, going forward despite the nagging awareness that she was walking into some carefully prepared trap. Whatever she found in Khora, whatever difficulty she would have in persuading David that she had left Antasteri last evening in a 'borrowed' open boat for the most innocent of reasons, Melissa knew she had no choice. Spiro the guard, the 'Katherine' file and the cages were leads she had to follow, She owed it to Andrew.

Unless she wanted to choose a killer for a lover, she owed it to herself.

Chapter 28

It lay in the middle of the track, a gold bracelet fallen from a woman's wrist or a man's pocket. Glad she had spotted it in the starlight, Melissa knelt to pick it up, intending to hand it in to the mayor's office in the morning.

There was something beneath it. Wary of scorpions, Melissa shook a camera release cord from her bag. She hooked the cord round the bracelet and her stomach turned over. The bracelet was attached to a knife: the hilt had been drilled so that the bracelet could be threaded through and fastened to it as some kind of barbaric ornament.

Without a sheath the knife was lethal: two edged, thick and perilously sharp. And even with a sheath no one could carry this in a pocket, it was longer than her spanned fingers.

Why had it been left on the track? To be found? As a message? A warning? Certainly not because the knife was damaged or blunt. Even if that had been the case, the owner would surely have tossed the knife into the sea, not left it for animals to cut their feet on. And he or she would be mad not to have first recovered the bracelet.

Carefully, aware of the danger of the slowly twirling blade, Melissa lifted the linked items higher for a closer look.

Shock lashed through her as she saw the bracelet clearly. First her name, spelt out in Greek letters on its central solid bar. Then the small golden charms running round from the bar, following each other in strict rotation: two linked fishes, the astrological sign of Pisces, then a golden seahorse. Fish, seahorse, fish, seahorse — there were no other charms on the sturdy gold chain.

Her birthday was 24 February.

Melissa's fingers tightened on the camera release cord. Her name, her birthsign, her favourite creature. Two coincidences she could accept, but three were too much. The bracelet had been meant for her.

Andrew must have had it made in one of the many jewellers' workshops in the old city of Rhodes. He had wanted a personal, special gift for her and here it was, cold in her fist two years after his death.

Emotion overwhelmed her: grief that Andrew was dead. She sat down on the track, knees drawn under her chin, and opened her hand. The bracelet was still there, hanging, with the knife, from her release cord.

How had Andrew's gift to her finished here on Asteri? He had not mentioned it to her in his final telephone call. The police couldn't have found it, or any bill of sale in his things, or they'd have told her. Had it been stolen from Andrew by a pickpocket?

Mechanically, she rose to her feet, opened her camera bag and dropped bracelet and knife inside. These would need to go to the police in Rhodes. Had the jewellery passed through many hands after Andrew's? She had no way of knowing. All she could hope was that here was another clue, which, taken with everything else, might finally reveal the identity of Spiro.

If left as a warning, was the knife meant for her or another?

Keeping her raw feelings and fear at bay by working, Melissa decided to use flash to photograph the spot where she had found the bracelet and knife. It was risky, with Andreas and Manoli due anytime along the track, but with her tripod she could bring camera and flash down low and also capture the vegetation growing on the track edge; another future guide to where she had found the gold and steel. A few fraught minutes saw it done and then she was away, half-running at first in her desire to distance herself from the men at Kemi.

Another hour saw her in Khora, where, passing the schoolhouse, Melissa broke into a cold, clammy sweat of relief. She had neither seen nor met anyone else on her midnight scramble, and now at last she felt relatively safe. Physically weary after her 'escape' from Antasteri and emotionally drained by her discoveries there and on her trek across Asteri, Melissa almost fell into her flat at Mrs Samouri's. Bolting the door, she dumped her cameras, slowly and clumsily stripped off her stained and sodden clothes, had a quick wash and went to bed.

Waking, her first thought was of Andrew and she immediately sought out the bracelet and its attached knife. Holding both in the light, she was as convinced in daylight as in darkness that Andrew had bought the jewellery. Sighing, Melissa left the two things on the bed as she washed and dressed, returning now and then to breathe upon a seahorse charm. Unless its shine and unscratched clasp deceived, she was sure the bracelet had never been worn.

Had it been a kind of trophy to whoever had seized it? wondered Melissa, carrying knife and bracelet with her as she went into the kitchen for a drink of water. Had the man who'd attacked her two nights ago seen or owned this bracelet, had he made a connection between the name 'Melissa', the golden seahorses, and herself?

'He knows I'm onto him, and he doesn't like it,' Melissa murmured, defiantly ignoring the sudden chill which had slithered down her spine. Catching a glimpse of herself in the reflection from Andreas Papandreou's picture she wondered if collecting water from the fountain and heating it for a bath was not the top priority but dismissed that as self-indulgent. Polaroids of her finds were first, then a rapid trip to the priest, who had a fax machine at his house. She would fax the polaroids to Rhodes police, then work out how to post Jonathan the negatives of David's Greek-Australian guard Spiro without arousing too much curiosity from Mr Zervos, who as well as being the chemist, doubled as the island's postmaster. More important still, she had to send Jonathan her pictures without arousing the suspicions of Manoli, who would take the post off Asteri. But there'd be a way round that problem: there was always a way.

Despite her determinedly buoyant mood, Melissa started as someone knocked vigorously on the front door to her flat.

Nicholas' voice. 'Melissa, we must talk

now, something's come up that I just don't understand —'

'We know you're in there.' Zoe Konstantinou interrupted Nicholas. 'Mrs Samouri told us she'd heard you come back last night. Aren't you going to let us in?'

'In a minute, I'm just brushing my teeth!' Her camera bag was in the other room. Melissa was heading for the cooker when there came another sharp series of raps at the yard door just to the side of her. 'It's getting like Great Yarmouth sea front out there. What's going on?' muttered Melissa, trying to be amused but instead feeling only a growing alarm. Caught on both sides she now heard Katherine.

'Melissa? I felt I had to make sure you were recovered from the dramas of yesterday.'

'Hang on, Katherine!' Melissa called.

'We're still waiting,' said Zoe sharply outside the front door.

'Come round to the side!' Melissa shouted: she might as well have all her visitors together. Glancing again at the camera release switch and its linked bracelet and knife in her tightly clenched fist, she flipped off the latch to the pink unit hanging precariously over the cooker to toss in the deadly blade and bracelet out of sight.

A shadow in the cupboard made her stand

on tiptoe, leaning closer over the gas jets. Melissa pushed the wooden door open to its fullest extent and, reaching in over the knife, thrust her arm deep inside.

'Busy, are we?' asked Nicholas behind her. He and Zoe had done as Melissa suggested and slipped down the side passage to the kitchen yard. It was he, not Katherine, who had entered first, finding her like this: startled, no doubt blushing.

'Mrs Samouri lent Katherine a key,' he said, accounting for how they had come in through a locked door. 'Hiding something?' he asked now.

'What on earth are you talking about?' Melissa demanded, yanking her arm out of the unit.

Disturbed by the violence of her act, a spill of documents hidden in the wall unit confettied round them over the tiles.

Zoe pushed past Nicholas and bent to pick up the papers, scanning them curiously. 'Two thousand seahorses, species *hippocampus*,' she read aloud from one. 'A live shipment, carried on an African airline from Turkey, due in America last week.'

'Anything else?' A new voice, Bailey's. Melissa sensed him standing in the doorway with Katherine as her gaze remained fixed on Nicholas. She couldn't believe he was being taken in by this . . . unless perhaps he was behind it.

Whichever, Melissa couldn't remain silent. 'I've been set up. Can't you see that?'

'Last month, six thousand cyclamen tubers,' Zoe continued.

'Did you dig them up in the woods on your last photographic trip?' asked Katherine sweetly.

'Don't be ridiculous, there aren't that many to gather in Asteri forest.' Melissa stopped, mentally cursing herself for that remark, which sounded as if she might have been plant-collecting, elsewhere if not here.

Nicholas broke eye contact with Melissa and looked beyond her into the open wall unit. 'I presume the ocelot fur coat's from Rhodes?'

That's what she'd seen, realised Melissa, as she twisted round to stare. Part of her mind had already suspected as much, but she'd been reluctant to accept it, knowing what suffering the coat represented. Now it came to her that whoever had dumped this 'shipment' of goods in her room had known exactly what to leave and from where the illegal skin coat could be obtained. And, no doubt, could provide a 'witness' who'd seen her buying the ocelot fur in Rhodes.

Sensing the trap closing, her enemy in the

doorway rejoicing, Melissa swivelled back to face Nicholas.

'Why would I have paperwork here?' she demanded, trying a different line of argument. She didn't want to mention the knife — or Andrew's bracelet — with Katherine present. 'Where would I get these documents from? You can check with Mr Zervos what postal deliveries I've had.'

'Then I say that you brought them with you,' said Zoe, brown eyes flashing as she glared up at the Englishwoman. 'These are order sheets.' She lifted another paper, let it fall.

'Greed makes people sloppy.' Nicholas lifted a rolled-up bundle of newsprint from his jacket pocket, tossed it across. 'That's how you've been found out,' he added, as Melissa caught it.

Three reports, written by the same person on the same subject: wildlife smuggling and Melissa Haye. One had been published that morning in a Greek English-language paper, the other two had both been produced yesterday in English tabloids. All three featured the same old photograph of her and a similar headline accusing her of hypocrisy. Again in all three, the report that followed claimed that Melissa had used her wildlife photo-journalism as cover for a lucrative sideline in supplying dealers with living or dead 'materials' for Asian medicine.

Both Greek and English pieces were under Ken's by-line, Melissa noted with disgust. Part of her was still stunned and disappointed that Nicholas could be so naive as not to realise the whole thing was a put-up job. Unless of course he knew and didn't care.

'I see that despite his nickname, Bruce couldn't come up with anything,' was her first fighting-to-stay-cool response as she folded up the final lurid report. She pointed the rolled up newspaper at Katherine, wishing, with an inner burst of rage, that it was a gun. She knew only too well who was behind Ken, who had promised to pay his legal fees if she sued for slander: after which time, of course, the damage would have been done. No smoke without fire, wasn't that what people always said?

'This rubbish was written by one of her friends,' Melissa continued, wishing her voice did not sound quite so shrill. 'Can't you see that the timing's just too good? The report coming out yesterday and this stuff now appearing in my flat? She knew to bring it round here last night; my staying on Antasteri gave her just the chance she wanted. Yes, you go and talk to Mrs Samouri — she's already borrowed a key off my landlady!'

'That's impossible.' Nicholas was shaking his head. 'Katherine was with me last night.'

'All last night, Melissa,' added Katherine.

Expressionless, Nicholas watched Melissa's incandescent blush. When he spoke, his voice was formal. 'There's a plane leaving tonight at midnight: be on it, Miss Haye. Police will meet you at Rhodes International airport — you've questions to answer, and after this morning, possible charges to face.'

'Nick, you can't believe this!' Melissa blurted out, stung by his unnatural calm. She could hardly stand the flat, bland expression of those usually fierce, intense blue eyes.

'Midnight tonight at the airstrip. I want you off my island.'

Something hard and sharp stung in Melissa's eye, slapped across her bruised cheek. Zoe had hurled a whole bundle of papers straight at her. 'I hope they put you in prison!' the Greek blonde spat as she left.

Katherine threaded her arm through Bailey's. 'Breakfast, I think,' she observed, lightly brushing the collar of his brown suit. 'Once we're gone, the mayor can get on with his job and sort out the rest of this unfortunate business.'

'Drop in to the chemist's and ask Mr Zervos to step over here right away, would you, Katherine?' Nicholas called after her.

'Certainly, Nicholas. And good luck, Melissa. Honestly.'

Then Katherine was gone.

Chapter 29

'It's not what you think,' Melissa repeated when Katherine had left.

Nicholas yanked a chair off the wall, crashed it down on the floor. 'Sit down, please.'

'Ken is paid by Katherine. So is Bruce.' Now she and Nicholas were alone, Melissa felt compelled to defend herself, even if Nicholas were involved with Spiro and the smugglers. She had never realised how much she had taken the man's talkative exuberance for granted until faced with its absence: this phlegmatic, Stalin-featured man was a stranger.

'There won't be any records or proof, only rumours, whispers.'

'You should know about that: whispers are all you've given me about Katherine.'

'What about the spotted cat fur coat?' Melissa lashed an arm towards the wall unit. She shook with rage as she thought of it. 'All the great cats are under pressure because of illegal trapping, shooting, medicines. Just one tiger cub will cost you ten thousand, minimum — this is a vast, grotesque business and Katherine is up to her neck in it! Remember what I said about the ocelot fur coat I saw in Katherine's TWC Italian store — she markets those things! Do you know how many dead animals there'll be in that "fashion statement" up there?'

'Your word against hers.' Nicholas would not look at her. 'The coat's in your flat.'

'Because it was dumped here! Do you really think after what I've seen of trapped animals I'd even want to touch one of those things? And the orders for seahorses —' Melissa scooped up a paper, thrust it at Nicholas, let it fall. 'Doesn't it strike you as too ironic that *I* should smuggle seahorses?'

She'd not had time to slip on her earrings, but even as she spoke Melissa recalled something she had said to Jonathan weeks ago: *If you want, you can tell Spiro when you meet that I adore seahorses. Maybe he'll offer to smuggle those, too.* The irony was there, all right.

'Katherine warned me you were very convincing.'

'Katherine — listen to yourself, Nick!' Never mind the tie she had chosen for him, thought Melissa in growing frustration and despair, Katherine was taking over his head, too. 'This isn't you: you should be hot as fire. You should be blazing out at me, not

385

playing at being Mr Calm!'

'Don't push it, Melissa. Right at this moment I'm real tempted to knock you down: your voice claims one thing but my eyes show another.'

Nicholas was intently studying the patterns of grain in the pine kitchen table. Once his hands came up, deliberately measuring and tracing the swirls and lines: all a pretence, Melissa knew. She remembered the last time they had faced each other across a table, how his eyes had never left her.

'Don't I exist for you any more?' The challenge was out, torn from her by anger, grievance and feeling. Yet also a crazy lightning blast of hope, because he had said her name; absently, as though he couldn't help it.

Nicholas' black wavy head jerked up. Melissa had the satisfaction of seeing surprise break across those dark, saturnine features, followed by a glowing indignation. 'You've some nerve, lady,' he said, the warm living rasp returning to his voice.

'You want to look in the cupboard, don't you?' Melissa goaded, stalking forward to stand beside the chair. However much Nicholas hunched his shoulders at her, she wasn't going to use the chair as a shield: she wasn't afraid of his anger.

'Before Zervos comes, why not look?' she

demanded. 'I can even try the coat on, if you want —' As she said that, Melissa went cold all over. An image of a dead Arctic Fox, its beautiful body jack-knifed in a rictus of agony, its teeth set in its own trapped back leg, flashed up in her head, an image from one of her own photographs. Fighting down the revulsion involved in handling the coat in any way, she tried to be calm, calculating. 'Don't you want to see if it fits me?'

Why are you doing this? An inner voice clamoured within Melissa as her heartbeat spiked upwards. *Do you want him to see the dagger, the bracelet, and if he does, what will that prove? You know you can't let him touch them.*

'Fur isn't my scene.' He was looking at her now, all right, blue eyes fierce as the first time they'd met, on Manoli's boat. His vigorous fingers closed tight on the faded cap tucked inside his jeans belt, then abruptly he walked swiftly round the table away from her to the kitchen shutters and burst them open. 'Need some air,' he growled.

Although deathly cold, Melissa made no move to totter into the wide river of sunlight flowing into the room. 'Where's Chloe?' she asked stiffly, thankful to glance away from that thing in the cupboard.

'Out taking Rox for a walk,' replied Nicholas. He grimaced, as though he had just given away a great secret.

'Can't we talk normally any more?' Melissa asked, hurt again by his attitude. Strangely, the personal hurt shut down the terrible run of pictures in her head: she began to warm up again, the icy cold in her face and cheeks tingling with clammy warmth. Now an irrelevant regret filled her that Nicholas would probably remember her like this: in simple blue sundress and sandals.

Nicholas' breathing seemed suddenly to fill the kitchen. 'Stop using Katherine's seduction techniques, they don't suit you.' He whirled about and prowled closer to the open shutter, leaning out of the window. 'I suppose Gordon likes you that way,' he added.

Melissa was indignant at being accused of stooping to Katherine's tricks, especially when she hadn't been doing anything. 'Well, I suppose you ought to know all about those "techniques" at first hand now,' she retorted. Katherine and Nick had spent the night together. For an instant, Melissa was so furious that all sense of tactics deserted her: from hoping to persuade a possible suspect to confront evidence of wrongdoing, she wanted instead to hurt, to pay back some of the pain she was feeling.

Because Nick had spent the night with

Katherine? Were her rival's affairs so important? Or was it that she felt disconcerted, aware that there was something alike between her and Katherine, something men could see, which attracted them to both women? For, as the last few moments had proved, Nicholas was still attracted to her, albeit reluctantly.

Nervous as any wild creature, Nicholas raised his blunt nose to the breeze. 'Can you smell it?'

'The plane tree at the end of the street? The judas tree blossom?' Melissa enquired pertly.

'No!' Nicholas' stiffened fingers drummed down the shutter like a jazz washboard player. 'The wind's wrong. Look at the olive leaves.'

It seemed now that Nicholas wanted to avoid all reference to last night and wasn't particularly keen on pursuing this morning's 'discoveries': the grisly fur item in the cupboard, or the incriminating mess of paper strewn over the tiles. Picking her way round the documents — Melissa hadn't bothered to peruse them closely just yet, she knew that if Katherine was behind their manufacture they'd be excellent forgeries — the young woman crossed to the window. For the moment she was quite prepared to play along with Nicholas.

He acknowledged her presence not by a glance but by an energetic jab of an arm and a pointing hand. 'See the way the olives in the field up there look silver?' he demanded. 'That means the prevailing wind's turned round. Could be we're due for dirty weather.'

Leaning out to watch the tumbling flash of the olive leaves, bright as falling silver coins, Melissa sensed Nicholas' gaze switch onto her as he said the words 'dirty weather'.

'So I won't be able to fly to Rhodes,' said Melissa. Deliberately using some of those techniques Nicholas claimed she employed, Melissa now ran a hand through her tousled hair, allowing the light to fall along it and along the curve of her profile, neck and bosom.

Beside her she heard the man's breathing stop. 'Will you be sorry?' she asked without turning.

Nicholas stepped back rapidly into shadow. 'A fur coat — not much to ruin a career for, is it?' he said, moving back now towards the wall unit.

Melissa turned, feeling the absence of her seahorse earrings against her closing throat. 'Aren't you going to ask me why, Nick?'

'I'm not interested in excuses.' Yanking

open the second door to the unit, Nicholas moved to put a fist inside.

Melissa rushed at him. 'Careful!' she exclaimed, conscious of the sharpness of the knife in there.

Stretching for the coat, his hand suddenly stopped in mid-air, black eyebrows raised in his puzzled square face. He spun round on his heel. 'A switchblade, Melissa?'

Surprise, bewilderment — no shock, Melissa noted, wondering just what that meant. 'I found it last night just past Kemi,' she replied, not mentioning the men she had seen. 'Do you know who it belongs to?'

Nicholas' head came down in sharp denial. 'No.' He turned. 'Must say, the decorations look like one of your touches.' Again his hand hovered closer.

Melissa grabbed hold of his arm. 'Don't!' She couldn't allow him to fingerprint the knife.

Nicholas looked at her, exasperation replacing surprise. Unpeeling her fingers with casual gentle strength, he said sarcastically, 'Don't worry, I'm not about to do one of your tricks and steal it — I'll leave it in the office for someone to claim, and we'll see who comes.'

'That has to go to Rhodes.' Melissa did not allow herself to be diverted from that vital point by insulting remarks about her supposed lack of honesty. 'Alexios should come to remove it.' She hoped she could trust the doctor, but in any case she had no choice.

A glint of suspicion surfaced in Nicholas' blue eyes. He allowed his arm to drop, the tip of his thumb accidentally scouring along one fold of Melissa's blue dress: they were now that close. 'Seahorse decorations, seahorse shipments — you really go for them,' he said. 'Is that knife yours, Melissa? Or was it bought for you, maybe?'

His eyes, watching her. Eyes which last night had no doubt seen Katherine naked.

'Don't you want me to try on the coat?' Melissa repeated her earlier question, trying to smile meanwhile but not succeeding.

Amazingly a grin lit Nicholas' face. 'Neither of us are any good at subtle changes of subject, are we?'

Melissa shook her head. 'No,' she said, still unable to return Nicholas' uneven smile. 'No,' she said again.

'If wishes were horses,' Nicholas murmured irrelevantly, remarking more loudly, 'Pindaros wants another meeting organised. I should be doing that, once Zervos finally condescends to appear.' Now he glared at the open door. 'What the hell's keeping that guy? I've a toy business to run, too, as well as Asteri.'

Outside, the wind moaned through the alley.

'You think I'm Spiro, is that it? You're not sure if that blade's mine?'

The unexpected questions almost caught Melissa off guard but she managed to answer lightly enough, 'Maybe. After all,' she added bitterly, 'you think I sell seahorses and go around draped in ocelot.'

'If I was convinced of that,' said Nicholas decisively, 'I'd be pumping you for answers right now about your trading runs and contacts. I definitely wouldn't be doing this —'

His arms clamped about her and his mouth covered hers. It was an angry, prickly sort of kiss.

Startled and confused, Melissa wasn't sure if she relished this development. 'Watch the moustache!' she mumbled.

'Sorry.' Nicholas twisted his head slightly and now it was better, his warm lips properly on hers. It was a relief to be closely kissed and held without acquiring backache or a crick in the neck, Melissa thought. His mouth tasted of mint.

'You're so pretty,' he was saying, kissing her chin. 'Silky.' His hand softly tugged her hair: he was letting her know that he remembered when he had yanked on her hair too hard.

The tug became a stroke, became a slow, tickly, tingling caress along her bare shoulder. They stiffened then flowed against each other, Melissa gathering tight, Nicholas playfully dropping his chin against her shoulder. 'I shouldn't be doing this,' he muttered, the admission seemingly torn from him.

A gleam of a knife from the cupboard flashed into Melissa's softly clouding eyes, waking her with a sudden hard jolt back into reality. Andrew's last gift was a part of that knife: even without the threat of bad weather delaying her enforced departure, she had only until midnight tonight to track down the smugglers before they disappeared from Asteri — probably forever. With a marina due for development at Kemi and Pindaros fighting to have his way with the mine, the island would be altogether too busy in future for Spiro and his men.

And, if her intuitions were right, Asteri would not be used again by Katherine in any of her undoubted 'transactions' in the wild-life trade.

Thoughts of Katherine were the final spur. Melissa drew back from Nicholas, aware that until she exposed the smuggling ring she could not be sure of trusting either him or David.

'Did you do this last night with Katherine?' she asked.

Nicholas' head jerked as if she had struck him. He stepped back from her, his features reddening, then, like molten rock, hardening a second later into dark immovable basalt. There would be no more yielding from him, his expression read.

'We talked business,' he growled. 'All night.'

With that final emphasis he broke from her, going to the door, where finally the chemist and the doctor — plus several on-lookers — were now gathering.

'She's all yours,' Nicholas said in Greek to the two men. He turned to stare at Melissa. 'These gentlemen will take a statement from you: Mr Zervos is our police representative here, as well as our postman,' he explained formally in English. 'You can talk freely with him and our excellent doctor about your concerns over documentation, and other matters.' Nicholas broke off, then resumed. 'After they've finished with you, you'll be free to go anywhere you wish for the rest of today, Miss Haye, so long as you don't try to leave the island — except, of course, on the midnight plane.'

'Wait!' Melissa was horrified by these injunctions. The computer files codenamed 'Katherine' were on Antasteri: today might be her last realistic chance to recover them. Everything was slipping away from her, every possible lead and piece of evidence. 'I'm due back on Antasteri this afternoon with Roxanne, for the modelling.'

The answer she received was a cold look and a silence before, clearly reluctantly, Nicholas spoke. 'Gordon kept phoning Mrs Samouri last night until you got home, so he could be in touch with you again. Anyway, I'll radio through to Antasteri, cancel your afternoon session.'

'But Nick —'

'In the circumstances, it's not appropriate. You leave tonight, no sooner, no later. Goodbye, Miss Haye.'

Chapter 30

It was St George's Day and already the festivities had been under way for several hours. Had that not been so, Katherine concluded, reflectively swirling a glass of sparkling wine in her hand, no doubt all the islanders would have turned out to witness the disgrace of her enemy Melissa Haye.

As it was, only about a score had bothered to leave the taverna and the tables set out under the loggia of the fish market, to go swaying up the long steps of Khora harbour in the direction of Mrs Samouri's. Katherine would have preferred more interest, would have liked the media there too, but on holy days the divine took precedence over the secular. Today, George Tanis and other reporters would no doubt be enjoying St George's at home.

Really, they would have very little choice in the matter, thought Katherine with amusement, since the only flights and ferries that were running around Asteri were private planes or boats and the odd hired caique. The harbours bustled with activity, but it was family reunions, not private enterprise.

Spiro and Bailey were right. Today was perfect cover for the run of the special shipment into Kemi.

Katherine raised her glass to her companion across the table from her. 'Bailey,' she said, nodding to him as she drank.

The Australian peered at her through his dark glasses. He was wiping the rim of a champagne flute with a tissue. 'Sir Oliver's late sailing in from Petra,' he observed.

'No doubt because of the traffic.' Katherine smiled at Bailey's sour disapproval, and turned to watch the bunting-festooned boats in the harbour. 'Look at all those little boats,' she said, the lilt of Suffolk creeping into her voice at this moment of relaxed triumph. 'It's utterly perfect. You're a genius, John Bailey.'

Sniffing at Katherine's use of his first name, Bailey put down the glass. 'The jeep's ready in the main square.'

'Ah, yes, for your afternoon "picnic".' Katherine's green eyes showed a gleam of satisfied gold. Sometime that afternoon, cruising round Asteri on a tourist spin, Bailey and Sir Oliver would be invited to attend a St George's Day celebration at Kemi.

Spiro and his men would also be there. On such a day of comings and goings, Spiro's caique, slipping through from Turkey, would be indistinguishable from the other dozens of small craft bobbing in and out of Kemi.

Spiro would already have brought the special wild shipment ashore in a large hamper. The creature inside would be drugged and comatose and present no problems. Spiro's men would ensure that no one tampered with the hamper, which would be put under shade ready for Sir Oliver's and Bailey's appearance.

After a brief enjoyment of hospitality, Bailey and Sir Oliver would leave for the Villa Michelangelo, taking the large special picnic hamper — with the creature safe inside — back with them in the car.

Simple, thought Katherine, aware that the St George's Day crowds would give them all the cover they needed. Bailey and Sir Oliver would leave Khora's main square just before the island band and dance troupes began their afternoon entertainments to send the shepherds and their flocks off up into the high pastures in style. The main square would by then be so packed full of gawping Greeks, sheep and goats as to make it impossible for anyone trying to follow. Meanwhile, to allay any possible suspicion Bailey would drive first towards Petra, then cut across the fields back to the Kemi road.

And all the time she would be on Antasteri,

thought Katherine with a small sigh of pleasure. She would entirely escape these bucolic delights and, secure in the plan's total success, would be able to concentrate on charming David Gordon another step closer towards her bed.

Katherine started as a blare of horns sounded another boat's arrival. Really, she reflected, after a glare at the offending yellow and blue caique, she wasn't sure yet whom to encourage first to take that final, voluptuous plunge with her: David Gordon, the handsome sculptor of Antasteri, or Nicholas Stephanides, the lively mayor.

'If he can use his tongue in as imaginative and active a fashion as he talks, then mayor Nicholas should be a highly stimulating experience,' she murmured to herself, smiling at Bailey suspiciously scanning the peeled orange on his china plate. Her dinner at 'Elysion' with Nicholas last night had not only been informative — lots of useful information about Nicholas' 'Stevies' — but also exceedingly well-mannered. Obviously that was the Greek and New Englander in Nicholas: men were just such conservative, culturally oppressed types. It would be a future pleasure to tease Nicholas out a little, one she would defer until she was off this island and she and the Greek-American could meet again in the States.

David Gordon was going to be the lucky one here, Katherine decided. Secretive himself, David would willingly agree to their need to be discreet. A three-week affair with the sculptor would be a very pleasant way of spending the rest of her holiday here, whilst she and Zoe worked on plans for their joint marina on Kemi beach.

Sir Oliver would by then have already been long gone, having taken his prize out by tonight's midnight flight. She and Bailey had made the arrangements for their client, the various flights and papers, but since Sir Oliver had insisted on taking his 'kitty' into Europe, then the attendant dangers of discovery would be on his shoulders, not theirs. Three weeks from today, when she left Asteri after having seduced David, her hands would be clean. Nothing — no link, no trace, no paper, no recording, no picture — would attach her to the smugglers: Bailey and his briefcase would make sure of that.

And, in a final, luscious stroke of irony, Sir Oliver was leaving tonight on the same flight that Melissa Haye had been ordered to take.

Katherine drew in a long sip of sparkling wine. *Melissa,* she thought, slowly swallowing as she addressed her former enemy, *You were warned that I'd finish you — now I have. Will I miss that long lens and those short legs? I don't think so. You and that dead lover of yours, Andrew Thornhill; you were both simply in my way. It's a pity, really, Melissa: in another age we might have been friends. We're both good at what we do — only of course I'm better than you. That's why I'm here, smiling at these ridiculous loudmouthed Greeks cavorting around the jetty in their baseball hats and cool shades and you're stuck in that flat, reviled by the Khora gossips.*

The double-pronged attack — newspapers and the discoveries in the flat, witnessed, as Katherine had intended they should be, by Nicholas — had done Melissa Haye's wildlife and conservation credentials serious, if not fatal, damage.

Katherine drained her sparkling wine: it was Greek champagne and the best the taverns had, but that was really all that could be said in its favour. But right now the quality of the breakfast laid before her on the gently rippling checked tablecloth didn't matter at all. The fresh bread, warm from the baker's, could have been sawdust. Her juicy orange could have been sour, the fragrant coffee cold. Nothing now could spoil her day.

Chapter 31

'David here. I'll be leaving a message next for my Venus at the Villa Michelangelo: I assume after this morning's revelations that Katherine must be as stunned as everyone else is about Melissa. Anyway, what I'm calling for is to cancel today's modelling session. I'm coming into Khora to see your father, and I'd like to see you — shall we say the harbour café at noon? Maybe you won't hear this in time or can't make it . . . Anyway, I'll be in touch. Take care.'

The time on the answering machine read 10 am, half an hour after the message had been rung in. Roxanne stopped the tape and depressed the rewind button. David had contacted her ahead of Katherine Hopkins. He'd wanted to talk to *her* about the shocking news of Melissa's involvement in wildlife smuggling. Whether consciously or not, David was aware of a connection, a sympathy between them. He'd arranged to meet her later that morning: an open-ended invitation. 'I'll be in touch.' A future promise.

Yesterday she would have been ecstatic:

kissed Chloe, kissed the phone, kicked off her shoes and gone mad for a moment. To-day Roxanne sat listening to the tape spin back, satisfied by David's attention as something due to her, happy in a selfish way — very happy. But overlying everything was an urgent sense of wrong.

Nicholas worried her. Her dad had been knocked flat by what he'd read in the papers and seen in Mrs Samouri's flat. He was fighting to believe it. Roxanne wasn't convinced that he could, or that he should. But then maybe she was being naive because she liked Melissa, too.

Dad was despondent and David stunned. Rolling on the sofa, Roxanne retrieved the English tabloid from the low table and, ignoring the sordid revelations of Ken Bend's report, stared at the photograph of Melissa. Just behind her, out of focus, was a man: a tall, dark-haired young man wearing an arran sweater.

On the evening of the public meeting, whilst she and David had been waiting outside Melissa's flat for Melissa to change, David had told Roxanne just how the wildlife photographer had come to lose her long-time partner. The man had tumbled off a cliff, David had said, unconscious of the grim humour in that statement, the faintly absurd image it invoked. David, like her, wasn't one of the world's great conversationalists.

And yet he often talked to her, Roxanne now admitted, bright head leaning low over the newspaper in her hand. Perched on the sofa, she drew her lanky legs up and settled in lotus position, the better to concentrate. David had at different times called her a canny and a kind listener: Roxanne knew she was a good listener, perhaps only children always were. Normally she'd a good memory, too, except that today, faced with her dad's greying features and stoved-in look, the power of recollection had been rather knocked from her. Now in the quietness memory returned, like water drawn up slowly from a deep well.

Roxanne was remembering a poolside conversation in David's villa on Antasteri. David had fallen asleep and she and Melissa were idly talking together when Katherine broke in, enquiring whether Melissa had ever been back to Rhodes since Andrew had died there.

After checking that David was still asleep, Katherine had continued, 'I believe he plummeted over thirty metros. Such a tragic accident. And the police finding retsina all over his clothes . . . such a pity.'

Melissa had looked at Katherine then quite steadily, although Roxanne's own heart had been sprinting and she'd felt her face scorching. To her ears, Katherine's remarks had been more than tactless; they'd been cruel and ghoulish. But Melissa's cold answer had shocked her more: 'Especially since Andrew always hated retsina,' she'd said, her warm brown eyes fixed on her adversary in silent, bitter combat.

Katherine had let the matter drop there as David's eyelids had flickered and it seemed as though he might stir. Yet the conversation had remained in Roxanne's mind and, now that she could think past the shocks of this morning, it came up as clear as sunrise.

Two years ago Melissa's lover, a man called Andrew, had died in a fall of over thirty metres from a cliff face in Rhodes. From the way she'd said his name and the way she'd looked at Melissa as she spoke, a man Katherine must have known. A man who'd died in suspicious circumstances.

From Nicholas and ASPW records, Roxanne knew all about the Athenian who'd been caught smuggling the Eleonora's falcon. The Athenian had claimed that an English tourist had been killed by wildlife smugglers in the south of Rhodes island. Was Melissa's Andrew that man? If so, reflected Roxanne, pensively tapping her front teeth with a forefinger, was it likely that Melissa would be involved in the wildlife smuggling trade?

The picture was complete, her sense of wrong confirmed. It was time she talked to Nicholas *and* David, Roxanne decided, coming out of the lotus pose and jumping to her feet.

It wasn't until she was outside and down two of five steps that Roxanne realised she'd rushed out wearing only one sandal and must go back for the other.

'You can go,' Alexios said to Melissa, without looking too closely at her.

'Be at the mayor's office by ten this evening, no later,' Mr Zervos said, head down as he packed away his police notes.

It was a little after eleven when Melissa pushed through the grudging, silent group gathered outside Mrs Samouri's and walked out along the street, away from the main square. Although in her working clothes and shouldering her camera and camera bag, she did not want to join the happy crowds strolling round the fountain to the brash music of the island band. Her expulsion from Asteri had put her outside the day's festivities.

Unfair! The thought pounded in Melissa's head along with the band's drum, but there was nothing she could do. Nicholas and the townsfolk of Khora had made up their minds: she was guilty of smuggling. Even Alexios, the doctor who had treated her, seemed to have forgotten how she had been attacked. All her negatives and the knife and bracelet had been taken from her by the part-time policeman and postman, Mr Zervos. She was on her own; and now she had less than eleven hours to discover who Spiro was and whether he had murdered Andrew.

Walking on the shadowed side of the alley, Melissa was aware of hard eyes staring, of glares from villagers on the street, from windows above her. Aware of whispers and pointing fingers, of hands thrusting towards her palm-out in the Greek gesture of offensive denial. She was the foreigner who had betrayed them. Ari Pindaros might destroy their mountain for his own gain, but he at least would give them a choice. And he was Greek, and a man.

Melissa had reached the long steps running down to the harbour. The road to Kemi grew out of the harbour road. If she wanted to go there, she would have to go down the steps and pass near the café where Katherine would still be enjoying her breakfast.

She had no choice, Melissa thought, staring down the white steps. Kemi was where Andreas and Manoli would be today. She'd found the knife and the bracelet on the Khora-Kemi track. Kemi was her only sure lead.

Farther down the steps there was a flash of blonde hair as Zoe and Ari Pindaros came out of a side alley. The millionaire must have decided to spend St George's Day with the people, thought Melissa, not really interested in Pindaros' movements. There was nothing more she could do to stop Pindaros Bauxite's plans for Asteri. Nicholas didn't trust her any more.

Sensing someone watching them, Zoe stopped and turned. Seeing Melissa she detached herself from Pindaros and walked up four steps. Sunlight emphasised the shiny lipgloss of her pursed little mouth.

'I'm surprised they let you out. Mayor Niko's soft.' Zoe lunged a step closer. 'Still hung round with cameras? But there's no sculptor to worry about today, is there?'

Clearly, her exclusion as a model still rankled; Zoe's usually soft voice was loud. People had begun looking out of their windows at the two women. Down in the harbour, Katherine's shadow, Bailey, came flitting out of a knot of bystanders. It was time for her to leave, thought Melissa.

'Excuse me.' She moved to go past Zoe.

Unexpectedly, the woman grabbed at the

strap of her camera. 'What are you trying to prove?' Zoe demanded, dragging at the strap, almost tearing the camera off Melissa's shoulder.

'Let go of that!' Alarmed for her equipment, Melissa pushed Zoe off; perhaps a little too firmly as the blonde teetered down a step and then cannoned into a house wall, knocking her sun-glasses off her nose.

Appalled, Melissa bobbed down to retrieve Zoe's fallen glasses. 'I'm really sorry,' she was saying, holding out the sun-glasses as a peace offering, 'But you really mustn't snatch at my gear like that —'

'Give those to me.' Pindaros had stalked up the steps and now tore the sun-glasses from Melissa's fingers. 'Don't you touch her!' he warned grimly as Zoe straightened up, grimacing with pain. Melissa backed away rapidly as the Greek went to Zoe, speaking softly to her as he gently brushed her clothes. They went off together down the steps, Pindaros with an arm around Zoe's shoulders, attentive only to her except for a single killing stare at Melissa.

'It was an accident. I didn't mean her to —' Melissa was still trying to apologise and explain when a sharp stabbing pain low in her spine made her break off. Hearing the pebble clatter and bounce away down the steps, she swung round.

'Katáskopo! Katáskopo!' A group of children had appeared and were ranged above her in a semicircle a dozen steps away. The eldest, a ten-year-old black-haired boy, lunged down to grab another stone from amongst the litter of pebbles and dust lying in the corner where the step met the wall.

'Turkish spy!' he yelled in Greek, a call instantly taken up as a chant by his half-dozen satellites. *'Katáskopo tourkikó!'*

In the house above Melissa, a window opened and two women leaned out to watch. Neither shouted as the ten-year-old made to throw the stone into her face.

Calmly, Melissa lifted her camera to her eye and focused. She snapped the shot as the child swung back his arm. Bracing herself for a sore head, or, worse, a smashed lens, she winced as a sharp piece of grit exploded against her legs, grazing her shin. At the final instant the boy had aimed low.

'Again!' a girl shrieked.

From the open window above Melissa, a woman blew a cloud of cigarette smoke into the fretful morning air. She had heavy features and a long plait of shining dark hair. Melissa recognised her from the public meeting as the wife of Andreas the shepherd. Beside her was Popi, Andreas' mistress, her face expressionless as her dark eyes met Melissa's.

At the edge of her vision Melissa spotted Stella standing on a house step, also looking up at Popi and Andreas' wife, but then Stella lowered her head and walked away into the shadows.

The lad squatted down for a third missile. Melissa raised her camera again. 'Come on, then, little boy,' she goaded, determined not to be bested by a bunch of kids.

The boy froze at the insult. The young children danced forward and then back, daring and jeering but never quite managing to egg each other on. A step at a time, Melissa backed away, never taking her eyes or her camera lens off the leader.

Suddenly, like startled wild sheep, the boy and his gang careered off in different directions, scrambling down side alleys and over walls. Melissa snapped the ten-year-old lunging straight past her at an incredible rate down the long steps towards the sparkling blue harbour.

'You are no longer welcome at my house,' called Popi from above. United in joint displeasure both Popi, Andreas' lover, and Andreas' wife withdrew and the shutters closed.

Melissa swallowed, checked again that her lens had not been damaged, and clicked on the camera's lens cap.

'That's her,' said a woman speaking Greek behind her. 'That's the foreigner who sells our flowers to the Turks.'

Melissa's head jerked up at the lie, just as Ari Pindaros came striding past her, smiling at her discomfort.

'You know that's not true!' she protested to the millionaire as he passed.

Pindaros shrugged. 'What do I know?' he said, and continued on his way, heading for the mayor's office.

Someone, by malice or by accident, had started this rumour but Pindaros could have killed it. By saying nothing he left Melissa floundering. More men and women had emerged out of the St George's Day crowds to point and accuse.

'You've stolen our flowers!'

'Sold them!'

'After telling us we shouldn't.'

'They come and pretend that they want to help . . .'

'More that she helped herself!'

People began closing in on Melissa, coming up to the bottom of the steps. The wind rattled the opening doors as men and women emerged from houses above her. In the bay the waves were flecked with angry white tops, mirrored above in a sky no longer blue but big with white clouds.

Suddenly an English voice, raised above the growing mutter of the crowd. 'What's going on?'

Taller and broader than most, David pushed through bystanders. He had landed his boat in Khora harbour and no one had noticed, but now his intervention was not welcome. 'Keep out of this, *Turkish* Gordon!' bawled one man. 'This isn't any of your business!'

'I'll decide what's my concern and what isn't,' answered David, coming to stand beside Melissa. Facing the mob, he asked in English without looking at her, 'You all right?'

'I'm fine,' Melissa answered briefly, intensely grateful and relieved at David's intervention but aware that at any moment the situation could turn ugly. 'We'd better get out of here.'

Conscious of David shielding her with his body, Melissa turned to walk up the steps. At the rim of her eye she caught a movement and yelled, stumbling aside. David was struggling with a Greek fisherman. There was the unmistakable flash of a knife striking from the seaman's fist.

'Drop it or I shoot!' shouted a clear young voice in Greek.

As the knife went clattering down the steps Roxanne burst out of the crowd to recover it. Throwing the blade out into the harbour, she mounted the steps. 'Ghiorghio,' she said sternly, addressing the man who had lurched forward at Melissa, 'this is your name day, the day of your saint.'

Shamed into silence by a girl, the fisherman stared at his boots. For a moment, no one wanted to look at each other.

'Thanks,' said Melissa softly to David and Roxanne.

Roxanne nodded. 'Please go now,' she said, indicating a way through the shuffling mass of islanders.

Even though he had sensed this in her, David could hardly believe it. Speaking in Greek, Roxanne's manner was older, her natural reserve transformed from charming shyness into a formidable composure. She stood on the steps, tall and slim, armed with nothing but fearlessness. She had no gun, yet it was as if Roxanne considered it impossible that any should disobey her. Self-contained, she scarcely looked at him.

Melissa, wisely, had already gone.

The idiot had certainly had too much to drink, Katherine reflected, when a few moments later Bailey came bustling briefcase in hand, to her harbour-side breakfast table with news of the confrontation. A volatile race, these Greeks, and prone to excess. Zoe had just gone scuttling back to see what was happening, although if Melissa had gone the play was surely over, and right now she'd not the time to consider David.

'Any sign yet of Sir Oliver?' she asked Bailey.

The Australian shook his head. As he opened his mouth to reply, a phone buzzed in his suit pocket. Lifting his briefcase onto a chair, Bailey took a small grey receiver from his pocket, put it to his ear and listened for a few minutes.

Snapping down the phone aerial he said quietly to Katherine, 'Cargo's running late. Problems with Customs. Not the usual contacts.'

Katherine exhaled deeply with frustration.

'As well Sir O isn't here,' said Bailey.

Considering that remark unworthy of an answer, Katherine looked across the harbour and its spill of little bobbing boats towards the large gardens at the other side of Khora bay. As her large green eyes scanned the harbour road she stiffened. 'Where's *she* off to?' she demanded sharply.

'Miss Haye can't do much now.'

'An unparanoid Bailey, that makes a

change,' answered Katherine, fingers tapping impatiently on her champagne glass. Suddenly she sat back in her chair. 'Well, I suppose you're right,' she conceded. 'Just every time I see those cameras of hers winking in my direction —' Katherine broke off. 'Look at that sky!'

'My God,' muttered Bailey. From a bright, faintly breezy morning the day had suddenly gone dark. On the jetty and along the front, people were scrambling madly to secure boats in the choppy harbour. Out at sea a waterspout gushed and tumbled, light against the greater blackness.

Spiro and Sir Oliver's special item were out in this.

'Maybe they'll have to dock where they can,' said Bailey, eyes screwed tight against the rising wind. The café owner was scooping tables indoors. Everyone was scattering.

Bailey caught hold of Katherine's shoulder. 'Time to get inside,' he said, as a cold blast of air ripped through Khora's streets and churned the steepling sea.

'No!' Katherine's chilled fingers tightened hard on the cold glass. It wasn't possible, a storm just wasn't possible. There'd been no warning, no local reports, no signs.

It was all going wrong, and her enemy was out there. Melissa Haye might, after all, see the smugglers land at Kemi. She had her cameras with her: she would be able to record everything.

'This can't happen to me,' Katherine protested, as a deluge of hard cold rain poured over her and her second breakfast coffee of the morning. 'This just isn't possible!'

Chapter 32

The last thing David saw before the rains hit him was the brave toss of blonde hair. The last thing he thought of before the storm came bellowing down the steps of Khora harbour and almost knocked him off his feet was the soft, living touch of Melissa's lips on his skin.

On Antasteri it had been, only the day before. She had kissed him so lightly, an impulsive happy gesture, because she was glad he had told Ari Pindaros he supported ASPW. A generous, joyous kiss, tingling on the memory, teasing in its brevity, promising in its warmth. Yet today, contradicting all of this, Melissa stood condemned as a wildlife smuggler.

David's features set in totem-pole solemnity. He had not thought Katherine devious either, and yet, according to Roxanne, *she* had conspired to blow apart Lykimi beach.

'All women are devious sometimes, you prat,' David murmured under his breath as his hand rose to his mouth, touching his own lips as he remembered Melissa's. He regretted now that he'd been so conventional, that he'd not done what he wanted: locked the blonde in his arms and kissed her without mercy.

David cursed as the gale broke round him and the cloudburst pelted his broad shoulders and back. Inside his head, he felt the storm's darkness and confusion: the weather matched his mood.

'David!' He flung his head up, squinting through the needles of water, but could see no more. Along the jetty, festive bunting flapped in ruins; a few stragglers clumsily slopped and stumbled off the cobbles towards shelter. Below in the bay the wave tops turned green then grey then blue, rainbowing over boat sterns, smashing into ship lights and tearing rigging. Manoli's antique ferry was ploughing and arching on the harbour mole, scraping and squealing. The wind plucked at David, sucking under his feet and between his legs, seeking any chink to get in and under, throw him off balance.

Fighting to hold his footing on the final steps, David suddenly laughed out loud and heartily, his mood flipping over from dark to light as, enchanted by the storm, he entered a world he usually only knew when he was working at full steam, wild and terrible and splendid.

A foot stamped hard on his. 'David, listen!' Roxanne yelled again — the rain had peeled off all of her reserve and quietness to show fully the strength beneath. 'Katherine's storm-crazy!' Wasting no more breath, Roxanne pointed to the café.

Standing sentinel by the last overturned table, Katherine Hopkins, his Venus, was utterly oblivious to Bailey's attempts to coax her from the spot. Her face was blurred by the pounding rain, but she was mouthing something, her mouth moving in coarse hard angles.

Aware of Roxanne whirling off to shepherd an elderly widow from the harbour front, David sprang down the steps, moving now with the gale. Buoyed by it, he seemed almost to float: he felt only the inky black mud crawling up his trouser legs. Away in his eye corner a conch shell, flicked from a wall by the gale, splintered over the cobbles.

In the midst of the flapping, noisy harbour Katherine remained fixed, stupid to danger, although her companion Bailey was trying to reason with her, shaking her arm and telling her to come on. It was as though, David thought, closing on them, that Katherine could not admit that here was something over which she had no control.

'David!'

Roxanne. Hair rising on his scalp, David twisted round to see a tall figure sprinting from a doorway, ignoring the calls of alarm from the men and women within the house.

She bawled at him in Greek, gesturing, but David had already heard it himself: the ghastly suck and splashing of a waterspout as it funnelled ashore, spiralling everything out of its path like so many children's spinning tops.

Katherine, classic features lit by the baleful glamour of the approaching waterspout, and Bailey beside her, seemed rooted to the spot. Even the flashes of lightning and the crack of thunder overhead could not break their mesmerised attention as the whipping column of spray gyrated nearer.

David reached Katherine and dragged her sideways, away from the table, down into the corner under the shutters where Melissa had once left her rucksack. Pushing Katherine down, David turned to help Bailey, but Roxanne had shoulder-charged him and the man came tumbling down, followed by the American girl. They huddled together as the spout roared past, bursting apart in a shattering of spray as it reached the steps.

A shower of torn bunting lashed down David's back and he heard Roxanne cry out as the coloured streamers struck her too.

Then there was only the sound of rain.

David wetted his salty lips. 'It's passing,' he said to her.

Somewhere sheltered beneath him, coiled and cramped, Katherine squirmed uncomfortably, but David, although he had saved her, glanced at Roxanne again. Her jeans and tee-shirt had been plastered by the deluge to every line and fragile curve of her strong, rangy body, but the rain had been unable to dampen down the gilts of her hair.

'Jesus!' exclaimed Bailey, raising his head and uncoiling a little from his crouch. 'You get many of those things?'

'Some,' said David, thinking how big Roxanne's stormy brown eyes were as she grinned at him. They both knew how lucky they'd been.

Pinned half beneath him, Katherine suddenly shuddered.

She was just a little shaken up, not shocked, thought Roxanne, as David and Bailey's attention instantly turned to Katherine, but no doubt the Englishwoman would make the most of her opportunity to be fussed over. Anyway, it meant that any chance for Roxanne to talk to David about Melissa and Andrew was effectively lost: she wasn't going to say anything whilst Bailey was about.

Now, thankful that the man's attention was fixed on his boss, Roxanne scrambled to her feet, away from the crouching David and the dishevelled Katherine. Nicholas she knew would from now on be constantly on call to deal with the aftermath of the cloudburst: no chance to speak to him, then, either. She stepped back into the heavy sticky rain, the last dregs of the cloudburst, and was herself instantly claimed by the boy Mikhalaki.

'Roxanne! Dr Alexios and Eleni need you at the surgery!'

'Okay,' she said, tearing her eyes away from Katherine and David, Katherine who was now sitting propped against the house wall and looking beautifully pale and interesting. 'I'll be right there.'

Chapter 33

Katherine wanted to return to the Villa Michelangelo as quickly as possible, yet in this weather no one was going anywhere. David's Rolls was heavy and robust enough to survive the battering gusts of wind, and to collect his car from its garage at the Villa Rodin, David borrowed Roxanne's bike.

Taking a break from graze and bruise duty, Roxanne saw him off along the Khora-Petra road, her heart bumping joyously as she saw the ridiculous picture a six-foot-plus former Olympic athlete made on a pink teenage bike plastered with Greek football stickers.

'Watch out for lightning,' she said seriously.

'If I hear thunder I'll leave the bike by the roadside and run, but the storm's passing now.' The rain was no longer pounding onto their heads or streaming down their cheeks and faces. Looking at Roxanne in a steady soft rain reminiscent of spring drizzle in England, David squirmed slightly on the seat. Increasingly whenever Roxanne was solemn he found himself tempted to kiss her: those stormy brown eyes drew him. This, in spite of his tangled feelings for Melissa, his admiration for Katherine. The bike-frame creaked.

'I won't laugh till you're out of sight,' said Roxanne, unkind to his dignity but appealing to his sense of humour.

David, glad she did not read his mind, glared at her in relief. 'Have you any notion of how foolish I feel on this contraption?'

The ebbing wind howled and snagged at the sodden handkerchief in his jacket pocket. Roxanne grinned, rain bouncing off her high cheekbones.

'Be glad you're not a shepherd,' she said. Crowded with frightened sheep and goats, a band and scores of villagers, Khora's main square was in tumult. Even as she spoke, Roxanne could hear through the dying wind a shred of her father's roar as he hollered yet again for calm.

David scowled down at the slender metal frame between his legs. 'Feel like a troll perched on a safety-pin,' he mumbled.

'Trolls are just fine with me.' Roxanne repeated her warning against lightning then turned and hurried away, looking round once to see David hanging low over the handlebars in a pose reminiscent of his swimming days, pedalling with a fast even beat towards Petra.

By the time David dropped Katherine and Bailey off in his blue Rolls at the Villa Michelangelo, the piercing gale was over.

'What's more, the cargo's secure at the Turkish base,' Bailey told Katherine and Sir Oliver a few moments later as the three of them relaxed on couches in the hidden courtyard of the Villa Michelangelo. Sir Oliver, it turned out, had never left Petra beach: the gale had blown up before he set out.

'Very thankful I was, too, my dear,' Sir Oliver now confessed to Katherine as, stretching out a bare, hairy forearm, he helped himself to a whisky from the decanter and glasses set on the table in front of his couch. 'But that's nothing to the relief of knowing my kitty's quite safe.' His nose and cheeks, caught by the sun, glowed against the tasteful wall paintings.

Inwardly approving of how warm and dry the room was, considering that its central portion was open to the sky, Katherine sipped her own drink. Shifting on her silken couch, comfortable in her freshly changed kimono, she too was relieved, if not exactly overjoyed, to see Sir Oliver. David had been extremely attentive on their drive over, but the sight of her client's high-coloured, cheery face had been enough to send the sculptor off at a brisk walk back to Khora. At Katherine's smiling insistence that they should join the St George's Day revels, the staff of the Villa Michelangelo — including the cook — had soon after followed their master.

Business should come before pleasure, Katherine now thought. Bearing that in mind she raised her head to Bailey, standing as usual before his couch — Bailey seemed to regard lying down in public as the height of decadence.

'Are you going to try contacting Spiro again?' she asked, nodding to the inner front pocket of Bailey's brown suit. Sir Oliver was dressed for the St George's Day festivities in short-sleeved shirt, light khaki trousers and sandals, but Bailey, being Bailey, had not changed. It did mean, however, that he had somewhere to slip his portable phone.

Bailey's hand hovered towards his left breast. 'Spiro may not want to be overheard right now. And this thing may not be secure. I'll have to use the guest computer.'

Sir Oliver heaved himself off his couch. 'Never mind that, man,' he said briskly, his former genial manner hardening as he addressed a male employee. 'I have to talk to him. This delay's going to mean changes in feeding patterns.'

Dead cargo was no good to Katherine, either. Instantly all attention, she motioned to Bailey to begin.

One of the conveniences of calling Spiro by electronic mail, thought Bailey as he logged in, was that the information was protected against all but the more sophisticated computer operators. No one on Asteri, not even Nicholas, had the necessary knowledge to eavesdrop on the news which appeared a few moments later on the screen.

Spiro was still in a Turkish port. The cargo, doped for the journey, had come round in the delay and had just been fed. According to local weather reports, the cloudburst had already spent itself: Spiro expected to set out in less than three hours. By late evening he, his men and their cargo would be at the rendezvous point at Asteri, where there need be no change of plan — the St George's Day celebrations would still be going on and would provide excellent cover. Spiro looked forward to a profitable conclusion of their deal.

Staring at the screen, Katherine smiled. Things were once more moving according to plan.

Sir Oliver pushed Bailey away from the

laptop computer and launched into a question and answer session with Spiro. After watching the screen closely throughout the interrogation — it was vital to ensure the creature's well-being — Katherine slipped away into the central garden courtyard before Sir Oliver finished and Bailey stepped in to delete the incriminating messages.

As she expected, Bailey joined her a moment later in the warming, herb-scented space. Both pretended to watch a bee busy amongst the newly opened hibiscus flowers.

'Melissa Haye will have a long wait at Kemi,' said Katherine.

'She'll be gone before Spiro docks.'

Nothing could be allowed to interfere with this transaction, thought Katherine: too much money was at stake. And not only money, if they were exposed. She folded her arms across her slender middle. Two years since Andrew Thornhill's death: would another 'accident' in a Greek island be too suspicious?

'Well, in case she hasn't, Bailey, just take care of it, would you?'

Chapter 34

It was long after eight in the evening and Khora was in festival mood. The storm was long gone, the evening soft, the cleaning up in the harbour over. Now people were settling down to celebrate the night of St George's Day around spitting pinewood bonfires on the jetty, by the fountain, and in the square of Khora's second small church — the one with the blue dome. The smell of petrol used to light the bonfires was heavy in the air, mingling slickly with mutton crackling on braziers. Bagpipes and lyras vied with each other in the main square outside Nicholas' office. Any other night, thought Nicholas, and he would have joined the dancers, kicked off his trainers and spun and stepped barefoot.

Not tonight. Not when in only four hours' time he would have to escort Melissa from Asteri in disgrace.

Nicholas put his fist to his mouth, grinding the bristles of his moustache harshly against his top lip. He'd seen the stuff in Melissa's rooms: Zervos said it was genuine, but still he did not believe it. His mind rang like a hollow empty shell. Nothing, not concern for Roxanne, nor satisfaction in seeing David Gordon earlier in the day pitching in to help clear the storm-tossed flotsam from the harbour, nor curiosity about Katherine — where she was, what she was doing — was enough to fill the emptiness.

Get off the personal track, Nicholas told himself, seizing a paper at his desk and trying to focus on that. Until fifteen minutes ago he'd been out of the office, making sure of the generators, the water supply, the safety of older houses. Setting up beds in the schoolhouse for those who didn't want the trek back over the mountain after a deluge, when flash-flooding might have drowned half the usual tracks. Now it was time to stop being an active mayor and start being a politician. In fifty minutes Ari Pindaros was due to see him, and Nicholas had no more debts to call in or tricks to pull.

Pindaros had given him Lykimi beach because of old history between them, unknown to any but the two men and a few minor embassy staff — Bailey, in spite of Katherine's injunction that he should find out what favour the head of Pindaros Bauxite owed the mayor of Asteri, had not turned up any details of the event.

432

Three years ago Nicholas had saved the older man from major embarrassment at a diplomat's house in the States where, thanks to a cocktail of cold-cure drugs and alcohol, Pindaros was blundering into everything and everybody. Before a fellow Greek could be made the butt of polite jokes, Nicholas had steered the taller man to a seat and grabbed him several coffees until Pindaros came out of his daze. A trifling matter, to be sure, but mortifying to a man as conscious of image as Ari Pindaros. The incident, taken with threats of bad publicity over the millionaire's plans to dynamite Lykimi beach, had been more than enough for Nicholas to extract a favour in return.

Tonight, however, both sides were even. Ari was bringing Zoe with him, and Nicholas anticipated a tough meeting. Yet, try as he might, he couldn't concentrate on issues. Not even the wildlife smugglers. By ten o'clock, Melissa would be out of his life. And that hurt.

It didn't matter that he'd known her only a month or so. Beside her, other women were less engaging, even Katherine Hopkins. His evening with Katherine had been one of the most stimulating in his adult life, laced with that kind of sexual tension which made every conversation, every glance, every movement, special and charged with meaning. Exciting, yes, stimulating, most definitely. But . . . ?

Katherine as an old woman: pinned and tucked, bright, dynamic, domineering. Wanting nothing but his wit and money and sexual all.

Melissa as an old lady. Trekking to Africa, or Antarctica or the moon with that enthusiastic gleam in her keen brown eyes, nagging him to come along, pattering at him about the elephants or penguins or moon-rocks. Probably about his weight too by then, and his opinions on Death Row. And look — had he seen that amazing yellow seahorse?

He couldn't believe Melissa sold seahorses to be left to suffocate slowly, dried, ground up and packaged. It flew in the face of everything else she was or hoped to be — and nobody, Nicholas acknowledged grimly, was that good at lying.

Nicholas spun out of his chair and stalked over to the back window. Chloe yapped at him from her basket. 'Stay down!' he rapped back at her, recollecting how his dog liked Melissa but wasn't over-keen on Katherine. Neither was Roxanne. Katherine seemed to have a knack of acquiring female adversaries.

Melissa and Katherine were more than that. Melissa claimed that Katherine was her enemy, that she was behind both the newspaper reports and the documents and illegal fur coat found at Mrs Samouri's flat. Yet where was Melissa's proof? And how much notice should he, as mayor of Asteri, take of such accusations?

Nicholas breathed heavily on the dusty glass, hearing Chloe stand up and start turning round and round in her basket. The glare from the bonfire in the main square shimmered on the left-hand side of the window; he could see nothing else out there at street level. Above the roof tops the sky had hung a necklace of clouds around Asteri mountain which ran all the way down into the forest. Signs of more bad weather if the wind rose from the south again.

Nicholas shrugged. The townsfolk dancing and drinking outside could see the looming clouds as well as he could. None of the fishermen were out tonight. He dismissed the weather for the moment and continued to consider Melissa and Katherine.

'Personally, I just don't know,' he said aloud, resting his chin on the cold window ledge. Katherine had not mentioned Melissa at all during their evening together, whereas Melissa seemingly could not stop yakking about her rival. 'You think Melissa's a bitch?' he asked Chloe.

Chloe was still going round and round, not

settling. She was only this unhappy when there was a really big storm brewing. Frowning, Nicholas stepped back from the window, yanked open a desk drawer and found the radio. Tuning to the Greek, then the Turkish stations, he listened for several minutes for any weather reports, head bent low over the drawer.

'Can't you tell it's started to rain without the local forecast?'

Nicholas switched the radio off. 'I'd like to know how long it's going to last,' he replied, rising to his feet.

He'd expected to find Pindaros smirking at him, but the millionaire's face was grave. 'Good evening,' said Nicholas, now hearing the steady pounding of water on the flags outside, 'Zoe dancing one last Sta Tria?'

A wind sighed outside the outer office door and Chloe growled, her neck ruff stiffening. Somewhere off in the square youths were splashing in the fountain, men and women still laughing and talking in spite of the downpour, the bonfire hissing and crackling.

'I'd hoped to find Zoe in here,' said Pindaros slowly, after looking back over one shoulder.

Both men started slightly as under the office window a bagpipe squealed and droned down. Instead of defusing the growing tension, Nicholas sensed that the sudden uncanny sound had only increased it. 'I assumed Zoe was with you,' he said gruffly.

'I've not seen her for the last ten minutes. Since the rain started.'

Out in the square the wind gusted suddenly stronger, catching a child's toy which went rattling away up an alley, the boy starting after it wailing and his mother dashing after him. The sound of feet running down the steps towards the harbour came as men began breaking from the crowd to make sure their boats were still secure.

'Does Zoe know anyone here?' asked Nicholas, thinking about Melissa, then Roxanne.

A knock on the inner office door and Alexios came in, dripping water. 'I've sent Roxanne home with Zervos,' he said. Then, 'There's something you need to see, Niko, out in one of the derelict houses.'

Behind Alexios appeared the priest. He looked straight at Ari Pindaros, then to Alexios. 'I will stay here.'

'Very well, Father.' There was nothing else to say. Following Alexios, Nicholas stepped out into the dark rain.

'It's getting worse!' shouted Alexios, as they ploughed through the now rapidly diminishing crowds towards the plane tree.

'No one will be able to get off Asteri tonight!'

Why had the doctor said that? thought Nicholas. 'Hurry!' he muttered through clenched teeth, as Alexios turned down Mrs Samouri's alley and then again down a smaller street, skidding on the slippery pebbles. Roxanne was safe, he had to remember: his child was safe.

'Here.' Alexios shone a torch into a tiny house, always a hovel, now roofless and stripped. A figure sprawled over a pile of rubble, face down, both arms flung out as though reaching for something. Everywhere around the head was a thick dark liquid which Nicholas knew was neither rain nor mud. The matted hair was blonde.

Nicholas stopped dead. Rigid with fear.

Alexios looked back at him. 'It's not her,' he said softly.

Nicholas closed his eyes, opened them. 'How did she die?'

'Clubbed down from behind with a chunk of concrete. A single blow. Fractured her skull.' Alexios too seemed reluctant to go closer.

'You're sure she didn't fall and strike her head?'

'The wound is too deep for that. No, Zoe was attacked.'

'Pindaros mustn't see her like this.' Now,

with the knowledge that the figure was not Melissa, Nicholas found he could move. He walked forward, knelt and brushed the blonde hair back from Zoe's face. Her eyes were open, her mouth frozen in a shout of agony.

Nicholas covered his own mouth. After a moment he looked up at Alexios. 'What needs to be done?' he demanded, his voice cracking for an instant, then, 'Let's get this over.'

Chapter 35

Melissa was threading her way across the fields towards Kemi, thinking hard about a conversation held a few hours earlier with Stella.

Stella, dressed in her usual black, with a small pack and water-bottle on one shoulder and an air-rifle tied with a piece of string slung over the other, had appeared from the oak woods with her goats. She soon caught up with Melissa.

'Good afternoon,' she said in Greek, raising her staff. 'It is a pity you could not keep the knife and the bracelet: they were the only things I could give you.'

Not even attempting to disguise her astonishment — she sensed that Stella would be disappointed and less forthcoming if she did — Melissa flipped off her storm-hood. *'Kalispéra,'* she replied, wondering what was coming next.

Acknowledging Melissa's return greeting with a blink of her black eyes, Stella said, 'We must get out of sight off the road. Follow me, please,' and glided on down the track away from the Villa Elysion towards Kemi, her few goats trailing after her.

For all that Stella moved with the ease and grace of an adder, she did not linger. Melissa found further questions impossible as she hurried to keep up. They walked another two hundred metres towards Asteri's south-east point, but when the track turned to cut the corner of the point, Stella kept going.

She stopped at a tiny shrine high on the cliff overlooking the sea to both east and west, motioning to Melissa to sit.

'Cold mutton sandwiches, water and raisins: scarcely a feast for a saint's day, but a fire here would provoke too much interest,' she said, producing two neat newspaper parcels from her pack and taking the water-bottle from her shoulders. She swept her free arm towards the wide blue water. 'Good place to watch ships from here. But enough of that. I would like to help you find Spiro. I want very much to see him in prison.'

Melissa almost dropped her parcel. Staring up at the widow she could only manage, 'Can you explain a little more? I don't really understand what you're talking about.'

'No!' Stella interrupted, settling down beside Melissa and ripping open her newspaper. 'I said we should speak again: this is the only chance I've had to keep my promise,

441

and we don't have that much time. So don't pretend you've never heard of Spiro: he is the reason you have to leave tonight.'

'Why should my going matter to you?'

'It doesn't,' answered Stella bluntly, her left cheek full of pitta and mutton, 'But I see Spiro's hand in it. Him I want. He's taking Manoli from me: stuffing a poor ferryman's head full of nonsense about money and young girls. We have a private under-standing, Manoli and I. He's too old to be a playboy.'

'Or a smuggler,' added Melissa, seeing Stella with new eyes. 'So you were Nicholas' source for the tip-off.' She had assumed when Nick had mentioned 'the guy' that his informant was male, not allowing for his American slang — or male chauvinism.

Stella nodded. 'I told mayor Niko: "Get Manoli out of it before he kills himself." '

'Or anyone else.' Melissa stared at her un-touched sandwich, thinking that no wonder Nicholas had been alarmed at her possibly revealing too much on Manoli's ferry. 'So how is Manoli involved?' she asked, recalling the time when the ferryman had appeared to be looking out for her at Khora, and possibly delaying her until Bailey and Katherine ap-peared. Yet it seemed unlikely that Manoli would deal with Katherine, at least directly.

442

Stella swilled the last of her sandwich down with a gulp of water. Around her the goats nibbled the sparse cliffside vegetation, their bells chiming faintly above the soft swish of the sea below. Stella wiped her mouth with a black sleeve and spoke.

'Three months ago, a man comes to Manoli in Rhodes: he wants a messenger, a lookout, a few local people. He calls himself Spiro, and he offers a great deal of money. Manoli told me this. I asked him then, "What does this Spiro do?" Manoli said Spiro smuggles cigarettes, and he wants to use Asteri for a few runs. Later, Manoli tells me the cargo is animals. By now I'm getting uneasy about the business. He tells me more, piece by piece — he knows I won't breathe a word to anyone. But for this last order I go talk to mayor Niko.'

'Spiro's last order?' Melissa was not happy with any of this account: Stella's motives seemed contradictory. 'Why bother saying anything, if it's the last one?'

'Manoli's kept talking about joining Spiro full-time on the mainland, or maybe in Italy or Spain.' Stella shook her head. 'I didn't like that, but didn't take much notice till two months ago, when I found the knife and bracelet in his things. That showed me Spiro was serious in keeping Manoli happy and maybe too in taking him away from Asteri.'

'So you went to the mayor.'

'Not straightaway,' Stella admitted. 'Not till Manoli started making excuses about not seeing me.'

Melissa gazed at the older woman steadily, and Stella flushed.

'Do you think this is easy, admitting such matters to a stranger? But now mayor Niko's business is in trouble —'

'Is it?' Painfully aware that she was outside the chattering classes of Khora, Melissa was oddly hurt that Nicholas had not told her this himself.

Stella thrust aside a lop-eared goat and leaned back against the shrine. 'That's what people are saying in Khora,' she responded. 'The man has money problems, big trouble! I don't trust a man who can be bought.'

'But Nicholas has factories in America,' said Melissa reasonably. 'Spiro would need a great deal of money to bribe him.'

'Spiro is only part of a chain. His bosses have money.'

'Are you sure?' Melissa tried to keep her voice casual. 'Do you know who they are?'

Stella shook her head. 'Manoli only speaks of Spiro — no one else. Not even the others who are involved from this island.'

'Have you ever seen Spiro?'

'Not to my knowledge.'

'Has Manoli ever mentioned what he's like?'

'Not to me.'

Melissa decided to be direct. 'Popi the seamstress told me mayor Niko was a smuggler. Could he be Spiro?' She waited, taking a quick bite from her sandwich, which tasted like rubber in her mouth, her face showing nothing of her inner confusion.

'Why do you think I left the knife and bracelet for you to find? I don't trust mayor Niko any more.'

Nicholas as Spiro. The idea produced an anguish so intense that for a moment Melissa could not speak. If Nicholas were Spiro then he had certainly had a hand in Andrew's murder. She waited for the saving anger to come, but felt only pain.

'I'm under suspicion of smuggling,' she reminded Stella, forcing herself to speak. 'That's why I'm having to leave Asteri to-night.'

'The very day the big shipment comes into Kemi: which should please Spiro very much,' said Stella. 'But even without that I know you are honest. Because Miss Hopkins is clearly Spiro's boss.

'People do not notice widows,' Stella went on, in Melissa's thunderstruck silence. 'Last night I see mayor Niko return from Antasteri with his daughter and her, Miss Hopkins. Later, when I am pasturing my goats around Khora I see Miss Hopkins' manservant slipping into your flat at Mrs Samouri's. I go down to the harbour where Manoli has heard on the radio that an unmarked dinghy has been found on the beach near to the convent: fishermen ask each other if the boat belongs to them. Manoli thinks of you.' Stella's voice hardened. 'He wonders if you have escaped from Turkish Gordon. I tell him not to be stupid. He tells me he's not coming to the church service for St George. I don't go, either: instead I take the only road from Khora to the west of Asteri and see if you are coming that way.

'So I see the men taking their braziers down to Kemi. They do not see me, a woman in black: nobody ever notices widows. I leave the knife and bracelet on the track and hide behind a wall. I watch you pick them up. I wait until Manoli passes my wall — you and he must have missed each other by only a few paces — and then I go back to Khora.' Stella paused, rubbing her knees with a hand. 'That bracelet was meant for you once, wasn't it? I mean the name and the seahorse charms — even Manoli made those connections.'

Melissa swallowed. 'I believe so,' she said quietly.

'A lover's gift, yes? But then perhaps you fell out —'

'No!' Melissa surprised herself with her vehemence. 'No,' she said again. 'Andrew . . . He's dead now.'

'Ah! Now I remember: from a cliff — Manoli said.' Stella stopped rubbing her knees and looked across at Melissa, closely scrutinising the younger woman's face. 'You think maybe Spiro killed your man?'

And if Nicholas is Spiro — Melissa's stomach clenched in on itself as she could not finish the thought.

'I see you want revenge. But you must promise not to harm Manoli.'

'Me? Harm men armed with automatic rifles?' Melissa laughed out loud. 'What?' she demanded, catching sight of Stella's rugged face frozen in shock, 'Did he not tell you that? Manoli is involved in a dangerous, illegal enterprise — very dangerous. People like Spiro don't care about the safety of old ferrymen: all they want is the money.

'We'll all be lucky to get out of this in one piece,' Melissa added, 'but now you explain something to me.'

Since she had surprised Stella, Melissa wanted to follow up her advantage. Playing devil's advocate, she asked, 'Why do you suspect Miss Hopkins? An English business-woman and a smuggler who employs Greek fishermen and ferrymen — not an obvious connection.'

'Why not?' Proud of Manoli, Stella defiantly raised her chin. 'Asteri's waters are not easy to sail in bad weather: you need the local knowledge. You saw the storm earlier today?'

'I was in it.'

'Even for our fishermen it came like a dragon, without warning. But we know where to land. Strangers . . .' Stella threw up her hands. 'Many are wrecked even in Khora bay.'

'Still, it's a big step from Manoli to Katherine Hopkins.'

'Not to a middleman — not to Spiro.'

'But why her?' Persisted Melissa. 'Why not a Greek? Ari Pindaros, say?'

Stella laughed. 'Pindaros is like my Manoli: he likes blondes. I was blonde as a girl,' she added proudly, tossing her now gray-brown head. 'So no, I do not think it is Pindaros. Were you even a brunette, I would not think it was Pindaros. The Athenian has no contacts outside Greece except in mining. But that Miss Hopkins: she has stores in the whole of Europe and America, many rich customers. It was her man I saw going into your flat last night: he had a bag with him then, but not when he left.'

'Why did you not say this to the mayor?' The question burst from Melissa's lips. 'Or if not to him, the doctor, the priest? This would vindicate me!' Furious, Melissa hurled her sandwich over the cliff. 'You think this is a game? You saw this morning! I was stoned by a mob: almost knifed —'

'Is it not better this way, where your enemies think you are finished? Do you not know, Melissa, that you are now safer than before? English I cannot speak much, but to hear and understand — I follow a great deal. And no one sees me.' Stella snatched a handful of stiff black cloth, shook it. 'Even you look straight at me but do not notice who it is behind the widow's clothes. Without my goats I am nobody — why do you think I want to marry Manoli? Will you promise not to turn him in to the police?'

Refusing to be thrown by the sudden change of subject, or troubling to deny Stella's accusation that she'd never noticed her, Melissa shot back, 'What do I get in return?'

'Information. Where the shipment will land.' Stella threw her a slanting, shrewd glance. 'Manoli would not tell me where until yesterday morning.'

'But thanks to your dropping the knife and bracelet I already know it's going to be Kemi.'

'I know what time the shipment comes, the name of the ship making it. And where you'll be able to film in safety.'

'What about getting the cargo off Asteri?'

'That I do not know. Nor — and I would swear to this — does Manoli.'

Melissa rose to her feet. 'Then I give you my word.'

Now, still a little shaken as she recalled this encounter, Melissa strode on and ignored the gathering darkness.

Chapter 36

Nicholas had the unpleasant task of breaking the news of Zoe's death to Ari Pindaros. Haggard but unflinching, the Greek millionaire allowed Nicholas to escort him through the revellers in the bonfire-lit square to the tiny side chapel in Khora's main church where her body had been taken.

Pindaros knelt beside his lover, put his greying head down to the cold marble and silently wept.

Helpless, feeling a horrible relief that it was not Melissa lying there surrounded by candles, Nicholas watched the taller man's shoulders shudder. He made himself look at the body again. Blonde hair and the same height and of similar build — had the killer intended this victim or another? He touched Pindaros' arm.

'I'll make all the necessary arrangements,' he said after a long pause. The Rhodes police would want an autopsy, but for today Zoe could rest in the cool of the church, in the priest's care.

Pindaros stared at nothing. Nicholas

doubted that his words had even registered. Faced with that blank mask of shock and sorrow, he had not intruded with the usual questions: When and where had Pindaros last seen Zoe? Had Zoe any enemies? Who and why would anyone wish her harm? The full-time police had been summoned from Rhodes. Let them do the asking.

Backing away, Nicholas found the priest in the main body of the church preparing the service for the dead. A nod was exchanged between them, a silent promise that the priest would take care of Pindaros. Nicholas had other business on his mind, beginning with an unpleasant but necessary curtailment to the St George's Day revels.

Until the arrival of the Rhodes police, Mr Zervos was their representative. A few moments after Nicholas had finally succeeded in stopping all the dancers and musicians, and had made his grim announcement, Mr Zervos was busy in the main square taking statements. Asking people if they had seen Zoe; if she had talked or quarrelled with anyone; if they had seen anyone approach or follow her. Later tonight perhaps, after the midnight plane had landed, after Melissa had gone, the Rhodes police might institute a wider search for Zoe's killer.

After Melissa had gone. A sudden gust of evening air chilled Nicholas. Plucking his faded blue cap from his belt, he jammed it low over his eyes and hurried away from the murmuring crowds in the main square. Ignoring shouts from Roxanne and David, Nicholas strode off down the steps of Khora harbour.

He was finding it impossible to stop thinking of Zoe and Melissa. This morning, Melissa had claimed that she had been set up by Katherine. That Katherine was the controlling force behind the wildlife smugglers. If so, how might Katherine turn Zoe's murder to her advantage?

If he were a smuggler, reflected Nicholas, flicking his cap backwards off his forehead, he would most definitely be tempted to run a very special cargo tonight, into a small island made safer by tragedy, its people distracted from observing the unusual because a truly shocking event now commanded their attention.

But to murder someone, simply to provide cover? Was Katherine really so ruthless? And why, out of the whole of Asteri, would she strike out Zoe — her ally in the marina development on Kemi beach. Katherine was not one to waste a good contact, Nicholas admitted, shoulders hunching slightly as he recalled her sassy smiles and walk. Wasn't it more likely that Katherine probably had a more personal target in mind?

Forced at last to consider that question, Nicholas broke into a run.

David interrupted his chief of security over the portable phone. 'Get all your people together, Spiro, and get over here,' he repeated. 'We need as many men as possible for a search team whilst we can still see our fists in front of our faces.'

'OK, boss. Sure.' Even over the telephone, Spiro sounded disgruntled. Clearly, he hadn't expected the order, but had no choice but to comply.

'Very public-spirited,' remarked Nicholas sourly, recalling the moment when one of the Antasteri guards had threatened to fire a machine-gun burst across his ship. 'Ask them to bring along the heavy artillery.'

'This is a search party for Melissa,' David quietly reminded. Neither wanted to talk about the fact that a killer was still on the loose.

Nicholas pointed at a man armed with a World War Two handgun and snapped at him in Greek, 'Get that safety catch on!'

David slipped the phone into his jacket

pocket. 'Spiro knows what we need.'

'Right — I'm forgetting that he and his men searched for Melissa. Only they couldn't find her. And then of course there's those mysterious fishermen your team can't seem to stop from using Antasteri harbour. Real professional security. Let's hope, where Melissa's concerned, they do better second time around tonight.'

Unable to deny it, David's black eyes narrowed alarmingly as his temper strained on its leashes. 'No security's perfect,' he said, not wanting to admit that his present team were going to be given their notices, Spiro included.

Spiro, thought Roxanne. Standing silently in the shadows behind the small posse of ASPW men gathered outside Nicholas' house, she was keeping very quiet — although at the same time aggrieved that such measures should be necessary. As the bulk of the townsfolk gathered in the main square continued to exclaim and theorise over Zoe's murder, Roxanne thought of the wildlife smuggler. Spiro: a common Greek name, suitable for an alias. Surely no man would be foolish enough to use his own name in illegal business. Besides, her father would certainly have already checked David's Spiro out.

Every time the name Spiro was mentioned, his heart went into overdrive, reflected Nicholas, rolling his tensed shoulders. He glanced at Alexios stooped under a streetlight, healing hands tightened into fists. It was a relief to know that Alexios reacted in exactly the same way. ASPW had nothing bad on Gordon's head of security, but at the same time nothing good. Apart from his name and Australian passport, Spiro was a mystery.

Too obvious, concluded Nicholas, as he had done since first hearing of a guard called Spiro on Antasteri, when he had immediately summoned the man to his office. Off-duty, Spiro went to Rhodes Mandraki harbour to take in the cocktail bars. He was often seen there, including every night of the month when the smugglers had done their run into Petra beach. And the guns Spiro liked didn't fit with the ammunition clip Nicholas had found on Petra beach. However much he might dislike Spiro or his boss, Nicholas had to acknowledge that both men seemed pretty much above board.

Did he still dislike David Gordon? Nicholas was no longer sure. Today Gordon had helped in the clear-up after the storm, tonight he had joined the search team. Were those the actions of a concerned or a very cunning man, anxious to cover his tracks? Nicholas had half-suspected Gordon of wild-life smuggling — he had the men, the privacy and those cages, supposedly for nursing injured birds of prey. And Melissa had supplied a motive: 'Much can want more,' she had said, when they first discussed the sculptor. Yet seeing Gordon's puzzled, anxious look, seeing the man notice and smile at Roxanne's brutal stuffing of her hair under a black woollen cap, Nicholas didn't know what to think.

He cleared his throat. 'We'll need to start here in Khora,' he said. 'Even though she was seen making for Kemi, Melissa might have changed her mind and doubled back. Alexios and I will take the streets, talk to people, find out if anyone knows anything —'

'Particularly after this morning's piece of mischief,' David Gordon broke in.

'What?'

Nobody had told Nicholas of Melissa's being stoned in the street that morning. Even Roxanne had not dared.

In a few terse words, David explained. Listening, Nicholas felt not anger but a deep shame: his own people had done this. And Melissa was even more in danger.

'The rest of you fan out, comb the harbour, all these boats. Don't forget the village fields, and the patches of scrub and derelict houses — What are you staring at? Let's get to it!'

Chapter 37

Two hours later David admitted the inevitable: the search would have to be called off for tonight. The street lights had gone off, the supply had failed again. The wind was rising, whistling shrilly through Khora's winding tar-black alleys. As he lifted his face to peer at the moonless sky and heavy clouds backing against Asteri mountain, it began to rain.

In seconds the whole search party was soaked and scampering for cover out of the blistering downpour. Behind him David heard Roxanne yelp as she skidded at the top of a greasy flight of steps and almost lost her footing. He whipped round to save her and fell heavily, cracking his shoulder.

'David!' Roxanne, reckless of her own safety, came whirling down the steps.

'I'm all right.' Cursing all the same, David grabbed a trailing bougainvillaea and hauled himself to his feet. A potted geranium spun across the cobbles, then a few metres away in the darkness he heard the pot shatter against an unseen wall. The rain was now so violent that he could scarcely see Roxanne's lean face swimming up from the murk below him, hardly catch her words:

'Alexios is taking everyone to the schoolhouse. I'm going home. David — Dad's going on — Stop him — He can't keep going in this!'

Lightning rocked out of the boiling sky above them and by the flare he found her lips and kissed her. For an instant the storm was no more: there was only himself and Roxanne, her lean warm body and mouth.

Reluctantly, they parted.

'I'll bring him back.'

'I'll be waiting.'

David plunged off into the gale.

Later, when David and Nicholas had returned to her father's home, when the three of them had retired to different bedrooms with the pretence of resting, Roxanne did sleep. Fully clothed, on top of the covers, not expecting to at all. Then she was aware, bristling, conscious of an eerie silence, an emptiness through the house.

Even before she'd forced her stockinged feet into her boots and her body off the quilt, Roxanne knew she was alone. No Dad, no David, no Chloe.

She called out for them anyway, expecting

and receiving no response. Shocked by Zoe's death, guessing what Nicholas and no doubt David had both thought — that Zoe had maybe been murdered in mistake for Melissa — Roxanne had forgotten to talk to either man about Melissa's dead lover, Andrew: how he'd probably been murdered by wildlife smugglers, how Katherine had seemingly known him, too.

'Where is everybody?' she asked aloud a second time, going out of the door. 'David?'

She tried their rooms, finding no one, then clattered downstairs, feeling the building around her rock slightly in the wind. In the low-ceilinged sitting room she flicked a light switch, not in the least surprised when nothing came on. At least her dad hadn't followed the usual island craze for knick-knacks and the cramming together of furniture and heirlooms; once Roxanne had felt her way round the rim of the sofa she could move quite quickly to the window, a ribbon gleam in the blackness.

Not attempting to open the clattering shutters, Roxanne peered through the gap, unconsciously rubbing her arms as pinpricks of rain bounced off her onto the already damp floor.

'Oh, my goodness.' Her eyes took in an underwater scene. The white house walls opposite were a running grey blur. Water hissed along the middle of the alley, carrying with it a griddle from an overturned brazier and, another moment later, a plastic toy trumpet. As Roxanne wondered at the craziness of Nicholas and David out in this — Melissa, she was sure, would have had the good sense to seek shelter — lightning blew up in her face. Taking the magnesium flare of the blast right in her eyes, Roxanne heard the metal griddle explode. Pieces of lethal shrapnel showered everywhere as the ground quaked with thunder.

'Jesus!'

Throwing an arm across her dazzled eyes, Roxanne's own shout was stifled by that pan- icked cry. Lurching back to the shutters, Roxanne was in time to spot a flattened shadow limping up and creeping along the opposite wall. A shadow frantically winding a strip of bunting round the metal clasps of a briefcase.

Bailey, scuttling round the Khora back- streets. Recognising the cringing figure, Rox- anne froze till he was past the narrow gap in her window and then began to tremble vio- lently. Fingers shaking so much she could scarcely grip the receiver, Roxanne scrabbled for and found Nicholas' phone.

It was dead. The radio and the spare two-way transmitter Nicholas kept at home were not much better, both fizzing with static and white noise. If she were to warn David and her dad that Bailey was up to no good, it looked likely she would have to do so in person.

Systematically Roxanne began to check over her clothes for metal. Bailey's attempts at lightning insulation were misguided: the safest way was to have no conducting material anywhere near you. Nicholas had taught her that, and her dad was with David; a comforting thought.

Running back upstairs for her overcoat, Roxanne decided that a warning wasn't enough. The men had to know where Bailey was heading, what he was doing. She jammed the black woollen cap back on, thought about a flashlight and decided against carrying anything.

Easing her way through the outer door against the storm wind pinning her to the doorjamb, Roxanne went out into the night.

Bailey did not know Khora as she did. In less than five minutes Roxanne saw him, head down as he teetered along a windy street leading down to the harbour: the man did not even understand which alleys to avoid so as to miss being battered by the gusts. No one else was stirring in the driving rain and wind, but Roxanne was careful to take paths parallel to those Bailey was using. If the man happened to look back during a lightning flash, she did not want her silhouette emblazoned on a wall.

Reaching the harbour, Roxanne had no choice but to follow directly behind Bailey, sometimes at less than twenty metres' distance. Keeping close to the buildings to avoid being struck by lightning, she ploughed along the sea-churned front, ignoring the tossing boats in the bay, their jangling lines and yawing wooden hulls making a strident endless round of music above the roaring ground-bass of the sea. Spray soaked coldly into her already sodden clothes as Roxanne strove to keep her footing in a dangerous shifting world, where at any moment a wave larger than the rest might curl over boats and jetty to blast her off her feet. Sure, it wasn't a Maine undertow out there, but it was just as deadly: it could suck her off the esplanade in less than a second.

Suddenly the narrow walkie-talkie, slung bandit-fashion over one shoulder down to the opposite hip, crackled. Roxanne desperately grabbed at the radio as Bailey clambered above the rolling pebbles of an area of beach and scrub, vanishing into the living wall of prickly pear at the end of the road and into Khora village.

Stiffened against a field wall and its overhanging mulberry tree, she waited as lightning, sheeting somewhere over Asteri mountain, was followed by a crack of thunder.

He wasn't coming back: he hadn't heard her radio. Bailey was making for Lykimi beach. Roxanne knew that for certain because now, as the thunder growled away into the breathing bellow of the storm, she heard it on the radio.

In swinging it over her shoulder, Roxanne had knocked the radio off its normal ASPW waveband. Incredibly, she had picked up a transmission: she could hear Bailey answering that he should be there in less than ten minutes.

Roxanne carefully memorised the frequency, then turned the needle back to the ASPW station. Nothing but static. She tried again, moving the dial very slowly with her wet fingers. Rain bounced off the walkie-talkie onto her face. She caught a blast of bouzouki music, then chatter, then hissing.

'Lunatic changed the frequency and forgot to tell me.' Roxanne jerked her head up and received a slap of wet mulberry leaves on the back of her neck. She set off again, meanwhile twisting the needle back to Bailey's station.

'Bailey's station' was the best way to think of it, Roxanne decided, as she copied the man and picked her way above the line of the rattling beach pebbles. Make it something of a joke.

Suddenly she stopped at the end of Khora village, wondering why in all the world she was doing this. Shouldn't she be trying to find David and Nicholas? But she didn't know where they were: they might even be waiting at Lykimi, ready to spy on Bailey.

Curiosity, she decided, was her only motive for scrambling on up the cliffhead path, but it was enough. She really wanted to know what was happening, what was being landed on the beach beyond Khora point.

'Over here!' The tense whisper came from a broom bush way off the track. Crouched low under the skyline, Roxanne snagged her way through thorns and scraped round a boulder to hunker down beside Melissa. They were less than a man's height away from Lykimi's desirable sands.

In camouflage, Melissa was part of the landscape, drab except for her eyes. 'No Nick or David?' she asked, sidelong, not wasting time with the obvious, *Why are you*

466

here? It's dangerous! However, any gratitude Roxanne might have savoured to be acknowledged as adult was swallowed in a larger alarm as she spotted the men.

Staring at them, she shook her head at Melissa's question.

'Probably done as I did and gone to Kemi: that's where Stella told me the smugglers would land for preference.' Melissa stretched briefly, cracking her left foot. 'But no one expected the storm to start up again with such a wallop.'

Her eyes narrowed at the figures lurching over the sands. 'Manoli, Andreas — both of them are at this beach party. I tracked Manoli and Andreas back from Kemi with two more, all of them scared out of their wits by their plans going so wrong.'

Roxanne thought she heard a chuckle then from Melissa, but wasn't entirely sure. Roxanne was sure she knew why the smugglers had chosen to land at Lykimi. A glance at the steepling sea confirmed her reasoning. Khora harbour was already crammed full of boats and, despite the foul night, too conspicuous. Yet away on the south-west coast of the island, Kemi was another thirty minutes' sail, highly dangerous in this weather. And Kemi was a narrow landing place, deep and secure, but difficult even for engine-powered ships to enter when the wind blew from the south. Lykimi, sheltered by Khora point from that wind, was both safer and closer to Turkey than Kemi in any Turkey-Asteri run.

Roxanne squinted through thick ropes of rain towards the point, but could see no ship riding at anchor. Not only darkness but the storm itself hid everything but the most violent of movements: men running, men wading into the rearing sea. The occasional spill of light struck through the constant downpour as they beamed a torch on the apparatus they were racing to build.

They were trying to run a cable from ship to shore, a gap of some thirty metres, a cumbersome business even when sheltered from the worst of the wind. Roxanne's radio suddenly spluttered with strident orders as the sailors and shore party lost patience with each other.

'When thieves fall out . . .' murmured Melissa. She glanced down at the radio, seemingly unsurprised. 'Well done there, Rox, that's the first real break we've had. I can't use my cameras with this lightning hovering — too much metal. To be honest, they're out of range of my flash unit anyway, and in these conditions I wouldn't get much detail from here even with my longest lens and fastest film. I've buried my gear in a sand pocket up the cliff. Pity we can't record this.'

Suddenly her matter-of-fact tone vanished. 'I wish I could get closer, really see what's happening!'

Melissa was frustrated and scared. Roxanne sensed the two emotions pouring from her as she turned her binoculars on the flexing cable. The fact that Melissa was frightened made Roxanne more alarmed — fear shared is fear doubled. Licking her lips, she strained to hear radioed instructions in language so foul that, had she not been chilled to the bone, she would have blushed.

'At least they have the sense not to carry their firearms as well,' Melissa breathed, as though telling herself rather than Roxanne.

'Quiet!' Roxanne cut harshly through her companion's fragile reassurance as another rapid exchange burst from her radio. By now the storm was blowing so hard that she could scarcely hear the bellowed instructions.

'Spiro's coming ashore first to check the rig will work,' she relayed, eyes puckering as she brought the radio right up to her ear. 'After he's landed they're going to send it down — yes, I've heard it right — they're sending the package next, with Spiro's lieutenant.'

Both young women leaned forward in their

hiding place to try to catch the clearest glimpse of Spiro. Roxanne, facing the moment, was thrilled.

Melissa was not. She was fighting an almost compelling urge to leap to her feet and strike out across the sand, to attack the man she held responsible for countless animal deaths and suffering, and most of all for Andrew's death. Staring at the stocky figure being winched across the clashing waves she saw the images of the wildlife trade: big cats with the bones cut out of their paws to make them easier to handle, 'more docile'; birds sprayed with aerosol paint to pass them off as more profitable rarities; dead tropical fish dumped down European drains by the thousand. And Andrew, murdered — she was still convinced of that — his beautiful head bandaged and his face in ruins, dead in a Rhodes morgue.

For all this the man being set down at the sea's edge was accountable. Now he was blundering up the beach. Beside Melissa, Roxanne gasped.

It wasn't Nicholas. Suddenly, with that realization, Melissa was free: Andrew became memory again, sweet but distant. Nicholas wasn't a wildlife smuggler. He had nothing to do with Katherine's little schemes — if this beach landing was one of hers,

Melissa amended. Despite the rain and danger, she felt new energy well in her, determination to expose her rival's links to this foul trade.

It wasn't David's guard Spiro, thought Roxanne. Yet the man was somebody she knew from somewhere. Who was it?

'Here they come,' said Melissa alongside her. 'If only I could get close! If this lightning would pass over —'

Swinging more than Spiro had done, another man had been winched ashore. A taller, thinner figure with a wooden crate strapped to his body was now landing on the beach, stepping out of the harness.

Bailey, who'd kept so far out of sight that Roxanne had forgotten him, now stepped forward to receive the crate. He carried it halfway up the beach, jaunty despite the rain, then set it down as Spiro and the others crowded round.

'What are they doing?' Roxanne asked as seconds became long minutes and thunder jolted the land behind them.

'Bailey will be checking that whatever's packed in there is alive and with no missing parts — also that it's the genuine item that he and Katherine ordered,' answered Melissa, glancing regretfully over her shoulder up the hill to where her cameras were buried and completely out of reach. 'Faking's very common in this business, even amongst associates and old trading partners. He'll have a checklist.'

'I wonder what the animal is?'

'I wonder. I'd like to grab a look at the crate, too.' Sensing Roxanne's surprise, Melissa explained. 'Wildlife traders sometimes add a little extra to pep up their profits on a smuggling run: a cache of drugs in a hollow cage bar. Or, as with a human carrier, swallowed by the creatures themselves.'

'That's gross.'

'I know,' said Melissa softly, wondering now what to do next — Roxanne's safety was an added complication, and even without her presence, Melissa wasn't sure what she should do. The storm had changed not only the smugglers' route and plans but also her own. Evidence! thought Melissa, her whole body jerking in frustrated anger. Now that she could finally watch Bailey handling smuggled goods, actually catch him in the act, she had no method of recording it. Again it seemed that Katherine had won.

'Oh, my goodness.' Roxanne's mild exclamation changed into stunned silence as Bailey and Spiro both stepped aside from the black shadow of the crate and seemed to strike poses. A flare appeared to issue from their bodies. Once, twice, three times, the gunshots echoed round the bay and then the survivors of this betrayal were fleeing in all directions, one clutching a side, another whose agonised screams were abruptly terminated as an answering burst of automatic fire from the boat sliced his head off.

A bullet hit Bailey's shoulder, blew him off his feet. As he went down, still clutching the gun from his briefcase, his other arm, flailing, struck the crate, smashing open the loosened top. Spiro made a desperate lunge for the dark shadow that leapt through the tiny gap, then tripped over the writhing Bailey and fell.

Lightning struck the mast of the caique, then forked into a sailor, exploding him and his rifle in a cloud of blue sparks.

Spiro staggered to his feet, lurching clumsily after the escaping animal. The shadow ran on, straight for the cliff where Melissa was waiting. As Spiro stamped down a boot to trap the creature she sprang at him, aiming for his face. The rock she was hefting caught the man's yelling mouth and the stone took away some teeth, smashing into the rough classic shape of a nose. With a slow bubbling sound, Spiro fell back over a stunted judas tree and slid down in a diagonal towards the dark edge of a patch of hottentot fig.

Roxanne picked up the mewing, cowering

creature, stroked its trembling body. Turning to Melissa, who was staring blindly at the havoc she'd just created, she said, 'Snap out of it, Mel. This way.'

Roxanne leading in a slithering crouch, she and Melissa fled swiftly from Lykimi beach.

Chapter 38

'What the devil's happening out there?' Sir Oliver demanded.

'Still raining.' Katherine flinched as thunder rolled overhead. 'And still lightning.' It was, she thought, almost as bad as a Florida hurricane, and it appeared to be going on forever.

'Poor little brute'll be terrified in this.' Sir Oliver glared at Katherine as though she were personally responsible. 'Why didn't you tell me Bailey was already setting out? I'd prefer to have gone with him.'

That's why we didn't mention it. Katherine scratched her long neck with a fingernail. Much as she disliked having to respond to Sir Oliver's complaint, she felt some answer was required. 'Bailey is utterly committed to the care of all transported stock. He'll make sure the creature doesn't suffer any stress.'

'And just how will he do that?' Sir Oliver put a hand to his head and mangled a fistful of dun-coloured hair. 'Can he stop this fearful din?' Disdaining an answer, he jerked to his feet off the creaking bed and began walking stiffly up and down the bare floorboards of this upstairs village room, his back straight, tense with fear and excitement.

Below the carved wooden stair, the Greek family from whom Katherine had rented this 'accommodation' for the night were asleep on chairs, slumped across the kitchen table: sharp-eyed mother, bronchitic father and modish daughter all snoring lustily. They didn't have to try relaxing in the fretful company of Sir Oliver.

A safe house, Bailey had told her before introducing Popi and her parents. Bailey had learned of the family's loyalty to Spiro when he and the smuggler had met by the Doric pillar last week to finalize details of tonight's run. In case they needed a place to stay in Khora, Spiro had told Bailey: Popi's was a comfortable, quiet house, lived in by a family whose silence he could personally guarantee.

Bailey had cracked one of his rare smiles in his retelling when he'd reached that point in the story. 'It appears our Spiro and Popi had an affair before she became the mistress of Andreas the shepherd — not something the young lady wants broadcast round Asteri, in case it ruins her business as well as her reputation.'

Well and good. The family would keep quiet and ask no questions — a prodigious sacrifice for Greeks, Katherine now thought sarcastically. Sitting on the narrow cot under sloping eaves, watching Sir Oliver's lantern-cast shadow loom over the made-up king-size bed in the centre of the room, she decided that Spiro had been being deliberately ironic when he described this house as comfortable. Popi's main claim to luxury was a running cold water tap in the kitchen. Katherine wouldn't have been surprised if the family hadn't slept with their animals as well as each other.

'How much longer?' Sir Oliver lifted a tweed-clad arm to the circle of hissing lantern light and tapped his watch. 'It's gone one o'clock.'

'Radio silence has to be observed for another hour,' Katherine reminded him. 'Since we haven't heard from Bailey it means everything's going smoothly.'

'Radio silence — what's that for exactly?'

Katherine stared at the dusty roofbeams. Except for the fact that the blue Nissan in which Bailey had driven Sir Oliver and herself into Khora was parked at the top of a very muddy track, she might have retired to the car for the rest of the night. But then, she hadn't anticipated needing to stay in Khora, least of all in proximity to Sir Oliver. At David's villa she'd been able to keep out of the man's way whenever she wanted.

'Bailey knows what he's doing.' Katherine wasn't about to admit Bailey's real concern: that ASPW, the Customs or the police might by mischance latch onto their radio frequency if it were used too often. And in Sir Oliver's fevered hands the radio would have been buzzing tonight.

'Keep that guy off my back,' Bailey had whispered to her, before slipping out from Popi's house on the pretext of going to the outside privy. 'I've enough on my plate this evening without that dumb bastard breathing down my neck.'

'He insisted on coming,' Katherine had hissed back, furious at Bailey. 'And you know I've got to be here —'

As soon as the message had come through tonight on the radio that the shipment couldn't make the Kemi landing and was going for Lykimi, her presence in Khora had become essential so far as Katherine was concerned. In case nature had any more tricks to pull, she didn't want to be miles away from the action at Petra beach: she needed to be on hand, to be free to react at once.

And — Katherine admitted this reluctantly — to be there as a support to Bailey.

Sir Oliver, feline-obsessive that he was,

had no idea what had occurred in Khora earlier in the evening. With no Greek and less attention, he had entirely missed any of the hue and cry connected with Zoe's death. Katherine was grateful for the aristocrat's narrow grasp on reality, except that just at this moment his endless walking and sighing was proving increasingly irksome.

Was it ever going to stop raining? thought Katherine, listening to the floorboards as they squeaked under her companion's plodding tread. Would Sir Oliver ever get on that plane out of Asteri — with his precious final 'kitty' — and let her resume the rest of her working holiday in some peace? The storm had trapped them all.

Finally she could no longer bear it. 'Do you mind not striding up and down? You'll wake everyone downstairs.'

'I told you to use more organised traders and routes. This whole affair' — Sir Oliver swung an arm around the primitive room — 'is a bloody shambles.'

The accusation nettled Katherine intensely. 'Sir Oliver: the item you requested is unique and for that very reason highly desirable. On the open market it could have been stolen or sold on to a higher bidder or substituted, and lost to you forever.' Katherine raised her hand to emphasise her final, deliberately cruel point. 'Shipped by some of the more "organised" traders, as you call them, your "kitty" would probably be in tiny little pieces by now. To speak frankly, to several "organised" traders, that cub's worth more dead than alive.'

Flinching at the brutal image, Sir Oliver dropped onto the double bed.

'Bailey knows that Spiro is reliable — so far as such people can ever be trusted.' Katherine ruthlessly pressed home her advantage.

'And how can he be sure of that?'

'Because they are half-brothers. Or rather stepbrothers. Spiro's widowed father married Bailey's widowed mother when Bailey was seventeen. Since then they've found their business interests often coincide.'

Taking advantage of the astonished silence, Katherine lifted her legs onto the bed and lay back. 'Put out the lamp and try to sleep,' she coaxed. 'Bailey will be back before breakfast — with your package.'

Her advice was taken. As the lantern sputtered out, Katherine closed her eyes in intense relief. She really had to keep Sir Oliver's good will because of the Beach International deal, but tonight it had been impossible to have a rational conversation with the man. The sooner the storm stopped and she could bundle him onto that plane the better.

In the darkness, Katherine could feel her mouth trembling. She had already lost an ally tonight and, more importantly, an old friend: Bailey the rock. Seeing him earlier tonight, dragging himself into the Villa Michelangelo whilst Sir Oliver parked the courtesy car, Katherine had known something was wrong. When he said he'd a headache and would take dinner in his room, she had followed him there.

'Where's our precious cargo?'

'Not coming to Kemi. Spiro's been delayed again — crew in dispute, threatening mutiny over their share of tonight's profits. Stupid bastards argued right the way through the good weather. Now the storm's raging again, Spiro doesn't fancy Kemi harbour in poor visibility and weather this rough, and isn't even sure the vessel will get that far.'

'But it's a totally new boat!'

'In a big gale. Sometimes, Katherine, I think you forget we can only plan so much.' Bailey looked at her, weariness scored into every line on his scrawny face. 'Tonight's no different. The storm's not the only thing.'

Leaving his briefcase in the middle of the room, he turned. 'Like to grab a shower.'

'What is it, John? What's happened?' For

Bailey ever to just drop his case in that casual manner was quite out of character. 'What is it?' she repeated softly.

'Zoe, in Khora tonight. I thought it was Haye. I thought she'd found out somehow, about the change of plan, about the shipment landing at Lykimi.'

'Ah,' said Katherine. 'Go on.' She put her hands on Bailey's shoulders, turned him so that he must look at her. 'Go on,' she commanded, bracing herself for what must surely follow.

'You said to see to it . . . I saw this blonde in the backstreets, with a camera.' He jerked his head away and pointed to the briefcase. 'Camera's in there: wasn't sure if she'd snapped me. But it was a very quiet part of town: everyone else was partying in the main square.'

Abruptly he shuddered. 'It had just started to come down again, really heavy rain. Could hardly see: all the lights went off. Ari wasn't there. It was semi-dark, she was small, blonde and with a camera. Thought it was Haye, poking around as usual. Had to stop her — at least for tonight, when we're landing the shipment. I guess I panicked, lashed out with the first thing to hand. Right now I can't remember all that clearly.'

Katherine, trying to think of something to

say in the face of that dreadful, tired confession, could only reflect on the sad fact that Zoe had probably been killed because she'd gone wandering the streets in search of a public lavatory.

In the end she said nothing, but drew Bailey to the bed and made him lie down. Covering him with a quilt, she left him undisturbed for an hour, until it was time he set out for Khora.

Now Bailey had been gone for hours and she was waiting, listening to the rain, the snorers downstairs, the wind. Zoe was dead by mistake and Melissa Haye was still around. Something would have to be done about it, Katherine decided.

Chapter 39

With Roxanne carrying the tiger cub and Melissa her retrieved camera gear, the two young women burst into Nicholas' house and slammed shut the door on the wind and rain. Instantly Melissa was heading through the living room towards the kitchen.

'Milk and a very little raw meat, cut up small. Food and warmth is what this baby needs, or we'll lose him.'

Roxanne, closing the door between living room and kitchen, now peeled off her soaked coat, the better to warm the bedraggled creature in the crook of her arm. Then she moved to light the lantern set in the middle of the big kitchen table.

'Not a good idea,' Melissa warned, glancing up from two warming pans on the gas stove. 'We may not have much peace here, if Nick and David don't come back soon.' She shivered. 'If I were Bailey and Spiro, this house would be the first place I'd come looking in Khora for my lost goods.'

Roxanne found that she, too, was shaking. With Alexios and Zervos, David and Nicholas watching at Kemi, who in the village could they apply to for help if the smugglers came after them from Lykimi? The full-time police, set to fly in after Zoe's death, were still trapped on Rhodes by the storm: no planes were flying in this weather. The police would sit it out, content in the knowledge that if they could not reach Asteri, neither could anyone leave the island.

But the smugglers were already here . . .

'Rox — put him down for a minute in Chloe's basket.' Melissa hefted the dog basket onto the table. Throwing out a plastic bone, she yanked her own sweater over her head, fluffed it in the basket and gently lifted the mewing cub from Roxanne's trembling hands. Settling the creature into the warm wool folds, she asked, 'Have you or your neighbours any feeding bottles? Hot-water bottles, too.' Without taking her eyes from the cub, she heard the milk sizzle and lifted that pan from the stove, leaving the water pan to boil hard. 'Sorry, Rox, I know it's pushing,' she added softly, 'but we really haven't too much time.'

Seeing that Melissa's hands were shaking as much as hers, Roxanne forced herself to move. Blessing the fact that her dad wasn't domestic and had never set foot in the kitchen for longer than he could help it, she found two dusty baby's bottles in the clutter of one of the kitchen's top cupboards. Sterilised by the boiling water, one was filled with the warm goat's milk. Checking its heat on her arm, and careful that the teat was not hot, Melissa settled on a kitchen chair, lifted the sweater-wrapped cub onto her knee and offered it the bottle, first splashing some of the milk onto its mouth.

After some chewing of the teat, the cub began to suckle noisily, a paw pressing Melissa's thigh. Stuck with tiny flexing claws, Melissa smiled and made a low coughing sound low in her throat. Still feeding, the cub purred in response.

Roxanne, taking refuge from panic in caring for this appealing little thing, stole quietly to the fridge and sniffed out the freshest meat. Chopping a steak into tiny slivers onto a plate, she left it on the table within reach, then slipped into the living room to run upstairs for fresh clothes for herself and Melissa.

When she returned, the cub had been fed, encouraged by simulated licking to defecate and was dozing in Chloe's basket surrounded by Melissa's sweater, its head resting on the chest of an old rag doll, Chloe's toy.

'You missed the messy bit,' said Melissa with something of her old grin as she described how to encourage the cub to empty its bowels.

Roxanne, dropping a bundle of clothes on the table, refused to be fazed. 'Sounds just like a large kitten to me,' she observed, catching a glimpse of a pink yawning mouth in the dog basket.

'A very puzzling kitten, though.' Melissa, camouflage trousers beginning to steam slightly as they dried, picked out one of Roxanne's sweaters and pulled it on. As she wound back the sleeves to her shorter arms, her eyes met Roxanne's. 'Are you as thirsty as I am?' she asked quietly. 'I think it must be the shock.'

Roxanne crossed to the water ewer, poured two full glasses and returned to sit opposite Melissa at the table.

'How long, do you think? Before they come?' She motioned with a thumb to the door, raising her water glass and drinking thirstily. Despite her dripping hair and clammy jeans, her throat was parched.

'An hour, maybe, if they're really determined. Bailey's been shot, and I knocked Spiro out, but we've already seen what they're willing to do to keep possession of this cub.'

Melissa tugged fretfully at the roll neck of the sweater. 'I suppose we should eat, too, only I can't face anything.' When she'd been feeding the cub with the meat, she could hardly bear to watch. Now she peered at Roxanne in the dim starlight from the open kitchen shutters. 'Have you any more trousers? Jeans don't keep their heat once they're wet.'

'You're that sure they'll come?' Faced with silence, Roxanne sighed, clambered to her feet and began stripping out of her damp jeans. 'I've some woollen pants, only they're really baggy.'

'Good,' Melissa said, poking the pile of clothes for a waistcoat. 'You can squeeze another layer on underneath.' Suddenly she flicked a pair of socks at the younger woman. 'Put plenty of these in your pockets. Have you a rucksack, too?'

'Melissa.' Roxanne paused until Melissa looked at her. 'You don't have to keep me busy. I'm not about to faint.'

'You're sure? You look very pale to me.'

'Have you seen yourself lately?'

Melissa chuckled a moment, then stopped. 'It's not funny, is it?'

'No,' whispered Roxanne, listening to the wind suck at the door. For several moments both were still, just listening, waiting for the footsteps to come pounding down the outside steps. The heavy knock at the door.

'We can get out the back way,' Roxanne said. She lifted the radio she had left on top of a kitchen unit and put the set to her ear. 'Nothing.'

'What about Nick and his group?'

Roxanne twiddled, listened. 'Nothing but static.' Knowing she had to try anyway, she spoke into the mouthpiece, sending a distress call in English and then in Greek. She kept repeating the call for five minutes before laying the radio down. 'Maybe the storm's affecting the signal.'

Looking more cuddly than ever in Roxanne's clothes, Melissa began unpacking some camera gear. Seeing the flash unit, Roxanne frowned.

'Animals think flash is just lightning,' Melissa reassured her. She ran off several shots near the rim of the basket and the cub only twitched once.

'How old is Buster?' asked Roxanne, resting her head and elbows on the table. Shock and the horrors they had witnessed on the beach came over her in waves; now close and terrible, now ebbing away. Seeing again in her mind Bailey's shoulder explode in a bloody pulp, she bit down on her thumb and concentrated on the tiny, gently rumbling, fat-bellied cub. Buster was a good nickname, she thought.

'He's a she,' said Melissa, with a certain gleam in her eye which quickly faded as she touched the rim of the wicker basket. 'Buster as you call her is about seven weeks old, and weighs around ten pounds. In the wild, cubs of this age might just be starting to follow their mothers on their regular trails, learn a bit about their territories.'

Melissa stared down at the sleeping cub, her face taut with a grief Roxanne did not understand until she spoke. 'Buster's mother was healthy and they were both eating well, until the smugglers decided to move in for the kill. They'd have to kill the mother, you see, in order to take the cub. Probably the father, too, for tiger parts. The last breeding family, gone.' She clicked her fingers as tears streamed from her eyes.

'What do you mean?' Roxanne whispered. 'There are a few tigers still left in India, Sumatra, Siberia —'

'Not like this. Buster's probably the last of her kind. The only one.' Melissa's hand bunched into a fist on the rim of the basket.

'That's why the smugglers only landed one package, isn't it? Because she's unique.' Roxanne was beginning to understand, although she still didn't know what was so different about this tiger cub.

'She will be now her parents are dead —

Oh, why do I keep hoping they won't be?' Melissa burst out, clapping a hand to her head. 'I know the smugglers will have killed them. You bitch, Katherine! You total heartless selfish bitch!'

In the basket the cub squirmed at her raised voice and Melissa instantly quietened. 'Sorry,' she said, after a choking gasp. 'It just makes me so *angry*. The smugglers know what they have — that's why we saw all that slaughter on the beach: a vast sum of money is at stake.'

'How much?' Roxanne hated sounding so mercenary, but the level of cash was a sign of the level of danger they would be in, now the final trade-off of money for the cub had gone wrong.

'If this were an "ordinary" tiger cub, say around ten thousand dollars. If Buster is what I think she is, then I'd say at least a hundred times that amount.' Melissa shrugged but failed to suppress the shudder. 'Total extinction simply drives up an animal's price, makes it sexier to the buyers.' She glanced at her watch. 'Have you a rucksack anywhere? We need to think about leaving.'

Roxanne, feeling lightheaded with shock and the grim realization that she, Melissa and the tiny tiger cub were in a million dollars' worth of danger, went running up the stairs again to her bedroom and hauled her rucksack off the wardrobe top. Padding it with more sweaters, she also stashed a water bottle into the side pockets and a Swiss army knife.

When she came downstairs, Melissa had pushed her binoculars through a rotten part of the front window shutters and was sweeping the street. 'No sign yet,' she murmured, turning to take in Roxanne's package. 'Pity about the day-glo football stickers: they really catch any light, but the sweaters are good. A nice comfortable den for Buster — Couldn't you have thought of a more appropriate name?'

'It's absurd and I like it,' said Roxanne lightly, watching Melissa stuff the pockets of the rucksack with both feeding bottles and, wrapped in a clean handkerchief, the rest of what was to have been her father's next steak. Where were Nicholas and David? she wondered, glancing a second time at the radio.

'I've tried but there's no answer,' said Melissa. 'I wish I knew Nick and David were all right.' She glanced again at her watch. 'By now I should by rights have been landing at Rhodes airport in disgrace.'

In Chloe's basket Buster purred in her

sleep, the white tips of her black rimmed ears twitching slightly. Now that her coat had dried out, Roxanne could see more clearly the contrasting stripes of her fur: patches of light and dark in the dim, shadowy light.

'What is she?' she asked. 'Why is she so special?'

'Have you a candle or a pencil torch: anything with less of a powerhouse beam than these lanterns?' Melissa flipped the metal base of one with a fingernail, the sound fading into the steady beating hiss of the rain. 'I'd like to be able to see for myself. I'm not exactly sure. It's just a guess, based on where this cub's been shipped from.'

'Where's that?' Roxanne brought a candle, lit it by the gas-cooker jet. 'And how can you be sure?'

'Buster's been shipped from Turkey, and comes from not far beyond. I know that because Stella told me and because of Buster's own good condition: she hasn't been travelling long. I'd say only last week Buster was with her mother. Since then I think she's been suckled and groomed by a bitch for part of the time — you saw how easily she settled into Chloe's basket? She's comfortable with the smell of dogs.'

'But where's she from?'

'Iran, possibly, Afghanistan or the remote Turkish mountains.' Careful not to tip burning wax onto the sleeping cub, Melissa raised the softly burning light over Buster's round ball of a head. 'You know, of course, that all tigers are marked by an individual pattern of stripes, just as we humans have different features from one another? These patterns are unique to each tiger, but their general colours and depth of shade and the width of banding tend to go by race. Size, too, varies between the races: the biggest tigers come from Siberia and the smallest from Sumatra. If Buster survives to maturity, I guess she'll come about halfway between the two.'

Melissa shone the candle over the cub. 'You see how her fur looks — thick, almost woolly? And the colour, a bit darker brown than usual, with the stripes close together?' She set the candle down and looked at Roxanne across the table. 'I'll get Jonathan to verify it, but I think what we have sleeping in your dog basket is the last surviving Caspian.'

Roxanne waited to feel a sense of awe but felt nothing. 'I've never heard of a Caspian tiger,' she said, glancing at the front window as the shutters creaked softly in a sudden gust.

'The Russians polished most of them off between the wars as part of a five-year plan. Agricultural development. The last few were spotted in the mid-sixties: odd ones and twos in Iran, a few pug-marks in Afghanistan. Then nothing.'

'And now there's one alive and in my kitchen.' Roxanne shook her head. Back from the dead, and so valuable to collectors that men would murder for it.

Murder. Melissa did not know yet about Zoe, Roxanne recalled with a violent start. Swiftly, watching the brown and yellow stripes of Buster's fluffy body rise and fall slowly in time with the tiger cub's breathing, she explained how Zoe had been found dead.

'So much death,' Melissa murmured, her drawn face unreadable. Perhaps she was thinking, as Roxanne was, of how she and Zoe had often clashed over the way Asteri should be developed. Now the Greek was beyond any reconciliation: shortly she would be buried in the island she had wanted to transform.

'How's Pindaros taking it?' Melissa asked from a sudden darkness as she pinched out the candle.

'Numb, like the rest of us.'

Roxanne heard the wind hiss against the

door. Tonight everything seemed unreal. She opened her mouth to observe as much when her readjusting night vision caught the sudden upward jab of Melissa's hand, raised in warning.

Quickly, before Roxanne could hear any sound, Melissa gently scooped the sleeping cub, the sweater and Chloe's old rag doll into the rucksack. Buster mewed once in protest, then, as Melissa put a hand into the sack and nuzzled the cub's body, relaxed and was quiet.

As she reached for the straps of the rucksack, Roxanne heard it herself, the scuff of a boot on a wall. Away in the north thunder drummed low and long, covering other creeping footsteps.

Roxanne snatched the rucksack and was off out of the back kitchen door, sprinting through the yard. Melissa had no chance to protest: a shoulder crashed against the front door in time to another thunder clap. Seizing her camera bag and starting after Roxanne, Melissa was just in time to see the girl roll over the yard wall, the rucksack now secure on her back.

As Roxanne dropped into the darkness, Melissa heard the front door cave in. Desperate to send the pursuers in the wrong direction, she scrambled over the opposite wall, deliberately hurling a flash unit down onto the flags with a splintering crash as she too rolled over the wall and down into the unknown.

Chapter 40

Alexios ducked back into the street through a front door barely hanging on its hinges. 'Roxanne's not here,' he said. 'No one appears to have seen her since last night.'

The tall doctor got no further, had no time to mention the scattered pans in the kitchen, the dog basket ripped to pieces on the table. Without a word, David tore the swinging door off its post and barged into the house. Alexios could hear his heavy feet thundering through the rooms, chairs toppling and beds shrieking as David tossed furniture aside. As he crashed out again into the alley, the sight of his usually immaculate jacket spattered with filth and sprouting twigs from its top pocket might have been ridiculous in any other circumstances.

Where was Roxanne?

David fell back against the house wall with something like a groan. As he caught a glimpse, in the rising purple dawn, of the carved lines of David's face somehow dissolving in the pelting rain, Alexios realised how close to breaking the man was.

Yet where was Melissa? Supposed to report to the mayor's office at ten last night, so far she had not been seen in Khora since yesterday afternoon. And where was Nicholas?

Niko and David had set out together last night, after ASPW and David's Antasteri guards had met at midnight in the main square to play one of Nicholas' hunches and go to watch Kemi beach. After the group had reached Kemi and split up on the way through the deserted village, Alexios saw neither man until first light, when he met David on his way to Nicholas' house. They had found the place deserted and wrecked.

'Tell me,' said Alexios calmly, 'are these extravagant demonstrations part of an artist's concern for his model?'

Blood rushed into David's face. He swung his arm up and Alexios ducked instinctively. They stood in the sloping street with the ruined door between them, two tall powerful men glowering at each other as rain water gurgled and splashed round their feet.

'Is Nicholas there?' a clear voice asked below them. Instantly both men's heads jerked round.

'Roxanne got away. The smugglers came after me. They're here somewhere on Asteri now: they landed last night on Lykimi beach.' Melissa sagged onto the final step just before Nicholas' house. 'Sorry, I've been up all night: must sit down.' Slowly she lifted the camera slung round her neck and showed it to Alexios. 'The film in here needs developing.'

About to say more, to add that she'd had to fling off most of her gear in order to escape, Melissa recalled David's possible involvement with the wildlife smugglers. True, as she had witnessed last night, David's guard Spiro was not the Spiro that Bailey had been with on Lykimi beach, but the animal cages and David's 'Katherine' file on Antasteri were yet to be explained.

Still her heart hammered in a glad, hectic kind of way as David strode across the fallen door towards her. Crouching on the same steps as Melissa was sitting, he brought a small flask from his jacket pocket. 'Take a sip of this,' he said gently. 'Whisky — it'll warm you.'

Alexios frowned. 'She's in shock,' he began, but neither David nor Melissa was listening.

Taking in her bedraggled blonde hair, the pale, ivory-translucent features, the water dripping from the soggy folds of her clothes and creating a tiny sun-shot puddle round her small, curiously unstrung figure, David wanted to comfort and cuddle her. Bundle her into warm soft sheets and let her sleep on him. Any possible connections between Melissa and the wildlife smugglers she claimed had now invaded the island were forgotten. As one warm brown iris slid tiredly towards the inner corner of her eye, David softly touched her trembling eyelid, struck with pity. He wanted to say something to her, but what?

'Have you any idea where Roxanne can be?' he found himself asking.

Melissa, taking the bottle from him with faintly trembling fingers, shook her head. Since their parting in the yard last night over opposite walls she wasn't sure. Even if she had any ideas, she didn't know whether David was the best person to tell them to. 'Where's Nicholas?' she asked again.

'Not back yet from Kemi.'

'He followed me there, did he? Good boy.' Melissa tried to blow the sodden fringe from her forehead but could not. Giving up on the attempt she yawned then shivered. David peeled off his jacket and threw it round her shoulders, gathering both cloth and woman close.

Melissa closed her eyes, feeling very safe. Perhaps it was a false sense of security, but what did that matter? She was so tired, and

David was as steady as a rock, a smooth, sun-warmed rock. Right now, even if he were the smuggler Spiro's boss, she couldn't have stirred from his embrace. She wasn't about to admit anything, so why not enjoy this physical closeness, the touch of a strong man's shoulder, the tang of pinewood after-shave, the long fingers smoothing down her back in a sweep of sweetness?

'Drink,' she heard him coax, but she was already becoming fatally intoxicated.

Out of all patience, Alexios stepped forward and firmly took the flask from her un-resisting hands. 'She's in shock,' he repeated. 'Warm tea would be better right now. Let's get her inside my surgery.'

Gently and as easily as though she were a fragile sunflower battered by the storm, David plucked Melissa off the step and carried her up the street.

In the surgery she tried to explain to Alexios about Bailey and Spiro and the smugglers, about the amazing Caspian tiger, which — pray God — was still alive and still safe with Roxanne, but the words that came out were just nonsense. Finally, as she braced herself for one last effort to make him understand, Melissa heard the nurse say to Alexios, 'She's rambling: I can't make out a single phrase, other than "extinct" and "Caspian".'

'I've given her a shot. Whatever she's seen or done, Melissa needs calming down for a few hours, or she's going to give out completely. If Roxanne's in this state, I hope we find her soon.'

Bailey was so late now that something must have gone wrong, Katherine reluctantly admitted to herself. Thank heaven for minor mercies, though: Sir Oliver was finally in a deep sleep, oblivious to the furtive scurryings and murmurings downstairs as Popi and her family prepared to face another day in Khora.

Stooping to a narrow window at the foot of her bed, unseen and unnoticed last night, Katherine pushed open the shutters. A puff of spray splashed her high cheekbones, but Katherine ignored that, as she ignored the purple and lemon dawn. In the street below was Ari Pindaros, walking with that dazed, closed-in look of a man going everywhere yet nowhere, walking because no doubt the priest had told him to step outside the church a moment for a breath of fresh air.

The priest and Zoe. She wanted to talk to the priest and attend the service for her former ally. Zoe would have approved of what she had in mind, so there was no disrespect.

Katherine slipped on her black dress and jacket over her pale cream silk camisole. Intended for evening wear, the dress was a touch slinky and bare, but with the jacket it would do. Sadly, for the shoes there was no remedy: she would have to do as she had done last night, wear an old pair out of doors and change inside into her black stockings and courts.

Slipping downstairs, Katherine smilingly refused the offer of breakfast, explained that she wished to pay her respects to her dear friend Zoe in church, and went out, bare-headed, into the relentless rain. If Bailey returned with the package for Sir Oliver whilst she was away, then so much the better: she would miss the aristocrat's ludicrous, gut-wrenching celebrations. For now she was acting on a decision from last night, on a plan inspired by her glimpse of Ari Pindaros, a lonely figure wandering the slowly lightening streets like an abandoned child.

'I must speak with you. The mayor is absent and this will not wait.'

The priest, accosted as he crossed the square from his house to the main church, stopped by the fountain. Ignoring the rain and the fretful squalls of wind sneaking round the square through the tossing branches of the plane tree, he acknowledged the young woman by an enquiring flick of his full beard, and said in English, 'Please continue.'

'Melissa Haye has not yet reported to the mayor's office. When she does, I suggest she is held in custody until the police fly in from Rhodes. She is a very dangerous person.'

'Oh? As well as a wildlife smuggler?' Somehow the priest sounded unconvinced at this, but Katherine ploughed on regardless.

'Zoe Konstantinou was afraid of her, and with good reason. Melissa Haye resented Zoe's plans to help develop Asteri. I saw her strike at Zoe in their last public quarrel.'

'Mr Pindaros spoke to me of this.' The priest folded his arms across himself, long black robes flapping slightly in the swirling wind. 'He, too, thought it possibly significant.'

'Zoe wasn't shot or stabbed, she was struck from behind with a stone . . . Last night when Zoe was killed — where was Melissa Haye?'

Warming to her theme, Katherine pointed to the narrow street entrance which ran after many twists and turns and junctions to the alley and derelict house where Zoe's body was found.

'Mrs Konstantinou was a bright, modern

woman,' she continued. 'She would never have wandered off into strange, unlit streets alone: the habit of living in a city such as Athens would be too strong. And she was a modest person; she would not have gone off with a man. But a woman, an unarmed woman . . .'

The seed planted, Katherine lowered her head, hiding her eyes. Any more would be to labour the point. Let the priest consider whether Zoe's 'fear' of Melissa Haye would have been strong enough to deter her from walking alone with her.

After a brief service for Zoe and at the insistence of the priest, Alexios locked Melissa, still sleeping, in his surgery. 'Just till the full-time police get here,' he explained to his nurse, but his eyes were dark. David and Mr Zervos, out searching Lykimi bay, had radioed in with an unbelievable tale of bodies strewn across the beach, one decapitated. Manoli and the shepherd Andreas were among the dead.

Told of Melissa's incarceration and the reasons and suspicions behind it, David cursed and shouted bitterly into the mobile that, although it was true that Melissa and Zoe had never got on, to his mind that was a pretty weak motive for murder.

'You'll have to keep her there now, for her own safety,' David added, and signed off after learning that Roxanne was still missing. 'Roxanne I'll find, however long it takes,' he vowed grimly.

The storm was not over yet.

Chapter 41

Roxanne and the cub settled luxuriously into the mound of duvets Roxanne had dragged from the villa bedrooms into the kitchen. At around ten pounds and the size of a small spaniel dog, the tigress was manageable for a girl of Roxanne's height and wiry strength, but it had been a long night for both of them. Now, safe for the moment at David's villa on Antasteri, Roxanne was determined that she and the cub should relax.

Until she had tried it, Roxanne never realised what a gift she had for housebreaking. With David and the guards on Asteri, and Litsa, David's daytime housekeeper, still with her family celebrating St George's Day and now grounded by the storm, disturbance had been no problem. A large stone through an unshuttered dining-room window had been enough to shatter the glass. Recklessly ignoring the jagged splinters left in the frame, Roxanne had clambered through it onto the sideboard, dropped onto the mosaic floor and pelted from the room to the shrill clamour of the alarm.

Inside the rucksack, even muffled in jumpers, the cub had been going mad at the ringing bell, which took several minutes to fall silent. Now, full of milk and meat — both taken from David's well-stocked fridge in the kitchen — she was gratefully asleep in a quiet house.

'Well, Buster, let's just hope the noise hasn't damaged your hearing,' Roxanne said aloud, spreading a hand over the dark and light softly breathing stripes of the cub snuggled against her. Already it was probably too late for the tigress not to have become imprinted on her, accustomed to her scent and her voice. In the future, when the cub became adult, she might not be wary of mankind: she might even consider herself more human than tiger, and so, as an adult, reject other tigers. Keenly aware of this problem, Roxanne had no remedy for it. She had snatched up the rucksack ahead of Melissa, the wildlife expert, and now she alone was responsible for this baby.

Changing a human baby had nothing on simulated licking to encourage the expulsion of waste products from a tiger cub's digestive tract, Roxanne thought with a shudder. She was becoming more proficient now, but it was hardly her favourite job. Still, compared to what she and the cub had already been through last night, it was a minor problem. Simply keeping them both alive so that they could enjoy their next meal was enough. Lying back, coiling herself protectively around the warm, trusting bundle of fur, Roxanne stared at her own plate of sandwiches balanced on the duvets. Sliced tomatoes and apricot jam: normally she would have wolfed these down, but having made them she just didn't fancy them. Weary as she was, Roxanne didn't fancy sleep, either. Even awake, she found her eyes invaded by the images of last night, tormenting her with their vividness.

Why had she snatched up the cub and the rucksack ahead of Melissa? Thinking back, Roxanne wondered again at her own sudden decisiveness, based on the cold, rapid calculation that although Melissa knew about animals, she did not know Khora or Asteri as well as a native islander. In darkness and storm, Roxanne still knew every twist and turn of the Khora streets: the dead ends and short cuts through house yards. And she was a faster runner than Melissa, with longer legs and a bigger body. The rucksack fitted her, and, filled with the squirming cub, was no bulkier or heavier than she had carried every year since she was fourteen.

When Melissa had sprinted for the opposite wall to create a diversion, Roxanne had escaped with the smugglers' prize. Thinking fast, she had run down the alleys, plunging through streams of draining water in case the smugglers had tracker dogs with them. Had Spiro, Bailey and the men at Lykimi beach somehow settled their bloody differences? Roxanne thought at one point, ducking under lines pegged out with the ghostly forms of dried squid, then yelped as one of the cub's claws came through the rucksack and raked her back. The infant tigress was going crazy: Roxanne knew she had to find a way to release the cub out of the rucksack or she'd have a dead Caspian — no, the last dead Caspian — on her hands.

Mike the butcher's bicycle was leaning against the wall of the blue church, its huge wicker basket on the front handlebars big enough for Mike's large dog. Roxanne, checking that no one was splashing down the street after her, shrugged off the rucksack, then her coat and packed the coat, lining side out, into the basket. She lifted the cub, hissing and scratching, from the rucksack, dropped it onto the coat and then wheeled the bike briskly away over the smooth flags alongside the church.

'Okay, Buster, let's find you some shelter,' Roxanne said, as the cub leaned out and stared curiously at the turning wheels. To her relief, the small tigress had chosen to stay in the basket with its tantalising smells of damp dog and raw meat.

The cub seemed fascinated, then hypnotised by the steadily clicking turn of the wheels. Roxanne pushed the bike across the square outside the church and then, reaching a junction of the Khora-Kemi road, settled into the saddle and rode past the olive press and out of the village.

She wanted to escape the claustrophobic walls and windows and doors: walls to surround and trap her, windows to spy on her, doors to be flung open in her path. She trusted no one in Khora except members of ASPW, and as they were not here she must leave.

No one, Roxanne reminded herself, rising from the saddle to tackle the first hill out of Khora, no one had come running into the street a few moments before, when someone had broken down the door to her father's house.

If David had been there, things would have been different.

'Yes — he would probably have been shot, protecting you, pal,' Roxanne said aloud, scornful of her own weakness in wanting David around in a time of crisis. But part of her was also astonished that she was holding up so well, no feeling of shock at all. Warm and steady, in spite of the rain, she pedalled to the crest of the hill, then freewheeled down the other side towards the Villa Elysion.

Nicholas' holiday home was empty now, so early in the season. Roxanne slowed, rumpling fur on the cub's head as the tigress pricked her ears forward and gnawed at the edge of the wicker basket. A muffled bang, probably a branch sheared off by the storm crashing down to the ground through the oak wood in the villa's grounds, had both of them looking in that direction, but since there were no other sights or sounds Roxanne did not stop.

She found herself keeping to the Khora-Kemi road, following a track she had known well in previous years, when on long summer nights she had travelled with her bike the whole breadth of Asteri, Khora to Hydra beach, and bathed there in the warm phosphorescent sea within sight of David's island. Now she travelled the same road again, almost in a dream, without conscious thought or choice, but going away from Khora, from danger, to a place where she had always known peace.

In the basket, the cub seemed untroubled

by the rain. Roxanne tugged off her sweater and wrapped it over one half of the basket and the cub crept under there, dragging with it Chloe's old rag doll, which had been stuffed into the rucksack.

'Man-eater, huh?' Roxanne said, grimacing at her own bad taste in jokes. But this was no laughing matter. 'I won't tell if you don't,' she told the cub, and stood up on the pedals again to put on a spurt of speed along the fork of the track down to Kemi.

As she rattled on, jolting despite trying to keep to the smoothest part of the track, Roxanne thought of the deserted Turkish village. Kemi gave her the creeps. When she was younger, about ten years old, she and some other island children had gone to Kemi out of curiosity, to check out the ruined mosque. Entering the courtyard of the mosque and about to wash their feet in the ritual low basins, they had been chased away by a stocky, bearded man.

Spiro, thought Roxanne, suddenly making the connection without any dramatic slamming on of the brakes or skidding of the tyres. That was where she had seen the smuggler before, in Kemi village. What had Spiro been doing there, all those years ago? Were his family of Turkish descent? Had he returned secretly to the village where his grandparents had once lived before they were expelled like the rest?

If that were the case, thought Roxanne, fixing her sights through the bouncing raindrops onto the distant black bell tower of the hamlet where Melissa had stowed the dinghy, then Spiro's choice of Asteri as a dropping-off point for his most valuable wildlife 'cargo' was perhaps ironic. Unless it was his way of showing contempt.

The men who had died on Lykimi beach: some were islanders. Roxanne gritted her teeth, telling herself not to think about tonight. After the smugglers had smashed their way into Nicholas' house she did not know if Melissa had escaped or not; all she could do was hope and pray and keep herself going. Towards the last part of the night, just before dawn, Roxanne had reached the hamlet. There she had fed the tigress and snatched a drink of water for herself. Staring over the beach at the open sea, she decided to take a chance. No one would expect her to do it, especially in a storm, yet right now, just before dawn, the wind was dropping. Roxanne was willing to risk that it would not rise again in any strength until the sky began to lighten with the sunrise.

She would take a dinghy from the hamlet

and sail it around Asteri's south-west point to Antasteri.

And that, reflected Roxanne, still staring at her untouched sandwich, was exactly what she had done. Now, taking up residence with the cub in David's villa, she had deliberately chosen the kitchen as their place of retreat. With its huge east-facing window, the kitchen had the best view in the entire building of Asteri and the strait: a vital point when keeping watch. Everything had gone smoothly except for a final, vital detail. Roxanne had expected to find David's telephone working.

But the line was dead.

Chapter 42

When Nicholas reached the surgery, Alexios was pacing the street outside.

'No, Niko,' he shouted. 'Not in there.' Then, seeing the bloodstains as Nicholas turned, he said in a quieter voice, 'Come into the house instead. I'll fix you up in the sitting room.'

Nicholas, ignoring Alexios and the matted patch on the right thigh of his jeans, rattled the surgery door. 'Zervos has just radioed to tell me that you're holding Melissa.'

'Do you know where Roxanne is now?'

'Sure, still at the house,' Nicholas replied without looking at Alexios. 'Let's keep to the subject, Doctor. I want Melissa out.'

'Niko — there's no easy way to say this — Roxanne's missing.'

Nicholas jerked round, his face alight. 'I thought you knew. I thought Zervos must have told you,' Alexios was saying, the breath suddenly tight in his chest as Nicholas sharply jerked his dark head back in denial. It had to be said. Injured or not, there was no easy way to tell his friend that his daughter was gone.

'Roxanne was with Melissa last night at your house. The smugglers broke in. According to Melissa, Roxanne got away with whatever the smugglers had brought with them to Asteri.'

'Roxanne's somewhere on the island with the special shipment,' broke in Nicholas tersely.

'Yes — and David's out looking for her.'

'Then you better fix me up fast, Doctor, because I want to find my daughter ahead of Gordon and everybody else. And give me that key.'

'David thought Melissa would be safer in my care.'

'Funny, I haven't heard that Gordon's been elected mayor in my place.' Nicholas, wincing as he moved, whipped back from the door to growl into Alexios' face. 'These guys have guns — will *you* stop them when they come here? Right now, Melissa's an easy target just waiting to be picked off — in fact, you and Gordon have fixed it now so that they'll know exactly where to call!'

Face darker than the storm, Nicholas turned back and hammered the door again. 'Melissa!' When there was no response, he snatched at Alexios' shoulder. 'Why isn't she answering? Get the door open, man!'

Alexios made no move. 'Melissa was in delayed shock when David and I found her this morning. I put her under sedation. She'll be sleeping it off: quite comfortably, I promise.' Alexios tried to remove Nicholas' heavy hand. 'Now, we need to look at that bullet wound: what happened? Looks like a shot at close range.'

'Close enough: an ancient Browning carried by one of our members. Happened at Elysion last night when we were scouring the bay there after no luck at Kemi.'

Nicholas snorted, unaware that Roxanne, riding on the road above the bay, had heard the shot but dismissed it as storm noise. 'After I'd told the fool to put the safety on, too,' he concluded, then snapped his fingers. 'Key, Alexios.'

Alexios coughed softly. 'I'm sorry, Nicholas, I know you've become attached to her, but in the circumstances . . .'

'Why in God's name is this door locked from the outside, anyway? When Melissa wakes she won't be able to get out.'

'The thing is — well, we thought you'd understand when Zervos told you Melissa was being held in my surgery.'

Nicholas' head came up in the steady rain, inhaling deeply through his blunt nose.

'What does that mean — exactly?'

'Melissa's in my custody as well as my care: just until the police arrive. She could be charged.' Alexios wiped rain water from the side of his nose. 'Zoe Konstantinou —'

Fresh blood spurted from his thigh as Nicholas barged the taller man against the door. 'There isn't time for this — Roxanne's being stalked whilst you stall. Either hand that key over or I break your arm and take it — your choice.'

'Don't threaten me, Niko.'

Nicholas suddenly grinned and flicked his injured leg. 'No key, Alex, and I tell the next ASPW meeting about that mink you bought in Athens for your mother-in-law. Still your choice.'

'Nicholas, be reasonable.'

'Melissa'll be awake soon, yes? Well, if she's what everyone thinks and is in with the smugglers I've got a few questions, like "Where's my daughter?".'

'Look, you're not seeing this thing clearly. You're too emotionally involved.'

Nicholas shook the taller man. 'She didn't kill Zoe!'

'Can you be absolutely certain of that?' Alexios was talking fast. 'Given their con- flicting interests — and mutual hatred?'

'What?' Nicholas flung his hands off the

taller man, and stepped back rapidly. 'What's got into you? What real motive is there for Melissa to murder Zoe? They scarcely knew each other!'

'They were business adversaries.'

'So what? Do I go round bumping off my rivals? Come on, Alexios.' Suddenly Nicholas paused, looked closely at the doctor. 'What's Gordon's opinion on this?'

'David's main concern was Melissa's safety. Especially since Miss Hopkins is not shy in broadcasting her suspicions about Melissa's possible involvement in Zoe's death. It was she who first suggested it.' Alexios, watching how Nicholas took that news found him utterly unmoved: his next statement showed where his thoughts were focused.

'I just bet Gordon's "concerned", but so am I.' Nicholas thrust out an open hand. 'Key.'

'Zervos told me not to let anyone see Melissa until the police get here from Rhodes.' Alexios paused. 'You still believe Melissa's totally innocent, don't you? Of even the seahorse shipments and those other things we found in her rooms.'

'Are you convinced that she's guilty, Alexios?'

Alexios shrugged, refusing to respond to

Nicholas' question.

'Have you never wondered, Alexios,' Nicholas went on, 'about Gordon's hospital for birds of prey on Antasteri? I have, lots of times. Litsa says she knows nothing about it. Those cages supposedly for injured hawks: they would take quite a few traded wild animals.

'What if Melissa is totally innocent?' Nicholas continued gruffly. 'What if she saw something she shouldn't have done on Antasteri? The police won't be due on the island for another half day at least. Are you going to keep her locked away until maybe Gordon or one of his security team come and deal with her?'

'But David's out looking for Roxanne!'

'So you've told me already. And now you're definitely going to give me that key and clean this mess up inside the surgery. No, on second thoughts we'll take your suggestion and make that the house; don't want Melissa seeing any more mess than she has to.'

'You don't give up.'

'No,' said Nicholas, blue eyes flashing, 'I don't.'

Chapter 43

Melissa came suddenly awake, heart thumping louder than the dying rumble of the thunder outside. She had been dreaming of last night, the lethal chase through Khora's backstreets. No time to stop Roxanne taking the tiger cub. No time to grab the two-way radio. No time to do anything but run and keep running, making sure the pursuit followed her.

Frantic to throw the smugglers off Roxanne's escape, Melissa dropped over the yard wall and landed on a carefully tended flower bed, then cried out and clutched at her ankle, calling out loudly, 'No, Rox, you go on!'

Caught up in her own white lie, she stumbled a few paces, limping between the roses and geraniums towards a latched gate in the encircling kitchen-garden wall, gasping as she heard a loud scrabbling behind her. With a show of panic not altogether feigned, she twisted back as two figures lurched over the wall at her, clumsy because of the guns strapped to their backs.

Lightning sheeted down, striking a nearby house roof littered with lobster pots, sending stinging wire and lethal shards of wood over the yard and its occupants in a loud hail of shrapnel. In the brief lightning flash as the men instinctively ducked and shielded their heads, Melissa was starkly lit, running for the gate, camera bag clutched close as though it contained something worth far more than camera equipment.

Yelling, the two men tore through the rose bushes towards her. Melissa yanked on the heavy garden gate and squirmed through the growing gap, pulling it sharply shut behind. Down the alley she plunged, her limp no longer faked as she had to scramble over the slippery stones and cobbles with a painful stitch in her side, fighting for every breath.

Slithering past a madly braying donkey rearing on its tether at the end of the street, Melissa tore open her camera bag. Reaching a junction of two narrow alleys, she deliberately spilled a wide angle lens onto the grit and pebbles of the larger path and took the smaller, jumping over a rolling narrow black bin and splashing through a huge dark puddle. For a few precious moments she crouched in the rubble of a crumbling barn, gulping in air as she heard feet sprinting the other way.

The trick had cost her an expensive lens but had worked: with her two trackers off on the wrong path she would be able to get away. Rising unsteadily to her feet, Melissa set off.

A few metres round a corner she was stopped short by a blank high wall: the path had petered into a dead end, with houses on one side and a small terraced field on the other. Cursing her bad luck, Melissa clambered over the field wall by using the cold slippery stems of a hibiscus bush and for the second time that night allowed herself to drop down into nothingness.

She landed on top of a chicken coop which erupted in noise, the bantams' hysterical alarm calls drowning even the final grumbling wind-down of the donkey. Instantly from an unseen street amongst the jumble of houses she could hear voices:

'That's her!'

'Bitch tricked us!'

'This way!'

Jolting her ankle fiercely as she leapt from the coop and landed amongst rows of beans, Melissa plunged across the rough oval field. Losing a flash unit from her gaping, flapping camera bag, she tipped down over the field wall into another black backstreet, this one with the pale gleam of the sea showing at its end, and pounded on, running for her life.

Now, even after the night was long over and her pursuers confounded, Melissa started awake, prepared to run again.

'Relax, woman, you're safe.'

It was gloomy in the surgery, the shutters not yet opened. Melissa sighed at the shadow sitting on the end of her couch. 'David?'

The shadow drew back farther on the couch.

'Nicholas. I should have known from the chauvinistic remark.'

Melissa slowly sat up and swallowed painfully: her mouth was very dry. This wasn't the time to untangle her feelings about David and Nicholas — even though she now knew for certain that Nicholas was not Spiro, not connected in any way to the smuggling gang that she was sure had murdered Andrew, and she still wasn't sure of the significance of the cages and the 'Katherine' file on David's island. And that was assuming both men would still be interested in her when Katherine was behind bars with the rest of the traders.

Nicholas padded from the couch to the white ghostly form of the surgery sink, returning with a beaker of water. 'Maybe this will sweeten your tongue as well as your breath, Bumblebee,' he muttered, thrusting the tumbler at her.

He had kept the shutters closed so she could not spot the bloodstains, and gritted his teeth to walk without limping, but Nicholas had forgotten Melissa's instinctive use of all her senses, honed after years of animal tracking. 'I smell dried blood on you. What's happened?' she exclaimed, eyes widening with alarm. Before Nicholas could speak she pushed herself from the couch. 'Have you seen the doctor?'

'It's just a scratch and it's already been fixed.' Nicholas shuffled sideways so that the bloody torn jeans and the bulky bandage were hidden, but Melissa caught hold of him, removing the glass from his fist, bustling him to sit on the couch.

'Where are you hurt? What did you do?' she was asking, smacking the glass down fiercely on a metal trolley of instruments. 'Nicholas, what happened? Are you quite all right?'

Suddenly questions weren't enough; she had to know, touch, see for herself. Turning away, Melissa moved to the shutters and tossed them open, gasping as the light streamed in and she saw —

'Nicholas!'

He was like a wounded stag, proud and wary and ready to charge — or at least prepared to defend himself. 'Bandages make it look worse than it is,' he said stiffly, 'So don't you fuss.'

Now she could see the good colour in his blunt face, the light in his eyes brighter than the storm-muted glare of the morning, Melissa laughed softly in relief. 'You're fine,' she said, leaning back against a shutter, trying not to stare at the man's full mouth, trembling a little under that bristling, wonderfully tickly moustache.

From not wanting a fuss, Nicholas was suddenly aggrieved. 'Well, now Alexios has dug out the bullet, I am,' he said, walking towards her, carefully, on the toes of his right foot to display his injury.

Melissa tried to keep on smiling, but at the word 'bullet', images of last night's carnage flooded her mind. She started, then burst into tears.

'Don't do that!' Horrified by the extremes of her reaction, Nicholas was at first bossy, then practical, yanking a clean handkerchief from his jeans pocket and thrusting it at her. 'Here, stop your crying.'

'Stop bossing me about, Nicholas.' Sometimes she almost hated him, Melissa thought. Snatching the handkerchief, she loudly blew her nose and vigorously mopped her face.

'There isn't time for me to do anything

else.' Nicholas, wanting to wrap his arms about Melissa and kiss her, remembered how on stirring she had asked for David. Hardening his heart at the sight of her blonde fringe ruffled by the breeze from the window, he added, 'Roxanne's gone and we've got to find her fast, before Gordon or anyone else.'

Melissa shivered with returning energy — or at least that was what she told herself it was. Her weakness in the face of this ferociously competent figure, still in control despite his injury, was alarming and humiliating. And last night, Roxanne had been tougher than she'd managed herself. Roxanne, who was now missing with a Caspian tiger.

'Nicholas! The shipment — it's a Caspian tiger cub, around seven weeks old. Caspians have been officially extinct for years! And Bailey's involved! He was with Spiro last night on Lykimi beach, where they gunned down their own people.'

'What? Bailey and Spiro are partners?'

'Yes! Katherine Hopkins has to be in on it too: you've got to arrest them, Nicholas! Bailey and Spiro can't have gone far: both were injured last night. Bailey was shot in the shoulder, I think, and Spiro — I hit Spiro in the face with a rock. Have Zervos go out to Petra — I tried to tell Alexios this morning but he'd given me an injection to make me sleep by the time we could speak privately.'

'Steady!' Nicholas strode closer to clasp Melissa by the shoulders. 'I'm not surprised the doctor gave you a tranquilliser: you look as though you could do with another.'

'But Spiro and Katherine and Bailey — they have to be picked up! This is a Caspian, and their thugs slaughtered its parents.'

'And, from what you say, several former associates. That should keep their profits healthy,' remarked Nicholas coolly, removing his hands from her.

Melissa tilted her chin at him. 'Should I care about them?' she demanded. 'When I know Spiro probably murdered —' Unable to continue as the old bitterness welled in her, Melissa broke off.

'Who, Melissa?' Staring at the raw look of weariness in her face, Nicholas took her cold hands in his. She looked different without her double pairs of seahorse earrings; younger, more vulnerable. 'Is he the reason you came to Asteri?' he asked gently.

'Roxanne — we must get on and try to find her.' Melissa tried to break free, but Nicholas shook his head at her.

'At least tell me his name,' he said.

'Andrew.' Melissa sighed heavily. 'Andrew Thornhill. I know now for certain that Spiro had a hand in his death. Maybe Bailey, too, although I haven't yet made any connection.'

Quickly she explained about her meeting with Stella and the true significance of the knife and seahorse bracelet. Nicholas heard her out in silence, his tanned face inscrutable. Only when she explained what Andrew had seen on Rhodes, and how he had later died, did a small muscle twitch briefly in his face.

'And now they're after Roxanne,' he said, when Melissa finished her rapid explanation. 'So we'd better hurry.'

Lifting the radio from his belt, Nicholas spoke rapidly into it, asking Zervos, Alexios and the other ASPW members for news of Roxanne.

The news was all the same: Roxanne was nowhere to be found.

'Anyone heard from Gordon?' Nicholas asked next.

'Not yet,' radioed Alexios.

'Niko — Zervos. I'm still at Lykimi, collecting samples before the storm washes our evidence away. Listen! I thought Gordon was with you. That's what he told me when he left me here, that he was walking back to Khora to speak to the mayor.'

'Well, he's not back yet. How long ago was this?'

'I've not seen nor heard from him in over an hour,' said Zervos. 'He's not answering on the radio.'

'Is that so?' Frowning, Nicholas shifted the radio receiver closer to his mouth. 'Think maybe he's run into trouble?'

'Gordon? Between Lykimi and Khora?' Zervos' tone of voice said it all, even before he added, 'There's been no other shooting here, so unless someone wanted to tackle him hand to hand . . . There's a trail of bloodstains near the cliff face as though one of the smugglers was injured —'

'That must have been Bailey,' broke in Melissa to Nicholas. 'He wouldn't be able to do much to stop blood falling from a shoulder wound.'

'But the trail peters out on the path,' concluded Zervos.

'Thanks, Zervos. Well, a second look in daylight can only be helpful. We should all keep trying to reach Gordon on the radio, too.' Nicholas exchanged a glance with Melissa: whether innocent or not, David's disappearance was a blow; one man less to join the search for Roxanne. 'What?' he asked Melissa.

'Bailey and Spiro tracked Roxanne and me to your house last night. I heard them shouting to each other when they were chasing me.' Suppressing a shudder, Melissa added, 'Maybe Alexios should look for a blood-trail here in Khora, although with the rain I doubt if any sign will be left by now.'

Scowling, Nicholas flipped the radio transmit button again and relayed this information and suggestion, which Alexios promised to act on at the earliest opportunity. Nicholas then returned to his main concern: Roxanne.

Officially it was too soon for her to be missing, and with no evidence of kidnapping Zervos could not leave the present murder enquiry — least of all since Manoli and Andreas, two men from Asteri, were laid out dead by gunshot in the main church. Nor had any more islanders come forward to help in the search: Roxanne was one of them, yet not one of them, being American by birth and living. If she had run off, it was for her own relatives to find her, or Turkish Gordon's men, and certainly no one else's concern.

Nicholas, listening to all this with an increasingly dark face rapped out, 'What about Gordon's people?'

'They're with me, Niko. I need help with the . . .' Zervos paused for a moment before concluding quietly, 'with the casualties.'

'Okay, okay. What about Pindaros?'

'I presume he's returned to Petra: after the

service for Zoe there was nothing to keep him lingering in Khora.' Zervos cleared his throat. 'I doubt if he'll be much use to you.'

'Right — so leave the guy out of this. Is there nobody else? Nobody in the whole of Asteri?'

'There's me,' said Melissa quietly beside him. For a moment it seemed Nicholas had not heard, then he turned to her.

'I think I know where Roxanne is,' she said. 'You don't need a search party.'

Nicholas gave her a strange look. 'I just need to trust you, right?'

'Why do you say that?' asked Melissa sharply. Sleeping in Alexios' surgery, she was unaware of the suspicion she was under. Now she waited with undisguised impatience as Nicholas continued simply to look at her. 'Well?' she demanded.

Nicholas jerked his head back and spoke swiftly into the radio set. 'Zervos, when you've finished at Lykimi I'd like you and David's security team to get over to Petra beach and ask Katherine Hopkins to accompany you back to Khora: nothing formal as yet, but I think we need to keep an eye on the lady. Watch out when you go there in case she's not alone: it could be that Miss Hopkins or her man Bailey are connected with Spiro. I'll explain the hows and whys later, and take any flak from the Rhodes police. If they complain, tell them I ordered you to do it as part of the official murder enquiry.'

'Okay, Niko, I'll go over there straight after Lykimi. And don't worry, I'll be careful.'

'Nicholas, before *you* do anything else, there's something here at the schoolhouse you ought to see.' Alexios' voice interrupted the exchange between the mayor and Asteri's part-time policeman.

Cursing, Nicholas snapped off the radio.

Out in the street the sun was shining wanly through a thick blanket of cloud but the southern wind had fallen and the rain was less heavy. In another hour the storm would have moved on and all travel would be easier — for the smugglers as well as for Roxanne, Nicholas and Melissa.

Responding to this, Nicholas set off down the street. In spite of his injury, Melissa had to jog to keep up with him.

'Is it a good idea to send Zervos to Petra?' she asked, breathless through concern, not speed. 'What if Bailey and Spiro are holed up there with Katherine?'

'He's armed, he's got a team of security men with him and Bailey and Spiro are both injured,' answered Nicholas shortly, 'And if

I know Katherine and she's involved as you say, then she'll have them keep out of sight.' He closed his mouth with a snap, as if that were an end to the whole business, but Melissa was not finished yet.

'What did you mean about finding Roxanne ahead of David?' she asked now as they hurried. 'Do you know more than you're saying about Antasteri?'

'No — do you?' he demanded, meeting question with question.

Melissa quickly told all she knew of the cages and the Katherine file. When she had finished, Nicholas said harshly, 'Why didn't you tell me this earlier?'

Melissa stopped herself from saying the truthful and yet corrosive, 'Because I wasn't sure of you,' and stammered instead, 'You and Katherine —'

'Did you really think I was that besotted with the woman?'

'You gave every impression of it.' Catching a welcome breath after that answer, Melissa was honest enough in herself to admit a quiet gratification at Nicholas' response — even now, in the midst of troubles.

Nicholas suddenly shook his dark head, surprising Melissa with his next question. 'Still, do you really think David's involved with this?'

'I don't know,' Melissa answered. 'I just can't be sure.'

Nicholas winced as they pounded down some steps. 'Let's go see what Alexios has for us.'

Until the police arrived from Rhodes, none of the men gunned down by Bailey were to be buried. Manoli and Andreas were laid out in the church, attended by their grieving families and the priest, but for the other smugglers the schoolhouse had become a temporary mortuary. Laid out on the stone flags under the high-roofed beams and Melissa's wall display of Asteri's forest and mountain, were three bodies wrapped in thick plastic sheeting. Through the ghostly wrapping it could be seen that one of the bodies was headless.

Zervos was still busy at Lykimi, leaving the doctor in charge of the dead. Nicholas now marched Alexios to the back of the hall and the dais where a few days earlier he had sat next to Katherine and Ari Pindaros.

'What's the point of this ghoulish exercise?' he hissed, jabbing a finger at the waiting Melissa. 'Want to show her that headless wonder, see if she knows him, or what?'

'No, to see if you know any, but remember, Nicholas' — Alexios caught hold of the man's sleeve — 'she still might have killed Zoe.'

Nicholas jerked his arm away so violently that his sleeve ripped. 'Melissa, can you wait outside, please?' he called down the school hall.

The small blonde figure standing near the entrance made no move to go.

'I'd like to see them, if I may,' said Melissa.

Alexios frowned. 'Considering your earlier shock, I wouldn't advise it.'

'Please' — Melissa walked forward slowly — 'I have to see.'

Before Alexios moved down the hall, Nicholas grabbed his sleeve. 'Not the last bag,' he warned, nodding grimly as Alexios acknowledged the command by a tense, 'You don't have to tell me!'

As the doctor came down into the hall to remove the layers of plastic, Melissa found Nicholas beside her, not offering his arm but rather clamping her to his side with a sinewy arm encircling her middle.

'I'm not going to faint!' she hissed at him.

'No, but I might,' Nicholas answered, trying to lighten the ghastly moment as the dead men's faces and upper bodies were revealed. Strangers to him, evoking no emotion other than relief that he was not like them, Nicholas felt Melissa beside him relax the stiffened posture she had steeled herself into in order to look. Glancing at her, he saw her features changing from a frozen anger to an open curiosity, then for a fleeting instant, a satisfaction.

'What do you see?' he asked, wondering at this unexpected response.

'Andrew was right: they are too smooth for Greek fishermen.' Not elaborating on that, Melissa stared another few seconds at the beardless, well-groomed figures. How she knew that these were two of the men Andrew had spotted in a Rhodes back street she had no idea, only that looking at them now she sensed a chapter in her life closing, a puzzle completed. She gazed for another second, then buried her face in Nicholas' shoulder.

'Let's leave the dead to themselves and go and find Roxanne,' she said. 'I just hope David has forgotten the place.'

'What?' demanded Nicholas. 'Where exactly?'

'There isn't much time now, the storm's dropping. I'll tell you on the way.'

Chapter 44

With Melissa safely out of the way in Alexios' surgery, David made the return journey from Lykimi beach to Khora in less of a dark temper than when he had set out.

Instructing his men to stay with Zervos, who was still shocked over the dead islanders, David had pressed on through the wet heathland, scarcely registering the purple-yellow dawn or the drenched and stirring scents of the early morning. The machinations of Bailey and the smugglers were nothing: where was Roxanne? How had she escaped? Where had she fled to?

Eighteen years old, a model, a young woman, a daughter. In a crisis which of these aspects would be the strongest? 'If I were Roxanne,' David talked to himself, striding heavily round the masses of prickly pear down to the road and the beginnings of Khora village, 'if I were an eighteen-year-old frightened girl, what would be my main concern after getting away? To let someone know where I was. To tell friends and family I was safe.'

The tiny shingle beach along which David was walking was spattered with dead birds and flowers, a child's plastic trumpet, a water-logged torch. Scrambling around a beached fishing boat, its sharp prow traditionally painted for protection with two watchful eyes, and barely noticing the shattered and gaping eye-socket on its port side, David continued his deliberations.

'Roxanne is considerate: she wouldn't want anyone to worry or waste time searching. I wonder if in the mêlée last night she had time to grab a radio set? Must go back to Nicholas' and have a look.'

Around him, now, stood figures disconsolately looking over their battered boats and businesses. A small group of mourners from Manoli's household had gathered around his rusting ferry. David, wrapped up in Roxanne, did not see Popi or Stella or the others. The women, huddled in their new but already soaked black clothes, slowly pushing brooms around the ferry's foredeck to clean out the mess of seaweed and dead jelly fish, were oblivious to Turkish Gordon's passing. The night of the storm had wrecked many lives.

A church bell was tolling. David registered it as he picked a way through the twos and threes of men standing smoking cigarettes on the long steps up from the harbour. Glancing over his shoulder, he saw now the jetty, half demolished by the sea, and the splintered remains of a half-dozen fishing boats.

Dipping into shadow, David walked straight into the mayor's house, its blue door leaning neatly against the pink house wall, no longer barring anyone's way.

Roxanne had not picked up a radio. One was lying near the overturned sofa. David ignored it, then jumped slightly as the radio in his jacket pocket popped and whined into speech.

'Niko? Zervos again. The body without a head, I've remembered who it is. His name's Yannis Korkonzilas. He was part of the Rhodes tourist police force a couple of years ago but then emigrated to Germany. Or so we were all told.'

'Where did you say he worked?' Melissa's voice breaking into the radio transmission was a surprise to David. Alerted by the tension in her question, he turned up the volume for Zervos' reply.

'Korkonzilas? Always in the city, Rhodes Town. Yannis loved the Old Town, and he loved practicing his languages with the foreigners.'

David frowned as Nicholas' loud rasp

came blaring over the set: 'Two years ago in Rhodes Old Town. You think maybe that Andrew reported what he'd seen to *this* policeman?'

Melissa, to whom the question must have been addressed, made some reply off-air which David could not catch, only the final, '. . . and Korkonzilas never filed it. He must have been corrupt even then.'

The signal broke up as David flinched, slewing round quickly, fists raised ready to defend himself. The crackling roar of the radio filled the space between him and the stooping figure of Ari Pindaros, now nursing one hand with another.

'I only put my hand on your shoulder,' he protested in English.

David clicked off the radio. 'You startled me.'

Pindaros pinched his narrow nose between finger and thumb. 'Stephanides has let that blonde bitch out of prison.'

David assumed so but said nothing, expecting Pindaros to add his own comment on this development. It came quickly.

'If he brings her near me, I'll kill her.' Certain of Melissa's guilt in murdering Zoe, Pindaros nodded his head to emphasise his resolution.

David still said nothing. A movement beyond Pindaros' fleshy shoulders had caught his attention.

'Katherine,' he said, stepping round the overturned sofa. 'I understood you were at Petra.'

'In the circumstances,' replied Katherine, smiling, 'that is scarcely appropriate.' Elegant in black, she made the wreck of the house seem even worse.

'Is Bailey with you?' asked David, noting how busy Katherine's green eyes were, scanning every part of the sitting room, fixing on the answering machine with its unlit cassette and stopped clock. Like him, it seemed that Katherine had come here to discover if there were any messages. Now, running the end of her shining brown plait through her nimble fingers, she answered smoothly, 'I haven't seen Bailey in hours. Sir Oliver's with me, though, he's waiting in the main square in the car. We thought we might go for a drive, put this sad business behind us for a while.'

She was so brazen a liar that David did not know whether to be impressed or appalled. She played for big stakes, Katherine Hopkins, and was unafraid to walk into a potentially lethal situation. Unless she had some means of communication, David reflected, Katherine would not know if Bailey was still at liberty, or if his smuggling 'cover' had been blown. Presumably, David thought, her present approach was to discover how much he and others knew. Well, he too could be deceitful and give nothing away.

Katherine glanced at Ari Pindaros. 'Zoe looked so beautiful at the service today,' she said.

'Yes.' Pindaros' eyes filled as he touched the left lapel of his grey suit, where a single dull blonde hair remained. 'She's at peace now.'

'And how are you?' Katherine asked gently, extending a hand towards the older man.

Her fingers accidentally brushed a low table, catching a mother-of-pearl shell stranded there. Puckering her mouth in irritation, Katherine put her hand down sharply on the spinning shell and suddenly her expression changed.

'Why, isn't this from Antasteri?' she remarked, looking straight at David. 'From your beach? You know, I think it is.' She lowered her eyelids slightly, Pindaros dismissed for the moment in an instant's delicious flirtation. 'Roxanne is obviously quite attached to your place, David.'

A tumble of black hair fell across David's

forehead as his head came back slightly, but otherwise he managed to stifle his response and answer steadily, 'I hope you were also impressed.'

'Oh, I was,' Katherine replied, 'Especially with the wildlife.' Smiling again at David, she gave Pindaros' arm a comforting squeeze and turned on her slender heels. 'Mustn't keep Sir Oliver waiting: I only popped in to see if Nicholas was back yet, or if there'd been any news of Roxanne. Poor girl, last night must have been quite terrifying for her. Goodbye, Ari, and take care of yourself. See you later, David.'

When she had gone Pindaros looked puzzled. 'Katherine wasn't here for Stephanides,' he remarked absently. 'What did she want really, I wonder?'

'Doing the same as I am, looking for clues,' said David. As he spoke, the thought of where Roxanne might be hiding, the true significance of the mother-of-pearl shell, made him duck down to watch Katherine's progress outside in the street. She certainly wasn't hurrying: maybe the message had been too subtle. Maybe he was wrong. A terrible thought, since he might have only one chance to recover Roxanne before anyone else.

So. Was Roxanne fleeing west or not?

David glanced a second time at the shell, plucked from the beach of Antasteri. He had ridden Roxanne's bike to Petra — had Roxanne herself taken her father's? Did Stephanides have a bicycle?

Suddenly, as David strained to remember, a mental picture of Mike the butcher's house came into his mind, a two-storey cottage close to the blue church and on the road to Kemi and the western half of Asteri. He'd brought it to mind because of the butcher's bicycle which was nearly always there, leaning against the house wall.

It was a sturdy machine, with, if he remembered it correctly, a big wicker carrying basket, perfect for transporting animals — Mike's dog often rode in that basket.

Now the pieces fell into place. 'See you later,' David said to Pindaros, and strode to the gaping door.

'Where are you going?' Pindaros was following him, almost like a lost soul. Which in a way he was, reflected David. He stopped in the street, turning in a puddle of stormwater.

'I'm going home,' he said simply. 'Want to come?'

Pindaros twitched his shoulders. 'Why not?' he said, and grinned a travesty of his conference smile.

★ ★ ★

David's security guards were still with Zervos and Alexios. They had helped to carry the bodies from Lykimi beach and now they were busy guarding the smugglers' remains from the curious villagers of Khora. David knew this but thought he would do very well without guards. Pindaros was more of a shadow right now than a man, yet even shadows have eyes and ears. He would find Roxanne: he already knew where to look.

With Pindaros always half a step behind him, David made his way back to the harbour. His own yacht was hemmed in by other little boats, and he spent an irritable ten minutes clambering in and out of craft, trying to find one that was still seaworthy and with keys and tackle on board. Finally a caique, its cabin crammed with fishing nets, seemed the most promising. David dragged out the nets and used the ship's own radio to hail Zervos.

Learning that Roxanne was not yet found — which did not surprise him — David answered, 'Nicholas and your people and mine can knock Kemi off their list of places to search: Pindaros and I are just going there now. I'll call you when we get in.'

About to add more, David broke off as two bodies landed heavily on the deck of the caique. Bursting from the cabin, he saw a stocky, dark-haired man punch Pindaros in the stomach, then tumble over the side to fall spread-eagled onto the deck of another fishing boat. As David lunged after the man, a brilliant orange light exploded in his head.

David shook his head and tried to rise, but a foot thrust him back onto his rough bed of fishing nets.

'Stay there!' ordered Pindaros sharply. 'It's years since I mastered a ship: until we've cleared the harbour you be still.'

'Be glad to,' croaked David. Now that his wits were beginning to clear he could feel the shudder of the caique engine: his ears were still throbbing from the blast.

'You took a flare almost in the face, my friend.' Pindaros was speaking in English: he sounded strangely sanguine, as if the conflict had released him from the obligation of grief. This was the free-booting bauxite millionaire David knew of old, although he still could not open his eyes to see if there was a true smile under that jutting widow's peak and bushy grey eyebrows.

'They were making ready the next ship. I caught that man listening to your report. Now they have a head start on us to Kemi.'

David rubbed his eyelids: all the lashes

seemed to have been burned off. He could feel his clothes ragged and torn, his jacket scorched and shredded. Almost afraid to meet blindness, he forced his eyes open.

Blue. The sky. Grey. The sea. Brown. David pinched his eyes narrower, and the brown haze became a rope. Cautiously, he lifted his hands up and examined the blackened palms. Instinctively, he had shielded his face with his hands. Now, callused and roughened by sculpting as they were, his hands were stripped raw under the smut. Immediately, David became conscious of them smarting.

'You were lucky.' In the cabin alongside him, Pindaros spun the wheel with the nonchalance of a veteran. The caique pitched more steeply as they hit the open sea. 'The man aimed badly: you were caught by the edge of the blast only.'

David pulled himself smartly to a sitting position, then instantly keeled over like a rolling ship and found himself back on the fishing nets again. He swore, the temper in him hotter than his reddened eyes.

'Not a pretty sight, though.' Pindaros laughed as David cursed some more. 'Good! Now you feel as I did when the black-haired man with the broken nose hit me in the guts. It's been years since I did any street fighting,

but to be caught that way is very sloppy. Still'
— Pindaros shrugged his hands and shoulder
— 'we shall get them, maybe, at Kemi.'

'Them? Did you see who else was with this
man with the bloody nose?'

'No, but somebody was in that boat's
cabin, unless Broken-nose could cast off and
steer at the same time.'

David caught hold of a swinging cable and
slowly this time hauled himself up against
the gunwale. Over the wooden boards he
spotted a school of dolphins tumbling and
spouting in the swirling seas: a rare and
happy omen for their trip, he hoped. The
spray wet his dry lips as he cleared his singed
throat to speak.

'You've forgotten what I said earlier, Ari.
We're not going to Kemi.'

'But on the radio —'

'Which anyone can listen in to. I told a
pack of lies.' David tapped the side of his
long sooty nose. As a knight errant he lacked
a certain sartorial charm right now, but that
couldn't be helped.

'No,' he repeated, 'we're not going to
Kemi.'

Chapter 45

'She's definitely been here.' Nicholas shifted one of the neatly rolled duvets with his foot. 'No sign of her leaving in a hurry or by force, either.' Nicholas, admitting this, now let a smile of relief bloom in his tanned, taut face. 'You were right.'

'Did you doubt me? No, don't answer that. Come on, we need to make sure Roxanne's not hiding in one of the villa rooms. I'll start in David's workshop.' Melissa turned to go, turned back, brown eyes quizzical.

'On the subject of doubt — do you believe I could have hurt Zoe?'

Meeting silence, Melissa took several steps closer to her companion. 'So I was right,' she said, feeling a curious relief now that the matter was out in the open, 'I am a suspect.'

Here the reason for Alexios' stifled manner towards her that morning, the reason why the doctor had pulled Nicholas so urgently to one side just as he and she were leaving the schoolhouse. It was whilst watching the two men whispering together, their eyes often fixing on her and then quickly withdrawing, that Melissa had begun to wonder if there was more to Alexios' tense stance than humanitarian or medical concern.

'Chloe!' Nicholas was patting the duvet. 'Down here, girl.' He waited until his dog flopped onto the bedding. She whined slightly at the puzzling scents of Roxanne and Caspian tiger cub.

Melissa watched impassively. 'I am, aren't I?' she demanded, as Chloe began to lick noisily at one of her white forepaws, her drying coat beginning to fluff out against the dark blue duvet cover. 'For some crazy reason I've become a murder suspect as well as a wildlife smuggler — strange though, isn't it, that as a smuggler I'm not out there, fighting for my cut?' She jerked her chin towards the long east-facing kitchen window and, through it, the sea and the tall pines of Antasteri, where the cages lay hidden.

'I never really had you down as a smuggler.' Nicholas dragged his blue cap from his pocket and pulled it onto his head. 'Don't flatter yourself that I think you're a killer, either — only maybe as a long shot,' he added gruffly.

Melissa lowered her blonde head, checking the number of shots she had left in her camera. 'But you concede that it's possible?' she asked sarcastically, picking up on 'really' and 'maybe'. Did he know so little about her still? she thought, reluctant to admit to the disappointment that Nicholas' statements invoked in her.

The man shrugged. 'Anything's possible.'

His answer could be a joke, but Melissa did not think so. 'Not big on trust, are you?' she answered sharply. 'And stop hunching your shoulders at me: I don't find it impressive.'

Nicholas picked up a plate from the metal sink, scowling at the flash of watery sunlight on metal and china. 'Only a fool trusts anybody completely,' he observed without meeting her gaze.

'Well, thank you very much for your unreserved confidence.' Melissa whirled round and started for David's workshop, calling back tartly over her shoulder, 'If you can trust me to search properly, I'll see you outside, all right?'

Without waiting for a reply, she flounced off into David's studio and smartly turned on the lights.

When they flicked into brilliance, Melissa saw almost at once that no one had been in the building for at least a day: sculpture dust had settled on the floor and not been swept, yet there were no tracks. Casting a rapid eye under the tables and tool racks, Melissa was ready to leave when she remembered the computer. This was a chance she should take to look again at the Katherine file, and snatch a photograph or printout. It would only take a moment.

Taking a deep breath to try to calm herself, Melissa switched on the computer, called up the relevant file and raised the camera to her eye.

Determined to concentrate on the technical details of how she should light her shots, Melissa did not bother to look round as Nicholas stalked limping into the studio, and refused to stir when he yanked back the sliding doors between the storage and working areas. She heard the man's low grunt of appreciation as he spotted the clay maquette David had produced to sell Pindaros the idea of his latest commission, and caught his grudging 'Good . . . good . . . ,' as he prowled round the easels displaying David's brilliant working sketches of his three models. Melissa likewise ignored Nicholas as he called down from the working third of the studio, his voice echoing in the apse-like chamber: 'You coming? What are you looking at over there?'

I will not allow him to upset me again. Melissa counted steadily to twenty, the main part of her mind wrestling with apertures and speeds. Since this computer did not appear to be linked to a printer, she needed a really clear picture of the screen and its damning information.

'Melissa —'

Some strain in Nicholas' voice made Melissa turn, the camera still to her eye, where her short zoom focus homed in on the barrel of a pistol.

Slowly she lowered the camera, arms trembling slightly. Had she made a dreadful mistake? Was Nicholas her villain?

'There's nothing here.' Nicholas motioned sharply with the pistol. 'Let's go.'

'Nick?' Melissa could still not believe it.

'I'd drop that if I were you, Stephanides.' David pushed open the studio door.

Plainly, David had not waited for his boat to land in the harbour alongside Nicholas'. Stripped to the waist and barefoot, the former Olympic swimmer was sleeked over with seawater. At the sight of his tall powerful figure stooped against the door-frame, ready to take on an armed man barehanded, Melissa cried out, 'Don't!' Whether she meant 'Don't shoot,' to Nicholas or 'Don't hurt him,' to David, she had no way of knowing. Events overtook feelings as David spat at Nicholas, 'Where's Roxanne?' and, as Melissa, glancing at the flashing computer file, cried out 'Don't!' a second time.

'Oh, yes, do,' came a new voice. 'Tell us all, Nicholas.'

Katherine appeared behind David and, at a touch from her hand on his damp shoulder, the man let her through.

As she strolled into the studio and David meekly followed, Melissa could not suppress a bitter comment. 'I'm not surprised you dislike cameras, David, when you've so much to hide.' And, as Nicholas lowered his pistol, 'I suppose you had me down as a fool, Nick, though I never trusted you completely.'

'Drop it!' The new voice was full of menace. Behind David three new figures had entered the long building — two armed with light automatic rifles aimed directly at David's back and Nicholas' broad shoulders. There was a dull clatter as Nicholas' pistol fell onto the concrete.

'Where's your girl?' the man demanded in Greek. Facing Nicholas, he was the same height and with almost the same depth of chest, but his black hair was both curlier and sparser and his moustache bloodstained at the ends. His nose was a misshapen sore. Looking at him, Melissa felt her stomach curl in a cold, then burning, horror. It took all her will not to launch herself at Spiro, the wildlife smuggler. Spiro, who had betrayed and murdered his own people on Lykimi beach. Spiro who, she was convinced, had killed Andrew.

Melissa dug her fingers deep into her palms as Nicholas flicked the brim of his faded blue cap and snapped back, 'Why do you think I'm still looking? Obviously, she's not here.'

Spiro's bloodstained moustache twitched but it was the second armed man who lashed out with the barrel of his weapon, flaying it across Nicholas' body. Melissa yelled 'Stop it!', but Nicholas never flinched.

'Down!' he hissed at his dog as Chloe tensed, a low growl issuing through her bared teeth.

'Where's my kitty?' demanded the second man, raising the gun to strike again.

'All in good time, Sir Oliver.' Katherine moved to the computer. 'Now, if one of you gentlemen could pick the gun up, and another make sure that Melissa isn't recording our reunion on some hidden camera . . .'

Melissa was briskly searched and stripped of her camera gear by Sir Oliver, who spitefully tossed her camera bodies into a plastic barrel and her zoom lens into a large lidded glass jar full of clay slip.

Spiro, battered features displaying a satisfied grin, motioned to David and Nicholas to throw down their two-way radios. Katherine meanwhile fixed her gaze on the humming computer screen, a faint smile on her perfect lips.

'What a coincidence.' Her green eyes widened as she took in the name of the file and the names and prices of animals. 'Bailey, come and look: you may be able to do something with this.'

Bailey, his left shoulder in a dirty bloodstained sling, was lowering himself by leaning against a sink. As he stretched a slow, twitching arm and retrieved Nicholas' firearm, he observed with some surprise, 'The safety's on.'

Instantly, Melissa's eyes flew to Nicholas, who said simply, 'I never meant to scare you. Being in a hurry to find Roxanne, I forgot how nervous you English get around guns.'

'Trite.' Katherine turned back from the computer. 'Sir Oliver, please help Bailey up: we need to get on before the police fly in.'

'Or the rest of your gang come and find out,' said David grimly. 'Those you haven't already got rid of.'

'Shut up, stupid bastard!' Spiro lurched forward and stabbed the tall Englishman in the groin with the butt of his heavy automatic.

'That's enough,' said Katherine coolly as David, with a strangled gasp, toppled sideways amongst the statuary. Ignoring orders, Spiro kicked him in the head.

'Call him off!' Melissa sprang at Katherine. Sir Oliver Raine, in a surprising turn of speed, hauled Bailey to his feet then smacked both hands back onto his gun, aiming it firmly at Nicholas' torso.

'Touch Miss Hopkins and I fire.'

Glaring into Katherine's flushed, triumphant face, Melissa grudgingly lowered her arm.

'That's much better.' Ignoring Melissa, Katherine scrolled through the pages of order details on the Katherine file, beckoning meanwhile to the shuffling Bailey.

'Can we use it?'

'Katherine — my merchandise,' said Sir Oliver, his florid complexion redder than ever in the unrelenting studio lights.

'In a moment.' Katherine held up a pacifying hand. 'Spiro, you take another look around. Perhaps Nicholas and Melissa missed something that will please our client.'

'No problem.' With a grin which made Melissa crimson with temper, Spiro went out into a morning filled with birdsong

'You're being very frank, Katherine,' said Melissa, when she felt cool enough to speak.

'No reason why I shouldn't be, Melissa. I don't see anyone present who will trouble me in future.' Dismissing Nicholas with a gold-edged wink of a green eye, Katherine glanced down at David, now sitting up and resting his bare back against a metal saw. 'Pity, really, David. I had you in mind for a TWC commission, but then, you being a recluse . . . it wasn't ideal.'

David fixed Katherine with his unblinking black eyes, his face paler and harder than marble. The burr in his reply was the anger, barely controlled, of a man promising himself revenge. 'If your creatures touch my girl, I'll take it out on you, woman. I'll carve your flesh till you don't know yourself.'

'Hear that, Nicholas? "My girl"!' Katherine swung round. 'Aren't you disappointed, Melissa? Oh, yes, I see that you are. But then, as you've already learned with Andrew, nothing's permanent where you and men are concerned.'

At the edge of her vision, Melissa could just see Nicholas scrutinising the pliers and pulleys. She dare not look at David in case she alerted Katherine or the fretful Sir Oliver, who, having only now spotted the lithely drawn bodies on the large easel standing close to the maquette of David's 'Judgement of Paris', was blowing lustily down his

561

sharp nose and averting his eyes.

Whilst the head of Beach International was so distracted, Spiro absent and Bailey laboriously tapping at the computer, Melissa guessed that she, David and Nicholas would not have so good a chance as now to seize the advantage. Yet Katherine had mentioned Andrew. For his sake, Melissa knew she must speak. Whatever the dangers, even if it meant a missed opportunity to escape, she had to know everything Katherine knew about Andrew.

A direct question might produce a lie: everything would depend on whether Katherine considered the truth or a falsehood the more hurtful. Quickly, before any of the men spoke and claimed her mercurial attention, Melissa addressed Katherine.

'What do you mean, about me and men? Andrew didn't leave me, he . . . he died.'

'Yes. Two years ago, almost to this very month. And you've never realised in all that time that his removal from Rhodes was down to me.' Katherine flipped a finger at a startled Sir Oliver to prevent his exclamation. 'Dumb blonde Melissa, always way behind.'

'Why?' Melissa needed no dissembling now: the question burst from her, urgent and hurting. 'You once cared for him, too — You and he were lovers!'

'A real black widow,' remarked Nicholas laconically, but Katherine ignored him. Swooping forward from the work bench, green eyes alight, she could not wait to skewer her enemy with every detail.

'Long ago, when he was fresh, but I found the bloom soon went off him. Andrew was too simple and much too curious. When Spiro told me about his spotting part of our Rhodes Town enterprise, Bailey here wanted him removed, but I decided to give him another chance. It was really a shame that Andrew blew it.'

Katherine's voice sharpened. 'When Spiro saw Thornhill again in that goat-infested village down in south Rhodes, only one day after their dawn rendezvous in Rhodes Town at the other end of the island, he and Bailey decided we couldn't take any more risks. At the time, the coincidence seemed unlikely and far too much of a luxury where our business was concerned. Thornhill was, after all, connected with you, a wildlife investigator. When Bailey phoned me, I'm bound to say I agreed with them. I suggested the retsina.'

Coughing slightly, Bailey hunched over the computer keyboard, his briefcase at his feet as he typed rhythmically with his free hand. Whoever had gouged out the bullet from his shoulder and roughly patched him up had not done too clean a job, thought Melissa, revolted by the man's sweaty pallor but even more by what she had just heard.

'I did hope, Melissa, that Andrew's death might slow you down a little, make you consider the risks in your line of work,' Katherine continued. 'Make you stop, that is.'

'You didn't know Melissa very well, then,' put in David quietly.

'Andrew always hated retsina,' said Melissa slowly. 'She didn't know him very well, either.'

Katherine merely shook her head at these interruptions.

'An understandable oversight,' she explained. 'One of our local Rhodes contacts bought him a few drinks whilst Spiro and Bailey were busy making the final arrangements for the shipment to land and for Thornhill's trip off the cliff.' Katherine gave a small, regretful smile. 'Andrew would have downed his retsina quite nicely, I'm sure. He was always polite.'

'You okayed a man's death by phone?' Nicholas seemed stunned by the ease of the decision.

Katherine missed the point entirely. 'Such are the wonders of modern international communication: fast, secure lines, even on a relative backwater like Rhodes. I suppose living on a real backwater, you're a little behind the technology, though as an American —'

'Can't this wait?' broke in Sir Oliver. 'You said that girl would be here, that my kitty would be safe here.'

At his petulant complaint, Chloe, who had been standing up rigidly on her feet and growling throughout the last few moments of sickening violence and glib accounts of violence, now laid back her ears and barked.

'Down, Chloe!' commanded Nicholas and Melissa together, and there was a moment's tense quiet, silent except for the swish of the pinewoods outside, then Bailey cut in.

'It's a long order for carved animal figures. When each one was completed or shipped: "all in soapstone as requested", it says in a letter at the end.' Bailey cleared his throat. 'The letter starts, "Dear Katherine".'

The Katherine file was now explained. Not as a smuggling record of animals and dates but as a sculptor's account to a customer. When she had discovered the file here on David's studio computer, Melissa recollected, she'd had no more than a few seconds to study it before being interrupted. Having not seen the end of the document, she had not seen the letter. Now, hearing the innocent nature of the file, Melissa felt a deep shame engulf her. She had been so quick to condemn, so ready to believe that David could be involved with the smugglers, and perhaps even with Andrew's death. All because the name on the file was that of her old enemy.

It was ironic — the thought ran through Melissa with the power of an electric charge — that, at the very moment when she discovered that Nicholas and David were genuine allies, both were helpless at gunpoint. If anyone was going to stop Katherine, it would have to be her.

Strangely that thought gave Melissa new heart, submerging shame in a fiery blast of determination. She had beaten Katherine before. Now her head came up as Katherine asked again, 'Can we use it?'

'Maybe.' Bailey wiped his pale forehead with the rumpled sleeve of his brown suit. 'These prices are way too low.'

'So adapt them,' replied Katherine with sweet patience. 'You and Spiro know the going rates.'

'Katherine!' protested Sir Oliver, allowing the semi-automatic to waver in his distraction.

'Watch them!' Katherine ordered sharply. 'Your cargo won't be going anywhere yet and this is urgent. I presume you want to keep the shipment? Well, this computer file will cover our tracks for good. When Bailey's finally stopped fiddling and gets on with the necessary changes — and don't forget to re-name it, will you, Bailey? — the police won't be looking for us at all.'

'I'd be careful of believing what she says,' said Melissa casually to Sir Oliver. 'You haven't paid her yet, I hope.'

The muzzle of the gun wavered towards Melissa. Katherine said viciously, 'We don't need all of them to tell us where Roxanne is.'

'The cub isn't with Roxanne,' said Melissa. 'I've hidden it.'

Sir Oliver gasped, his grip on the gun barrel slipping.

Katherine slapped Melissa hard across the face. 'Liar!'

'There again, perhaps David's hidden the Caspian. Or Nicholas.' Despite the ringing pain in her head, Melissa smiled. 'We were here before you.'

'Not so much before *him*,' said Katherine, pointing at David.

David's jaw set as the gun muzzle was trained on him

'Antasteri's mine,' he said quietly. 'I know every inch of it.'

'It's just a baby, right?' put in Nicholas.

'Kill me,' David continued quietly, 'and if Melissa is lying, you may not find the cub alive. If you find it at all,' he added, after a pause.

Sir Oliver moaned.

'I've seen the Caspian,' said Melissa. 'I can describe it to you. Can she?' She jerked a thumb at Bailey, still furiously typing. 'Can he? If your little tigress is ill after her long journey, will Katherine have the knowledge to save her?'

Sir Oliver looked uncertainly at Katherine, who said quickly, 'I was right about the mother-of-pearl shell and Roxanne coming here, wasn't I? You've dealt with me and my people before, and haven't you always been satisfied?'

'The Pallas cat, remember who shipped it for you?' asked Bailey, wiping his sweaty fingers on his lapels as he switched off the computer. 'We've the know-how and experience.'

'And efficiency,' added Katherine.

Melissa laughed softly. 'Now the commercial's over, Sir Oliver, you've still the same problem. You can't afford to lose any of us right now, and if we all rush you —'

A smell of the sea drifted into the studio as Spiro hauled the door open.

'Nothing!' he told the expectant faces and,

without further comment, he marched into the long building and seized hold of the nearest block-and-tackle.

'Chain two and bring one,' he said. 'Maybe the girl will give herself up rather than watch her people suffer.' He pointed his gun at Nicholas. 'We'll start with him. Bring the dog, too: the bitch will lead us there, even if its master won't.'

Chapter 46

David yanked again on the chains padlocked to his arms and torso, staring and cursing at the solid beam above himself and Melissa which obstinately refused to budge. A thin trickle of blood and sweat ran across his shackled wrists and muscled forearms. As he strained again a drop splattered onto the easel with its drawings of Melissa, Katherine and Roxanne as Athene, Aphrodite and Hera.

'I'll try climbing up again in a moment,' Melissa panted. She had just attempted to heave herself up the thick metal links to the level of the roof beam. But the chains around her body, designed to shift and hold blocks of stone, were too heavy.

'Bugger it!' David stopped struggling and glowered across at Melissa. 'I wish to God I knew what was happening out there! Do you know where Roxanne is?'

Melissa tried to nod but found that the chain wrapped close around her body made it impossible. Spiro had used only the lightest chains on her and David, not from consideration or kindness but because they lay close at hand.

'I believe so,' she said, her breath tight in her chest. Light as they were for stone or wood, the metal links weighed hard on flesh. 'You mentioned the place yourself.'

'Ah.' David's sound of recognition was also a ragged breath. Both of them were tiring quickly under the drag and strain. He looked sideways and down into her face. 'Don't worry, Melissa, this is my workshop. I'll think of something.'

Chest heaving, he paused, hands gripped tight on the chains above and around his shoulders and torso. He was already naked to the waist, and his tailored cream trousers were now filthy. David the immaculate perfectionist had come down in the world, Melissa thought wryly. So had she.

Gasping, she admitted, 'These last few hours, I've learned I'm not as strong as I thought I was.' Scraping her chin slightly on a metal link, she looked at David. 'Your Roxanne's tough.'

'She's too young for me.' David frowned, but then he smiled at Melissa, smiling even with his glossy swan's eyes. A look which made her conscious, not of her sticky, smeared camouflage clothes, but of the taut links across her hips, her cinched waist.

'Do you think I'm an animal smuggler or a murderer?' she asked. The questions had no meaning now, but later, should they come out of this alive . . .

David laughed, showing his strong teeth. 'That wouldn't matter.'

'Why not? It did with me.'

'Ah, the Katherine file! I suppose you found the hawk cages, too? Poor little Melissa.' David lifted a chain with his fingers, let it fall with a harsh metallic clash. 'Now are you convinced of my innocence?'

'Yes — but what about me?' answered Melissa, chains digging deep round her waist and breast.

'I never believed either charge — ever.'

Meeting his solemn eyes, Melissa was thrilled for an instant, but then Nicholas' rugged New England voice sounded in her head: *Only a fool trusts anybody completely.*

Suddenly, in their moment of intimate silence, David worked off his temper on the lifting gear he was encased in, wasting his strength so recklessly and furiously that Melissa cried out, 'Stop! That isn't getting us anywhere!'

'What's happening out there?' David's voice dropped suddenly as he was still. 'Listen!'

Both were so quiet they could hear the

drone of bees, the lisp of the sea curling up the tiny beach of Antasteri harbour. Through the open studio door poured a molten bar of light, stinging in its promise of heat.

A man's shadow impressed itself on the golden bar, then Ari Pindaros was in the room with them; so shocked by their trussed figures that for a moment he stopped and did nothing.

'Hurry, man! Get these things off us!' David ordered.

Starting to, Pindaros moved and rushed to the work-benches. Passing close to Melissa, she saw how his hair was stiff with sea-spray, and caught a whiff of his thousand-dollar suit, fragrant with crushed hyssop and sage. In any other circumstances, the millionaire's dishevelled appearance would have been amusing.

Pindaros meanwhile was rummaging along the work-benches to find the keys to the padlocks.

'Use the cutters on that far wall,' David said. 'Those hanging close to the shutter.'

Finally Pindaros looked where David was pointing with his head and lifted the correct tool down from the wall. Moving more fluently now, he thrust the blunted point of the cutters into the first of the padlocks holding David's chains. One after another the locks snapped, showering like flashing steel confetti onto the floor. The chains followed more slowly — speed here would have cut David's back to ribbons.

Unwinding the last chain, David seized the cutters from Pindaros and set to work on Melissa, lifting and throwing the metal links off her. 'What happened to you?' he demanded of Pindaros as he worked.

'Katherine Hopkins and the others sailed into the bay two minutes after you'd anchored at the edge of the harbour wall and dived overboard. They saw you run along the jetty and assumed you were alone.

'I hid in the cabin, saw them rush up to the villa,' continued Pindaros. 'I dared not radio for help in case any of them had a transmitter.

'I followed and waited in the woods.' Pindaros flushed slightly, as though perhaps ashamed that he, an unarmed man, should not have instantly confronted four opponents, two of them armed. 'When they led Niko out alone, I slipped in.'

'Good, good.' David steadied Melissa as the final suffocating metal bond came off and her numbed legs and feet took her own natural weight. Her wrists and ankles were sore but not chafed. Silently she pointed to David's raw forearms.

'It'll keep,' said David. Though not fooled by his briskness, Melissa knew there was no choice: time was running out fast for Roxanne, Nicholas and the Caspian cub.

She stamped her feet on the concrete. 'Which way were Nick and the rest going?' she asked Pindaros.

Pindaros stared at her flushed, determined face and glanced at David, who was coiling a rope around his middle and tucking a chisel into its folds. Again, the man's gaze returned to Melissa. He seemed suspicious and astonished. Facing him down, Melissa decided to be blunt.

'I didn't hurt Zoe and I've never wished anyone's death. If she were here now, Zoe would help us: she wouldn't let these — these people succeed.'

In spite of Melissa's best intentions, her voice wavered when she thought of everything Spiro, Katherine, Bailey and Sir Oliver had done, or allowed to be done, for the sake of ownership and riches. Thinking of Andrew drinking the retsina of his death from good manners, she felt the colour drain from her face.

Pindaros' features, ugly yet arresting, did not soften: he was unconvinced by her little speech. No reason why he should be convinced, reflected Melissa bleakly. She tried again to reach him, appealing to practicalities. 'I'm here now with you and David. I can't leave Antasteri.'

'You did once before, as I recall,' said David to her under his breath, full mouth stretching a wicked grin. Showing he had forgiven Melissa for her 'escape' from Antasteri on that occasion, David now added, 'Melissa won't be going anywhere except with us, Ari.'

Pindaros scowled, then nodded sharply. Having made his choice, the Piraeus accent sounded in his voice as he said briskly to David, 'Katherine was leading them. She had Niko's dog with her. They were moving south.'

David's black eyes took on a further gloss. 'Towards the cages,' he said, and Melissa laughed.

'They're wrong,' she said. 'Even with Chloe — but then Katherine's no use with dogs. Chloe could be whining and scratching to go off in a completely different direction and Katherine wouldn't know.'

'Yet Spiro or Bailey might be good with dogs.' Pindaros added that unwelcome thought as Melissa also reluctantly admitted, 'So might Sir Oliver.'

'Then let's move,' said David, as Pindaros stretched over a packing case for one of the hammers hanging on the studio wall.

Kneeling, Roxanne swished Chloe's old rag doll across the dry sand again whilst looking elsewhere. For the last two hours, ever since scrambling down the slender hair's breadth of a path to this place with Buster mewing in squirming outrage in the rucksack, she had been on watch.

The sea cave was her last mystery in this game of hide and seek. David had explained where it was when he had taken her, Melissa and Katherine on that fast guided tour of Antasteri two days back. Only two days, but Roxanne was reckoning on Katherine having clean forgotten the existence of the cave. Katherine had been listening, but not really paying attention to David's words, only to David the man.

Yet would David remember? Had he noticed her interest in the cave? thought Roxanne, tugging sportingly on Chloe's old toy as she felt Buster seize it. The tigress cub growled and struck the rag doll with a lashing paw.

'Ow! You little demon, I felt those claws!' Flinching slightly but then ignoring the tigress' sharp growing teeth, Roxanne rolled the cub over and tickled its belly, marvelling again at the warm thick fur, the beautiful pattern of stripes. The engaging white ear tufts she could see clearly, even in the half light of the cave. She wanted the cub to live, but where now would a Caspian tiger flourish?

Roxanne looked about the low-roofed cave. Certainly not here, she thought. The sand and pebbles of the cave floor were both dry, although the sea ran in and out of the cave, frothing slightly where the cave met the beach. Roxanne had entered its limestone mouth from the beach and kept well back from the blue rushing water and its foamy swirls. The cave was level, ran twenty metres back into the cliff and had a high platform of sand and pebbles where the sea did not reach. Even the recent storm had not dampened these stones, nor the tiny stalagmite slowly forming at the very back of the cave.

It wasn't much of a secret place, Roxanne was forced to admit, but for a few necessary hours it would do. It would have to.

With one of David's telescopes she had watched the sea around Antasteri through the villa's big kitchen window. Spotting the small motor-boat rounding the north side of Asteri half an hour before it landed, recognising it neither as her father's nor David's, Roxanne had decided on discretion. She guessed that after the storm Nicholas and

David might be unable to manoeuvre their boats out of the crowded and chaotic harbour at Khora, but still she could not risk waiting openly at Antasteri harbour. Nicholas or Melissa would be welcome, David she longed for, but other visitors might be deadly.

Suddenly there came the sound of running footsteps outside. Heavy footfalls on crumbling sand. Roxanne swept the cub up in her arms and started to her feet, eyes fixed on the cave entrance.

Another heart-jamming moment and David had his arms around her and the cub, the sledgehammer rush of his embrace bringing himself and Roxanne to their knees on the cave floor.

'Thank God!' he was saying, 'If you hadn't been here, I'd have gone mad, but you're safe now.'

'Easy there,' Roxanne started.

Unheeding, David held her closer. At the touch of his strong swimmer's torso, half-naked and cold, human and vulnerable against her belly, the last of Roxanne's shyness vanished. She did what they both wanted and pitched a kiss, her lips taking the salty sweetness from his mouth, silencing his tender nonsense.

A moment only, and then Roxanne drew back.

'Tease,' murmured David, shifting his grip. Between them, soft and warm against his chest, he felt the living cub, saw the dog-sized baby claws digging into the shoulders of Roxanne's shirt.

'You're too much,' whispered Roxanne. 'No time.' She glanced down at the purring cub, her lean features glowing.

And you're still too young. The thought struck David as he heard Melissa scrambling into the cave, saw reality in the shape of Pindaros' bobbing shadow across the low cave roof. Now, as he broke from Roxanne, as they both rose to their feet, David looked at the Caspian tiger for the first time, his heart jumping as he watched the round, almost downy head nuzzling near Roxanne's breast. Surprisingly, he found himself privately disappointed in the tiger's size and general drabness, although the cub seemed lively enough, expertly worrying at Chloe's old rag doll with strong little teeth.

Melissa, rushing across the pebbles and sand, demanded and received the cub, her face alight with relief and a kind of wonder. The tigress dropped Chloe's rag doll and snapped at Melissa's hair, then growled and mewed. 'How long since she's been fed?' Melissa asked Roxanne, nodding to her by way of greeting. There was no time for long reunions, not with Nicholas still in Katherine's and Spiro's power.

'Buster?' Roxanne broke off from staring at the deep scrapes on David's shoulders and playfully blew across the cub's nose. 'About two and a half hours ago.' She raised her head to Melissa and asked the questions Melissa had been dreading. 'Something's wrong, isn't it? Where's Dad?'

David answered, his tone hard with suppressed anger. 'Katherine Hopkins has taken him hostage. But we have what she wants,' he continued grimly. 'We'll trade the cub for him.'

It won't work, thought Melissa, her cradling fingers spreading in a protective gesture across the cub's thick pelt, although just then her main concern was not for the Caspian. Sick with foreknowledge but conscious of Roxanne's sudden pallor, she said nothing.

'No,' said Roxanne slowly. 'It can't be done. We're witnesses: after she's got the cub, Katherine will be satisfied. Then Spiro won't hesitate.' She motioned harshly, slashing a finger across her throat.

'So what now?' Pindaros addressed David, another male. So far he had done no more than glance at the Caspian. Even without the threat of sudden death, the millionaire was not interested in infant creatures, however rare.

David had crossed to the cave entrance. 'We need to get off this beach if we're to have any chance,' he said, then backed abruptly into the shadows, motioning the others to the back of the cave.

Over the gush and spout of the sea Melissa heard the faint dragging swish of feet across soft sand. Gradually the sound grew more distinct, breaking up into separate patterns of movement. Melissa kept staring at the cave mouth. A flock of gulls took off from the other end of the beach, and she was briefly dazzled by their white wings as the birds crossed the sky directly in front of their hiding place.

An angry voice suddenly boomed from the beach. 'This is a waste of time,' Spiro burst out in Greek.

'Be quiet!' Katherine's scornful answer, though less loud, carried clearly to Melissa. 'David mentioned a cave on this beach: the girl could be holed up there, and now because of your mouth, she'll know we're here!'

The swish of feet stopped suddenly. In the dreadful, absolute silence that followed, Melissa could not bear to watch. Averting her eyes from Roxanne's haggard, suffering face, she stared fixedly at the stalagmite, dully wondering how many years it had taken to form under the age-long dripping of water.

A long moment passed. Outside the cave she heard the slow creaking of pine trees as a breeze spilled across the island. In the cave she felt to be stifling. *If Nicholas is dead . . .* Melissa pinched out the thought, straining to hear through the low bubbling whine of the waves.

'Roxanne?' Katherine again, her voice now sugar-sweet. 'Your father's here with us. Say something nice, Nicholas.'

Flinching, Melissa listened to the sound of heavy repeated blows against a body, and then, after an excruciating pause: 'Rox, if you can hear me, I'm fine.' Nicholas gasped in a huge lungful of air. 'So don't you give up!'

'Wait.' Before Spiro could strike again, Katherine had another idea. 'Go on, Chloe. Find Roxanne. Go on now, girl —'

The swift patter of paws, the yip of greeting, a wagging tail. In another instant, Melissa knew they'd be betrayed by Chloe's innocent pleasure.

'Call out to them!' she whispered. 'Say the cub's sick.'

David squeezed Roxanne's wiry shoulder, agreement in his eyes. Pindaros, also recognising surprise as their only advantage, flattened himself against the dark side of the cave.

Clearing her throat once, Roxanne called from the darkness. 'Dad — I've got the cub here and she's not moving much any more, just lying on her side in my lap, panting.'

'No!' The anguished bellow cut through Chloe's bark as she scented Roxanne and came trotting into the underhang. Behind Chloe, a riot of voices:

'My kitty —'

'Sir Oliver, stop!'

'No, you don't, Stephanides. You walk with me. Slow.'

Bailey wasn't with them, Melissa guessed. Maybe he'd been left at the cliff top or by the shrine, which Katherine had finally remembered.

Even as Melissa twisted round to whisper this to David, Sir Oliver staggered into the cave, tossing his gun aside as his fevered eyes searched for the Caspian.

'Here!' Melissa bounded forward to meet him, showing the prize.

Sir Oliver's cry of warning became a gasp of pleasure. Ignoring David, Roxanne and the yapping Chloe, he grabbed for the tigress.

Growling and bristling at the strangers, noise and disruption, the cub struck out from

Melissa's arms, sinking teeth like tiny razors into Sir Oliver's grasping hand.

'But you're mine!' the baronet protested, snatching back his bleeding fingers.

'Not until you've paid us,' said Spiro. He had Nicholas in front of him, hands crossed over his head, the muzzle of the rifle pressed against the middle of his back.

David, moving slowly from the shadows near the cave entrance, had quietly retrieved Sir Oliver's discarded weapon. Now he aimed it straight at Spiro's head. 'Drop the gun.'

Sir Oliver, caught between trying for the cub again and lurching forward to charge David, found his way blocked by Ari Pindaros.

Slowly, with extravagant care, Spiro tossed his gun out onto the beach and Ari walked over to retrieve it. Nicholas instantly slammed an arm back across Spiro's already broken nose. Crying out, the smuggler staggered against Katherine, who shrugged him off with a patrician expression of total disgust.

Melissa felt the tiger cub licking a rasping tongue against her neck. Warily, in case the Caspian should try its teeth again, she shifted the infant tigress a little in her arms. Then, face to face, as she had done three months before on the cold, blue English estuary, she confronted Katherine.

'It's finished,' she said. 'For good.'

From outside the cave came a sound of scuffling ended by three gunshots, and Katherine turned white.

'Bailey,' she said softly. 'Bailey.'

Chapter 47

Bailey was dead. Clutching briefcase and pistol, he had clambered down from the shrine to help out Katherine and his half-brother, Spiro. When Ari Pindaros stooped to recover Spiro's gun, Bailey dropped his briefcase and fired. Hampered by his injured arm, he missed. Returning fire, Pindaros dispatched him with two shots.

Stunned by Bailey's death, Katherine, Spiro and Sir Oliver offered no further resistance. Ordered out of the cave by Nicholas, they remained standing — listless, silent, scarcely moving — on the tiny beach, whilst David and Roxanne climbed up the cliff track and sprinted down through the woods to Antasteri harbour. Later, as the white sails of David's yacht appeared round the northern point of the islet, Sir Oliver sighed and sat down in the sand: his only positive action for over an hour. Spiro stayed fixed. Katherine, oblivious to everyone, wandered slowly along the slip of sand to stare at Bailey's body. It seemed to Melissa, as Katherine and her co-conspirators were shepherded warily onto David's boat, that her enemy was only now beginning to understand that the final price one paid was never in cash.

Her enemy, thought Melissa, as on the boat journey back to Asteri she turned away from the others to look across to the island's central peak. Asteri's forest mantle came gradually nearer as the yacht sailed on, but Melissa herself felt that she had never left the beach. The sands of time: how well that symbol stood for her now! Every decisive point in her life seemed to have been played out on sand, on beaches. Her confrontation with Katherine, two months ago. Andrew's death, which Katherine had ordered. Now this.

No, thought Melissa, fingers curling tightly over the low gunwale in her place by the stern, there was no comfortable end to this business, nor to her long-standing enmity with Katherine. Forgiveness would not bring Andrew back.

Dully, careless of her wind-blown, sea-sprayed appearance, she watched Khora come into view: those low pink and white houses and narrow, stepped streets. Behind her, Nicholas carried a rifle trained unrelentingly on the men and woman in his custody. Melissa sensed his energetic concentration, his commitment as mayor and felt by contrast only her own numb weariness. Bailey's death had brought it all back to her: the loss of Andrew. Eight years of happiness snuffed out in an instant.

Ahead, his back to her, David swung hard on the tiller. He had grabbed a shirt from his house on the way down to the harbour and now his clothes were an incongruous mixture of clean white shirt and sweat, grease and bloodstained trousers.

Studying him for a moment, Melissa took in the tanned, perfectly proportioned body without a tremor of mystery. Without the spell of possible danger, the sculptor had lost something to her. She could not see a future for them.

Sensing eyes piercing his back, David turned briefly. He looked first to Roxanne, seated alongside Melissa, his handsome face first tender, then uncertain as he watched Roxanne check again on the sleeping cub in her rucksack. He glanced at Melissa; a conventional look of reassurance. Since their reunion in the cave, only Roxanne was more than flesh and model-material to him. Only Roxanne. His dark eyes swept sympathetically over Melissa's drooping, grimy figure, then turned back to Roxanne.

Farther ahead, black figures were emerging from across the blue harbour water, out of the day's biscuit-coloured haze. Melissa rubbed her tired eyes with a dirt-smeared arm and the still, dark shapes became real people: the pale, grieving families of the newly dead. Grouped along the undamaged portion of the jetty in their black clothes, their pose was as formal and telling as that of painted mourners on a funeral urn.

Stella and Popi were at the head of this unhappy group. Silently, with burning eyes, the two black-dressed women watched the white yacht slip quietly into a mooring. Above them early swallows twittered and skimmed, but Stella's gaze scorched along the passengers on the boat, stopping at Melissa.

Men in green uniforms gently guided Stella aside and came to catch the lines from David's boat. The police had arrived from Rhodes to restore order formally to the island. Briskly efficient, they swarmed onto the yacht to handcuff the prisoners. Politely then, sure of their role, the nine policemen waited as Melissa and the others slowly came ashore. Their officer indicated to Nicholas that as mayor he would still be needed: Melissa, Roxanne and David were for the moment free to go. Zervos would take their statements later.

Glimpsing the waiting body-bag on the quay side and a brown briefcase already bagged in plastic in a policeman's fist, Katherine lowered her head and wiped her eyes.

Mewing at being wakened, the tiger cub, unaware of the carnage its pitifully 'unique' status had inspired, was handed over by Roxanne to Dr Alexios for safe-keeping until better accommodation could be found. Ignoring Sir Oliver's groan, Popi and Andreas' widow watched coldly as Alexios left the harbour front gently cradling the cub.

Stella's eyes had not left Melissa. Meeting and holding the Greek woman's look of silent confrontation, Melissa unflinchingly stared back at the final cost of bringing Andrew's murderers to justice. She had felt she'd had no choice but to find his killers: Stella's hard, bleak face told a different story.

She'd had no choice, but that didn't make the revulsion which hit Melissa then any less sickening, in the way that sickness can make a person cold and hot and turned inside-out all at once. Shuddering inwardly, she was struck again by grief. Stella's pain seemed to have drawn it out of her, out of its old familiar place. Standing on that Khora harbour with Bailey's body-bag a few metres away and the black widows whispering on the jetty, Melissa felt as she had in the Rhodes mortuary two years back. The same numb horror and bone-dry mouth. The relentless grinding in her stomach.

David spoke to her then and she almost gagged, instinctively recoiling at the sight and sound of him. 'What?' she demanded sharply.

'What are you going to do now?' David repeated patiently. Yet there was a dash of temper or stress there, too, hard beneath the faint Northumberland accent.

Into the gaping hole his question opened in Melissa's mind — What was she going to do, now that she'd finally tracked Andrew's killers down? — Nicholas strode with his own answer. Replying for her, he said smartly, 'She's coming to my place to clean up.'

'No, I'm not,' said Melissa quietly. Seeing his hand reaching for her arm, she jerked away from Nicholas. Catching sight of his blunt, rather homely features freezing into a look of angry pain, feeling the fretful Chloe brush against her, Melissa found herself twisting back again. 'Please —' All she wanted now was to be left by herself.

Nicholas' fierce blue eyes narrowed. Rebuffed, suspicious, he was about to take a step closer to Melissa when he was claimed by half a dozen different people, all clamouring for attention.

'Mayor Niko —'

'There are papers to sign, *kýrie* —'

'Can the police really take Manoli and Andreas to Rhodes?'

'*Kýrie,* can you explain . . . ?'

'Mayor Niko!'

'We shall need a statement from you —'

And so it went on. Forced to answer, to remain on the jetty and fulfil his function as mayor, Nicholas could only plunge into the thick of things. Twenty minutes later, when he and the commander of the police unit walked together up the long steps to the mayor's office on the main square, Melissa was long gone.

Returning alone to Mrs Samouri's, Melissa closed the door and shut out the present.

Grudgingly, plainly wanting to be elsewhere and doing something else, Nicholas led the police and their prisoners off to his office in the main square. Chloe, confused, padded after them. In twos and threes the mourners turned away from Manoli's ferry on the harbour front and stumbled slowly along the backstreets to their stifled, shuttered homes.

Soon, only David and Roxanne were left. Roxanne had settled on the bottom of the long steps, looking out beyond the tumbled-down half of the jetty and across the yellow fishing boats to the dark swell of the Turkish mountains over a blue sea.

'There were dolphins in this bay when I was little,' she observed quietly, as David sat beside her. Sadness tugged at the corners of her mouth. 'No more.'

Above her, a pair of falcons swooped and dived, reckless in their mating displays. Tracking their flight to Asteri's central crag, David was suddenly tongue-tied. Now that they were finally alone, there were things he wanted to say to Roxanne, but he was no longer sure where to start. In the cave they had been natural, spontaneous with each other. Now he was conscious of a restraint in both of them. Roxanne was still looking at the mountains.

'Am I too young?' she asked after a moment's silence.

David shook his head. 'I'm too old for you.' Leaning towards her, tenderly fussing, he picked a cave cobweb from the bright bob of hair. Feeling the fine strands spark through his fingers, crackling a response in his groin, he wished they were in the cave again, meeting danger together as equals.

Colouring slightly, Roxanne leaned back on her elbows and fixed her eyes on the hazy sea below. She watched a butterfly bustle past the long, still figure, then motioned beyond David. 'I'm due to go to college at the end of this summer. I already help out at Alexios' surgery.'

'I know.' Roxanne in repose looked very canny and knowing, thought David, his heart lurching. Wanting to touch her again, he remembered the soft skin, her wiry body, the rangy walk, her mouth, her lips. His jaw set. 'In the meantime — I was hoping you'd be the model for all three goddesses.'

'Me? For all of them?' For a moment surprise brought renewed hope, but then Roxanne recollected that since Katherine had been arrested and Melissa was due to return to London to clear up her photographic business affairs, she was the only one left of the three models. 'Sure — whenever I can,' she said, her face glowing, but without pleasure.

He *was* too old, thought David. By rights, he shouldn't be asking her to model at all, not wasting her summertime here, but the thought of her being so close, all summer, and not seeing her again, not talking to her again, was not to be endured. Before winter came she was going away and he'd no right to stop her, to stand in her way with his middle-aged demands of permanency.

Close by in one of the inner village fields grasshoppers began sawing, piercing the uncomfortable silence. 'I suppose you'll want me on Antasteri?' Roxanne asked, wishing as soon as she'd spoken that she could have a second strike at the sentence.

'Naturally — besides, what would I do without my Hera? But I should warn you,' David added quickly, despising himself for being so falsely hearty, 'we'll be largely by ourselves over there. I'm going to dismiss the guards. Spiro — *my* Spiro — was always a touch extravagant. Did I tell you about the time he frog-marched a widow down to the harbour after finding her instead of Litsa spring-cleaning the little woodland shrine?'

Roxanne shook her head, reflecting to herself that the lack of guards meant nothing. Clearly from now on her relationship with David was going to be strictly professional.

Suddenly, in an echo from his competitive swimming days, David thrust himself off one fist to his feet, standing down from the steps between Roxanne and the sun.

'Right! I'll be in touch then, pet.' It wasn't enough, he thought, forcing a smile as he held out his hands to her. Nothing was really settled between them. And at the end of summer, Roxanne would be leaving. The idea ground inside him, a bitter thing.

Roxanne watched a strange light come into David's black eyes, felt the throbbing heat of his fingers as she placed her hands in his, herself in his hands. Rushed to her feet on the second step and at once released, she suddenly understood. David was trying to do the decent, English thing — he didn't really want her as a model at all, he wanted *her*.

Artlessly, she laughed with sudden happiness. She danced along the step, her stormy, now wildly merry eyes level with his. 'David: do you know what your name means?'

She saw him swallow, heard the tense intake of breath. ' "Beloved",' he said softly. 'It means "Beloved".'

'And so you are,' said Roxanne. She opened her arms. 'I want you to love me, David.'

The wonder and relief in his face then. His broad body blocked the sun to her, but his handsome face had its own light, flooding up the tanned neck, jaw and high cheekbones. With a yell of delight he whirled her off the steps, kissing her, telling her how much he loved her. Roxanne was a moment before she could get him to listen.

'David! Put me down, now,' she commanded for the third time, 'No — not there, here, on this step. That's better! Now we're a height.'

Grinning, Roxanne hugged him.

Chapter 48

Several hours later, escorted in handcuffs onto a light aircraft by the Rhodes police, the prisoners left Asteri.

In the days that followed, Spiro revealed under questioning that the Turkish side of his family came originally from Kemi, but he refused to give any name but 'Spiro'. Faced with a long prison term, he gave in and divulged a large part of his involvement in the wildlife smuggling trade, including his introduction — through Bailey — to Katherine Hopkins. His trafficking had increased, he admitted, to supply her specific requirements.

Denying to the last any part in the killings on Lykimi beach or in Andrew Thornhill's murder, Spiro did acknowledge that he had paid Manoli, Popi and Andreas to undermine Nicholas Stephanides' standing as mayor and head of ASPW by rumour and gossip. But it was Bailey, Spiro claimed, who had bribed Mrs Samouri to turn a blind eye so that he could dump the fake wildlife 'shipment' and documents in Melissa's flat. And it was Bailey who, acting on Katherine's orders, had roughed Melissa up in the street on the night of the public meeting.

Back on Asteri, Stella went to see Mr Zervos and the last pieces fell into place. Still in mourning for Manoli, Stella would not be denied her day in the witness box.

Katherine had said nothing. Even when Spiro related a conversation with Bailey during which his half-brother confessed to killing Zoe Konstantinou by mistake, Katherine remained silent. She had said nothing about her shattered reputation, her ruined future. Bailey's death had broken her.

And now she was gone from Asteri, as were the other survivors from Katherine's last smuggling run. The Caspian tigress, much photographed and hyped by the media, was soon to begin her new, safe, but orphaned and lonely life in a progressive German zoo, whilst the wildlife and zoological community scrambled for research grants and sponsorship to begin a new series of expeditions in the Near East. Sir Oliver, stripped of his directorship of Beach International, had been taken to Athens and would face charges in Greece and Britain.

After witnessing the media circus around the Caspian tiger, Ari Pindaros decided that it was better to throw olive branches at the

Greens. He now made a public commitment against any bauxite mine on Asteri mountain and for an 'ecologically sound' marina at Kemi. Its foundation stone would be dedicated publicly to Zoe's memory, but privately to greater profits. The Asteri mining operation had always been a borderline decision: in the circumstances, the marina would produce better media coverage and the shares in Pindaros Bauxite would remain high.

The fact that there is no such thing as an ecological marina was neither here nor there.

Chapter 49

A few rainy Norfolk days later, Melissa parked the car at Lady Anne's Drive to spend the day on Holkham Sands. She'd been alone the last time she'd visited the sands: a long day spent in photography and note-taking, a day for absorbing the windswept landscape and thinking of Andrew. Now, finally released and set to rest, Andrew was beginning to fade from her life.

The morning had started quite cold, a damp sea-fret sweeping over sky, sea and sand in a chill grey mist. Walking slowly up and down the beach, Melissa began to feel the warmth of an early English summer breaking through.

As the hours passed, the sky cleared and the sun grew stronger, prompting Melissa to return briefly to the car to cast off her padded jacket and change her footwear. Into her mind flooded other memories, of Andrew smiling at her as she left on some expedition, waving her off, wishing her well. She smiled just a little herself, remembering. This time there was no pain, only a quiet valediction.

A flock of gulls rising suddenly from the sands startled her.

'Thought this is where you'd be — your next-door neighbour said you'd be kicking your heels along Holkham beach.'

Melissa swung round, astonishment showing in her face, whilst the breeze, scooping round the wide sandy bay, frothed her golden hair across her warm brown eyes. She looked drained, Nicholas thought tenderly, understanding at once why she would come to these open miles of sky and sand.

'Chloe's with Roxanne and David,' he went on, as Melissa continued to stare. He put a hand to his head, found no cap to tug so ducked down and grabbed a pebble instead. 'Still can't quite get used to thinking of those two as a couple — Rox was saying only yesterday that when she goes to college at the end of the summer, David will visit for Christmas. Otherwise they'll write and phone. And Roxanne is going to model for all three figures — she says David thinks her slimness is not only no problem but "truly beautiful".' Nicholas frowned, hunching his shoulders. 'So David's cleared it with her and with Pindaros. They've got it all worked out,' he concluded, a touch peevishly.

Melissa chuckled and the pebble slipped from Nicholas' fingers, splashing into a slender silver puddle which lay between them. 'Brace yourself,' she observed wryly. 'You could be entertaining a future son-in-law there.'

Nicholas scowled. 'You really think so? There's time yet for change, lots of separations whilst my girl's away at college . . .' Words failed him as the English afternoon sun lit the soft curves of Melissa's figure. No cameras or camouflage today, only a broom-yellow button-fronted dress and silver sandals. And, naturally enough, the seahorse earrings.

'David willing to leave Antasteri for Roxanne. Sounds promising to me,' teased Melissa. The freckles over her top lip were suddenly submerged in a fresh blush. 'I'm pleased for them,' she added softly.

Nicholas was still looking at her. 'You're the only woman I know who'd walk through dunes in high-heeled sandals,' he said.

'And you're the only man I know who can sneak up so close to me.'

' "Hobble", not "sneak", Bumblebee.'

Unable to help it, they grinned at each other. 'Your neighbour certainly knew my name,' Nicholas went on. 'As soon as I said who I was, the speed of her speech increased by I'd say fifty per cent. She couldn't wait to tell me where you were.'

Refusing to be thrown by this admission, Melissa shrugged. 'Probably read about you in the papers,' she said. 'Under Ken Bend's by-line,' she added drily. Since her return home, Melissa had found messages of support on her answering machine from both Ken and Bruce. So much for their loyalty to Katherine.

His wits blown away by their resumed closeness and scarcely attending to what she was saying, Nicholas stared at Melissa's lightly tanned arms, mentally comparing their smooth roundness with his own sinewy, hairy forelimbs. He wanted those arms round him. He wanted Melissa, every bit of her. The last few days without seeing her had been the absolute pits: nothing had been right.

'I thought you were still needed on Asteri for the next week or so,' said Melissa now. 'I thought we'd said goodbye last week, on Khora harbour.'

Yeah, with what felt like half the cops and criminals of the region watching and listening in, thought Nicholas. Irritated by the recollection, he snapped, 'I thought you had to come home to sort out your photo contacts in London, so what are you doing up here in Norfolk? Couldn't believe it when Jon Saunders told me where you were.'

So that's how he'd found her. Melissa tilted her chin at Nicholas. 'Did you go and see Jonathan, too?' she demanded.

'This morning. Soon as I'd flown in.' Nicholas' expression became smug. 'Knew you couldn't keep away from a recuperating wildlife officer.'

'Jonathan's job has nothing to do with my visiting —'

'Oh, don't be shy about bragging about your coup. I did plenty of it on your behalf. And none of your English understatement, either.'

'Nicholas!' Melissa struck out at him playfully with her fingers: hitting his chest was like hitting a rock. A warm rock. 'Will you ever stop interrupting me?'

He seized her hand, laid it flat against his body, over his heart. 'Only if you say "yes" to a few simple questions,' he said, smiling at her with his light blue eyes.

A horse and rider galloped by across the flat grey sands, but it was not the pounding of hooves which Melissa could feel in her head.

'You're real cuddly, you know that?' No longer trying to wait, Nicholas swung an arm round her flanks and pert behind, lifting Melissa over the narrow puddle and setting her down closer still to him, her body clamped along his.

'This your favourite place?'

Holkham West Sands were special to her, Melissa thought. Not to Andrew, but to herself. Which was why she had returned here to reflect on the happenings of the last two months and not Andrew's favourite estuary. She opened her mouth to answer, felt Nicholas' hands circling her hips and found herself snatching in a breath instead. Feeling as tickled by his fingers as by his moustache, Melissa nodded.

'Good!' Nicholas' heartbeat peaked under Melissa's tensed hand. 'And now that we know the system works, we'll begin.'

The hand caressing her hip paused as he cleared his throat. 'I love you, Melissa —'

'Yes!' Melissa kissed him, feeling the blood in her own veins sprinting and leaping. 'Yes, Nick!'

She felt him tremble. 'You're sure?' he asked, drawing back and looking at her in an amazed kind of way, as though he could scarcely believe it. 'We've only known each other two months.'

'Yes.'

'It'll take some sorting, you travelling all the time.'

'Yes.'

'We'll have to get used to being apart.'

'Yes.' Melissa licked her lips and kissed him again, her free hand now going on its own voyage of discovery.

The sound of children's voices came from behind the dunes. Nicholas grasped Melissa tighter, the rush of heat showing even in his darkly tanned face. 'We are going to be alone, soon?' he asked gruffly.

Adoring his bluntness, touched by the way he'd come chasing across Europe for her, loving his teasing fingers, Melissa nodded. 'Later, handsome,' she said, and silenced his 'When?' with another long kiss.

The pines behind them moved in the light breeze. The wide sandflats stretched, it seemed, for miles, with at their farthest edge the thin blue line of the sea.